FAKE DATING THE FOOTBALL PLAYER

MOST LIKELY TO ★ BOOK FOUR

SARAH SUTTON

To those who blast music with their windows down.
You've got a bit of Lacey Churchill in you.

CHAPTER 1

I wasn't sure I'd ever get used to waking up in a room that wasn't mine. I always woke up disoriented. My brain was slow to turn on, like an old V8 car that used to run like a beast in its prime, now misfiring each time its key turned in the ignition. There were mornings when the bedroom was wholly unfamiliar as sleep slowly receded. Mornings that the posters on the wall weren't recognizable, and I couldn't remember why my normally thin sheets were so thick. Sometimes I got through the whole description of the room, scanning all the details at a panicked pace, before the ignition caught.

And each time that happened, a weird mix of relief and disappointment blasted through me.

Friday morning, though, my mental stall only lasted a moment, but it was jarring enough that I instantly became wide awake. The dull gray light of the early morning snuck through the parted bedroom blinds, and I swung my legs out from underneath the hot blankets, grateful for the cool air that swept over my skin. The bite of it grounded me.

It was strange sleeping in someone else's bedroom, even though it'd been weeks at this point. Two months. I needed to get used to it. I didn't have a bedroom of my own anymore.

As silently as possible, I went about my morning ritual. I slid my open suitcase out from underneath the bedframe, grabbing a change of clothes. From there, I shoved the items inside my school backpack. Scraping my hair into a messy ponytail, I tied it off with an elastic before throwing the bag over my shoulders, easing the creaking bedroom door open.

Three other people lived in this house with me, but the air was absolutely soundless as I made my way through the short, narrow hallway. Once it opened up to the living room, I spotted my cousin, Hudson, sleeping on the couch. His long body didn't fit on the cushions, and he had his legs propped over the edge, and his neck looked like it craned at an uncomfortable angle. Despite the contortion, he slept faithfully.

Seeing him on the couch caused a sick sense of guilt to spear through me, like always, but I shoved it down.

I had about made it to the front door when a soft voice stopped me. "Sneaking out again, Lacey?"

My hand froze on the handle. *Caught.*

The mobile home was pretty large, all things considered, but from the front door, I had a straight shot into the kitchen where Uncle Dean sat with a steaming cup of coffee and his e-reader in front of him, his sparse hair dripping. He had a house robe and a pair of long pajama bottoms on, despite the lingering summer heat.

This was normally the time he was in the bathroom,

about ten minutes before he left for work, so I thought I was in the clear.

With a flick of his head, he summoned me over. "I don't like you leaving before the sun's up," he said without looking at me, swiping a page in his reader. "We might live in a relatively safe area, but don't all towns say that before something bad happens?"

One corner of my lips quirked up. "Never would've pegged you for paranoid."

"I'm not paranoid; I'm realistic."

"*Fatalistic,*" I countered, planting a hand on the table. It wobbled a bit beneath the sudden weight. "Don't worry, Uncle Dean, I can protect myself just fine."

I knew he had proof of that statement, but he didn't say anything. Instead, his gaze went over my shoulder to my backpack, almost like he had X-ray vision to see inside. "You know you can shower here, kid."

"The run to school always leaves me a little grimy," I told him. "I'll shower in the girls' locker room again."

"You could ride the bus," he insisted. "With Hudson."

"No senior would be caught dead on the bus. Hudson's an exception, since the entire school jokes that he's already dead."

I'd said it with enough tease that Uncle Dean smiled, attempting to hide it in his mug of coffee. He took a long, slurping sip, flicking another page on his e-reader. "If only the student parking pass prices weren't so high, or you could take that hunk of junk to school."

Uncle Dean was referring to the semi-ancient dark blue metallic van that we had parked in the backyard. In late

June, Uncle Dean had talked about how a coworker was selling a work van for cheap, since he knew it was one of my dreams to go traveling around the country in a van—#VanLife. Ever since I was little, and realized it was possible, it had been all I wanted. It'd been like Christmas morning when I got the news about the sale, and I scrounged up my savings from serving tables to buy it. My chance to skip this godforsaken town and go exploring had finally waltzed within reach.

And then Hudson came along and bought it before I could, putting his name on the title. I still had no idea where he'd gotten the money. He'd said he bought it as a graduation present for me and he'd help me fix it up, but I knew his true motives.

"It's *not* a hunk of junk," I argued. "It needs a little more TLC, that's all. She's just...noisy." And yeah, it cost a near fortune to be able to park a car in the student lot. That was Brentwood High for you—ridiculous.

I readjusted how my backpack straps dug into my shoulders. "I should get going."

Uncle Dean nodded, not quite looking me in the eye. "You've got your cell phone, right? The one I got you?"

"Yep."

"And you have your pepper spray?"

I thought of where it sat in my backpack pocket. "Yep."

"And you turn it in to the secretaries before school begins, right?"

My lips twitched. "Yes, Uncle D."

The wrinkles around his eyes deepened as he frowned. "Tell Hudson to do the same thing about his pocketknife, you hear me? That boy doesn't listen to a word I say. One of these days, it's going to bite him in the behind."

Both of us looked over toward the living room, where a sleeping Hudson was barely visible. He'd shifted since I'd walked past, more of his legs hanging off the couch now, his jaw dropped as he mouth-breathed. He was probably even drooling. *Dweeb.* "Not that he listens to what I say, but I'll try to be a good influence."

Uncle Dean grumbled about how Hudson could use one of those, but the volume was buried by another mouthful of his coffee. With a farewell salute, I made my way back to the door.

Brentwood High was easily a forty-ish minute walk from here, but more of a thirty-minute run. I was a slow runner. With my backpack, it was always an awkward, bumbling journey, but a refreshing one. I tugged down my elastic bike shorts where they had ridden up and started off.

This had been another element of the new Lacey Churchill morning ritual—running to school. I'd never really run much before. From the brief stint of sports I played in middle school—and the half-season I attempted at volleyball my freshman year—I learned that running was actually a form of torture. And even now, as I ran down the main road of the Vista Villas trailer park, I still hated it.

Except I learned that running made the pressure on my chest that already existed a bit more bearable. If my lungs ached because of running, not for any other reason, then it was okay. I was okay. I could deal with that pain. That pain was allowed—pain for any other reason was not.

Vista Villas sat on the outskirts of Brentwood, but I saw

more signs of life the farther I got into the city. I passed by a few running cars and a slow-moving SUV stamped with *Brentwood Daily News* on the back of it, and it paused every few feet to stick a newspaper in someone's mailbox. The sky slowly began to lighten as I continued my route, and I took breaks between pumping my arms and gripping my backpack straps, trying to alleviate the chafing burn of the fabric. Dew clung to the bits of grass and weeds that'd popped up from the gravel road, and the toes of my tennis shoes darkened with it.

Eventually, after multiple starts and stops of running, I got to Brentwood High with sweat gathered in places I didn't even know sweat could gather. Even my eyelids were sweaty.

Like I said, running? Ew.

This morning, though, my ritual pumped its brakes nearly as soon as I stepped into the school.

Out of Order. The sign that hung on the girls' locker room door was unforgiving, and I froze when I saw it. I tugged on the handle, but it didn't budge. For good measure, I pulled again. No entry. No way.

No way could I sit in class like this. Unwashed hair, no makeup, clothes that I'd literally worn to sleep. Sweat clinging to my eyeballs. Sure, I could change in one of the bathrooms—and *attempt* to salvage this grease pool on my head in the sink—but there'd be no escaping the stench of Sweaty Lacey. My five-dollar Target perfume could only do so much.

It left one option.

I glanced down the narrow hallway to the last door on the left.

The boys' locker room.

I should've thought about it longer. Should've considered any potentially horrifying consequences. But then again, it was barely seven o'clock. First period gym class wasn't for fifty-five more minutes, and no one really went in there before school. Probably. And honestly, it would only take me five to scrub my skin and wash my hair. I could do my makeup in one of the many girls' rooms in the school. All I needed was five minutes.

And, of course, the boys' room opened *sesame* when I tugged on the handle, making me grumble at whatever sexist gods were in control of my morning.

I listened first, straining to hear the slightest sound of a human being inside, but the locker room was empty. A fresh Lysol scent clung to the air, which made me feel a little better about venturing deeper. There were lockers on each side of the room, and then four rows of lockers in the middle, providing a barrier from the showers and bathroom stalls that were positioned at the back. I passed a few benches and made my way to the showers. Thank God they had curtains like the girls' room had, and after setting my backpack down on the nearest bench, I unpacked everything I needed. Shower shoes, shampoo, conditioner, body wash. Easy-peasy.

I grabbed two towels from the rack by the laundry return chute in the corner, and once I was behind the safety of the shower curtain, I stripped down.

Five minutes, I reminded myself, because now that the hot water beckoned me, it was hard to resist.

The water felt absolutely glorious on my sticky skin, and I massaged shampoo into my hair. *Five minutes*, I told myself again, squeezing my eyes shut. *Or maybe six.*

Seven-ish minutes later, I flipped the handle, cutting off the heavenly flow, and quickly grabbed my towel from the hook. I squeegeed as much water as I could from my hair—which wasn't a whole lot, since my hair only fell a little past my collarbones, anyway—and then wrapped the thick towel around myself. Was it me, or did the guys get bigger ones? Maybe I'd need to shower in here more often.

I tore back the curtain, intending to grab my clothes from where I'd left them on the safety of the dry bench, but froze instead.

And there it was. The biggest reason why showering in the boys' locker room was a terrible idea.

Exhibit A stared at me with the widest eyes I'd ever seen, lips parted in shock.

The quarterback of the football team, Landon Settler.

I recognized him immediately, but then again, it'd be impossible *not* to recognize him. There wasn't a student at Brentwood High that looked like Landon. He looked more like a college student than a senior in high school with his tall frame and thick muscles, and his shock of reddish-brown hair was hard to miss. It was pasted to his temples now, and even from here, I could see sweat clung to his skin too, in a way that looked much hotter than I'm sure I'd appeared stumbling into the school building. Much, much hotter.

Pressure built in my throat, and I clutched the knot of my towel near my armpit tighter. Though mortification and horror simmered underneath the surface of my skin, I shot Landon an awkward smile. "Uh, hi?"

He blinked, and then blinked some more. His skin was flushed, but from how sweaty he was, I had a feeling he'd been flushed even before he came in here. Probably a morning workout in the weightlifting room—which, admittedly, I hadn't thought of being a possibility until now.

I would've facepalmed if that didn't mean letting go of my towel.

Landon's gaze swept from my face down the rest of my body, a rapid peek that almost seemed against his will. He didn't linger, though—he forced his head away to stare at the lockers. "You—you need to leave," he said to them, tone flat and low.

A part of me bristled at the blunt order, even though I *was* the one in the wrong locker room. "I was here first," I replied, but turned to collect my bottles of shampoo and conditioner. "But trust me, I'm not sticking around to watch you shower. And I'm not giving *you* a free show of watching me get dressed either. So, if you could hand me my—"

"I mean—there are others," Landon cut me off, and as he spoke, his voice increased with frantic fervor. His eyes were wide on the lockers, like *they* were now standing dripping in a towel. "Guys. Coming into the locker room. Like, they were right behind me."

It wasn't even a second after he got that out that the murmur of voices went from nonexistent to *loud*—chatting in the hallway to having opened the locker room door. They were obscured by the rows of lockers, but they wouldn't be for long. "Landon, I know you finished your set, but you could've waited for us to finish ours, too," someone called. "What, you not like us anymore, bro?"

Landon burst into action before I could even react. He hastily snatched my clothes off the bench and stuffed them into my bag. Then, he grabbed the handle of my backpack and whipped it off the bench, closing the distance between us in a matter of a few steps.

My confidence from a moment ago, boldly chatting with him in just my towel, vanished in an instant at his sudden proximity. I tried to tug the curtain shut between us, but his large hand closed over mine, the warmth of his fingers swallowing mine whole. Our gazes locked. Up close, I could see the freckles that dotted across his nose and along the tops of his cheeks, swimming in the warmth of his skin. "This is where they're coming," he hissed, and without preamble, he grabbed my slippery upper arm. The grip wasn't tight, but his fingers practically wrapped around the entirety of it, and he hurried me from the showers to the toilet stalls in the corner of the room.

He dropped my backpack down at my feet, and without another word, he snapped the stall door shut.

"*Landon*," one of the voices sang, and then it switched to normal. "Jeez, what's the point of working out together if you're not going to hang around until we all finish?"

"Not my fault you all take forever to finish your sets," Landon said from right outside the stall door, voice clear. Not a single tremble. Nothing in the way he spoke would've hinted that he hid a girl on the other side. "It's supposed to be a workout, not a gossip hour."

I shivered like a dog as my hair dripped onto my shoulders, adrenaline pouring through my veins. I spotted lewd scribbles all over the interior of the stall, which made this whole situation skeevier. The lockers creaked open as the boys grabbed their things from them. With the rattling noise, I took the opportunity to frantically get dressed. I locked the stall door, but I didn't drop the towel from my body, maneuvering getting dressed around it. No way was I getting fully naked, not with Mr. Quarterback's shadow lingering underneath the door.

My bottom half was fully dressed before I noticed an important article missing from my backpack. *Where did it go?* I shifted everything around, growing increasingly panicked, when a voice cut through my movements. "Wait, *whoa*. What do we have here?"

"Dude, who had fun in the locker room?" the second voice demanded, laughing. "Left behind their *unmentionables*. You think it was Bray and Jade?"

"My money's on one of Reed's extracurriculars." The first voice snickered. "Although, I don't think he's dated anyone with a rack this big."

My hand digging in my bag stilled, and I let my forehead fall against the stall door. Right against the lewd drawings. Germs were totally scrambling from the metal onto my skin, but I couldn't even care.

The first voice continued, "It's not Jade's. She'd have to stuff that bra to get it to fit."

Of all the things Landon didn't grab... Kill me. Just kill me.

One of the locker doors slammed shut. "Nate and Riley, maybe? Don't they know that's what the hookup closet's for?"

"Maybe you should tell him, Kyle. Maybe you should give him a *tour*." The first voice made a strange noise that caused the other to laugh, and I squeezed my eyes shut tighter, gripping the knot of my towel. Was my bra being passed around like a hot potato? If so, the Neanderthals could keep it. "Whoa—hey! You taking it as a trophy, Landon? We all know it doesn't belong to your girl—you know, because you don't have one!"

"Neither do you, if I'm remembering correctly," he quipped back amidst their laughter, but this time, there was an edge to his voice. One that hadn't been there when he'd stumbled upon me. "Someone got rejected last year."

The first boy muttered something underneath his breath, something like *dumb witch.*

"I'm putting it in my locker until Connor or whoever can grab it," Landon went on. "You know Tito—he'll probably take it home with him."

One of them teased, "Add to his collection."

I held my breath, but could only hear the two boys laugh. Landon never joined in.

I could hear the sounds of the shower curtains being drawn aside, and a second later, the rush of water filled the air. Something knocked into my head, startling me enough that I nearly made a noise. When I looked up, I came face to face with my bra slung over the top of the stall door, the strap dangling from Landon's finger.

Of course I'd picked out the neon pink one with white daisies. It couldn't have been one of the other plain-Jane bras I owned. *Kill me.*

Face burning, I yanked it off from his finger and hastily put it on. From there, it was a race of getting my shirt over my head and grabbing my backpack, all while fighting to remain as silent as possible. I bumped into the stall door once, but Landon quickly covered it by clearing his throat.

I cracked the stall door open, finding the wall of Landon's back facing me. Now that I was fully clothed, I felt semi-calm enough to take in a few more details about him. He wore a black cutoff, one that hugged his body and exposed his arms. A total football player's body. I even let myself be impressed, ogling for only a second before I poked him in the shoulder blade. *Firm. Mmm.*

Landon turned and scanned me, this time not as quickly as before. He took in my black T-shirt and ripped pair of jeans, and the backpack that I already had slung over my shoulder. I still had my sneakers in my bag—it was too hard to put them on in the cramped space. Even though I was dressed, I had to look rough with my dripping hair and bare face, but for the world's briefest second, Landon looked starstruck.

He probably was starstruck, honestly. He just got a free show of me half-naked.

"Landon," one of the boys called. "What are you doing over there? Are you—"

Without hesitation, Landon shoved his way into the

stall, and when I took a startled step backward, my socks slipped on the tile. My balance went out the window, and I sucked in a gasp as Landon wrapped his arm around my waist without hesitation, catching my fall. His hand fell on my lower back, the strength in his arm holding me upright.

I might've swooned a little if I weren't literally hovering over the toilet in the boys' locker room. Sure, it might've smelled like cleaner, but I would've literally rather died than touch the porcelain.

"I—uh—bathroom," Landon blurted as he stared down at me, chest to chest in the tiny space. "I—I'll be a minute."

Once I found my footing, I wedged my arm between us and pushed him back. Immediately, his arm dropped from me as if I burned, and he pressed himself as far apart as he could. His eyes darted around me rapidly, like he was thinking. Not fast enough. "How am I—"

Landon pressed a finger to his lips to cut me off, eyes flaring. He lifted his hand up, palm facing the ceiling, and held it to me. "I'll get you out," he whispered, his voice barely a sound even in the space between us.

I stared up at the broad boy as a trickle of amusement broke through the panic that'd been building the second his posse walked in. *I'll get you out.* Like I was in some James Bond movie on the brink of getting caught rather than crammed in a bathroom stall. Even though I was a complete stranger, all that mattered to him was getting me out of the mens' room unnoticed.

Despite knowing I fully could've gotten out of the locker room myself—and would've—I slid my hand into his, a tiny, incredulous smile building along my lips. He gripped it tightly, in a bold way I'd never have pegged him for. He held my hand as if he was afraid I'd let go.

Landon turned and eased the stall door open, peeking out. Using his body to shield me, he hustled us away from the showers—I absolutely did *not* risk a look—and back toward the locker room entrance. He never faltered, never looked back, never let go, even after we'd put the lockers between us and the showers.

A little flutter tickled my stomach when I looked at Landon. It was the sort of sensation I got when I drove too fast down a gravel road. A little reckless, a little unsafe, a whole lot of fun.

Landon pushed open the locker room door and let me walk through before dropping my hand. His fingers spread on the door and propped it open, looking like he wanted to say something, but only went as far as to part his lips.

Something about the sight of him made me want to smile again. Like the way you laugh at a kid who does something cute and funny at the same time. I wasn't sure what it was about him in that moment, if it was the doe-eyed look on his face, the dusting of freckles across his nose, or the blush that still clung to his cheeks. Something about him made me feel light.

Even though I definitely still felt awkward, I'd learned over the years to pretend things didn't bother me. To shove down all the emotion and play it cool. I took my shoes out of my bag and dropped them onto the ground, shoving my feet into them. Swinging my leg up, I propped my foot on the wall right beside Landon's hip. "Listen," I began, leaning into my thigh to tie the ratty laces. "You tell anyone about this, and I'll make you wish you were never born."

I dropped my foot and propped my other leg up, tying the laces tight. "I won't tell," Landon answered after a beat, his eyes glancing along my leg before jerking back up. "I promise."

I leaned into Landon's personal space, and though the height difference wasn't that much, I had to tilt my head back a little to look into his eyes. "It was kind of fun, though," I said, raising my eyebrows. "Thanks for an exciting start to the morning."

He still didn't say anything, but now it looked like the flush across his freckled cheekbones was from more than just working out. I patted his hand where it held the door open before turning around, jostling my backpack further up my shoulders.

Before I rounded the corner out of the locker room hallway, I glanced over my shoulder. Landon hadn't moved—his expression hadn't even shifted—and that tickling feeling didn't disappear from my stomach.

With a chuckle, and a small smile that lifted my lips, I ducked out of the hallway.

CHAPTER 2

"**A**nd then Landon Settler walked in while I was showering."

Hudson, who'd taken a bite two sizes too big for his mouth, coughed on his BLT. "*What?*"

I leaned my chair back on two legs and looked at my fingers. It'd been a while since I painted my nails, but remnants of my purple polish clung on the nail by my cuticles. It made my hands look dirty. "I mean, I wasn't, like, fully commando or anything. But he still saw me in my towel. The nerve."

Hudson choked down his food before attempting to speak again. "You *were* in the guys' locker room. But, c'mon, Lacey. I know you're not naïve to how guys are. What were you thinking?"

"I was thinking 'man, I stink, and the girls' locker room is locked.'"

"Well, what happened after he came in?"

I rocked farther back in my foldup chair. "He ogled a bit, and then stuffed me into the bathroom stall before his

17

friends could see me. So, despite him totally checking me out, I guess he gets some points for chivalry." I winced as I remembered Landon with his finger hooked around my bra.

Hudson rolled his eyes as he stuck the straw of his chocolate milk into his mouth. "You're lucky it was Landon and not Ashton Shaw. At least Landon has *some* morals left."

"I thought you hated Landon Settler."

Freshman year, my cousin was involved in his first fight. Though the true details of it never circulated around Brentwood, I knew the full story. The narrative that spread was that Hudson tried to beat up Ashton Shaw, Kyle Filmore, and Landon Settler one day after school, going from zero to one hundred for absolutely no reason. Ashton and Kyle claimed it was because Hudson's mom passed away, and that it'd knocked a screw of his loose. They claimed Hudson pulled a knife on them.

The true story was that Ashton and Kyle thought it'd be fun to pick on the twiggy freshman that was Hudson Bishop, which resulted in Hudson needing five stitches in his cheek. Landon had been a bystander that didn't step in until the action was already underway, and got a few punches of his own when Hudson began defending himself.

Because of the rumors Ashton and Kyle spread, though, Hudson went from a normal guy to an outcast. Hudson began dressing the part, acting the part. Sometimes I wondered what life would've looked like if things had been different, if he hadn't fallen so easily into the role of the bad guy, but I couldn't picture it.

"Oh, I don't like him," Hudson said now, shaking his head. "But I at least trust the guy not to try and rip your towel off."

I made a face at the unseemly visual, but then again, he had a point. Especially with Ashton, the guy who truly seemed unable to take a hint. Last spring, he asked me on four separate occasions to junior prom, and I declined all of them. The final time, he'd asked me in front of all of his friends, no doubt thinking I'd say yes out of peer pressure. He'd been wrong, and I may or may not have embarrassed him in front of his buddies. I'd rather go alone than be subjected to his company all night.

Then he cornered me after my waitressing shift and demanded to know why I wouldn't go out with him. Stalker material. It seemed summer had finally killed his fatal attraction, but then again, it *was* only the first week of school. Our paths hadn't crossed yet, thank God.

I glanced around the space Hudson and I had been put in during the lunch period. The first day of school, Principal Oliphant told Hudson that he could either sit in Cafeteria A with all the underclassmen, *with* a teacher shadowing his every move, or he could eat in the school counselor's office. Ms. Murphy, the forty-something whose PhD status was questionable, had graciously given us the space to ourselves, but she'd told us not to tell. "I'm technically supposed to be in here with you," she'd said, and then winked. "But I trust you two."

I wasn't sure if that made her a cool person or a bad counselor. Probably a bit of both.

Hudson chewed before attempting to speak. "Where's your lunch?"

I looked at the empty table space between us with an inward groan. Then again, I should've expected it. "I forgot my wallet."

Hudson's angry eyes came out in full force, but even though he was frustrated, I struggled not to laugh as I looked at him. His bright blue colored contacts—prank courtesy of *moi*—made me want to snort every time. "Why didn't you ask me for money? Even better, why didn't you make yourself a sandwich from what's in the fridge? At least grab an apple off the counter?"

I ducked my head to rest on my folded arms, peering at the array of printout quotes on Ms. Murphy's wall. They were hung by tape, and some were crooked. "I'd rather eat things I buy."

"Oh, our food's not good enough for you?"

"Please. You know what I mean."

Hudson muttered something that suspiciously sounded like a swear word, but I pretended not to hear. Without saying anything, he shoved his bag of carrot sticks my way, nudging the hummus within reach, too. My pride told me not to reach for them; my stomach told me I should. "You can have your room back, you know," I told Hudson as I fished out a stick, dipping it into the hummus. "I can sleep on the couch."

"What makes you think that now, after two months of me saying *no*, I'll change my mind?"

"I'm waiting until you realize you're beginning to form a hunch." To emphasize my words, I ducked my head and bunched up my shoulders. "You're turning into that troll guy."

He kicked me underneath the table, and with his boots, it was hard enough to hurt. "Hey, it'll help my image. No one expects the Grim Reaper to have perfect posture, right?"

Even though I'd joked about it this morning with Uncle Dean, it always rang differently when Hudson talked about the nickname. Like he was *attempting* at humor, but it never really landed. To the entirety of Brentwood High, Hudson Bishop was better known as the Grim Reaper. The nickname came after the fight, and the rumors around it stuck all the way to his senior year. Whenever I asked about it, Hudson said he didn't mind the nickname for the most part. It got people to leave him alone.

But it also isolated him in other ways, like having to eat lunch in the counselor's office.

"Hudson. Take your room back."

"No."

"I'm not asking."

"And I'm not negotiating." And with that, he effortlessly changed the subject. "I didn't tell you what happened yesterday after school. I got home and you'd already left for work."

I dipped another carrot stick into the hummus and narrowed my eyes. "You get detention already? Is Oliphant giving you a hard time?"

He quirked an eyebrow as if to say *what's new*. "She's making me do this mentoring thing."

"She's having *you* mentor someone?"

"Other way around."

I laughed out loud, not even bothering to slap a hand over my mouth to cover the sound. Hudson needing a mentor. That mental image was perfect. "*That's* rich. Truly. Who, pray tell, is mentoring our favorite high school senior?"

Hudson sighed as he looked down at his sandwich, giving his head a shake. "Some sophomore."

"One who will probably pee their pants five minutes into the session." Okay, sometimes Hudson's reputation had a funny side, like seeing kids in the hall part like he was Moses and they were the Red Sea. Especially the underclassmen. They absorbed the rumors the upperclassmen told them, which only seemed to get crazier and crazier each year. "Go easy on them. Who knows, maybe you'll have an underclassman to do your bidding for you. Homework, class projects, buying your lunch. Wouldn't that be nice?"

The bell was muted in Ms. Murphy's room, but it still cut through our conversation, causing us to collect our things. Hudson let me grab one more hummus-coated carrot stick before he shoved the Tupperware container into his backpack. "What would be nice is not meeting with her at all."

"*Her?*" I waggled my eyebrows at him, tossing my head back with a laugh. "Principal Horrible's playing matchmaker now, huh?"

Hudson flicked me on the back of my head with his fingers, but it did nothing to dull the swift stab of amusement. "I'll be staying after pretty much every day except Fridays, so can you make sure Paisley gets off the bus okay those days? If you have to work, you can drop her off with Mrs. Maria on the corner."

"Sure," I said, tipping my chair back farther as he got to his feet. "You sure Mrs. Maria can handle her, though? Paisley's had an attitude lately."

"Maybe Maria's sweetness can rub off on her."

"Here's hoping." I scoffed out a laugh, but leaned back too far in my chair. The two legs of the chair slid out from my balancing act, sending me clattering to the ground with a yelp. Hudson's laugh burst out as he headed toward the door, a light sound, echoing even as he walked out with me grumbling behind.

My life drastically changed on a Friday night in June when my mom called the police on me. I'd been living in our two-bedroom, two-bathroom house on Grisham Street all alone since April, when she'd unofficially moved in with her boyfriend. She'd stop in sometimes to get clothes, use our washing machine, but otherwise left me alone. That wasn't anything new—I'd gotten used to her staying stretches of time at someone else's house as I grew up. And now that I was older, and learned how to talk back, it was kind of nice to live on my own in that house. To pretend I was an adult, all on my own.

Until she stopped paying the electric and water bills, and the shutoff notices followed through on their threats. In hindsight, I should've known nothing good would come from me confronting Mom after she got out of work. I should've known she wouldn't listen, because she never did. I should've known her boyfriend would've stepped in and escalated things, like he always did.

Except I didn't think it through. That's the problem with anger. It tastes good in the moment, but the consequences...not so much.

After living practically on my own, I found being thrust into someone else's routine suffocating, the way it felt to wear a jacket two sizes too small. I didn't have a chance to prepare myself for the sudden and swift change either, which made for a hard transition. I'd caught the atmosphere shift a few times after I stepped into the room. Paisley's laughs would always die off and Uncle Dean would clear his throat before trying to strike up a conversation that always left me feeling hollow. They could never really relax around me.

A guest who'd overstayed her welcome.

So, as often as I could, I picked up shifts at my part-time job or worked all afternoon outside on the van, affectionately dubbed Petunia. Saturday, though, I had homework, and shared the dining table with Paisley as we worked. Paisley swung her legs off the kitchen chair and doodled on her homework sheet rather than doing it. The drawing was quite good for a seven-year-old—the sun was shaded with various shades of yellow, and the butterflies were multi-colored as she drew them around the page. Instead of doing my own homework, I watched her, wishing my life was as difficult as second grade mathematics.

She didn't look up. "Take a picture."

"Huh?"

"Take a picture of me. It'll last longer."

Something that was also new ever since I moved in—Paisley's attitude. She was like a little growling chihuahua. If *her* nickname was the Grim Reaper, I would've believed it. Maybe she was the third grade Grim Reaper. At first, I'd been patient with her, but with each jibe and dig over the past two months, it became increasingly hard to hold back.

"Wow," I said with a little scoff. "A comeback from the eighties. Super impressive."

Paisley pursed her lips a little, saying nothing.

When she fell silent, guilt ebbed in at the fact that I'd made fun of a kid. I tapped the surface of my history textbook in front of me with my pencil. "How was the first week of school?"

"Fine." She frowned then, looking up at me. Unlike Hudson's, her eyes were brown, and dark enough that they were a little unsettling. When she had a flat stare, she kind of looked like she belonged in *Children of the Corn.* "How was your week?"

I'd been expecting a quip from her, so my defenses went up. "Fine."

"Homework?"

I glanced down at my textbook. "A little."

She scribbled her happy little sun with happy little butterflies and let her harshness linger in the air. "Why don't you worry about that instead of me?"

And just like that, my guilt vanished.

Uncle Dean came out of his bedroom with his e-reader in one hand. He took in my expression and focused on Paisley. "Are you being bratty again?"

"Never," she replied, scribbling.

Uncle Dean let out a withering sigh as he dropped into the seat on the other side of me. "I've told you time and time again that we are polite to our guests."

"I thought she's family," Paisley said. "Not a guest."

Uncle Dean's expression faltered, like he realized a mistake he made. It was the same shift in expression that always came, and discomfort bloomed in my stomach as silence fell over the table. "I'm family *and* a guest," I told her, picking at the remnants of my nail polish. "But besides, you shouldn't be mean to family, anyway."

"Maybe you should keep that in mind too," she threw back at me, and with that, Paisley snapped her box of crayons shut and walked away.

My uncle ducked his face into his hands and scrubbed, letting out a sigh. "I thought the rebellion was supposed to come in middle school."

"I'd say that conversation was a success for the most part," I told him, leaning back into the seat. "No one cried."

It was a joke. A bad one, given the fact that neither of us laughed, but I still tried. Lately, Uncle Dean had started to devolve into the textbook definition of *exhausted*. Puffiness underneath his eyes, prickling skin as he went days without a shave, slumped shoulders. He'd been picking up extra hours at the factory he worked for, and between that, keeping house, and maintaining one extra kid, he had to be drained.

"Do you want me to pick up groceries this week?" I asked him, tapping the textbook again. My fingers had picked up the tempo, an increasingly nervous beat. "If you have a list, I can do the shopping."

Uncle Dean straightened from his slouched position, letting his fingers slide from his eyes. "No, I've got it, kiddo. The store's right outside the factory. I'll swing in one day after work."

I flipped open my history book to a random page and picked up my pencil, nodding.

Uncle Dean set his e-reader down on the table and loaded up the latest novel he was on, but by the way he kept fidgeting, I knew he was trying to work up the courage to say something. Learning his tells had come easily for me, especially since he shared a lot of them with my mom.

"Lacey," he began slowly, still not looking up. "Has your mother contacted you at all?"

"No." I didn't miss a beat, but I did grip my pencil tighter. "Why?"

"This isn't something I want to get into too much with you." I waited, because I knew despite what he wanted, he would go on. "She hasn't dropped off this month's check for child support yet."

Once Uncle Dean found out Mom had left me unsupervised for months—and let the electric get shut off—he put his foot down. Mom and Uncle Dean came to the decision about temporary guardianship quite quietly, without the court getting involved. He never told me the entirety of their conversation, and Hudson claimed he didn't know when I tried to pry it from him, but from what I gathered, Uncle Dean told Mom that she could give him guardianship, or he'd call Child Protective Services. They agreed on a set amount for child support, unofficially, and that was that.

I stared at the gibberish printed in the textbook in front of me, a throb building in my temples. Uncle Dean's words stung like a slap, and it was clear to see why he hadn't wanted to bring it up. Mom made the first two payments without trouble—the checks showed up in the mail on the first of July and August. It shouldn't have been a surprise she eventually gave up, but something about it stung, like I wasn't worth the fight to stay nor the money she agreed to pay Uncle Dean every month. "Do you want me to call her?"

"No! No. I'll...I'll try getting in touch with her." Uncle Dean gave up with looking at his e-reader and raised his chin. "The last time you saw her, it caused nothing but problems. Which isn't your fault—" He had to rush to get that in there "—but I want us to be safe. Not that seeing her isn't *safe*, of course—"

"I get it, Uncle Dean. I do."

The last time I saw Mom, it *did* cause nothing but problems—problems that ended with me with scraped palms and Hudson with bleeding knuckles in the back of a police cruiser.

I waited for Mom to call me after that night, waited like

an idiot by my phone. It never rang. In fact, it was only a week later before my phone plan had been canceled, and Uncle Dean had to add me to his.

I curled my hands into fists even now recalling the memory, eyes tightening. "How much is it? The money she said she'd pay? I have money saved up from work—"

"Don't even think about it," Uncle Dean said sharply. "I already hate the fact that you pitch in for groceries. Just... don't worry about it, okay, kid? These are adult problems."

Adult problems. I wanted to laugh. I wasn't sure when a parent not wanting to see their child anymore became an "adult problem," but it still crushed the same.

"You worry about you, okay, Lacey?" Uncle Dean coasted his hand down the back of my head in an affection gesture, one he often did with Paisley, and it once more caused my eyes to sting. There were waves of moments like this—when the guilt and shame of forcing him into this situation was hard to swallow. I tried to tell myself that it really wasn't my fault, that it was my mother's, but it didn't silence the thoughts for long.

Something must be wrong with me enough that she didn't even try to keep me.

I nodded, swallowing past the emotion that built in my throat, and gave him a quaky, encouraging smile. "Will do, Uncle Dean."

CHAPTER 3

Whatever was "out of order" in the girls' locker room got fixed by Monday morning, thankfully, and I went about my ritual getting ready in there. No beefy football players would be barging in and scarring me for life, so I took my sweet time massaging the shampoo into my roots.

I laid out all my makeup on the vanity on the far wall and got ready easily, readjusting my towel wrapped around my head. My makeup routine was probably a bit complex for sitting in a classroom for the entire day, but the repetitiveness of it comforted me. I'd been doing my makeup since the seventh grade when I stole Mom's eyeshadow palette, and I'd experimented with it almost daily since.

Ah, it was peaceful to not have to worry about being spotted in my towel. I'd probably have a nightmare about the whole Landon Settler situation sometime soon.

I'd just finished up applying concealer underneath my eyes when the locker room door creaked open. The person who walked in was obscured by a section of metal. Their voice, however, was not. "You *didn't* put me on it...right?"

"If you're so worried about being on it, you should've voted a label for someone."

A third voice chimed in. "It's not that big of a deal, Mads."

From the corner of my eye, three people stepped out from around the lockers, stopping when they saw me. Now, the voice registered as familiar. "Can't you do your makeup at home?"

I let out a pained sigh, not even bothering to glance up. "Ah, just my luck," I muttered without being quiet about it, pulling out my tube of red lipstick. "It's the evil stepsisters and the wicked stepmother."

"Does that make you Cinderella?" Jade Dyer stepped into the view of the mirror and frowned at me. She was that kind of perfect that made you want to wring her little neck, at least appearances wise. Blonde hair that probably cost a fortune at the salon. Nails that were never chipped. Her personality, though, was about as beautiful as a garbage can. The girl wouldn't know what kindness was if it bit her in her stuck-up little butt. "I don't know how to say this, but Cinderella didn't look so...trashy."

I grinned, popping my lips together with a smack before turning to face her head-on. Her piddly minion, Madison Oliphant—yeah, Principal Horrible's equally horrible daughter—stood at Jade's side, though her expression was more neutral rather than looking like she stepped in dog poop. On Jade's other side stood Riley Huntington, public enemy number three. They looked a little like Jade copied and pasted. "Thanks, babe," I said, twirling my lipstick tube.

"It wasn't a compliment."

"Then why did I take it as one?" Girls like Jade, who got angry when you didn't conform to their social cues, tickled my funny bone. Seriously. She expected me to drop to my knees in worship because she knew how to do a backflip, and there was something so ridiculously amusing about it. "You wear makeup, too, you know. What makes me trashier than you?"

"Please, you're obviously trying too hard. A red lip? Who are you, Taylor Swift?"

I narrowed my eyes. "Don't bring her into this."

Madison broke away from us then to pop open one of the lockers, shoving her duffle into it. Her interest in the conversation was obviously waning, but she had to get a quip in. "Red lipstick is a little...bold for school."

"And the nose ring," Riley added, curling her nose with distaste.

"You're afraid I'm going to draw the attention away from you, huh?" I gave myself one more once-over in the mirror, trying not to be annoyed with how my winged eyeliner wasn't quite lined up. I touched the glittering stud in my nostril, wiping off any foundation that might've gotten on it. Satisfied, I glanced at Jade. "Afraid I'll give you a run for your money with Connor?"

"Connor wouldn't go for you." The smug surety in her voice made me want to hit her. "In fact, no guy on the football team would."

I looked over to Riley. "When did Ashton quit the team?"

The girl didn't answer me, but her lips thinned. Then again, she didn't need to answer—we all knew Ashton was one of the defensive linemen. "Ashton's over you," Riley said, tilting her head, and her curls hardly moved, like she used too much hairspray. "He was texting me all weekend."

"Wonder how your boyfriend feels about that," I replied, watching as her lips thinned even further. She'd be baring her teeth soon.

I knew better than to engage with the three of them, but parrying the banter back and forth was so satisfying. Confrontation tasted *so* good.

I gathered my makeup back into its bag and headed toward the bathroom stall to change, contented by my last quip, ready to dust my hands of the situation.

"Just remember," Jade called after me in a weird, ominous tone. "If you ever find yourself wondering why you don't have a boyfriend, remember this moment."

"Yeah, yeah." I waved my hand in the air without turning. "I'll never get a date because I wear red lipstick. Guess my life has no meaning."

I closed myself inside a stall and got dressed, imagining Jade's probably still twisted expression, and allowed myself to smirk.

"Most Likely To: Never Get A Boyfriend?" I demanded with my phone an inch from my nose, reading the words once more before scoffing out a breath. "Oh, that's rich. Clever. Truly. Someone needs to give that girl an award."

Hudson got home from his "mentor" thing ten minutes ago, and he joined me outside to work on the van. I only had an hour before my shift, and I'd wanted to get as much done as possible. The heat of the sun began to die off, but it didn't stop sweat from gathering along my skin as we worked in the small space of Petunia. We had the two side doors open along with the trunk doors propped, allowing the barest breeze through.

Today, I worked on building the platform bed. When we'd first gotten Petunia, we'd taken all the back seats out and stripped the interior down bare. We added vinyl flooring and put up paneling, which took us longer than I cared to admit—it turned out I wasn't the best at taking measurements, and Hudson had to recut the boards several times—but we were almost able to start on the exciting stuff. The stuff that'd start to make the van feel more livable.

Except right now, I let Hudson work while I gaped at the stupid PDF on my phone.

"I didn't tell you so you'd get upset about it," Hudson muttered, leaning his weight into his power drill, drilling one of the last boards down for the bed frame. "Or else I would've kept it to myself."

In all honesty, it was kind of surprising I hadn't picked up on the Most Likely To list earlier at school. The list was monumental in Brentwood High society, but then again, I normally kept my head down from all that—no point in worrying about popularity and gossip when I couldn't care less about who anyone talked about. I was probably one of the only students *not* subscribed to Babble, the school's gossiping site, so that must've been how I missed the memo.

If I knew Jade was going to put me down on the stupid list, I might have actually wrung her neck this morning.

"I'm not upset. Seriously." I scoffed again, folding my arms over my chest, glaring at my phone. "This is ridiculous, you know. This whole...Most Likely To list business. Ridiculous. I'll never understand gossip, Hudson. Like, what's so funny about this? Why does everyone give that stupid Top Tier so much power?"

All through my ranting, Hudson drilled, pausing only to flick his hair from his eyes.

"Never get a boyfriend," I muttered, scrolling through the list. "I mean, what the heck? I'm on here, but you aren't?"

"Yeah, yeah, not the first time I've heard that today."

I took in more names on the list, remembering a few, not really recognizing others. When I ran into Jade this morning, had she already put me on the list? I wouldn't put it past her to write me in as a last-minute addition out of spite.

"You know." Hudson's voice took on the soft sort of leading quality that his dad's got sometimes, especially when he was broaching a subject he didn't know how I'd react to. "Maybe you *should* date a bit more. Well, wait, *more* implies that you date a little. You should go on dates, though, Lacey. Not with Ashton, but someone... Are you listening?"

My gaze had gotten stuck on who'd been paired my opposite, in a way. Most Likely To: Never Get A Girlfriend. *Landon Settler.*

This boy, I swear, I thought while raising my eyebrow at my phone. He just kept popping up. Weird that he'd been put on the list, though—his Top Tier status should've given him a pass.

"Lacey." Hudson waved his hand in the air, catching my peripheral. "I think I know where Paisley's getting her selective hearing from."

"I'm listening, I'm listening." I put my phone down and gave him my full attention, one filled with attitude. "Dating. Tell me—why would I date anyone around here? Aside from the fact that everyone's brain cells have been consumed by football and stupid popularity lists, I plan on skipping town the second I graduate. What's the point of dating?"

"You never know what will happen."

"*You've* never dated either, Mr. Hypocrite." I walked over to him and tugged the power drill out of his grip, picking up a screw from the bin. "Maybe you should worry about your own love life. Move over."

Hudson scuttled along the plywood toward the open back doors, watching as I hopped on and took over where he'd been drilling. I lined up my screw with the joist and put pressure into the drill, holding it steady. The plywood vibrated, and the sound echoed inside the van. "Once we get this finished, it's painting time," I said cheerfully. "I'm thinking a forest green. Cute, right?"

He watched me work for a long time before he sighed. "Why do you want to leave Brentwood so badly?"

"Come on."

"Is it really because of your mom? Or is it something else?"

I knew getting angry was the last thing I should do. I knew it in a distant way, like I knew that Hudson was only worried about me. But it was that worry, that concern, that left me feeling suffocated, like someone had their arms wrapped around me too tightly in a hug I never wanted. Talking about my mom was a necessity sometimes, but others, I wished we could never mention her at all. I wished Mom could've been a pet frog that hopped away, or a hamster that snuck out of its cage—something that's absence was noticed, but brought up once and then never again.

"You shouldn't leave because you're afraid to face her," he said quietly.

I felt my body stiffen up. "I'm not *afraid of her*," I got out through gritted teeth. "Please. *Afraid?* More like she should be afraid if we ever run into each other. I've got a laundry list of things I want to say to her. None of them pretty." With a hard sigh, I picked up another screw. "Is it so wrong that I want to see the world outside of Brentwood, Hudson? Huh?"

"I just don't want you to live your life running away, Lacey."

The drill bit slipped against the screw as I put on pressure, slicing up the notch, ruining the cheap metal. I tossed the screw to the side with more force than necessary, and it rolled along the plywood. "I'm not running away." I forced myself to relax, to absorb the truth of the statement as I reached for a new screw. *I'm not running away.* "Let's talk about something else."

The beauty of my cousin was that he always backed down from confrontation, contrary to Brentwood High's popular belief. He was the most nonconfrontational person I'd ever met. He'd say things that would toe the line, but when it came down to an actual conversation—*ahem*, argument—he never pulled the trigger. He always let things go.

Hudson hopped out the back and moved around to the side door, picking up his water bottle. As he did so, he leaned a shoulder onto the van's door and eyed me. "I bet you can't get a boyfriend by homecoming."

I actually laughed aloud, a high-pitched, sudden sound. "That's a stupid bet idea. There's literally nothing in it for either of us except me wasting my time."

"If you get a boyfriend by homecoming, I'll give you the keys."

"Uh, the keys? To what?"

Hudson reached up and knocked his knuckles against the van's roof, creating a rattling sound that seemed to echo in my ears.

"Hudson, I *have* the keys. I already drive Petunia around. The keys are literally on my keyring in the kitchen."

"Yeah, but it's not *yours*. Not legally. The title's in my name, remember?" He shrugged. "I wasn't going to sign it over to you until graduation, but if you get a boyfriend and actually let yourself have feelings for him, I'll sell Petunia to you early."

"Why?" I asked, scanning his gaze. The bet seemed horribly skewed in my favor. So much so that I sat in silence, trying to figure out if Hudson was *really* proposing such a terrible wager. "Why not hold on to the van until graduation? You know what will happen if you sign it over."

Growing up, I'd wanted to leave this city behind and never look back. I'd planned it all out, time and time again. I printed out pamphlets and directions and did my research on GEDs and campgrounds I could park at. I consumed all the Van Life content YouTube had to offer. If Uncle Dean hadn't intercepted in June, as soon as I turned eighteen at the end of September, I was going to leave. I'd find a van, fix it up, and leave the second the clock struck midnight.

That was why Hudson bought the van out from under me in the first place. To take my escape route from me and hold it hostage until graduation.

"I know," Hudson said without missing a beat. He glanced around the interior of the van, jaw tight. "But if you really want to leave Brentwood, Lacey, I'm not going to be the one who holds you back. I think you should give the dating world a shot before ditching this place. You only live young once."

"I know what you're doing." I set the power drill down and faced him. "You're thinking that I'll fall head over heels for a guy and stay in Brentwood. That I'll choose to stay because I'm in love, or whatever. I'm right, aren't I?"

Hudson shrugged. "Does it matter?"

His nonchalance made this all feel like a trap, but he had to see the flaw in his plan. There were only two and a half weeks until my birthday, the same day as homecoming. Even if I spent every day, all day with a guy, no way would they be able to talk me out of leaving as soon as we transferred the ownership of the van. No way. "*Any* boyfriend?"

"A *real* boyfriend. I need to see him with my own eyes, so don't pull some 'oh, he lives in Canada' crap or whatever. And not Ashton."

"You keep bringing up Ashton like *I* was the one stalking *him*."

Hudson sighed at the thought of the boy in question, no doubt, but he didn't shift from the subject. "What do you say?"

I didn't know the first thing about dating, let alone in real life. It couldn't be like the movies, where the main character catches the eye of a guy in a coffee shop and they have some sort of chemical reaction. Love at first sight? It would've worked in my favor for this, but it didn't exist in the real world. And in the real world, I didn't have time to wait for a guy to waltz into the picture.

But I couldn't pass up the chance Hudson offered.

Like always, I'd play this by my own rules. That was the only way I knew I'd win. With the decision made, I smiled up at Hudson. "It's a bet."

CHAPTER 4

The dinner rush at Le Petit Bateau was no joke, especially when management perpetually understaffed servers on weekday nights.

"Behind," I called with a tray full of hot dinner rolls—three servings worth, to be exact. One basket went to table two, one needed to be dropped off at table eighteen, and this was the fourth batch table thirteen had gone through. Apparently, they were taking advantage of the unlimited bread, which I couldn't blame them. With the price tags on the menus, I'd fill up on free bread, too.

My warning had been directed at the two other servers posted at the POS system—which really meant point-of-sale system, but with how much the computer lagged, the acronym totally could've meant something else—and without even looking, the two girls leaned closer to the computer to let me slip past them.

The chatter of the dining room was loud, so were the clattering of forks and knives against ceramic plates. I smiled at anyone I locked eyes with, feeling my red-painted lips stretch wider than they would've if I wasn't on the clock. People here got to see my good side. When they got my good side, I got good tips. It was a trade I could concede to.

After dropping off all the rolls, I tucked the circular tray underneath my arm and made a beeline back for the server line.

Kelsi, a freshman at the community college a few towns over, rocked back on her heels and leaned against the station where the plates were, groaning. She had her natural curls smoothed up into two buns on the back of her head. "This is the last time I'm pulling a double," she announced.

I shot her a grin as I moved to the POS. "You say that every time you pull a double."

"This is a *Monday*!" She threw her hands up. "I didn't expect to be working my tail off on a freaking Monday night. Why's it so busy?"

"Maestro gave out coupons for a free appetizer last week," the other server, Cha, said beside me. Her first name was Jenny, but she told us to call her by her last name when she started here last year. She was a senior with me at Brentwood, but despite that, we never really spoke outside of work. "You two haven't noticed people cashing them in?"

"Who gave Maestro the right?" I demanded with mock outrage, but my smirk fell when I looked at my ticket time. "Is it me, or is the grill line taking forever tonight?"

"Not just you," Cha said.

"It's because Nate's not working," Kelsi added, and then she was off to check on her tables.

Cha moved over to the salad bar to make a few bowls, still within earshot. "Hey," I said, grabbing her attention. "Do you know of any guys at school looking for girlfriends?"

Cha snorted. "I'm sure there are hundreds."

"Any...cute ones?" Cute wasn't *necessarily* important, but it'd make the next two and a half weeks pass quicker. "In our grade, preferably."

"Why?" She propped her hip on the salad bar, tongs in hand. "Looking for a hot date to homecoming?"

I crinkled my nose. "I haven't gone to a single dance since I've been in high school, and I'm not starting my senior year."

"I get it, hating Brentwood is one of your character traits." Cha shook her head and loaded her salads onto her tray, patting my shoulder lightly as she passed by. "I'll keep my feelers out for you." And then she headed out onto the floor.

I took turns shifting my weight to one foot and then the other, trying to alleviate the pain radiating from my soles. There hadn't been a single second of peace tonight, let alone a moment to get off my feet, and I'd be paying for it tomorrow when I attempted to run to school.

The wad of cash in my pocket was deliciously large, though, and I patted it again to give me a boost of energy.

Our manager shoved open the door that led to the back of the restaurant and peer around. He was a short man with a head of curly black hair, a guy who looked like he'd be meaner than he was. Once he was satisfied with the number of filled tables, he turned to me, nodding. "How's it going, Lacey?"

"Ship's in good shape, Maestro," I responded, giving him a salute. His name was Michael—super boring—but the nickname Maestro came after an angry customer practically cussed him out. They were probably looking to call him "captain," since Le Petit Bateau meant *the little boat* in French, but instead sarcastically called him Maestro. It stuck, much to Michael's chagrin. "Though next time you give out coupons, you could give a girl a heads up."

"Not that you're complaining with the tips," he returned with a teasing smile, dusting a crumb from the counter into his palm and dumping it into the trash. "Little miss 'I'm going to move away and never come back.'"

I stuck my tongue out at him, and that was the precise moment that the grill line decided to intervene. Table thirteen's shrimp scampi and seafood bake came up with steam rolling off it, and I loaded it up onto my serving tray. Right before I stepped out from the serving line, the hostess waved me down. "Lacey! I just sat table fourteen."

I nodded as I passed her, though I felt like sticking my tongue out. Surely she didn't mean to double seat me. Surely it was accidental. But if she wasn't careful, I was going to *accidentally* bump her into the lobster tank.

"Plates are hot, so please be careful," I told the two elderly men, not even wincing as the ceramic seared into my fingertips. "Can I get you anything else? More water? More napkins?"

They took their time looking over their plates, in which

I forced myself still and to not bounce on my toes. I was thinking of ten other tables at once, but the key to getting a good tip was to make sure the guests I was with felt like they were the only ones. So, despite Maestro calling out that table eighteen's order was ready—and the fact that I still had to greet table fourteen—I waited patiently for the men to answer.

"No, no, Lacey, this is great. Thank you."

"Enjoy your meal," I told them sweetly, tucking my tray underneath my arm. "I'll be back to check on you."

And then I was off. Hot food always took priority over new tables, so I ran table eighteen's order out quickly before stopping by table fourteen. Ugh, it wasn't a small table either. The host double sat me *and* it was a seven-top. The lobster tank was looking more and more like a viable option.

"Hey, there, sorry about the wait," I began my spiel with a peppiness that had begun to fade over the night, but I made sure to maintain a cheerful expression with each set of eyes I locked onto. A man, a woman, another man, another woman... "My name's Lacey, and I'll be taking care of you tonight. Can I get you something to drink?"

I'd gotten all of the words out before I settled on the last person at the round tabletop, freezing. No one else had looked familiar except for the last person, a boy with broad shoulders—Landon Settler.

Landon looked completely different than last week, when he'd been sweaty and wearing workout clothes. His hair was parted down the middle, loosely pushed back out of his face, and the collared shirt he wore had the top two buttons undone. He looked like many of the other young guys who came in here for dates or with their families—sophisticated and untouchable.

He was probably thinking that I looked different too, given the fact that I actually had clothes on this time around.

It was a good thing I was trained to multitask, because while I was shocked at the sight of him, my server brain still registered what everyone wanted to drink. "All waters," I said with a slight chuckle, locking eyes with the dark-haired girl beside Landon. "Easy-peasy. Back in a flash."

And then I booked it from the table.

"Anyone want to take fourteen?" I asked when I was behind the safety of the server line, peering over the POS system to stake out the table. Landon had his head tilted toward the girl on his left, murmuring something. "I'll give you ten bucks."

Kelsi stopped filling her sodas to look over. "Ew, a seven-top? No, thanks."

"Is that Landon Settler?" Cha asked, raising her eyebrows. "Aw, he's with his family. That's his sister, I think—did you know he had one? A lot of people don't. "

Hope sprung like a well within me. "Ten bucks and he's yours."

Cha grinned like she was thinking about it before she shook her head. "I would, but a seven-top would put me into cardiac arrest territory."

I'm already there, I thought miserably, trudging to the drink station.

I shouldn't have worried that much, honestly. Of course

Landon wasn't going to be all "hey, looks like you actually do hang out in places other than the men's locker room" or with his family there, and again, he wasn't that kind of guy, anyway. He practically embodied the word *shy*. Friday morning had been the first time I spoke to him ever and he barely stuttered out a full sentence. It'd be easy to ignore him entirely.

I carried the seven waters back to my table with my spine straight, mentally coaching myself into the role. Everyone happily chatted when I approached, allowing me to reach around them to set their drinks down. "Are we ready to order or do we need another minute?"

"I think we're ready, dear," the redhaired woman told me. She had to be none other than Landon's mother, with the same hair color and freckles. There was none of Landon's gentleness in her face. "I'll start."

Working my way around the table, I jotted everyone's orders down quickly, and when I got to Landon, I kept my gaze trained on my server book, scribbling down his meal.

"Oh, and dear?" The woman with red hair laid her hand on my arm, causing me to jump before I could tamp the surprise down. "My husband wants *extra* garlic on his scampi. He always forgets to order it and he'll grumble about it all night."

"Extra garlic," I parroted back to her, making a show of tugging out my book and writing *XG* down. "Got it."

When I risked a look at Landon, his gaze was focused at where his mother's hand rested on my arm, not my face. As I walked away, I heard his mother say something about *"facial piercings,"* no doubt commenting on the glittering stud I had in my nose. That was a common quip I got, especially in a fancy-schmancy place like Le Petit Bateau, but if Maestro didn't care, no one else should've.

Despite the relative ease of taking the order, I knew it wasn't the hard part. The hard part came fifteen minutes later when I was delivering food, and the thin boy I didn't recognize dumped the crab legs' butter into Landon's sister's lap. Hopefully he wasn't her boyfriend, because the look she gave him promised nothing good. I snatched extra napkins off my tray, apologizing for the fault even though it wasn't mine.

"I need a five-minute smoke break," I told Maestro when I got back to the serving line, dumping my tray in the return and wiping my hands on my apron. "All of my tables have their food or their check, so they should be good for a few."

"Clocking it now," Maestro returned, twisting the grandma-looking kitchen timer he kept on the counter by the POS system.

I didn't smoke. In fact, I wasn't even old enough to, and Maestro knew it. Asking for a "smoke break" was an easy way of asking for a mental checkout—five minutes to decompress from the pressure dinner rush put on. Everyone got two per shift, and I definitely needed one now.

Once outside the side door, I crouched down beside the outdoor ashtray, balancing on my toes and wrapping my arms around my knees.

I'd been working at Le Petit Bateau for almost two years. As soon as I got the worker's permit from the school,

I picked up as many shifts as I could. During the school year, I was limited to three days a week for only five hours per shift, but sometimes Maestro let me pull extra hours under the table when he was desperate—which, due to his seriously crappy scheduling skills, was often. Anything for the extra money.

I slid my hand into my apron pocket, clutching the crumpled bills. Maestro's off-the-cuff line of moving away danced through my head, tantalizing enough that all of my cells ached for it. One of the great things about serving was that restaurants all over the country were hiring. I wasn't stuck in some elitist town in Connecticut working at Le Petit Bateau my entire life. If I wanted to, I could work at any one of the number of chains LPB had across the country.

I would've left right then if I could've. Taken Petunia and hit the road. The buzz of that freedom was as tempting as could be, the image of myself behind the wheel, escaping into the night. Ditching Brentwood, leaving everything bad behind.

Hudson's warning the day he got Petunia, though, kept me from acting on that impulse. *"You can drive it until graduation, but if you take the van, I'll report it as stolen. You know that taking a stolen vehicle across state lines is a felony, right?"*

Even though I was nearly certain he'd never do it, it felt like too big of a risk to call Hudson's bluff.

But...his offer. His bet. The ticket to freedom was almost within reach.

"Hey."

I jerked my head up to find Landon Settler standing before me, approaching as silently as he had Friday morning in the locker room. The wind tugged at the left side of his hair, trying to brush it across his forehead, and he batted it back.

I didn't rise from my crouched position. I still had three more minutes. "Hiya."

"Sorry for earlier," he told me, awkwardly holding his hands in front of him. His gaudy blue and gold Brentwood High class ring on his ring finger caught in the light. "It wasn't your fault. With the, uh—with the butter falling on my sister."

"Oh, I know," I answered confidently, tilting my head. "You came out here to tell me that?"

"I came out here to apologize." He cleared his throat, but didn't look away. "For that. For my mom."

His cheeks were already red from our ten second conversation. He was an easy blusher, and for some reason, that made me want to grin. "Your mom?"

"About the—well, the nose piercing comment. I know you heard it."

I wasn't totally sure how he knew that I knew—I thought I'd hid my reaction pretty well—but I didn't question it. "A gentleman, are we?" I asked as I got to my feet, dusting my apron. "After you saw me naked?"

Landon cleared his throat again, but it quickly turned into him coughing, and this time, he did look away. I'd been looking for that reaction, and even though he'd interrupted my five minutes of well-deserved silence, I didn't mind it.

That strange urge to smile came again, but I kept my expression neutral.

"Don't sweat it," I said while patting his chest, secretly just so I could see if his pec was as firm as his shoulder blade had been. It totally was. "Except, if you really want to repay me, I think it's only fair to reciprocate, no?"

"W-What?"

I was going to tell him *you saw me half-naked; when's my turn?* with as much teasing flirt as I could muster, just to see his face turn firetruck red, but it was at that second that I saw her.

At first, I thought I imagined it, watching the tall and slightly muscular woman step out of the red SUV in the parking lot across the street, separated by two lanes of road that didn't have any traffic. Her loose brown hair picked up in the wind, and even from here, I could see the tattoos lining up her arms. She scanned the parking lot of the strip mall she'd parked at, but as if in slow motion, I watched her gaze swing toward Le Petit Bateau.

Mom.

Ice water poured over my flame, dousing it completely. All of the confidence, the boldness, the teasing—it was gone in a flash, and not even a smolder remained.

I gripped Landon by the front of his button-down shirt and yanked his chest to mine, narrowly avoiding getting lipstick on the fabric. He was a wall of a boy, perfectly shielding me. My chest rapidly rose and fell with panic, and I stared at the buttons on Landon's shirt, unable to swallow the saliva in my mouth.

What are you doing? I demanded in my head, the words

loud and jarring. I should feel rage at the sight of her, living her life. I should be furious that, even after two months, she still hadn't called me once. I should be angry that my own mother had ditched her own daughter.

But now, in the smoking section of my work, practically breathing onto the chest of a boy I'd spoken with a total of two times, I suddenly wanted to cry.

In that instant, I could remember the last time I saw her with perfect clarity. I had been on the ground with my palms scraping the grit and gravel, staring up at Hudson, whose own fist had curled at his side. It had all happened in the briefest flash—Mom's boyfriend pushing my shoulders, Hudson hitting him to get him back. Mom had rushed out of Allen's Alley to find her boyfriend playing the victim while holding his bloody nose.

She had to have seen me on the ground. She had to have. I waited for her to turn, to glance my way, but she never did.

Landon brought his hand up and touched the side of my arm now, the same one he'd grabbed to haul me through the locker room. His fingers were warm against my skin. "Are you okay?"

I risked another glance around him, but Mom was no longer anywhere in sight. The parking lot was one for a row of stores, so she could've gone into any one of them. Shopping for who knew what. Shopping, even though her daughter was gone. I was fairly certain Mom had no idea where I worked—besides signing the work permit papers, the topic had never been brought up again. However, the idea that she was so close, could've spotted me, could one day waltz into Le Petit Bateau and see me, left me feeling sick to my core.

Landon's hand gently rubbed up and down on my arm, an inch of gentle movement that slowly lulled me back into focus. I looked up into the storm of his eyes. When he blinked, his lashes brushed against the constellation of freckles along his pink cheeks. I had to smell like fried fish and grease—real attractive—but he smelled nice, like lemon and something sweet.

My mental awareness took its time creeping back in, the air around me slowly coming back from the white noise blur it'd been in. I let go of Landon's shirt, staring in a mild sort of horror at the now-wrinkled fabric. I should've apologized for getting grabby, but that would open the door for him to ask what that was about. I couldn't let him ask.

Instead, I lifted my chin and met his gaze again, and that was when it happened. Lightning flashed in my brain, like a *ding, ding, ding* of a lightbulb going off. Angels were totally singing, because staring up at Landon, I didn't see a freakishly tall quarterback.

I saw my ticket to freedom.

Hudson's words resurfaced in my mind. *A real boyfriend. What do you say?*

I opened my mouth, but the side door of the restaurant flung wide, and Maestro appeared with his kitchen timer in his palm. "Five minutes are up, Lacey." His gaze slid to Landon, eyeing the senior boy up with suspicion. "Let's get back to work."

I smoothed my fingers down the fabric of Landon's shirt, rubbing out most of the wrinkles, patting him once more on the chest. "I'll see you in school," I told Landon, staring him down as I made my promise.

At school tomorrow, in fact, because I needed to get this "boyfriend" ball rolling, and I found just the guy to fill those shoes.

CHAPTER 5

When the third period bell rang Tuesday morning, signaling the break for lunch, I was the first out of my seat and launching into the hallway. Thankfully, my classroom was near Cafeteria B, where most of the seniors sat—and where the Top Tier camped out. Normally, I avoided the place like the plague, but today, I was on a mission. Tucking my textbook underneath my arm, I picked up my pace.

I got to the mouth of the cafeteria doors and poked my head in for a quick peek. Some members of the Top Tier were sitting at their usual table in the middle—I could see Jade and Madison in particular, tossing their coiffed hair like they were on the set of a photoshoot instead of the grungy lunchroom—but not the tall, broad-shouldered boy I'd been hoping for.

I looked down at myself. I didn't have a lot of impressive outfits to choose from in my meager suitcase, but I'd borrowed one of Hudson's oversized band tees and tied it into a knot at my waist, pairing it with the only denim skirt

I'd packed. My hair hung loose around my face, and the brief check in the bathroom before last period told me that my makeup was still intact from this morning.

I'd looked at my mouth a little longer than I should've in the mirror, debating on whether or not to scrub off the red lipstick.

No. I refused to let Jade Dyer get to me. Refused.

When it came to guys at Brentwood High, I had experience with very few. Most of the experience sucked, anyway. And besides, this was important. Serious. The idea of putting the fate of my life in the hands of any random upperclassman made my armpits sweat. No, I needed someone I could trust, and while I didn't know Landon...I felt like I could trust him.

And speak of the devil.

Landon Settler walked down the hallway with his head down, brown paper lunch bag in his grip. The only issue was that he wasn't walking alone—Ashton Shaw walked at his side, his arm draped over the quarterback's shoulders. Ashton was a pretty boy, with his stupidly puffy brown hair and deep eyes. He was the kind of guy that, if put in a lineup, someone would've assumed was nice. Held doors open for the elderly. Saved kittens from trees. He definitely put on that persona for the rest of Brentwood High.

From my experience, he was more likely to shut doors in the elderly's faces and set the tree on fire.

He laughed about something, but Landon had no amusement on his face. In fact, he looked like he was even leaning away from the boy.

I almost bailed at the sight of Ashton, but forced myself

to stand my ground. They were about to pass me when I reached my hand out like I was a roadblock, halting their progress. Landon's expression filled with surprise.

"Hey," I greeted, trying to keep my voice light. "Can I talk to you?"

"We're talking right now," Ashton replied, tilting his head to the side, accompanied by a teasing smirk. "Looking good, Lacey. I see the summer sun treated you well."

I instantly resented the fact that I was wearing a skirt and Mr. Skeevy got to see my legs. "Landon," I said pointedly. "Can we talk? *Alone.*"

Landon stared down at me, eyebrows drawing together. Weirdly enough, they were a shade lighter than his hair, redder against his skin. "Uh...sure." He came out from underneath Ashton's arm and didn't spare him a backward glance.

Perfect. I diverted my path into the opposite direction of Cafeteria B, away from his friends and away from anyone who might've wanted to eavesdrop. After all, what did Lacey Churchill have to say to all-star Landon Settler? Surely Babble would've wanted to know.

Then again, maybe Babble *should* know...

No. Not yet. I was getting ahead of myself.

When we walked around the corner into a secluded hallway, I spun around, catching Landon, who'd only been two steps behind me, off-guard. He backed up, gripping his bag tighter. "Is it about the Most Likely To list yesterday?" he asked before I had a chance to begin. "Because I didn't know they'd put you on it. I swear."

"Did you know they were going to put *you* on it?"

Something minute in his expression shifted. "I wasn't surprised."

Interesting. "That's actually why I called you over here. In a way." *Here goes nothing.* "Want to get dinner with me tonight?"

Landon blinked once. Then two more times. He probably thought he heard me wrong, because his expression didn't change for the longest, longest moment. Long enough to make me wonder if he hadn't heard me to begin with. Or was searching for a polite way to say no. I hugged my textbook closer to my chest, a flutter of anxiety tickling my ribs. "Dinner?"

"Yeah. Dinner. Like, a date." Without giving myself time to debate any possible repercussions, I leaned into it, shrugging on my best *gushing* girl voice. "I know it's, like, super last minute, and super random, and I'm not sure where you like to eat, but—I don't know, I thought it could be fun. You and me hanging out. How funny would that be? Both people voted most likely to never get into a relationship go on a date together?"

Aaaaand, more blinking. I wasn't sure if I was relieved or annoyed by Landon's perpetual state of hesitation. At the very least, I thought he'd be interested. I mean, last week, when he'd found me in the locker room, he hadn't hesitated then. In fact, he'd *looked* at me then. He could deny it all he wanted, but he totally checked me out. What, was he more of a "look for free" kind of guy? Or was I not his type?

Now I really wished I'd scrubbed off the lipstick, Jade's snotty voice like a buzzer in my ear.

"Dinner," Landon echoed, still eyeing me with a confused sort of suspicion. "I—I have football practice, and I'll have to shower afterward, but—"

"So that's a yes?"

"Y-Yeah. That's a yes."

I sucked in a breath that cooled the anxiety swelling within me and stuffed down a triumphant smile. "Let's meet at Le Petit Bateau, then." High schoolers that went to LPB's on a weekday for dinner were few and far between, which gave us privacy. Cha might've gone to Brentwood—and so did Nate on grill line—but they'd be too busy working to listen to what we were saying. Plus, the employee discount was too hard to pass up. "Say...seven?"

"Seven."

A thrill shot up my veins at the idea of my plan in motion, and I was sure that it showed on my face. Good. Let whoever was walking past interpret *that*. "I'll see you tonight, then," I told Landon, clutching my books tighter before turning around, cutting back toward my locker.

Lunch period had only just begun, but I wasn't sure I could go meet Hudson in Ms. Murphy's room. Not with my scheming brain still running a mile a minute. He'd see through me easily, and I couldn't risk it. Instead, I opted to go to the west side staircase, to wait on the steps until my next class.

Phase One, complete. Now on to Phase Two.

Le Petit Bateau was slow for a Tuesday, which was a kids eat free night. Not that it was that much of a lure in the first place—our kids' menu kind of sucked. Then again, it made LPB's the perfect place for scheming. I showed up a few minutes before our agreed-upon time, sitting in an empty section.

"Cha," I said as she walked past my table, grabbing a few straws from the front pocket of her apron. I added them to the little straw cabin I was building from the straws I'd stolen out of the apron of another server. "You'll never guess who I'm on a date with."

Cha glanced at the empty booth across from me. "Danny Phantom?"

"Witty," I said with zero humor. "Landon Settler."

She laughed, leaning her palm on the tabletop. "Now *that's* witty. Wait, seriously? How'd you score that?"

"You mean, how did he score *me*?" I waggled my eyebrows at her, and she promptly swatted me for it. "It's a long story, but do me a favor? When he sits down, can you take a picture of us?"

"Did you seriously ask him out for a boost in popularity?"

Giving her my best server smile, I laughed. "I asked him out because I like him. Can you blame me for wanting a photo to commemorate the fact that he actually said yes?"

I wasn't sure I sold her on my laugh, but in the end, it didn't matter. A shadow appeared over us a moment later, and we both turned to find the broad quarterback behind Cha. He wore the same jeans he'd been wearing at school, but his shirt was another button-down. It was a forest green color that made his hair appear much redder under the lights. The top two buttons were once again undone.

"You made it," I greeted him, gesturing to the seat across from me with one of the wrapped straws. "Have a seat. Cha, can you get him a water?"

Cha snatched up my straw cabin and stuffed them back into her apron, all the while giving the quarterback her flirty eyes. "You *sure* you want water, Landon? We have teas, soda, lemonade. Something *sweeter*."

I made a face at Cha's shameless flirting with my date, which she blatantly ignored.

"Water's good." Landon slid into the booth, and his gaze cut almost cautiously to me. But, no—that wasn't right. It wasn't caution. It was...nervousness. "Thank you, Jenny."

She giggled—actually *giggled*—at hearing him speak her first name, and flitted off to fetch the drink. I smoothed my hands down my skirt and sat up straighter, wondering if I should launch into my offer now or wait until after we ordered. Landon hadn't picked up his menu, and my impatience nagged at me.

And apparently it nagged at him too. "Be honest." Landon sat still in his seat and eyed me like I was a rabid dog and he was waiting for it to lunge. "Who put you up to it? Connor? Kyle? Did they give you twenty bucks to ask me out?"

My jaw actually dropped open at that, but I managed to snap it shut as naturally as possible. "No one put me up to anything. But if I knew there was going to be money involved, I might've let them persuade me a little."

"So you're saying you asked me out because you really wanted to go on a date?"

I glanced around to see who sat closest, and the only person was the guy behind Landon, collar up, head bent over the table. I hadn't noticed when he sat down. As I peered around, I saw Cha lift her cell phone and point the camera at us. Taking the cue, I leaned across the table, laying my forearms flat against the top of it. Landon shrank back a little at my sudden closeness, but I surged on. "I was going to say it in the hall today, but I wanted...privacy. I have a proposition for you."

Surprise completely engulfed his features now, eyebrows shooting up and eyes going wide. It was exactly how he'd looked the day he'd walked into the locker room to find me in a towel. "Whoa, I'm—I'm not like that."

"Is that seriously the only definition of proposition you know?" I barely contained a sigh. "I have a *business proposal* for you, how's that?"

He shifted in his seat, glancing around the restaurant. "What do you mean?"

I had one last chance to reconsider what I was about to ask. One last chance to bail on the plan I'd been building ever since last night. I'd walked through every angle, thought about every possibility of it going wrong, and had an answer for each issue. If I wanted a boyfriend, this was the simplest, surest way. I just had to go all in.

"We were both on the MLTs this year for the same thing, right? Apparently, your popular friends think you're never going to get into a relationship. Sounds like your football buddies are having a ball poking fun at you for it, huh?"

Landon tilted his head as if to say, *your point?*

Here went nothing. "How fitting would it be if we—oh, I don't know—got into a relationship with each other? Stick it to their faces and remedy our casting, or whatever that stupid phrase is everybody calls it."

Landon's face scrunched up as he frowned, the area around his eyes wrinkling. It was definitely more of a *WTF* frown than a confused one, which didn't feel like it would bode well. "You care about the list that much?"

I stiffened, offended at the prospect. "No."

"Sounds like you do. Sounds like you care a whole lot about it if you're willing to fake a relationship with a stranger."

Fine. If he was going to point all the fingers and arch all the eyebrows, I'd give him full transparency. "My cousin made a bet that I couldn't get a boyfriend by homecoming—"

"You made a bet to date me?" Landon's voice got a little too loud for my liking.

"No! Not you specifically. Just...in general."

"And you thought I'd be the easiest mark?" Something strange crossed his expression as he laughed a little, the way someone does when they don't really think something is funny. He pressed his palms to the table as if he were about to stand up. "I should've expected something like that, honestly."

I reached out and wrapped my hand around Landon's wrist, freezing him to the spot. I'd prepared for this. This had been one of the "going wrong" scenarios that popped into my mind. "I didn't want to do this," I began, shaking my head with a sigh. "But if you leave, you're not giving me a choice."

"You don't want to do what?"

I slid my thumb along the skin of his wrist, lifting my eyebrows. "You and I both know the truth about what happened with Hudson freshman year. If you walk away, I can't promise Babble won't get a certain submission tonight. How do you think Brentwood High will function when they learn that their freckle-faced quarterback and his beloved besties are really bullies?"

Everyone had a weak spot, a secret, and it worked in my favor that Hudson was Landon's. Really, *popularity* was Landon's weakness, something he'd do anything for. Though Landon hadn't *really* been involved in the fight— Hudson was the one to split Landon's lip, not the other way around—Landon *had* been there when his friends jumped Hudson. Landon *had* been the one to keep the truth about it all a secret.

If I'd confronted Ashton or Kyle, they would've laughed in my face, I was sure. Would've told me that no one would believe me.

Landon, though, was like a fish on a hook. I watched the blood leech from his face, and I knew that he took the bait. "You're *blackmailing* me to be your fake boyfriend?"

"You can look at it like that, if you want." I turned my hand over to hold his wrist more naturally, almost like I was holding his hand. "Come on, though, it's not like it's *that* bad of a deal. You get your friends off your back, I win my bet, and we both walk away happy campers. Do you have a crush?"

"W-What?"

"A crush." I leaned forward farther, feeling his pulse jump underneath my touch. "We could make her jealous, you know. Some girls need a bit of a push to like a guy, and sometimes they can't picture dating a guy until they've seen him in a relationship. I could help you win her over. Less blackmailing, more of an I scratch your back, you scratch mine sort of deal. Only until homecoming."

Landon's blue eyes darted back and forth between mine, reading the sincerity there. Landon was my airplane ticket. A first-class seat to my freedom. Without him, I'd never arrive at my destination. And even though I'd never actually post the truth about the fight—Hudson would be thrown in the limelight once more for something he'd tried to put behind him, and, honestly, I doubted anyone would believe his side of the story—I had to let Landon think I would.

"What—" Landon began, but then stopped, sighing. The next breath he sucked in was low. "What would us dating look like?"

I suppressed a grin. *We are now boarding the plane.* "We'd act like we were actually in a relationship. See each other at school, meet up outside of school. Take photos together. I'd go to your games, meet your friends—"

"What would I have to do?" His gaze flicked up from where my hand still rested on his wrist to my eyes, the storminess in the depths stilling the air between us. "To be your boyfriend."

I used my free hand to lean my head into my palm, looking at him from this new angle, and even though it was weeks down the road, I saw the finish line. "Just say yes."

"And the girl that I like...this could convince her?"

It depended on a lot of factors, really. Whether or not they were close, whether or not he had already been friend-zoned—which, for his sake, I hoped not—and whether or not she had a boyfriend. But showing doubt now wouldn't work in my favor. "It's worth a shot, isn't it? What do you say? Yes?"

Cha was finally bringing back Landon's water—I could see her maneuver around from the server line with her ordering book in her hand—which meant this conversation would have to abruptly pause, but Landon didn't need the chance for a pause. He nodded slowly, almost like he was damning himself to whatever consequences were next, diving all in. "Yes, then. Yes."

The grin I'd been suppressing bloomed now. And just like that, I had a boyfriend for two and a half weeks.

CHAPTER 6

*I*t turned out that fake dating required a whole lot more strategy than I initially anticipated. Naturally, Landon and I couldn't announce that we were exclusive after one date, especially not twenty-four hours after Hudson offered the bet. Like *that* would go unnoticed with him. Then again, we couldn't wait too long either. Time was precious, and if I was going to help Landon capture the girl of his dreams, I needed to go all in. Might as well act like his genie with one wish during my last few weeks in Brentwood.

Landon and I left Le Petit Bateau after we finished our meal, mostly because Cha kept walking by to catch a hint of the conversation, and it was impossible to talk about anything secret with her around. We postponed our official chat until Wednesday after school, which proved tricky, since he had football practice and then had to drive his sister home. When I told him I'd pick him up once his parents got home—because, weirdly enough, the sophomore wasn't allowed to be home alone—he'd tried to refuse. "I can meet you someplace."

But I'd held firm. "It makes more sense for us to ride together."

In the end, Landon conceded in giving me his address, but told me to park along the street instead of in the driveway.

At four twenty-five, that was exactly where I sat now. I felt like I was at a stakeout, resting my arms on the worn leather steering wheel and staring out the windshield. The glass was dotted with dust and water spots, in desperate need of a wash, but I'd get to it sometime. I could wash the car wherever, but for right now, the construction of the interior was more pressing. I had a lot of work to do before homecoming.

A black SUV zoomed up alongside me and drove a little ways down the street, turning into the driveway of a small gray house. A man popped out a moment later, smoothing down his blazer and readjusting his grip on his briefcase. I raised my chin from the steering wheel and squinted. Something about him was familiar. He walked to the mailbox and popped it open, retrieving whatever was stashed inside, but that's when I saw it. The letters were white against the black box, in a font that was easy to read. *Settler*.

That was why he looked familiar—he was the man from Monday night at Le Petit Bateau. Extra Garlic. I glanced at the red house at my right, at the numbers Landon claimed were his address, and scowled.

Landon really told me to park at the wrong house. I wasn't sure why, but it irked me.

It took Landon ten more minutes to show up, driving his faded red coupe down the street and turning into his driveway. He didn't look over once from traveling between his car and the house, and then it took him ten more minutes to reemerge wearing different clothes. He kept his head down as he walked along the sidewalk on the opposite side of me, and as he got closer, I saw his hair was damp.

I tapped my fingers as I waited for him to cross the street, and the second he popped open the van's passenger door, I pounced. "Did you seriously give me the address of someone else's house?"

Landon didn't hesitate before sliding into the seat, slinking down. "Yeah."

"Care to tell me why?"

He tugged his seatbelt across his chest, but looked like now *he* was the one on the stakeout, afraid to be spotted. "If you parked in front of my driveway, my dad would've tried to talk to you. I saved you from the awkward conversation. Can we go?"

I didn't reach for the shifter. "We've been dating less than twenty-four hours and you're already embarrassed to be seen with me?"

"My parents—" Landon broke off with a rough sigh, rubbing his forehead. "They're intense, okay? Neurotic. I'd rather *not* introduce them to this whole plan of ours."

"You mean, introduce them to *me*?"

"What's the point of you meeting them if we're going to

break up by homecoming, anyway? Can you, just—can you drive?"

Something about the way he spoke made me refuse to move. "We need to make this as realistic as possible."

"I get you haven't dated, but do you *really* think it's realistic to meet the parents the first day you're dating someone? If you think that's a green flag, you're colorblind."

I wasn't sure I liked this version of Landon. I liked the version that was quiet and blushed a lot more.

I'd grabbed the shifter when the door to Landon's house opened again, and his dad walked back out into the yard. I don't know if he forgot something in his car or what, but as he stepped onto the paved walkway, his gaze locked on Petunia. And narrowed.

"Drive!" Landon's voice was a sudden whisper-shout, making the situation ten times tenser. "Drive, drive, drive!"

Spurred by the sudden order, I slammed my boot onto the gas pedal, hard enough for the tires to squeal at the sudden heave. We both lurched back into our seats, and I shot down the roadway past the Settler house. I shouldn't have looked—definitely should not have looked—but it was like I had no choice as we drove past Mr. Settler.

In slow-mo, our gazes locked. I could see the surprised expression on the man's face, like a blurry snapshot.

Landon and I sat silent for a solid minute as I continued to drive—and he stayed in his practical fetal position half on the seat and half on the floor the entire time—before I spoke. "I feel like that was way more suspicious."

He closed his eyes as he groaned, settling into his seat with a defeated slump.

I kept peeking glances at him, because it was super weird to have someone other than Hudson in the passenger's seat. Petunia was a personal thing for me, since it was going to be my home on wheels, so it felt odd introducing someone new.

"First things first," I began, waving my hand at him. "Take out your phone. We should exchange numbers. It'd be really weird if we didn't."

Landon complied, but slowly, unlocking his phone with a click. I opened my mouth to recite my number to him, but stopped at the last second. The number I knew by heart, the number I'd had my whole life, wasn't my number anymore. It belonged to a phone on a plan that my mom had stopped paying.

Swallowing down the rush of unease, I tugged out my phone and tossed it to him. "Text your number from my messages."

He muttered under his breath about something being "complicated," but I let him bask in annoyance while he typed. A second later, his phone pinged. "Done."

I glanced to see him saving my contact info, and then reached to cover his cell with my palm. "Hey, no, no—you can't save me as *Lacey*."

"What? Why not?"

"It should be something cutesy. Like a pet name."

"Why would we be at the pet-name stage *already*?" He shook his head, leaning away from me. "I'm saving it as Lacey."

"Then I'm saving yours as Frecklefaced Football Player."

I listened to him sigh in exasperation as I turned onto Walnut Street, smiling at how identifiable the sound was becoming. "Fine."

I tried peeking, but he angled his phone in a way that made it impossible to read the screen. "What does it say?"

He saved his contact info on my phone too, locking the screen before I could see what name he set for himself. "My Blackmailer."

We were off to a fantastic start, honestly.

I chose Jefferson Park as our meetup spot, easing Petunia into a parking space, rolling the shifter into place before shutting the engine off. The cab instantly became quiet without the rumbling transmission. "So, I've figured out there are five questions that every couple should know about each other to be believable." I turned toward Landon and propped my elbow on the steering wheel, raising my eyebrows. "Just in case someone asks."

Landon reached up and rubbed his fingertip against his temple. "Okay."

"How did we meet?"

"You were showering in the men's room."

I closed my eyes briefly. "What if we say we started talking because of the list? We were both on it, both thought it would be funny to go on a date, and really hit it off? It's close enough to the truth."

Landon nodded slowly, leaning onto the console between us as he looked out the windshield. "Le Petit Bateau's. We hit it off. Got it."

"What trait about each other drew us in?" I pressed my

palm to my chest. "I really like how broad your shoulders are."

He looked like he wanted to say something to that, but held himself back. "I like...how bold you are."

Bold. Normally, when people called me that, it was never a good thing. It was almost always an insult. I tipped my head to the side. "When's your birthday?"

"May ninth."

"Mine's September thirtieth."

He tilted his head to look at me, which brought our heads close in a split second. His eyes looked almost green up close, and his pupils were large. "So, the last day of our agreement is your birthday?"

He'd never know the true reason behind all this—the van, the freedom, my mother—but I nodded, not elaborating. "Now, friends. The only person you'll have to worry about interacting with on my side is Hudson—it's mostly going to rely on us playing it up for him when our paths *do* cross, which definitely won't be often. Probably just at school. The proof he's looking for is me being gone mostly. Taking photos together. That sort of thing. Who's your best friend?"

"Connor," he said, and I could picture Brentwood High's most beloved immediately. "And Reed Manning. They won't be hard to convince. They'll be...happy for me."

"Do we need to worry about your sister?"

"Gemma? No."

The surprise in his tone took me aback. "What are you going to tell her? She'll ask, right?"

"She doesn't have Babble, and she doesn't really listen to gossip around school. I'm hoping I won't have to tell her."

For some reason, him keeping this from his sister felt a little...insulting. Just like how he hadn't wanted me to meet his parents. On one hand, I could understand it. Of course he wouldn't want to lie to his family. If mine hadn't pushed me into this in the first place, I might've kept us separate, too. It still made me feel small, though, like something that was embarrassing that you didn't want the people closest to you to find out.

I straightened my shoulders and faced the park through the windshield, wondering, briefly, what it would've been like introducing a boy like Landon to my mom. It was impossible to tell how she'd have reacted. She wouldn't have been angry about me dating, but I could imagine her not caring at all. In a weird way, that felt worse.

Landon dropped his hands back into his lap. "If we're going to convince the girl I like, that means we should be around people more. Around the Top Tier."

It made sense that the girl he crushed on was in the Top Tier—those in that popular group tended to date within the clique. "I work three days a week, but otherwise I can be free." Being out with Landon would also be a good excuse to be out of the Bishop house more. This whole fake dating thing was going to kill a lot of birds with one stone. "Is there any other base you think we need to cover?"

"Consent." The word came out so swiftly from him, but it took me several seconds to catch up with what he meant. At first, I thought he meant like a contract—like we both needed to sign consent to dating—but then he said, "I don't want to randomly touch you without you being okay with it."

I wanted to tell him that I didn't care if he touched me, but I realized that might've been more for his benefit. That *he* didn't want *me* touching him without consent. It wasn't even something that'd popped into my mind. Of course, though, we'd have to touch each other. Frequently, if we were going to fully sell a romance. "It has to be subtle. Something people won't pick up on. Something easy. Quick."

He looked at me like *I have no clue.*

I racked my brain for a few seconds, trying to picture us together. "What about 'hi'?"

"Hi?"

"Yeah, *hi.* Maybe if one of us feels like it'd be a good moment to be cutesy, we say *hi,* the other person says it back, and then we touch. It's subtle, casual, and no one would suspect a thing."

"I don't see how *hi* could even work. Why would I randomly look at you and say 'oh, hello'?"

"Not a *hi* like a greeting, but more like...conversation filler. We say it because we want to say *something.*" I shook my head, popping open my door. "Hop out. I'll demonstrate."

"You're having too much fun with this," Landon muttered under his breath, but he obeyed. He probably realized fighting would be useless—which was a good thing to learn now.

The wind tugged at my hair as I rounded the front of Petunia, coming to where Landon stood in his open doorway. He tucked his hands into his jeans pockets and tried to look everywhere but at me. "So, I'll say hi, and touch me when you say it back. Got it?" When Landon nodded, I turned away from him, focusing on the trail that led deeper into Jefferson Park. And then, causally, I glanced over, locking onto his blue eyes. I gave him a faux shy smile. "Hi."

Landon couldn't seem to lose the twist to his features as if he'd smelled something bad. "H-Hi." And then, as awkward as could be, he reached out and patted my shoulder. Like we were football pals. Like I had a bug on my shirt.

I smacked his hand off. "Never mind, you start. When we make eye contact, say it."

I went back to glancing out over the park, slowly letting myself look over at him, letting our gazes connect. "Hi," he said.

"Hi," I replied, and with zero hesitation, I leaned in and wrapped my arms around his waist. All at once, our bodies pressed along each other, the firmness of his muscles all up in my soft body's business. My heart jumped at the contact, not properly prepared for how a boy would feel so close. Even if it was just pretend. I tipped my head back and looked up at Landon, trying to inject as many stars into my eyes as possible.

The wind caught at my hair again, and a few pieces stuck in my lashes, but I didn't pull away. I could see myself in the reflection of Landon's eyes, almost like a fish lens. Gosh dang, those *muscles*. The firmness of his stomach was pressed against my chest, and the sides of my arms felt the toned skin of his sides. I thought high school students were only built like that in the movies, but it was apparent that Landon must've lived and breathed physical activity. That, and he was blessed by whatever physique gods existed.

Landon looked wholly unaffected as he cleared his throat to get my attention. "How long are you going to stay like this?"

I spoke through my smile. "Until you stop acting like a statue and start acting like a boyfriend."

He reached up and tucked the flyaway pieces out from my gaze and behind my ear, and the action was smoother than I thought it'd be. Not nearly as awkward as his shoulder touch. Not quite lovey-dovey, but the quiet movement was very much so *him*. No complaints.

With a satisfied nod, I took a step back. I cleared my throat, ready for attempt number three. "Hi."

He didn't miss a beat this time. "Hi." Landon swiped up my hand that lay open at my side and threaded his fingers through mine, giving them a squeeze.

"Nailed it," I said happily, but looked down at our hands. My fingers were awkwardly splayed from how thick his were, to the point where it almost hurt. I maneuvered my hand out from between his and cupped our palms together, so all of my fingers lay over the side of his hand. Except now it felt a bit more platonic, less couply. I slid my pinky between his index and middle fingers, and it fit our hands closer, in a way that felt much more natural. "Your hand is big," I said.

"Your hand's small."

Snorting, I let go. "Consent, check. I think everything

else that comes up, we can tackle pretty easily. We're still in the early stages of a relationship, after all. It makes sense to get to know each other as time goes on, so we don't have to hash out *everything* right now."

"You're so calm about this," he said, and folded his arms across his chest. In an odd way, it made him look younger. "Like touching and being couply is easy for you."

"It is easy," I insisted. "Because it's not real."

And really, there was a lot riding on this. I had to give it my all.

Something popped into my head at that moment, and I reached for my back pocket. "You know what we should do? Send a tip to Babble." I didn't know how to work the site, but upon loading the interface, it was surprisingly simple. The school colors were emblazoned in a way that was cute and cool, not too hard to read—so unlike the horrible Most Likely To list PDF. Whoever had designed this site really did a great job. "Oh, perfect, you can make anonymous submissions."

"Why are we doing that again?" he asked as I loaded up the photo Cha had snapped of us at Le Petit Bateau. She captured the photo of Landon perfectly—you could practically count his freckles from how high-res the picture was— but she really only caught where the tip of my nose protruded from my face. The rest of my profile was covered by my hair. Humph.

"Building the narrative. It makes everything more believable. '*Landon Settler was out on a date,*'" I typed with a theatrical voice, adding a few gasp-face emojis and a whole lot of exclamation points. I tried to channel all the breathless, gossiping students I heard chitter and chatter through Brentwood halls, imagining what their submissions looked like. Hopefully I wasn't too far off. "'*I think I heard him call her his girlfriend.*'"

"Is that too on the nose?"

"Time is of the essence," I told him, and without letting him look it over, I sent it off to the Babble gods. My phone made a cute staccato chime as it did so. I looked up at Landon's expression, one that had crunched eyebrows and twisted lips, and I winked at him. "So. When's our second date?"

Landon's strange look persisted. I didn't know him well enough yet to read the emotion in his eyes, no matter how hard I looked. "I should probably..." He lifted his hand, and his class ring caught in the glimmer of sunlight that leaked through the clouds. The split blue and gold gemstones brightened. "I should give you this, shouldn't I?"

Automatically, I scrunched my nose up at the idea of wearing it. For one, it wouldn't even fit, not even on my thumb. For another, the bulky thing *screamed* Brentwood Pride. There were two stones in the center, one blue and one gold, with a football etched into the side of the metal. Across the front of the ring, in tiny letters I could barely read from here, read *SETTLER*.

"Maybe...not." I tried to smooth my expression out. "Not right away. I'd hate to lose it. Those things are expensive."

Landon used the tip of his finger to straighten out the ring before dropping his hand. "It's probably an old-fashioned thing, anyway."

The tips of his ears were reddish, and I felt the strongest urge to take the ring from him anyway, if only to make him feel less embarrassed. "I—I feel like that's something you should give your girlfriend for real," I said gently. "Not your fake one."

"You're probably right." He squared his shoulders, reaching up and laying the backs of his fingers over the side of his face. He left it there for a moment before curling the hand into a fist. "I should save some of the firsts for the real thing."

It didn't occur to me that by fake dating, it was taking away some of Landon's firsts. I'd held his hand—had he done that before? Had a girl wrapped her arms around his waist before? The date with me—was that the first he'd been on?

I made the decision then and there to take as few of Landon's firsts as possible. Firsts didn't matter much to me, but I wouldn't be the one to take Landon's from him. Despite literally threatening him with blackmail, I wanted him to come out of this with ease. And hopefully with a new girl on his arm.

And by the time I skipped town, I'd make sure to leave Landon barely remembering the girl named Lacey Churchill, just like everyone else.

CHAPTER 7

*H*aving a boyfriend with a Brentwood High parking pass meant that I didn't have to run to school every morning anymore, and *dang*, I didn't realize how nice that'd be.

It felt nice to be able to sleep in Thursday morning, even if it was only twenty extra minutes. I could hear the house begin to stir as I slowly blinked my eyes open, listening to the floorboards creak as someone walked across them. The bedroom door opened almost soundlessly, but the shout that came not even a second after was not nearly as quiet.

"*Lacey!*" Hudson had entered the room a few steps but slammed into the threshold upon seeing me, slapping his hands over his eyes. He still wore his pajamas, and his hair was pushed up and tousled. He must've just woken up. "What are you still doing here?"

"You're acting like you walked in on me in the bathroom instead of your bedroom," I told him, rubbing my eyes. "I'm fully clothed, you know. I even have a bra on."

"*Gah*, okay, don't say that word." He pressed his hands more firmly against his face. "I was going to grab clothes. You're usually gone by now."

I threw the comforter back and swung my legs against the side of the bed. "Don't let me stop you. I need to brush my teeth anyway."

Hudson parted his fingers to peer through, and even then, he kept his gaze on his feet as he shuffled toward his dresser. "Why didn't you run to school today? Aren't you planning to shower?"

"Not today."

"Are you riding the bus with me?"

"Not ever."

Hudson plucked a shirt out of the drawer, and apparently he gave up his disgust at seeing me on his bed, because he looked over to frown. "How are you getting to school, then?"

I couldn't hide my smirk, but I hopped up and turned before I gave him a full view of it. I swiped up my morning bag from my backpack. "My *boyfriend's* picking me up," I told him, and then escaped into the hall.

"Wait! *Boyfriend?*" Hudson's voice carried after me. "Lacey, hang on, what?"

There probably was a smoother way to drop that bomb, but the shock was too good. I knew more would be following, and *that* shock might not be as gratifying. Hudson had told me to get a boyfriend, a guy not like Ashton, but I was sure he wouldn't be all that happy about me choosing Landon, either.

"Who's got a boyfriend?" Paisley asked as I passed

where she sat on the couch watching morning cartoons. She already had her school clothes on, and her hair was braided into two little buns at the nape of her neck. A product of her brother, of course. "Is it Hudson?"

I laughed loudly at that.

Even though I knew I needed to be quick in the bathroom so as not to hog it up, I carefully did my makeup. Today was a big day, after all. Winged liner, blush, red lips —everything needed to look just right. I had a relationship to announce. After scraping my hair back into a low ponytail, I went to get dressed.

My phone chimed as I made my way back to Hudson's room, and I peeked at it.

LANDON

You said the corner of Hillcrest and Villaview, right?

Of course, he'd saved his name as just *Landon*. Boring.

LACEY

Yeppers. I should be ready in about ten

LANDON

K

I scowled at the letter, and knew that the first thing we'd need to work on were his texting skills.

Hudson had waited for me to reemerge from the bathroom, arms folded as he sat on the edge of his now-made bed. He must've pulled the duvet up while I was gone. "Boyfriend," he said.

"Boyfriend," I confirmed. I bent to tug out my suitcase, and lightly punched his feet so he'd move them out of the way. "Shall I give you more information?"

"You better *shall.*"

I cleared my throat as if about to begin a fairytale, piecing through my clothes. "It's a funny story, actually. Coincidentally enough, after our agreement, I went out with a guy on Tuesday. That's where I went. We hit it off, met up with each other yesterday, and he asked me to be his girlfriend."

Hudson narrowed his eyes. "After *one date?*"

"One cannot put a timetable on love."

Hudson shoved his foot into my knee, nearly off-balancing me and sending me flopping onto my butt. "This doesn't count, you know. I didn't bet you to get a boyfriend just to have a boyfriend. I want you to actually like the guy."

"I *do* like the guy." Despite putting on the performance, the words were honest. Sure, I didn't know much about Landon, but they still felt genuine. "We've been talking since last week, so it's not like we've only spoken once." *Technically true.* "He's really nice. I mean, yeah, we established labels a little early, but it's fun getting to know him. Learning what pushes his buttons." The last bit made me snort. "But I haven't won the bet yet. I have to last until homecoming to make it count, right?"

"Right." His suspicion narrowed his eyes. "Who is it?"

"Oh, look at the time—we're going to be late." I nudged him until he sat up. "Go shower before you miss the bus."

Hudson grumbled, but did just that. The conversation

would come up later, but I'd rather him find out through the masses than me telling him alone in his bedroom. At least if he found out at school, there'd be witnesses.

The air was crisper today, a perfect September morning, and I hurried down the dead-end street. I tugged at the hem of my skirt, hoping the extra inch of real estate would keep the chill at bay. When I was one house away from the intersection, where Hillcrest met Villaview, I saw him. Landon parked his coupe exactly where he'd said. He sat up straighter in the driver's seat when he saw me, and even from here, I could see his shoulders lift and fall with a big breath, almost as if he was bracing himself.

I popped the door open, and the tune of a country song leaked out. "Morning, sunshine. Happy to see me?"

Landon gave me one of those smiles that wasn't a smile. The kind you give someone when you pass them in the hallway and you're too awkward to say hello. "You could've taken more time if you wanted. I don't mind waiting."

"It doesn't take *that* long to get beautiful," I retorted, and then slid into the passenger seat. The faint scent of grass hung in the air, along with what could've been a trace of sweat, but the air freshener plugged into the vent masked most of the smell. It was like Caribbean Waters mixed with a little football player. "But if you don't want Hudson seeing you as he walks to the bus stop, we should go."

Landon almost looked alarmed. "You didn't tell him? Wasn't that the whole point of this?"

"I didn't tell him that it's *you*." I gave him the side eye. "Yet. He's more indifferent to you than Ashton and Kyle, but he really doesn't like football players."

"He'll have to find out at some point, won't he?"

"Yeah, but school is probably the safest bet for that. No telling what his reaction will be." I was only half-kidding.

Landon gripped the steering wheel tighter as we drove down Villaview, back toward the entrance of the mobile home park. He took it slow—much slower than the locals drove this road—and we bumped along with the sound of a country singer's twang filling the air. I wasn't sure if I should make small talk or sit quietly in my seat. I meant what I said when I told Hudson I liked pushing Landon's buttons, but there were still moments like this that I didn't know how to act around him.

"How come you don't drive the van to school?"

"The price to park in the Brentwood High lot is criminal." I tugged the seatbelt away from my neck where it'd begun to chafe. "I'd park it at one of the businesses and walk to school, but with the two-hour parking limit, I'm too afraid someone would tow it. Hudson doesn't really have money to pay for the parking pass, and I'm saving as much as I can."

"For college?"

"No." College, in fact, was the last thing on my mind, despite how often seniors are told college is their only option. Even being back to school a week, the obsession with applications and scholarships had already started spreading around the school like the plague. If someone had dreams of being a doctor, sure, then it's necessary. But for me, a girl who was completely content with the idea of bouncing from restaurant to restaurant around the country, never tied down to one place, college seemed like a money suck. "How about you? Do you have college plans? Is that something I should know as your girlfriend?"

Landon turned off of the Vista Villas lot and onto the main road, his car giving a slow purr as he accelerated. "I can't imagine it coming up in conversation, but, yeah, I have college plans."

"Anywhere cool?"

"I've been offered an athletic scholarship at Central Connecticut State University," he said somewhat indifferently. Maybe to him, all of this was blasé. "It's a D1 school. So that's...cool."

Ah, yes, football scholarships for the quarterback. It made sense. "You don't sound that pumped about it."

"I'm pumped," he replied, but his voice was much more mellow than excited, further proving my point.

We'd left early enough for Landon to swing into a coffee shop's drive-thru, though we had to wait in a line that nearly wrapped around the building. The sun was beginning to rise, and its brightness was visible in my side mirror. I stared at it until my eyes ached, and then turned to Landon. "Hi," I said suddenly.

He blinked. "Hi?"

He had his elbow propped on the console between us, which left his hand dangling, and I swept it up in a flash. I didn't weave my fingers through his, but held his hand as I did yesterday, with my pinky wedged between his index finger and middle finger.

Landon stared at our hands for a long moment before he lifted only his eyes.

"We should get comfortable with each other. That way it'll be more natural in the moment."

"Right."

I stared at his profile as he inched forward in the line, one car away from the ordering station. He was so reserved, which wasn't a bad thing, but I wanted to crack him. I tried to imagine a version of Landon Settler sitting in the driver's seat with a grin on his face and not the slightly downturned tilt to his lips he wore now. *So serious.* I wanted to make him smile. I wanted to make him laugh. Just to see what it sounded like.

He rolled down his window as the car in front of us began moving forward. "What's your coffee order?"

"Caramel macchiato with an extra pump of caramel. Hot."

As he ordered, Landon shifted his hand around mine, going from awkwardly letting me hold his hand to fully returning the grip. For no reason except for my girly hormones, my heart fluttered. Just a little. I mean, come *on*. With a face and body like he had, of course it would a *little*. It wasn't much, but it left me feeling like we were moving in the right direction. Maybe convincing everyone wouldn't be so hard.

We got to Brentwood High with about a half hour before the bell, but there were still students parked and lingering by their cars, chatting as the sun rose from the horizon. I wasn't prepared for the number of prying eyes that turned toward Landon's car almost as soon as he turned in to the parking lot, and I watched as they did a double take—they were turning initially for Landon, but those widened eyes were for the figure in his passenger seat.

"Everyone's staring," I said as I slunk down in the seat, hugging my backpack and my coffee to my chest.

"Isn't that the point?"

I hunched lower. "I guess."

Apparently, there was a known rule that no one could park in the front spaces of the lot—those spots were reserved for the Top Tier. That had to be the only explanation why Landon was able to snag one of the best spaces in the entire lot, with a few surrounding us empty. I was surprised no one—ahem, *Jade*—didn't stake a sign in front of them saying TOP TIER ONLY.

Landon put the car into park and picked up his macchiato from the cup holder. "Anywhere between five and ten minutes, everyone else will get here. Connor will show up with Jade and Madison, Ashton will be with Kyle, and then Reed'll show. The plan is to wait for them, right?"

That *was* the plan, but now I felt like booking it for the blue and gold-painted doors. My hot macchiato sloshed in my stomach. "This is the best time to meet them?"

"Yeah, or at lunch."

Lunch would've been infinitely worse. I could picture it now, sitting across from Jade while spooning a clump of mashed potatoes into my mouth. "Now's...fine."

Landon brought his coffee cup to his lips but stopped short of taking a sip. "You don't have to be nervous."

I looked out the side window to find a girl with a yellow beret pointing her camera at Landon's car. It was clear what she was doing, and it was so much weirder to see someone take your picture when you had no idea who they were. "I'm not nervous."

"You look like you're about to bolt."

It was almost laughable how well he could read me already. "When do I meet the girl you have a crush on?"

This time Landon did take a sip, if only to prolong his answer. I wasn't sure why he was so secretive about it, anyway. Of course, I had to know who it was—I had to know who to play up my flirtatious eyes in front of. He had to know this too, because after wincing, he said, "She'll be with my friends."

There were only two girls he'd mentioned among his friends. A wave of horror passed over me. "Dear God, please tell me it's Madison and not Jade."

He winced again, this time almost as if I struck him. "Definitely not Jade."

Ooh, Madison, then. Huh. Quite honestly, it made a world of sense. Quarterback dating the co-captain of the cheer squad. They'd look sort of cute together, with his red hair and her blonde. They'd make cute, freckle-faced babies. She was so much shorter than him, though, in a way that would probably look comical if they posed together.

But, come on—he was crushing on one of the evil step-sisters? *Why?* I shouldn't be judging him, but I'd been hoping he wasn't that clichéd. "Well, that's good. Aside from the fact that she's the antichrist's BFF, it's good that she's single. Clears up the waters a bit."

The corner of Landon's lips twitched. "The antichrist, huh?"

"Don't get me started." My hatred for Jade was a rabbit

hole I could get lost down for hours. "You have my permission to touch me when they come up. Like a preemptive *hi*."

"Got it. Same here...I guess."

A car slid into the space on the other side of me, and without even hesitating, they blared their horn. I jumped hard in my seat, my belt scraping against my neck, and I turned to come face to face with none other than Ashton Shaw. Recognition flared in his eyes as he stared me down, lips curling into a Joker-like grin.

"Of course, he shows up first," I muttered.

Landon didn't say anything in response, but clicked his belt off, popping open his door. Immediately, I could hear Ashton's voice. "Well, look what we have here. Landon, you giving out free rides now?"

I stared at Landon's dashboard, drawing in a deep breath as Landon forced a chuckle. This felt like the moment in a card game where I had two choices—go all in or fold my hand. I *so* wanted to do the latter. *You can do this, Lacey,* I thought as fiercely as I could, unclasping my seatbelt. *These people don't matter anyway. You've got this.*

Right. They didn't matter. I had this. All in.

Steeling myself, I shoved open my door, clipping Ashton in the hip hard enough for him to stumble back. "My bad," I drawled, stepping out onto the asphalt. He was way too close for comfort, but I didn't look him in the eye. "Didn't see you there."

"Bet you didn't," he returned, sounding like he was smiling. "You go from whisking my boy away in the hall one day to climbing out of his car the next? My, my, you move fast."

It was last year that I was very nearly swayed by that dimpled grin. If Ashton hadn't been the one who'd hurt my cousin, I probably would've been swayed. Kyle got out from Ashton's car and looked at us all over the hood, a silent spectator.

"So, your date went well on Tuesday, I take it?" Ashton went on, his gaze flicking toward where the quarterback stood on the other side of the car. "Are you two *official?*"

I hadn't realized Landon told his friends about the first date, and for some reason, a spark of panic darted through me.

"It went really well," Landon said, and in a moment, he had rounded the car and came up beside me. "We, uh— yeah, we're official now."

Before anyone had a chance to react, Landon swiped my hand up with his and maneuvered my pinky between his fingers, like I'd done earlier in the car. The fluidness of the movement came so naturally that it was almost a little shocking. Whatever nerves he'd held on to a moment ago were gone now, and his expression was totally assured when I looked up.

Ashton's smug smirk deepened as he dropped his gaze to our hands. And then, as obnoxious as could be, he began to laugh. He glanced over his shoulder to look at Kyle, who interjected a snort. "Isn't that surprising, Kyle? Landon, I know you were feeling crappy about the Most Likely To label, but I am surprised. *Lacey Churchill?*"

In my left hand, I weighed the contents of my coffee,

wondering how much splatter would cover his white shirt if I tossed it at him.

Landon tucked me closer to his side, and our shoulders brushed. "I'm surprised too. I didn't think she'd go for a guy like me."

Time to get my game face on, because he was doing all the heavy lifting. I dropped Landon's hand and wrapped my arm around his waist, curling my finger through the beltloop on his jeans. He tensed, but hopefully not enough to be noticeable. "I guess someone else should've been voted Most Likely To: Never Get A Girlfriend, huh?"

I watched Ashton's eyes tighten behind the mask of a smile he wore. It almost made him look like a serial killer.

In the middle of our showdown, Connor eased his blue SUV on the other side of Ashton's car, and even with the doors closed, I could hear the blare of music pumping from the speakers. It was abruptly cut short as the car shut off, and a beat later, three doors opened. "Oh, bite me, Connor," Jade said in a voice that sounded distinctly *not* romantic.

The roof of Connor's car was too high for me to see Jade around, but Connor was visible, and his gaze zeroed in on me in an instant. "Oh, hey. It's Lacey, right?"

I lifted my chin at him. "That's me."

Jade came around Connor's car to stand beside him, Madison trailing behind her. The queen bee raised her eyebrow at me, looking at the way I hung off Landon. "Ever hear of personal space, Lacey?"

"They're *together*," Kyle answered for us, speaking for the first time in the whole exchange.

The reactions were mixed across the board, and it was a struggle who to look at first. Madison's eyebrows shot up in a look of pure shock, and I scanned her. There wasn't any jealousy, not that I could see. I wasn't sure if that was a good sign or a bad sign yet. Jade's expression was a bit like Ashton's, with amusement lighting up her features, though she didn't laugh. Connor's lips stretched into a grin as he looked between us. A *happy* grin. "Wait, really?"

Landon threw his arm over my shoulder, and I jolted with the sudden heavy pressure. I brought my coffee to my lips to hide my surprise. "Yeah, we bonded over the list. So, I guess I should be thanking you all for putting me on it, huh?"

Landon said *thanks* to his lame friends while I was fighting the urge to show everyone who stood here my middle finger.

"Well, that's super cool," Connor said, gripping the strap of his backpack. "Lacey, be patient with our boy here, okay? He's a little shy, but you'll get him out of his shell eventually."

"You'll have to sit with us at lunch," Jade said, voice suspiciously light. There was that trace of amusement on her face, buried under her own mask. It sort of gave her a serial killer look too. "We can hear the full story of you and Landon."

Yeah, count me *out.* "I actually—"

"She sits with her cousin at lunch," Ashton answered for me, smirking. "You guys know him, right? The Grim Reaper?"

I forced myself still. "Stalker, much?"

With Landon's heavy arm over my shoulders, he eased me back a step, away from Ashton, almost like he was afraid I was about to lunge. "We should get inside," he said, glancing around his messed-up friend group. His eyes lingered on Madison for a second. "I'll see you all later?"

Madison gave the barest nod, which caused my suspicions to rise.

As soon as we got a good distance away from his friends, that was when things morphed back to how they'd been in the car. Landon practically jerked his arm away from my neck, but quickly fumbled to pick up my hand. His fingers were stiff, holding mine as loosely as possible. "I didn't realize you knew Ashton," he said when we were out of earshot. His voice sounded accusatory. "Why didn't you say so?"

"I thought you knew," I told him, grimacing. "I thought guys talked about that sort of stuff."

"What sort of stuff?"

"Girls they like. Or, in his case, girls they never leave alone." Because I truly didn't think Ashton ever liked me. He might've just liked the way I looked. "He asked me to prom last year. Seven billion times."

"That was *you*?" The shock in his voice was near palpable. "He never said who."

I rolled my eyes. "Unfortunately."

Landon hummed a little. "That explains it, then."

"Explains what?"

"Why he was so...intense." He opened the entryway door for me, but I didn't let his hand go. Though we were about to walk down a hallway filled with spectators, something about his grip was reassuring, like as long as I held his hand, I wouldn't be nervous. "We'll try to avoid him from now on, then."

My eyebrows knitted together. "But he's your friend."

"If he makes you uncomfortable, it doesn't matter who he is."

I looked up at him at the same time he looked down at me. His features were neutral for a second before his lips stretched into a little smile, one that indented the corner where his lips met. It was like a dimple at the corner of his mouth, and I stared at it, surprised I'd never noticed before.

If he makes you uncomfortable, it doesn't matter who he is. It was such a *boyfriend* thing to say. "You know," I began, pausing before we faced the masses. "You secretly meeting Madison later will torpedo our chances of this working."

"W-What?"

"I saw that little 'ooh, I'll meet you later' head nod you two shared." I jerked my thumb back toward the parking lot as if he needed more clarity. "If you want to make her jealous of your new relationship, you can't let her think she takes priority over it. And you shouldn't be meeting other girls while you have a girlfriend."

"I was going to ask if she'll make sure the others are cool about us," he said, blinking innocently like I'd accused him of kicking a puppy. "About...you. Jade may be high up in the Top Tier, but Madison *is* still co-captain. She has some influence."

Maybe that made sense. In a way. And if Landon went to Madison asking for her to spread all the happy rumors about us, maybe that would make her see Landon in a different light. Less in an *oh, he's such a nice friend* way and more of a *wow, he's a sweet and caring boyfriend* way. "Maybe...hold off for a day. Let her wonder a bit more."

Landon nodded eagerly, taking his trusted sensei's advice without question. He readjusted his grip on my hand, warming my palm. "We should get going, yeah?"

Get going to our lockers, which were at the other end of the school. Past the freshmen, sophomore, and junior lockers. The chatter and noise of the hallway around the corner came back into my awareness. All it took was one step out into the flow of traffic, and there'd be no taking this back. Landon could always make some excuse with his friends, and I could give one to Hudson, and we'd both walk away from this without the public of Brentwood High having known anything but rumors.

This was the point of no return.

"Are you not nervous?" I asked softly, swallowing hard.

"I guess a little," he said, fluttering his fingers against the back of my hand lightly. His eyes were steady and intense as they met mine, causing my spine to straighten. "But it's not like I'm facing this alone. I've got you."

I readjusted my palm to fit tighter against his, my fingertips brushing the edge of his class ring as I did so. The metal felt cool, and I traced the outline for a moment, something about it calming me. "You've got me," I echoed, adding in my head, *and I've got you.*

And then we were off.

The freshmen eagerly packing things into their lockers faltered at the sight of Landon, doing a doubletake when they spotted our hands tucked together. Social hierarchy wasn't a hard thing to grasp, so even though school had only been in session a little over a week, they all knew who Landon Settler was. It was clear, though, by the questioning looks on their faces, that they had no idea who Lacey Churchill was. By the end of the day, I bet they would.

The thought made me squirm.

Game face, Lacey, I told myself, straightening my shoulders. *Get on your game face, because this is going to be your life for the next two and a half weeks.*

Oh, joy.

CHAPTER 8

*H*udson's response to Landon being my boyfriend went about as swimmingly as I'd hoped.

"*Landon Settler?*" Hudson had his fry coated in ketchup suspended between the tray and his mouth, and a big glob of red was about to drip off. His eyes were more rounded with shock than squinted with anger, so I counted that as a win. "You're kidding me."

"Why is it so shocking we're together?" I demanded, looking down at my own lunch tray. Brentwood High had slim pickings today—pizza sticks and french fries, which was a weird combo, but I wasn't complaining. The only day I refused to even enter the cafeteria was on spaghetti day. How one could mess up noodles and sauce, I had no idea. "Is it shocking that he'd go for me? Or that I'd go for him? Either way, it feels offensive."

I knew why Hudson was more shocked. It wasn't the fact that I was dating anyone from the Top Tier—it was Landon Settler specifically.

"Listen, I know he's not your first choice, but I've always thought he was really...cute." I fumbled for the excuse I'd preplanned. "I mean, those broad shoulders—"

"You know why I'm *shocked*," he said, emphasizing the word with a malicious twist. "Did you forget what happened in the ninth grade?"

In my head, it was perfectly justifiable—it wasn't like I had real feelings for Landon, so there wasn't any betrayal. Plus, given the fight, I could use it against Landon to my advantage. But Hudson couldn't know any of that. I leveled my stare at him. "And did *you* forget that you were the one to beat *him* to a pulp, not the other way around?"

"Jerk could've at least told the truth," Hudson grumbled now, shoving his fry into his mouth. Some of his angry posture had leaked away, though.

"If I'm recalling correctly, you never tried to tell the truth, either." Hudson had swallowed the public opinion ruling the first day he went back to school after the fight. Rumors had already spread, labeling Hudson as the perpetrator. "You never tried to tell anyone that you were really the victim."

Hudson's scowl only deepened, hating that I was right.

Though I'd been lighthearted, I watched Hudson eat with a solemn expression, feeling my thoughts tumble and toss in my head. I tried to dissect the barest amount of emotion he had on his face. He didn't look angry anymore, didn't look frustrated—the shock had begun to wear off, leaving something that left me feeling a smidge hopeful. "He's different from back then."

"I hope so," Hudson said. "With the arm he's got, hopefully the guy learned how to actually throw a punch by now."

"Hopefully he's learned how to stand up when his friends are being idiots," I countered. I thought of Ashton from the parking lot.

"Listen." Hudson put down his pizza stick and looked at me steadily. "If you actually like him, then I'll...deal. Really. He can count toward the bet. Just as long as you hit him at least once for me. *And* as long as he doesn't convert you to the Top Tier."

Now it was my turn to be shocked, though I tried to hide it as quickly as possible. Hudson wanted me to get a boyfriend so badly that he was ready to throw his three-year grudge out the window. I thought he'd be more resistant. I didn't *quite* think he'd say "never mind, I'll sell the van to you now," but I thought there'd be a bit more negotiation. "Please, I'm dating Landon, not his *posse*. Rubbing elbows with Jade? *Barf*."

That got Hudson to smile.

I dug my spork into my pasta salad, watching as it squished like mush beneath the pressure. "Has my mom paid your dad yet?"

His reply came quick. "Pretty sure my dad told you not to worry about that."

"How am I not supposed to worry?" I hated the fact that I was forced into their house to begin with—I couldn't stay there rent-free too. "You guys are doing so much. I'll chip in—you know Le Petit Bateau pays me enough."

"Careful." Hudson leaned closer to me across the table, dropping his voice. "Who knows if Ms. Murphy has a hidden recorder somewhere. She hears that you're struggling, and you'll be stuck in the recliner four days a week."

I flicked a french fry at him. "I'm being serious."

"So am I."

I sighed as I looked at him, knowing that as much as I poked and prodded, he wasn't going to give me my answer. I watched him as he studiously ignored my intense stare, continuing to eat.

"Back to the topic of your boyfriend," he said, finally glancing over and giving me an intense stare of his own. "Just have fun, okay? Forget about how hard everything is right now and be a normal teenager."

A normal teenager. I wanted to laugh—maybe even make a joke that would've made him choke on his chicken sandwich—but the humor dried up in my throat. A normal teenager. Sitting in the counselor's office, I was certain I'd never been one, even before moving in with the Bishops. In fact, before moving in, my life more closely resembled that of an adult than a senior in high school. A normal teenager. I wasn't even sure what that looked like.

After my shift at Le Petit Bateau that night, I didn't go straight back to the Bishop residence. It was almost ten, so the sky was dark, and all of the streetlights were lit. The fish scent was stronger today—normally I became noseblind to the terrible stench, but I actually reeked of cod and whitefish. Which meant I had to smell *really* bad. The thought of a hot, blissful shower was the only thing getting me through the car ride, and then sinking into my bed. Hudson's bed. Whatever.

But, for now, I let the fishy scent absorb in Petunia and drove around aimlessly, wasting gas, unable to shake the shadow that had fallen over me since Landon's text.

LOVER BOY

A few of my friends and I are going bowling tonight at Allen's Alley. Do you want to tag along?

It was a harmless enough text. It would've been a good excuse for us to "bond," or at least show off our new relationship. But even if I hadn't had to work, I still would've said no to the invitation. Bowling was fun, but Allen's Alley was distinctly not. It was a bowling alley and a bar, and there was one bartender that made me break out into hives just thinking about her.

Mom would still be there, probably. I didn't know how long her shifts lasted, but she always stayed until closing, whether she was bartending or not. If I would've gone, I would've run into her. And if I would've run into her, I didn't know what would happen. The last time I'd gone there, it hadn't ended well.

That thought made my stomach turn.

I wasn't afraid to face her. I wasn't. In fact, the thought of her filled me with so much anger that it was a wonder the steering wheel didn't bend. Confronting her there, in front of my new fake boyfriend and his lame friends, wouldn't be a good look. That was why.

I stared blankly out the windshield, giving Petunia more gas as we chugged up a hill in a residential area. I didn't look closely at my surroundings, making mindless turn after turn. When I'd told Landon I had to work, he hadn't replied. Which was...whatever. I already established how abysmal his texting skills were. What would he have said, anyway? *Okay?* It wasn't really anything that warranted a response. But still. Seeing the *read* pop up under my text left me feeling hollow.

I turned into a random driveway to turn around, reaching for the gearshift before freezing. When I blinked and focused on the garage door in front of me, the breath I tried drawing in lodged itself in the middle of my throat.

It was that sort of scary realization where you arrived at your destination but you couldn't remember the drive at all. And it was even more jarring because I was home. Not at the Vista Villa mobile home. Not the Bishop home. *Home.*

It was small, but had been perfect for two people, especially when one rarely came home. Mom and I lived on Grimes Avenue, which wasn't the best part of Brentwood, but Mom used to always make sure our yard was maintained. She hadn't been the world's best mother, but she'd been pretty close to the world's greatest gardener. Lawn perfectly clipped, plants watered, a wide range of flowers planted in the front. Now, though, the flowerbeds looked jungle-like, the plants near the walkway wilting onto the sidewalk, and the lawn overgrown. If she didn't mow it soon, she'd get a letter from the city. She might've already gotten one.

No lights were on, and I wondered if that was because she made sure to turn them all off before leaving or if she hadn't paid the electric bill again. I also couldn't help but wonder when the last time she'd been inside was. Now that I was gone, did she come more often, or even less?

The house looked so ghostly. A haunted house kids on the street made up stories about. In the grand scheme of things, nothing *bad* happened within the walls, but the thought of them unsettled me all the same.

My phone began to rattle in the cup holder, its chiming ringtone snapping me back into the moment. For a wild, crazy moment, I thought I'd pick up my phone and find Mom's number across the ID. Finally reaching for it, I drew in a sniffling breath before checking the caller ID. *Lover Boy.* "Hello?"

"Hey." Landon sounded a bit breathless, as if he'd run up a set of stairs. "I just realized that my last text never sent. I meant to say, 'We can plan something again a different time' but service is crap in Jefferson. Is this a good time to talk? Are you out of work?"

I gave a humorless chuckle as I stared at the dent in the garage door. "Yeah."

"Is everything okay?"

"Why wouldn't it be?"

"You sound different," he said. "You sound upset."

After turning my phone on speaker, I shifted the van into reverse. "Am I that transparent or are you a super good judge of people's voices?"

"You don't sound like how you normally do," he said. "Normally, you're cheery and confident, I guess. Now you sound..."

"Tired?"

"I was going to say sad."

My knee-jerk reaction was to deny it, because I wasn't sad. I wasn't. It wasn't like I was crying. How did I *sound* sad? I let the accusation linger in the air, shifting uneasily. "I had a long day at work. What's up?"

"I was just going to tell you about tonight." He cleared his throat and spoke even lower. "Do you know Ava Jenson? She runs Brentwood Babble. She was at the alley tonight, and I talked to her a bit about...us. About how we're together. She's going to post us to the site, so everyone who doesn't know about us will know by tomorrow."

A few days ago, I'd been almost giddy about the idea of posting to Babble, entertained by the idea that we'd be shaking up the masses and kicking my freedom plan into gear. Now, I was too exhausted to care as I backed out onto the road. "Why are you practically whispering?"

"I'm not supposed to be on my phone after nine-thirty."

Despite my mood, amusement cracked through. "Little Landon Settler has a *curfew?*"

"Only my phone does."

I flipped on my blinker to turn off Grimes Avenue, but even when I left the road in the rearview, I didn't leave behind the icky feeling that rooted underneath my ribcage. "I think for our first day, it went okay. Meeting your friends and everything, I mean. What do you think?"

I could *hear* Landon thinking over the phone, like him debating whether or not to speak made an actual sound. "Do you want to sit with me at lunch tomorrow?"

Ha, did I? Did I want to surround myself with people all decked out in football jerseys and cheer uniforms? Since tomorrow was a game day, the entire table would be filled with Brentwood High's blue and gold color scheme. Filled, except for me. "Well, I..."

"If we're going to make Madison jealous, I should bring you around more, right?"

"Right, right," I rushed to say, but *ugh*. "I can...sit with you tomorrow. But if you make me sit next to Jade, so help me God, I'll—"

"Don't worry," Landon said with the tiniest amount of humor. Something shifted on the other end of the phone, sounding like shuffling paper. "I wouldn't subject you to that kind of torture."

"Good."

"Good," he echoed, almost like he hadn't thought about it. "I can, uh—I can let you go. I just called to let you know about what happened at the bowling alley."

I glanced down at where my phone sat in the cupholder. Landon hadn't ended the call yet, but the pressure behind my ribs tightened at the thought of it, to the point where the pain was piercing. I gripped the steering wheel with white knuckles. "Landon?"

"Yeah?"

"Can you stay on the phone with me until I get home?" I hadn't realized how desperate the words would sound until they came out, rushed, pathetic. Landon's voice had a lulling quality that made it easy to forget the world around me—easy to forget the driveway I'd backed out of. "I know you have curfew, so I get it if you can't, but it's nice to talk to someone."

Normally, this was the time that I decompressed. I spent the entire night serving with a smile on my face, making mindless small talk and staying constantly on edge, and normally I basked in the silence the van provided. I could let my resting bitch face free. But the hole yawned wider inside of me as soon as I parked in my driveway, and Landon's voice was filling it up.

I braced myself for him to turn me down, mostly because his silence had lingered much longer than necessary. If I wasn't driving, I would've checked to see if he'd already hung up. "Uh, yeah, sure," he said instead, voice carrying a gentle quality. It was less of a whisper now and more of a murmur, like the way someone spoke when they laid beside you in bed. "How long until you're home?"

"Less than ten minutes."

"Do you want to talk, or do you want me to?"

Something about the question caused my throat to tighten, and I had to clear it to speak. "You can."

There was another shuffling sound, crackling almost like static. "I'm sitting at my desk right now," he told me. "It's the same desk I had when I was eight, and my legs barely fit underneath it. It's so cluttered, too. Papers and pencils all over it. I need a better organization system."

I drew in a slow breath, equally stunned at the number of words that came out of his mouth and their mundaneness. But as he spoke, I could picture the scene in front of him, picture the moment he was in. While he spoke, it was almost like I was there with him.

"Not many people know this about me, but I, ah—I draw. For fun. Nothing special, but it's relaxing. I usually wind down for the night by sketching something out. And before you ask, no, you can't see any of my work. Seriously. I think I'd shrivel up into dust if anyone ever saw it."

I flipped on my blinker and slowed for the stop sign. The intersection was dead, not a headlight in sight. "Don't you think your girlfriend should see what you're working on?"

"No. Never. Ever." He tried to stifle a chuckle, but it still crackled through the phone. I realized now that the shuffling sound *was* paper. It was easy to identify now, and I imagined Landon picking up the sheet. "But it's relaxing for me. It's... I like it."

"What do you draw? Landscapes?"

"Portraits."

"Ooh, what are you working on right now? Describe it to me."

His hesitation was back in full force, but instead of refusing—like I'd been expecting—he slowly began. "I'm working on a girl who's sitting in the passenger seat of a car. I'm trying to work on my shading with graphite, and I'm working on her hair right now."

I tilted my head at the mental image, bobbing my head. "That sounds cool."

"It's just me goofing off."

"Have you ever drawn someone you know?"

"All the time. It's easier to draw someone I know." He faltered a little. "But not—not always. I don't want to be creepy. I'll use them for the base, but change little things. Like the eyes, the lips—things like that."

"It's not creepy. Not to me. If I could draw more than a stick figure, I'd be drawing people I knew all the time." I'd draw Jade with a unibrow, for example. I trailed my hands down the steering wheel. Vista Villas wasn't far now—two turns left. "Have you ever drawn Madison?"

Landon was quiet on the other end of the line for a long moment, answering me before his words did. "Once or twice, yeah."

I flinched as headlights swept into my eyes, and gravel crunched as the van slid onto the shoulder. As gently as I could, I veered back onto the roadway. "Maybe you can draw me sometime. Would that be weird?"

This time, Landon didn't answer, but the shuffling on the other end of the line quit.

"I'm almost home," I told him, slowing down for the entrance of the mobile home park. "I'll see you tomorrow morning. Same time?"

"Same time," he confirmed, voice much quieter than before. A whisper. Hearing it reverberate through the interior of the van caused something along my skin to tickle. "Lacey? You know, if you ever want to talk on your way home from work, you can call me. Curfew or not."

Definite tickle. It pierced through my skin to heat my blood, and the lonely, hollow feeling that'd been lingering since before seemed to lift in that moment. The air was warm, but in a pleasant way, the way a supportive hug might feel. That was the effect those words had. Smiling, I twisted the steering wheel into the Vista Villas drive. "Deal."

CHAPTER 9

I intercepted Hudson as he headed to Cafeteria B the next day, his gait slow. Despite not being allowed to eat in the cafeteria, he still had to go in to buy his lunch when he didn't pack one, and it was almost comical to see people jump out of his way. I hurried up behind him, grasping his shoulders. "Kill me," I told him.

Hudson shrugged my touch off. "Hello to you, too."

"You might as well kill me, because I'm not going to make it through lunch." I looked all around us, but most of the students had scurried ahead of us or lingered way back, giving the Grim Reaper his personal space. "I'm sitting with the jolly green giant and his posse today."

"That sounds like a you problem."

"You're not even the slightest bit concerned for me?"

"Concerned for *you*?" Hudson glanced over, giving me the glare of his electric blue eyes in their full glory. "I should be concerned for *them*, don't you think?"

I latched onto Hudson's arm and yanked him to a halt,

wheeling on him with wide eyes. "I've got it. Landon should come eat lunch with us in Ms. Murphy's office!"

Hudson's expression was less than thrilled. "No."

"He wants to meet you. Cross gaps, mend bridges, all that jazz." More or less. I mean, I could *see* Landon doing that. "You haven't talked since ninth grade—the last year of high school is a perfect time to make up, right? Besides, us sitting with you makes *much* more sense than me sitting with his friends."

"I'm sure the idea of him eating lunch with me would make him feel the same way as you do now." Hudson shook my arm off once again and continued his walk down the hall, running a hand through his hair. "It's going to be as good as you make it, Lacey. And besides, you're going to sit with Landon. To eat lunch with your *boyfriend*. Shouldn't you be excited about that?"

I sucked my lips into my mouth, for a second panicking that I'd slipped up. "Uh, right, right. I *am* excited to spend time with my...boyfriend. Because he *is* my boyfriend. And I like him. A lot."

Hudson made a face. "Good for you."

I needed to be more careful on all fronts. I couldn't go blab everything to Hudson, because he'd see through the boyfriend BS if I let the wrong thing slip. It was a wonder he hadn't noticed already—that new mentor thing he was doing must've been taking all his concentration. And I needed to hold up my end of the bargain with Landon. The world couldn't revolve around just me.

At least, not yet.

But man, I wanted nothing more than to whine my way out of this.

I clutched my blue food tray tightly, tapping it against my chest as I tried to see around the row of students. Cafeteria B was packed, like always, and so many people actually left me feeling a bit claustrophobic. I was so used to eating in Ms. Murphy's office where the only sound was the ticking of her wall clock. Hudson, standing in front of me in line, looked barely affected. "How are your mentor meetings going?" I asked him, stepping up on my tiptoes to speak over his shoulder.

"Fine," he returned, voice flat. "It's not like it can go badly."

"Staying after school sucks, though."

Hudson nodded slowly. "I guess so."

"What did you say her name was again?"

"I didn't."

We shuffled forward in line until we got to the counter, and Hudson set his tray down. The lunch lady barely passed him a look as she slopped the gray-looking mashed potatoes onto his tray, giving him the world's barest amount of gravy, and picking the burnt-looking pieces of roast beef to pass his way. Hudson took it all without batting an eye, though he did stare the lunch lady down as she served it.

When it was my turn, my gravy overflowed onto my tray, and my roast beef slices were juicy and fresh-looking. My mashed potatoes still had a gray tint, though.

I couldn't stand the way everyone treated Hudson differently, but true to his temperament, he remained unfazed.

Once we paid, I grabbed his tray and yanked it as hard as I could without spilling anything. Then I shoved my tray with the gravy river into his open hands. "You know I like the crispy stuff, anyway," I said, winking at him.

Hudson let out a sigh, one that sounded like a death rattle.

"Pray for my soul." And then, without letting him get another word in, I dove into the sea of lunch tables.

Like I said, Cafeteria B was always crowded. If there was a lunchroom I'd ever sit in willingly, it'd be Cafeteria A, even with the freshmen and sophomores. Mostly to avoid the large table at the center of the room.

Most of the tables in the cafeteria only could fit eight people, but of course the Top Tier had snagged the largest table in the room. It was a long rectangular one, not the circular ones most other kids sat at, and it could fit ten people per side. From a few tables away, I gripped my lunch tray tightly as I stared at the assault of blue and gold. Numbered jerseys were everywhere, and so were cheerleaders in their short skirts. My combat boots and flannel so wouldn't fit in.

And hang on, where was Landon? I didn't know his jersey number, but that redheaded skyscraper would've stood out, and there wasn't a boy like that in sight. I danced over every single head, gaze settling on the two empty spots at the table.

No way was I going over there if he wasn't sitting down. Heck no.

Except in my scanning, the she-devil caught my eye.

"Lacey!" Jade called, shooting her hand into the air and

waving it like a flag. Students from other tables turned toward the sound of her voice, and then looked to me, where I stood like a statue. "Don't be shy. Come sit."

At her side, Madison flipped her ponytail over her shoulder and eyed me up, lips curling.

Connor, sitting at Jade's other side, beckoned me, too. "We saved a seat for you, Lacey." He gestured at the spot across from him, beside a blue lunch bag partially unpacked.

Of course they would've had to save my seat, because every chair at the large table was filled. As my combat boots shuffled me closer against my will, I couldn't help but wonder who I'd kicked out to gain entry.

They could *so* have their seat back.

"Where's Landon?" I asked as I got to the back of the chair, ready to flee.

"Here," came a rushed response, and a shadow appeared at my shoulder. Ashton trailed behind him, but I only focused on the quarterback. "Sorry. I needed to warm up my chicken tenders in the microwave."

The relief I felt at the sight of the blue-and-gold-clad boy made my knees weak. His bright jersey caused his skin to look paler, but his blue-green eyes were vivid. "Hi."

I hadn't said it for him to touch me, but he jumped to attention. "Hi." He coasted his palm over my shoulder in a quick, delicate touch, and then he scraped my chair out for me, taking my tray and setting it on the table.

"Yeah, have a seat, Lacey," Jade said from directly across from me, flashing her shark teeth. She had a green sandwich wrap in front of her on what looked to be beeswax paper, cucumber slices in a tiny Tupperware container, and a tall sparkling water uncapped to wash it all down. It was like she was attending high tea and not school lunch. "Ugh, I could never eat *that*." Her gaze slid over my gray mashed potatoes and burnt beef strips.

"I could never eat a moldy wrap, either, so it's a good thing we don't have each other's meals."

"It's a spinach herb wrap." Jade gave me a haughty look. "Can't you see the grease in that meat? Disgusting."

I sucked in a breath to respond when Landon's hand closed over my leg, on top of my denim shorts. He wasn't looking at me—with his free hand, he pulled off the lid to his own Tupperware container—but the meaning behind the touch was clear. *Don't engage.*

Right. This wasn't the prime opportunity to have a snark fest with the she-devil. I reached down and patted Landon's hand, silently assuring I'd behave.

"That looks delicious," I said while eyeing his container, leaning closer. He had one Tupperware for his tenders but another for what looked like pasta salad. "Can I have a bite?"

Landon's gaze darted from his container to me and then back, and for one moment filled with disbelief, I thought he was about to say no. "Sure," he said instead, and held his fork out to me. "Go for it."

"Which piece should I have?" Pointedly, I looked at Landon's fork, at his container, and then back up to him.

Landon held the fork tightly in his grip as he stabbed a piece of pasta salad, and as stiff as could be, he turned to offer it out to me. I took the bite graciously, making a dramatic *mmm* sound. "Really good. Did your mom make it?"

Landon mumbled something about his mom buying it from the store, but I kept sneaking peeks at Madison. Nothing. No reaction. Madison didn't even bat an eyelash as she continued to eat her lunch. She wasn't remotely jealous? Nauseated at the very least?

I scanned the lunch table once more, desperate for a familiar face besides Landon's. Desperate to find *someone* with a gaze that didn't look semi-threatening. Connor was a safe choice, but he kept his head down most of the time, shoveling his food into his mouth like it was a race. Jade looked at him with disgust while he did so.

But as I looked around, I realized that I wasn't the only one not wearing Bobcat blue and gold. A boy at the other side of Connor, holding a grape juice box, wore a simple T-shirt with an unzipped jacket over it, looking wholly unbothered.

He realized I was staring. "I'm Reed," he said, offering a nonchalant wave. "Lacey, right?"

"That's me," I said, lifting my chin. "No jersey? You're allowed to be in the Top Tier if you're not playing sports?"

Reed gave a teasing eyeroll. "Apparently."

"Our pretty boy over here quit the team this year." Ashton clasped Reed hard on the shoulder, but Reed didn't even flinch. "Played with us for all these years and then abandoned ship."

"And you were so heartbroken," Reed said, biting down on his juice box straw.

"Not really," Ashton replied. "Maybe we'll finally have a decent starting lineup."

Reed lazily flipped him off.

"Are you coming to the game tonight, Lacey?" Madison asked, causing my eyes to dart back to her. I kept expecting the same snotty expression that Jade normally wore, but Madison's face was blank, making it impossible to read her. "To cheer Landon on?"

I sat back in my chair, dragging my fork through my mashed potatoes. I needed to play this tactically. "Oh, so *that's* why you all dressed the same."

Jade scoffed, and if she hadn't had a mouthful of moldy wrap, she probably would've fired back. "Fridays are game days," Madison said, like *duh*. "Did you really go your whole life here at Brentwood not knowing that?"

"My life doesn't revolve around school spirit," I said apologetically, spreading my palms. "But, uh, to answer your question, not sure. Football isn't really my thing."

Landon put his hand back on my leg, this time missing the hem of my shorts and landing on my bare skin. We both jumped in surprise—my knee popped up an inch and his fingers spasmed over it—but he didn't pull back.

"Oh?" Madison raised an expertly sculpted eyebrow, gaze narrowing a little. *There we go, crack that façade you've got going there.* "Then why are you dating Landon?"

"You must not know him as well as you think you do." I reached down and grabbed Landon's hand, bringing it up to rest on the tabletop, putting it on display. Almost every set of eyes dropped to our layered fingers, just as I intended. "There's more to Landon Settler than being a quarterback on a crappy football team."

The reactions all around were exactly what I'd been looking for, from almost everyone. Jade's expression turned livid. Madison's jaw dropped an inch, offended I could've said such a thing. Ashton's eyes narrowed. The only two who seemed amused were Connor and Reed, who passed each other a glance.

"We haven't lost a single game," Ashton said, drawing my attention to him. His voice dripped exasperation. "I wouldn't say that's *crappy*, would you?"

"How many games have you had since the beginning of the school year?" I asked. "Two?"

Landon tightened his grip on my hand, no doubt wondering what the heck I was doing.

With my free hand, I patted his fingers before letting go, sliding my lunch tray closer to me. "That's one of the things I like about Landon—that he doesn't make Brentwood High his entire personality." I glanced around the table again before falling back to Madison and Jade. "Unlike some people."

"Your attitude could use some work," Madison said to me, leaning back into her own seat and folding her arms. "I'd be embarrassed, talking to a boyfriend's friends like this."

"Oh, honey." I brought my forkful of roast beef to my lips. "I think you've got a whole lot more to be embarrassed about, Ms. Most Likely To: Peak in High School."

The boiling point had been reached. Madison surged forward in her seat as if she wanted to stretch across and strangle me, but as her chest bumped the table, Jade's uncapped sparkling water jolted. It fell over almost as if it had a grudge against the she-devil, too, toppling into her lap and glugging out its insides. Jade screeched, pushing the water bottle away from her—and, evidently, onto Madison's lap, because the girl shot to her feet with a gasp.

Connor laughed loudly in the cafeteria, but to his credit, he did try to stifle the sound.

Landon ducked his head toward me in the midst of the chaos, his lips brushing my ear. "What are you doing?"

I turned to face him, our noses coming an inch apart. "Trust me," I whispered through my smile, and bumped my nose gently against his.

Once I turned back to Madison, I knew I had her. Her eyes were lit up with fire as she stared down at me, her soaked gold skirt sticking to her thighs, expression twisted into something that promised fury. The first real reaction I'd gotten from her since Landon announced that I was his girlfriend. It was the sort of *how dare you* look I'd been waiting for. Making her jealous *might've* worked in time, but this was just as effective—possibly even more so.

Making her mad.

"Oh, dear," I said while I chewed, sweeping my fork into my mashed potatoes and taking a large helping. The two girls looked at me as if I'd personally flung the bottle at them, and it made me want to join in on Connor's laughter. "You're not melting, are you?"

I knew the end goal: get Landon and Madison together. My route had to change. Because there was no world in which pretty and perfect Madison Oliphant was going to be jealous of *me*, the girl with so many flaws it was a wonder how she held it together. I needed to trigger this thought in her: *Landon would so be better off with me.*

"I'll get napkins—" Landon began, but I wrapped my arms around his, holding him in place. He could *not* be her knight in shining armor.

"Can I have a bite?" I asked him, looking at his chicken tenders with as much of a puppy-dog stare as I could muster. I'll admit, I felt a little silly, but I held the eye contact like my life depended on it, telepathically sending Landon, *Stop looking at the girls and play along.*

At first, I thought he would tug away and get the napkins anyway. Even though my grip was tight, with his biceps, he definitely could've broken free. But somehow, my telepathy must've gotten through. He picked up the tender and held it out to me, but instead of taking it, I ducked my head and took a bite.

Madison and Jade rushed into the bathroom to use the air dryers, leaving the table's atmosphere so much sweeter, and I ate my mashed potatoes in peace. Landon didn't touch me again the entire period, but then again, the girl we were performing for had left.

At the end of the period Landon pulled me down a hallway opposite of the classrooms, the same hallway I'd tugged him down to ask him out Monday. He paused to make sure no one followed us before dropping my arm. "What was that?" he demanded, features stiff and frustrated. "The whole point was to *bond* with my friends, not piss them off."

"No, the whole point is to make Madison fall for you. Am I wrong?"

"How is insulting her going to do that?"

He wasn't shouting, but he sure wasn't trying to sound sweet. I glanced around, assuring once more that no one was lingering to listen in. "Five bucks says that before the day is over, she'll come up to you and demand you dump me."

"And that's helpful *how*?"

I poked him in the chest. "Because *you're* going to say something like, 'I feel like Lacey really gets me, you know?'" I had pitched my voice lower to mimic his before switching back to normal. "Or whatever cutesy thing you need to. And then Madison will think 'no, I really get him—he should be dating me instead.'"

Landon listened with increasing incredulity—I could see it in the way his head slowly tilted to the side as I spoke. "She—she won't ask to see me."

"Five bucks," I repeated, batting my eyelashes. "We should get going before we're late to class."

He stared down at me warily, and once more, I got the strongest urge to grin. He kept resisting, but soon he'd realize I was right. He'd stop doubting me. His blue-green eyes darted over my face until he finally gave in. "Hi," he said with a sigh, holding his hand out.

"Hi," I replied cheerfully, wrapping my palm around his. My fingers brushed over his class ring as I swung our hands, and for the first time ever, I felt content by Landon's side, uncaring of the eyes on us.

Convincing Madison to fall for Landon would be

messier this way, but the end result could be the same if Landon and I played our cards right. I didn't mind taking the brunt of her anger either, since I'd be gone in a month's time. And, you know, this way, I at least got a little fun out of it. Get Landon his girl and finally take my chance to antagonize the evil stepsisters a little.

I swung our hands with a little more happiness. What more could I ask for?

CHAPTER 10

A new discovery was made later that night: I hated football.

Or, more specifically, I hated the amount of times Landon was hit on the field.

Granted, it wasn't many, since Landon didn't seem to be on the field when the other team had the ball. But the times he was tackled—three—were when he was in the process of making a pass or running the ball toward the goalpost. I knew next to nothing about football, other than the fact that the guys ran around for touchdowns, but each and every time someone slammed into him, I waited for one of the referees to call a foul.

No one ever did, but someone in the stands kept yelling at Landon as if it was *his* fault.

What made it even worse? No one sat beside me. I sat in the front row—which I would've assumed would've been the most coveted spot—and no one sat down the entire game. I might've been Landon Settler's girlfriend, but I was still Hudson Bishop's cousin. Still my mother's daughter.

This town may have been big, but the animosity was inescapable.

"Should've stayed home," I muttered to myself once the game was over, awkwardly standing behind the bleachers with the rest of the football parents, waiting for the Bobcats to finish their post-game huddle. I dug the toe of my boot into a clump of grass, wishing, not for the first time that night, that I had someone I could talk to. Someone that would've made me feel less alone in a crowd of people who I definitely didn't fit in with. Wouldn't stick out like the awkward sore thumb.

Yeah, did I also mention I was the only one *not* wearing some sort of Bobcat spirit gear? Because I was. Even down to the ninety-year-old-looking grandpa sitting on one of the benches, wearing a sweatshirt with his grandson's face on it.

To pass the time, I buried my face in my cell phone.

After beginning the fake relationship with Landon, I started making a checklist of things that needed to be done in order for me to skip town the second I could. It turned out that Van Life required a ton of planning, and though I'd been prepared for it, I did think that I would at least be in Brentwood until graduation. Now, I'd expedited that by seven months. There were so many things to figure out, and I scrolled through the list I created on my phone, thinking.

- Finish the van.
- Have Hudson transfer Petunia title (after birthday).
- Figure out GED.

- Get birth certificate.

The GED was a bit tricky. My mailing address would technically still be in Connecticut even though I traveled, and in Connecticut, you had to wait six months from unenrolling from school to take the test. Which gave me enough time to practice, I guessed. During those six months, I had enough money saved up that I could travel to different cities to find which was the right fit to settle down in. Which Le Petit Bateau to call home. Once I settled down, then came the harder stuff—like getting my own car insurance. I could stay on Uncle Dean's policy until my permanent residence changed.

Ugh, so much to think about.

I glanced up from my phone to find the football players finally emerging from their post-game huddle. The chattering of everyone around me grew to a crescendo as sons and grandsons emerged, and family members congratulated the sweaty boys. I scanned the crowd for the massive player and found him almost immediately.

I took a step forward, a mere second from calling out his name, when people stepped in front of him, shielding my view. "Your overstriding was terrible today," the man said, but almost in a conversational way, like he was trying to hide the fact his words were scolding. "You got lucky for the final play, making that pass with how deep your stride was. You noticed it too, right? I know you know to keep your stride short when you throw."

I stepped closer, my eyebrows coming together. I didn't know who the man thought he was, and all I could see was his back, but he could go take a hike if he was going to yell at a high schooler. My fingers twitched into a curled fist.

But then I stopped, because despite being ready to tell the guy off, I recognized the dark-haired girl and the redheaded woman who stood beside him. *Landon's parents.*

"I think the main problem is that you're elevating your front shoulder too much," Landon's mother interjected, reaching out to pat one of his shoulder pads. "You need to remember to keep this shoulder down when you're leaning back to throw. It'll keep you from overextending your spine."

Landon kept his head downcast during the scolding, taking it all unflinchingly, but I couldn't miss the rigidness of his spine, even with his shoulder pads still on. *Don't do that*, I wanted to say to him. *Don't let them walk all over you. Say something back.*

Growing up with my mom, arguments were common. Both of us tended to let a snide comment slip whenever we were around each other, and the other would never just turn the other cheek at it. I blamed her for my tendency to lean into confrontation—I'd never learned anything else.

His dad gave a hard sigh. "I swear, Landon, we've been doing this for years, but sometimes it feels like it's not sticking." He reached out and thumped Landon on the shoulder pads.

Landon didn't flinch; he didn't even look up.

"Eavesdropping?" I jumped at the sudden voice in my ear, whirling around to find Connor Bray standing over my shoulder. He leaned back on his heels with a small smile, though it looked a little guilty. "Sorry. I didn't think I'd scare you."

"It's okay," I said cautiously, shoving my bag strap higher up on my shoulder. Out of any guy in the Top Tier to come up speaking in my ear, I guess he was the most preferable. Connor's chestnut-colored hair was wet, almost like he'd had the chance to take a quick shower in the locker room. He held his shoulder pads in one hand. "Uh, good game."

"Thanks." Connor glanced past me to where Landon was convening with his family, and Connor sucked in a breath through his teeth. "They're putting him through the ringer today. Don't worry—they do it after practically every game. I think they just like to feel useful."

"The definition of parents living vicariously through their kids, huh?"

Connor smirked. "Ah, you understand it. Don't worry about Landon. He knows to hear them out and then put it behind him."

I glanced back at Landon's bent head, at the way his parents stood before him, almost a united front of scolding. "You'd think they'd be praising him for making a twenty-yard pass."

"You'd think." Connor's eyebrows rose once and fell quickly.

Jade and Madison came up behind him, both carrying their duffle bags. Their cheer outfits looked a whole lot less glamourous without the stadium lights to catch the glitter and sequins, and their makeup much more smudged up close. "What'd you think of the game?" Jade asked me, wrapping an arm through Connor's.

"I honestly didn't understand much of it," I told her. "I played Candy Crush on my phone mostly, really."

Jade's lips twisted. "Seriously?"

"Seriously. I'm close to a new high score."

I wasn't. Did anyone still play Candy Crush nowadays? I did, however, poke the stick into their side further—the way they wore matching expressions of mild disgust proved it.

Jade propped a hand on her hip. "Then why did you come?"

"I'm here for Landon, duh. Since that's what girlfriends do."

"Not that you would know." She snorted at that, pressing her hand against her mouth. "You've never had a boyfriend before. You can never keep them around long enough."

Connor stiffened, turning his head toward her, but I caught his low warning tone. "*Hey.*"

"I'm kidding," Jade said, slapping him on the chest. "Lacey knows that. Right?"

I know that I want to shove my combat boot down your throat. "Madison, do *you* have a boyfriend?" I batted my eyelashes innocently.

She clutched her bag strap tighter, knuckles whitening. "Why?"

"I was wondering why you weren't voted most likely to never have a boyfriend, but I guess your label does fit you a bit better."

Connor looked between all of us nervously, eyes never staying still. "Why don't we—"

"How come you aren't by Landon now, then?" Madison arched an eyebrow. "You know, since you're his girlfriend and all."

Was that suspicion I detected in her voice? I tilted my head. "His family is talking to him."

"So? As his girlfriend, you haven't met his family?"

"After two days? If you think that's a green flag, you're colorblind." On the inside, I smirked a little at the phrase Landon had used once, feeling witty even though I'd stolen it. "Besides, they're having a family moment. Wouldn't want to intrude." Or *accidentally* kick Mr. Settler in the shins.

Madison scoffed a little. "You don't want to intrude because you know they won't approve."

"I don't know if you've noticed, but I don't really care about what people think of me." I leaned forward onto my toes, ducking my head closer. "Unlike some people."

"Hey, here comes our quarterback," Connor said a little bit too loudly, relief tingeing the words.

Landon had parted from his family, who apparently moved off toward the parking lot, and now came toward us. He eyed us all warily as he approached, as if the tension had reached him even across the way. Our eyes met last. I'd thought it was strange seeing him all dressed up on the field, but it was even stranger up close. The shoulder pads made his torso look massive, the jersey stretched tight across it. "Hi," I greeted him warmly.

Landon's gaze lightened, if only marginally. "Hi," he

replied, and then swiped up my hand. His fingers were cold, making me jump. He had grass stains on his arms and on the front of his jersey from the few times he'd been tackled, but otherwise seemed unscathed. It was a little wild to think about, after him being wrestled into the ground like that, he'd only come out of it with a few stains on his clothes. "What were we talking about?"

"How Lacey hates football," Jade chimed in, helpful as ever.

"What I hated was how many times you were tackled on the field," I said, laying my hand on the front of his shoulder pads and giving him wide eyes. His red hair was sticking to his temples in a few places, but otherwise his hair was dry. "I think my heart stopped every time."

My cheesy tone made me die a little on the inside. Though he clearly tried to hide it, Landon's expression belied much of the same feeling.

Now that he was here, and we got to show off a little for his friends, I was truly ready to go home. But I couldn't—not until we were convincing enough.

"Madison," I said, taking my phone out of my back pocket. "Can you take a picture of us?"

Her expression went a little deer-in-headlights as she stared at my phone. "Uh, I guess." Hesitantly, she took it from my grip.

I inched closer toward Landon, but he jerked back in a way that was both obvious to everyone who stood around us and mortifying. "I—I stink."

Way to nearly blow our cover. To compensate, I pressed forward and wrapped my arm around his waist before he could flinch away again. "Boo-hoo." I curved into his side, feeling the shoulder pads that protected his chest and curved around his shoulders. He hadn't been lying about the smell, but it wasn't that bad. Grass mixed with perspiration, but in a way that was more rich than gross. In a way that was definitely *him*.

It took Landon a moment to fall into the embrace, but his hand eventually lifted to wind around my waist. His palm curled around my hip, and the way we posed, we had to look like a couple. Without a doubt. This was our first real picture together. Cha had taken the one at Le Petit Bateau, but this would be our first *real* photo as a couple. Our first posed one.

Madison's gaze was partially obscured by how she held up my phone, but I eyed her closely, trying to pick apart the expression. She looked flustered, but I couldn't tell if that was from how close I stood to Landon or if it was leftover emotion from our conversation. Ticking her off was definitely the route to go, because there wasn't the obvious jealousy for me to play off of. It made me wonder how deep in the friendzone Landon was.

"There," Madison said, offering my phone back by the barest grip. "I think I got one."

Landon dropped his arm hastily and went as far as take a step away from me, and I fought the urge to yank him back.

"Revoltingly cute," Connor said with a grin, giving us a thumbs-up. He'd pulled his shoulder pads over his head, and they rested on the ground by his feet now. "Send it to me and I'll print that photo on magnets for everyone."

It was clear then. Connor was my favorite out of Landon's friends.

"Landon, a bunch of us are going to the Wallflower," Madison said, shifting her duffle bag on her shoulder. She gave him her full attention, batting her eyes in a way I couldn't tell if it was flirty or not. "You joining us?"

"I'm beat," he said, and then stepped back to draw off his shoulder pads. He shook his hair, and in the dark, it looked more brown than red. "I'm going to take the bus back to the school and then go home. I should go before I miss it."

"Or you can ask your girlfriend to drive you," I reminded him, poking him in the side. His extremely *firm* side. I'd never get over it. "She does have a vehicle, you know."

We *really* needed to work on Landon's happy face. He looked crossed between uncomfortable and constipated. "Can you drive me?"

"Of course." Hopefully my enthusiasm made up for his reaction. I turned to the trio, but mostly focused on Connor. "Maybe we can do something soon, all of us."

"We'll definitely plan something," Jade replied, and I knew that if she was planning it, I wanted no part. I didn't trust her as far as I could throw her—but hey, I'd love to see how far she'd get. "Have a good night, you two."

Madison gave a little wave, one that Landon nodded to, and we parted ways there. Silence followed our now-duo, but it was a comfortable one. Landon's shadow blended together with mine as we moved away from the stadium lights, two long black shapes that seemed to disappear into the darkness more and more. I'd had to park way out in the boonies since I'd arrived so late, and I squeezed the button on my fob so the headlights would flash.

When we got to the van, though, that was when Landon's hesitance began again. He slowed a few paces from the side, gripping his shoulder pads tighter. "These will stink up the back—"

"Landon, if you talk about smells one more time..." I let the potential of a threat linger in the air, mostly because I wasn't sure where I'd go from there. I popped open the side door and gestured for him to put the pads in there, and with great reluctance, he did. "Your parents weren't going to give you a ride?"

"*They* don't like the way I smell." He straightened as he faced me, expression blank. No trace of that smile that flipped my insides moments ago. "They prefer if I ride the bus back for away games. My car is at the school anyway, so it works out."

I jingled my keys at him. "Well, now you have your personal chauffer. How's that sound?"

He responded by tugging open the passenger side door and sliding in.

Ooookay. I slammed the sliding door shut and rounded the front of Petunia, tapping the cool, bug-coated grill as I did so. Landon already had his belt on when I climbed into the cab, sitting quietly in the darkness. The atmosphere was exactly as it'd been the first time we'd driven together— awkward. His eyes were on the dashboard, but it was clear that his mind was elsewhere. I wondered if he was replaying the conversation with his friends over, thinking about the game, or if he was thinking about what his parents said.

I thought about what Connor had said about Landon listening and then disregarding their reprimand. Hopefully it was true. "I thought you did great today," I told him to fill the silence, hoping that would alleviate any of the stress on his shoulders. I backed out carefully from my space, looking at all my mirrors to make sure I didn't flatten someone in the parking lot. "I mean, I don't know the first thing about football, but you looked pretty cool running around."

"You didn't have to come if you hated football."

I felt my features darken. "If Jade ends up missing her ponytail, don't check me for scissors. How does Connor put up with such a mean person?" I slowed down for an elderly couple who passed between the aisles of the parking lot, slow moving with their stadium cushions tucked underneath their arms. "She's just mad that a girl like me infiltrated the Top Tier."

"A girl like you?"

"Lower class. Grungy. Cousin of the Grim Reaper. Wearer of red lipstick."

From the corner of my eye, I saw Landon's head turn toward me. "She said all that?"

"Not in so many words. She definitely said the lipstick part." I smirked a little. "She said no guy on the football team would go for me. She's pissed I proved her wrong."

Except I didn't, really, because Landon wouldn't *actually* go for me under normal circumstances. My smirk dissipated. Now I felt even more stupid for opening my mouth.

"That wasn't why you started this, was it?" Landon

asked, his voice sounding strangely serious. "Because of something Jade said?"

"No! God, no. I told you it was a bet with my cousin."

His expression didn't change. "With Hudson."

"Yes, with Hudson."

He turned back toward the road as we pulled out of the parking lot, merging in with traffic seamlessly. The engine rumbled between us, interjecting its own line of dialogue. "Why me?" Landon didn't look back over. "Like you said before, you could've dated anyone. Why'd you choose me?"

Ha, had he read my mind these past few days? I'd been asking myself the same question. "I knew you'd say yes."

"Because you could blackmail me for the fight freshman year?"

That hadn't been totally the reason I'd been sure he'd agree. It was the convincing factor, sure, but when the thought about asking him to fake date me first popped in my head outside Le Petit Bateau, I hadn't thought about the fight at all. "I feel like I can trust you," I said after a beat, mulling it over. "Don't ask me why I feel that way—maybe it's because you're shy."

I could pinpoint the exact moment that my opinion of him shifted. That very first day in the locker room, where he packed up my things and hid me in the stall. And even later, at Le Petit Bateau, where he held me to him after I spotted my mom. There was no hesitation on either front, no second to reconsider. He could've left me standing in the locker room when his friends came in, and he could've shoved me away outside the restaurant, but he didn't.

"How about you?" I asked, taking quick peeks at him. "Why did you say yes?"

Landon traced the bumps in his football pants. "To make Madison jealous."

"You'll have to do better than what you did back there, then. We didn't exactly put off couple vibes. More like I was holding you at gunpoint."

"I was nervous. And I was thinking about the way *you* acted today at lunch. Not really couple vibes then either, do you think?"

"I told you earlier, it's called being strategic," I fired back.

He frowned. "You being antagonistic is strategic?"

I hit the brake, pitching us both forward. I jerked onto the shoulder, causing the car behind me to blare its horn as Petunia kicked up dust. When we came to a halt, I glared at Landon with enough ice to freeze over the football field we'd just left. "Are you kidding? *Me*, antagonistic?"

Landon's chest rose and fell steadily—if I'd been hoping my display of poor driving skill startled him, I was sincerely mistaken. "What would you call it then?"

"Defending myself. Something my *boyfriend* should've been doing."

"'*There's more to Landon Settler than being a quarterback on a crappy football team.*' That was you defending yourself?"

"I was defending *you.*"

Landon blinked once, and then twice more. "I never asked you to."

I let out a disbelieving scoff and slumped back into my

seat, staring at the road as car after car passed us, their tail-lights red eyes glaring back. *Do not strangle the quarterback,* I thought to myself, simultaneously counting to ten. *Connor, Madison, and Jade all know he's with you. Your alibi* so *doesn't check out.*

"How is it strategic?" Landon's voice was significantly quieter than it'd been a moment ago, like he was backing away from the ledge we both stood on. "Explain it to me."

My blood still pumped hot in my veins, not yet ready to give up my frustration. I wanted to cling to it, wanted to rub it in his face, to snap at him again. I wanted to call this whole thing off. I wanted to make a mess of everything. "The idea," I began through gritted teeth, "is to make Madison so ticked off that she convinces herself you're better off with her. I told you this earlier. Because I don't know if you noticed, but you are so far in the friendzone that making her jealous by being lovey dovey with someone else isn't going to get you out."

Landon had no reaction to hearing that his love might be a lost cause. He reached up and pressed the backs of his fingers along his right cheek, and then his left. "She'll get so mad that she'll want to be with me?"

"She'll get mad enough to take you away from me. At least, that's the goal. Then it's up to you to keep her." I raised my eyebrows. "Did Madison or did she not find you after school today? We made a bet on it, remember? Did Madison find you?"

Petunia's engine hummed loudly between us, almost like it was growling with me. "She did," Landon eventually answered, no reaction.

"And what did she say?"

"Exactly what you said she would." A muscle in Landon's jaw jumped. "That I deserved better."

I leaned my elbow against the car door and rested my fist against my temple, suddenly feeling so weary. It had been exactly what I thought she'd say, but hearing it come from Landon didn't quite feel so rosy. "Then we're on the right track. You owe me five bucks."

He shifted to sit lower in the passenger seat, his hair rucking up a bit against the back of the headrest as he closed his eyes. "I don't like the idea of you fighting with them, because there *is* a time after this, you know. After homecoming, after we've...broken up."

"And you're worried they'll target me?" This time, I actually did laugh—it was a dark, hollow sound. "It's not going to matter."

"Why not?"

Because after I get the title to Petunia, I'll be out of the state in a heartbeat and won't ever look back. Landon still hadn't opened his eyes, wasn't waiting on me for an answer. Seeing him so relaxed, so at odds against how fiery I'd felt mere moments ago, had my shoulders losing some of their tension. "Once we break up, they won't care about me."

"Once we break up," Landon said softly, "it will be infinitely worse."

He was right, of course. If I didn't leave once Landon and I went our separate ways, I could imagine the sort of ridicule, taking everything I'd rubbed into their faces and throwing it back into mine. *See,* they'd say. *He never liked you. No one likes you—you, Lacey Churchill, are unlovable.*

A hole yawned open in my chest, the last thought echoing from the darkness. When I spoke, my voice sounded hollow. "You obviously don't know me if you think I'd be bothered by that kind of thing."

"What are you doing this weekend?" Landon asked suddenly, and I blinked to bring him back into focus, to bring my mind out of the pitch. "I think...I think we should spend more time together. Outside of school. Just to...get used to each other."

"So you won't stiffen every time I wrap my arm around you?"

He finally glanced over, locking eyes and flitting away. "Yeah."

My first reaction was to say no, that I was busy. After a draining day like today, I wasn't sure I had it in me to put on any more performances. But if it was only us, it wouldn't be a performance. The only way to get comfortable with someone was to spend more time with them, right? Especially for someone as introverted as Landon. And whether he intended it to be or not, his offer was a white flag to our bickering, a request to defuse the tension.

So even though I knew I didn't have to, I waved my white flag too. "You free tomorrow?"

CHAPTER II

Igasped awake from a dream that I instantly couldn't remember, heartrate skyrocketing as I batted at the heavy covers, frantically glancing around the space. My back slammed against the headboard as I took in the posters and the curtains and the furniture, my mind all at once screaming *this isn't your bedroom.*

It only took a few seconds for realization to sink in, for the fog of sleep to evaporate, for the adrenaline and panic to recede enough to realize that it was Hudson's bedroom.

I slumped against the headboard and knocked my head against it, drawing in breath after breath to calm my racing pulse. The dream that'd brought the panic was blank in my mind, but the feeling lingered in a weak way now, its teeth still embedded underneath my skin.

Just when I thought I'd finally gotten used to it, I'd wake up expecting to find my purple bedroom, my stuffed animals, my lightweight yellow duvet. After three months, I still woke up the same way.

I threaded my fingers through my hair near my part,

tearing through the tangles, the pain grounding me. It was early—early enough for the light not to filter through the blinds yet—but I knew for a fact I wasn't going to be able to fall back to sleep.

Saturday mornings at the Bishop household were sleepy. Uncle Dean had a night shift at the factory on Friday nights, so he slept in late the next morning. Despite the windows streaming in light, Hudson usually stayed conked out on the couch until Paisley stirred, when she booted him off so she could watch her cartoons. I usually lingered in Hudson's room until there were signs of life from beyond the door, because there was nothing more awkward than trying to navigate a house that wasn't yours when no one was awake.

My hair was short, so the braids only hung a bit past my shoulders, but it looked pretty cute. Instead of putting on my usual makeup, I slapped on some tinted sunscreen, winged on some waterproof liner, and applied my usual red lip. *Perfect.*

When it finally turned eight o'clock, I lifted my phone and rapidly texted.

LACEY

You got a swimsuit?

I wasn't sure if he would've been up or not yet, but my phone chimed quickly.

GRUMPY BUTT

It's the middle of September

Yeah, I totally changed his name after yesterday.

LACEY

Have you seen the temps today? 80s!
Last chance to get a good swim in before
it's too cold. Don't tell me you're a
chicken :P

GRUMPY BUTT

bawk bawk

I smirked at my screen before throwing it on my bed, grabbing my swimsuit from my suitcase. It was one I'd had to buy post-moving out since I hadn't thought ahead to pack one, and it was a two-piece blue set. I moved back to the bathroom to change into it, sending another text.

LACEY

Picking u up in 10. If you don't have swim
trunks on, you're swimming in your
panties

GRUMPY BUTT

I don't wear panties. >:(

Can you park on the street corner of
Willow?

So I wasn't even allowed to park on his *street* now? Sheesh.

LACEY

Still embarrassed by me? Way to hurt a
girl's feelings.

But yeah, fine, I'll park in a secret spot.
Got any snacks to bring on the road?

GRUMPY BUTT

I'll scrounge something together.

Locking my phone with a click, I set it on the sink and tied the straps of my bikini top tight, throwing my tee back over it. Hopefully hanging out today helped Landon feel a bit more relaxed about everything. Even our text conversations felt a bit more conversational. He used emojis. That, my friends, was what I liked to call progress. Baby steps, baby steps.

As I made my second pass back through the living room, the sound stirred Hudson awake.

"Where are you going?" he asked from the couch, voice still thick with sleep. In fact, he hadn't moved whatsoever from his sleeping position, except that he squinted his eyes open at me. "It's too early for a Saturday."

"I've got a date," I told him, coming close enough to kick his leg that hung off the couch. "I'm taking the van to the beach, just so you know. Don't report me missing or anything."

"The beach?" His features twisted up further, like he was thinking *am I still half asleep?* "It's over an hour away. And September."

I kicked his foot again before turning away. "Not sure why you both think that's a good excuse."

Hudson's voice trailed after me, "Don't lump me in with him."

"You're lumped!" I called back, ducking back into his room to grab my wallet and keys.

It was already warm when I got outside, and I rolled my

windows down to air out the van as I drove. A few stray hairs broke free from my braid, tickling my face as they were tugged around in the wind. Even still, I relaxed at the sight of the open road and the sun shining in. It was a taste of freedom that would be coming soon.

Two weeks. I could handle two weeks.

Surprisingly enough, Landon was waiting on the corner of Willow when I got to it. He leaned against a tree with his one hand in his black sweatpants pocket, the other holding a plastic grocery bag filled with something. When he spotted the van, he straightened, ducking his head as he rounded toward the passenger seat.

"Those are not swim shorts," I said with a scowl as he opened the door. "Did you think I wasn't serious about making you swim in your underwear?"

"I knew you were serious." Before climbing in, Landon reached for his waist and tugged the band of his swim bottoms out from underneath the band of his sweatpants. I caught a glimmer of his stomach as he did so, the sun once again feeling too hot. "I couldn't walk out of the house in a swimsuit. My parents would've thrown a fit."

I watched as he climbed easily into the seat. "It's a speedo, isn't it?"

Landon choked on the breath he drew in, eliciting the exact reaction I'd been hoping for. He saw me grinning, and though his face was slightly annoyed—and pink—I saw the amusement that lingered in his eyes. "You're ridiculous."

Not a laugh. Amusement, but no laugh. I'd get him eventually.

I navigated through Brentwood's backstreets to get to the main road, reaching for the aux cord that dangled somewhere between the seats. I used my knee to steady the steering wheel and slipped my phone out from my back pocket, trying to balance looking at the road with plugging in the music. "It's about an hour drive to the beach, so hope you brought some good snacks."

"I've got it, I've got it," Landon said, taking my phone from me and plugging in the aux cord. He opened my music app that was on the main page and pressed the shuffle button. "And I brought a variety of things. A few waters, crackers, candy, sandwiches—"

"*Sandwiches?*" I glanced at him. "Aw, did you pack a picnic? That's what couples do, right? Pack a picnic for the beach? We can take cute, cringey, couple photos." Landon brought the plastic bag onto his lap and fumbled through it, searching for something. When he pulled out a red bag, I brightened. "Twizzlers!" It was a share-size bag, one that I could easily demolish by the time we got to the beach. "Ooh, and you got the cherry kind!"

Landon broke them open, and their sweet, artificial sugary scent carried its way to my nose. "I thought I should bring them."

"Totally the supreme candy. Not a lot of people our age like them. I'm surprised you do."

"I don't, actually." Landon picked out a little bite-sized piece and offered it out to me, which I greedily accepted. He didn't look at me, but sifted through the plastic bag again. "I grabbed what I found in the pantry."

I shot him a thumbs up. "Well, you crushed it."

"So, what's with the construction zone back there?" Landon asked as we pulled out onto the main highway, glancing over his seat to peer at the van's back area.

"A work-in-progress." This weekend's plans *had* been to start painting, but I would do that tonight. My next shift at Le Petit Bateau wasn't until tomorrow, so when I got back from the beach, I had plenty of time. "Have you ever heard of van life?"

"You mean where people live in their vans and travel around the country?"

I nodded with excitement. "Exactly. That's what I'm going to do. I think eventually, I want to make my way toward the west coast, but I want to take my time. I'm not sure where I want to settle down yet. I've got a lot saved up from serving, but van life is pretty inexpensive."

The corners of Landon's mouth turned down as I spoke. "Where do you shower?"

"Gyms, the Y, places like that. Not sure if you knew, but I'm not picky about where I shower."

When I glanced over, there was no doubt about it— Landon Settler was totally blushing. "You're not going to college?"

"Not *everyone* has to go to college, you know." I reached across Landon for the glovebox, my hand brushing against his knee. He jumped, but held still as I fished out my sunglasses. "I don't know what I'd go for, anyway. It's not like I've got twenty grand lying around for basic classes, and if I *did* have twenty grand, I wouldn't sit through another however many years of school."

"You could get scholarships."

"Could. Maybe. But I don't want to." I held my palm out, and after a second's hesitation, Landon put another Twizzlers piece into my palm. "Don't tell me you subscribe to the thought that *everyone* has to go to college. I think I might have to fake break up with you."

"No, no," he hurried to say, shaking his head. "I don't think that. I...I don't know. I guess it's strange to me because I've never really thought of an alternative."

I chewed thoughtfully, sitting up straighter in the driver's seat. "Let's play a game, then. What would Landon Settler do if he didn't have a football scholarship?"

"Probably still go to college."

"What for?" I leaned a little closer to him. "*Art?*"

Landon visibly cringed. "No, probably something practical."

"*Practical.*" I scrunched my nose up as if the word smelled bad. "You sound like an adult. No. You sound like a *parent.*" It was easy to guess that it was probably his parents who fed him that line, and I wanted to sigh at how easily he bought into it. "Come on, give me *something,* Landon. Stop being quiet and shy and tell me how you feel. Take yourself out of the box you're in and really think— what would you *want* to do?"

"I don't know what I want." The words rushed out of Landon forcefully, defensively. "I want to say I'd probably major in sports management, but then I know you'll ask if that's what I *want* to do, and honestly...I don't know. Doing something with sports administration sounds okay, but is that what I want or what my parents want? I wouldn't want to major in art, though. What I like most about drawing is that no one's putting a grade on it—no one's scrutinizing it. It's the one thing that I do that no one judges. I might take a class or two, but I like keeping that side of me to myself."

When Landon stopped speaking, he seemed to realize how rapidly he'd been talking. He shrank back into his seat, hunching his shoulders up a little. He seemed embarrassed, but I, for one, couldn't stop grinning at the highway in front of me. It was easily, hands-down, the most I'd heard him say in one stretch, all over something he was passionate about. He went from Shy Landon to Expressive Landon in a matter of seconds, and then back again.

"Don't laugh," Landon all but whispered, refusing to make eye contact.

"I'm not laughing," I insisted, smile still twisting my lips as I flipped on my blinker to pass a semi. "I just think you're cute."

Landon slouched lower. "That doesn't sound like a compliment."

"I like that you want to keep your art to yourself. I think it makes sense, given how all of your other moves are watched. Babble, football... I bet art for you is a true escape."

"I just goof off with it."

"Don't," I ordered sternly, tapping the steering wheel. "Don't brush off something that's important to you. You're allowed to cherish it."

Landon didn't answer, gazing down into the Twizzlers bag like it held all the answers to the universe.

I wanted to pat him on the shoulder, even though I wasn't sure how much of an encouragement he'd find it. I learned more about him in the last five minutes, though, than the past few days of us spending time together, so that was something. A baby step in the right direction. Once we got past that awkward acquaintance barrier, moved into the friend zone, we'd be able to fully sell the relationship. Fully convince Madison.

As the silence lulled in the cab, the music that had been playing from my phone caught my ear, and I gasped. "Oh, I love this song!" Without warning, I reached out and turned the dial, the volume blaring like a concert. Landon jumped and he braced one hand on the side of the door as if we were about to crash. Instinctively, I knew that Landon would never truly relax around me if I didn't relax around him, too. Not that I was *that* on edge, but I needed to let go. Act around him the way I acted around Hudson. Landon had been vulnerable with me, so I'd be open with him.

As we drove down the highway with the music loud, I sang along with the lyrics of the chorus. I wasn't a great singer. I, arguably, wasn't even a good one, but the volume of the radio masked most of my voice.

I pointed at Landon when the first round of the chorus was over. "You know this song, right?"

His eyes were perfectly round as he looked at me, almost like he questioned whether or not I was sane. "Uh, yeah. I mean, a little."

I sang the next lyrics with more volume, and then held a closed fist to him, acting as if it were a microphone. Landon looked at my hand like I held a bug, his expression no less freaked out. In fact, my effort of making him more relaxed only seemed to increase his discomfort.

I tilted my head back and forth to the beat as I sang, jamming as much as I could while focusing on driving. My high notes cracked like I was a prepubescent teen, and I laughed at the sheer *horribleness* of it all.

But what really made the moment so great was that it wasn't only me laughing. Landon tried to cover his mouth to hide it, but I caught the barest hint of his chuckle over the noise of my voice and the music. My lips stretched in automatic response to it, heart giving an impulsive flutter.

When the song was over—and I ended it with a dramatic flourish of a jazz hand—he offered another Twizzlers piece to me, but instead of reaching for it, I opened my mouth.

Careful not to touch my lips, he popped it in. "It's going to be a long hour, isn't it?"

"Don't worry," I said as I munched, smiling at the flavor. "I'll get you to sing at some point."

I didn't end up getting Landon to sing. Traffic got crazier once we passed Rothsville, and my concert session had to be put on hold. Growing up in Brentwood had me knowing the route to the beach by heart—because anyone who was anyone knew that the county communal swimming pools were fifty percent bleach and fifty percent kid pee—so it wasn't too stressful of a drive. Landon faithfully kept me supplied with Twizzlers and even a few Reese's

Pieces, and we reached the beach by the time the heat truly set in.

"See?" I said as I hopped out of the driver's seat, turning my face up toward the sun. It burned like a kiss. "Definitely beach weather. Probably one of the last days for the year."

Landon shut the door behind him and looked around at the empty parking lot, twisting the plastic bag in his grip. "I wondered if we'd be the only lunatics to go to the beach in September."

I walked around to the passenger side and jerked the side door open, revealing more of Petunia's work-in-progress. Hudson's black duffle sat behind the seats, and I dragged it closer to me, dragging out the couple of beach towels and a water frisbee. "You were the one that said you wanted to hang out together more."

"'Hang out' isn't synonymous with 'swimming.'"

"It could be."

After swiping my sunglasses from my face, I tugged my tee over my head and shook my braids loose of it. Even though the sun was warm, the cool breeze from the ocean tickled my stomach, and my traitorous skin began forming goosebumps. I stuffed the shirt into the bag before I reached for the button on my shorts, freezing when Landon's hands came down over mine.

His skin was flushed as he looked at me, his freckles nearly lost in the color. "Y-You could keep those on."

"Uh, have you ever worn wet denim?"

His eyes were almost fiercely on my face, like he was afraid to look anywhere else.

I narrowed my eyes at him, trying to figure out why *he* was the one embarrassed. He didn't let go of my hands. "You've seen me in less."

"*Technically*, yes, but you were more covered."

Okay, so he wasn't wrong. Technically. The towel *had* covered more skin than the bikini, but I was surprised he was even thinking twice about it.

As we spoke, the back of his fingers brushed the skin of my stomach, causing me to suck in a low breath. He jerked away, his fingers curling into fists.

"You're so modest." I couldn't help but smile as I said it, swiping up the towels and tucking them over my arm. Not that I would've expected anything different from him, but I didn't even know the last time I'd interacted with a guy my age without them sneaking glances at my chest or butt. "Your football buddies could learn a lesson from you. Especially Ashton."

Landon didn't say anything, but he distinctly refused to look at me, and it made me wonder if this *was* a bad idea. Good thing we weren't fake dating over the summer—it'd be really hard to explain why he was so freaked out by the sight of my bare skin.

I knew I didn't have the body of a cheerleader, but I didn't exactly think he'd be so...*uncomfortable*.

After grabbing everything, I slammed the door shut. "All right," I said, turning to him with as much nonchalance as I could muster. "Let's go."

The walk to the ocean was a slope downhill, filled with prickly crabgrass and pathways that needed weeding. When we got to the sand, I sighed at the warm top coating of it while burying my toes in the cooler middle. The beach was completely empty, which felt like a major win in terms of what we were here to do. There'd be no prying eyes and no pressure.

I dropped the towels off at the edge of where the dry sand met the damp, turning to look at Landon fiddling with the hem of his shirt. "Are you going to take it off?" I asked, tilting my head. "Or are you going to swim with your shirt and sweats on?"

"I'll take it off," he insisted, but didn't tug the hem up.

"What did I do to make you so nervous?" I stretched my arms wide. "I'm just a girl who drives a van, likes cherry Twizzlers, and totally would've been booed off *American Idol*."

"I'm not nervous."

"Then why aren't you looking at me?"

He lifted his chin as he focused more intensely on the ocean. "I—I don't want to make you uncomfortable."

"You acting like I'm a ninety-year-old grandma wearing a bikini is making me uncomfortable. Is that why you won't look at me? Because I'm ugly?"

"N-No—"

"I'm not as pretty as your cheerleader friends, is that it?"

Landon started to shake his head, pressing his fingers to his cheek. "*No.*"

"You're afraid I'm going to jump you in the water or something?"

"I don't want you to think I'm weird." A muscle in his jaw jumped as he ducked his head a little. "I'm afraid that if

I look at you, you'll think I'm being creepy and checking you out."

The sudden urge to smile came again, but I maintained my poker face. "*Are* you being creepy and checking me out?"

"No." His voice dropped to a murmur. "Not on purpose."

Without warning, I rocked forward on my toes and took Landon's face in my hands, forcing his head to turn toward mine. His cheeks were warm underneath my palms, his eyes widening at the sudden closeness. He didn't tug back, but froze solid. "Landon." I kept my voice firm. "For this fake relationship thing to work, you have to seem interested. If someone were with us right now, they'd never buy in to the fact we were dating, would they?"

Landon blinked, almost as if dazed. "No," he whispered.

"No. They wouldn't. The whole point of today is to get used to each other, right? So, we can act like a real couple. You wouldn't think your girlfriend creepy and weird for checking you out once you take your shirt off, right?"

His lashes fluttered as he shook his head.

"Exactly. So just look at me and pretend like we're actually dating. Look at me and pretend you're at the beach with Madison." I leaned closer, giving him my most determined expression. "Stop being shy, stop overthinking, and just *be*. Can you do that?"

Maybe I should've approached it like that to begin with. *Pretend I'm Madison.* In hindsight, that seemed like the simplest thing.

I watched the decision wash over Landon's expression, like the trepidation that had been weighing him down vanished in an instant. With my hands still on his cheeks, he gave me a nod. Now, I did smile at him, and I watched his gaze flick down to my lips. Something inside me twisted at the movement, and I dropped my hands instantly, almost like his skin burned me.

Without any hesitation this time, Landon grabbed the back collar of his T-shirt and tugged it up over his head in one fluid movement, shaking his now ruffled hair free of the material. He reached for the ties of his sweatpants next, untying them, kicking them off to reveal green swim shorts.

And holy *hello muscles*.

Everyone had their quirks, right? Some people loved forearms. Some people loved hands. Some people even loved ankles, which seemed bizarre, but I wasn't going to question it. I, however, *clearly* had an obsession with muscles, at least when they were on a body as well-built as Landon Settler's.

Obviously, I should've been prepared to see how firm his biceps and pectorals looked. I'd touched his side enough times to know what it felt like. But the boy even *looked* like he lived and breathed football, from the curve of his muscles to the grooves at his waist. The tops of his shoulders were filled with freckles, trailing like starbursts across his skin. Goodness gracious.

"I—I think I take it back. It does feel weird...you staring."

I was sure that it was me who had the blush on their cheeks this time, but I just rolled my eyes. "Have you looked in the mirror? You look like a Greek god or something."

His face crunched up as he cringed. "I do not."

I unfastened the button on my shorts and slid them off, kicking them into the pile of belongings before picking up the water frisbee. I waved it at him. "Race you to the shoreline."

The sun hung high above us, but it seemed to glow on him and his open expression. The guardedness he'd worn like a second skin dissolved as he looked down at me, and whatever I'd said, whatever mindset shift he had, worked better than I could've hoped for.

"Three, two, one, go!" Landon rushed to say, and before I had a chance to process, he raced off toward the shoreline kicking up sand in his wake.

"Hey!" I shouted, sprinting after him. "You're such a cheater!"

His laugh echoed with the crashing waves, and I couldn't help but think it was such a beautiful sound.

CHAPTER 12

Swimming around as teens wasn't as exciting as swimming as kids, but Landon and I did take turns splashing each other, throwing around the frisbee, and seeing who could hold their breath the longest. Landon won each time, due to his giant lungs, but it was close. Once we were pruney, we made our way back to the shore to lie out in the hot sand. Landon sat on the towel beside me. He'd pulled his T-shirt back on to protect most of his pale skin from the sun. He'd found a stick in the sand and used it to draw out a picture on the surface. I watched him as he did so, letting the sun warm my stomach.

A stomach he'd gone back to averting his gaze from.

"What time is it?" he asked, turning his head but not looking with his eyes.

I picked up my phone. "A little after one."

"I think if we left now, we'd dodge the most of the lunchtime traffic."

He was probably right. That was why we hadn't left at noon, when we'd actually gotten out of the water. That, and I didn't want us climbing into the van dripping with seawater. So, instead, we laid out and let the sun dry us.

But leaving... Was it weird that I didn't want to? Not that sitting on a towel was overly exciting or anything, but there was something so peaceful about hearing the waves roll into the shore, smelling the salty air, listening to the steady breaths Landon pulled in and let out.

I lifted my head to get a better view. "What are you drawing?"

"The water."

"I thought you said you drew portraits."

"I do." He gestured down at the sand. "Hence why my waves look like wiggly snakes."

"You could draw me." I tucked a hand underneath my chin like my head was on a pedestal. "Come on, this face is *begging* for a portrait."

Landon let out a soft breath, one corner of his mouth quirking up. "Some other time."

I made a face but relaxed back down on the blanket, closing my eyes against the warm sun. "What got you into drawing, Picasso?"

"Uh, I guess those little assignments you'd get in elementary school. I was paired up with this girl and had to draw her, and—I guess from there, I enjoyed it." Landon hummed a little, and I could hear his stick scratch into the sand. "That first picture sucked, but I liked it enough to keep drawing."

"Do you still have it? The drawing?"

"Probably in some box somewhere." He cleared his throat. "Do you have any cute elementary school stories?"

I shook my head. "I don't really remember much of elementary school. I didn't sleep much as a kid, didn't have friends, had family issues. My poor childhood was traumatic."

I'd said it as a joke, a flippant off-the-cuff line that I never should've let fly, but Landon's sand scratching sounds stopped. "Traumatic?"

All at once, I snapped back to reality, tensing at the idea of going down that road of conversation. I opened my eyes and stared up at the bright sky, letting it burn my eyes. "I was just kidding," I said, and I sat up. "You know what we should do? We should take a picture to send to Babble. Come closer."

When he didn't move fast enough, I sidled up beside him, whipping my phone out and turning it on selfie mode. I wrapped an arm around Landon's neck and brought our faces together, the skin of his cheek brushing mine. "Smile," I commanded him, looking at his distinctly unsmiling face in the screen.

When he obeyed, I could feel his grin against my skin, and something like a rush raced down my spine. I stared at him in my phone screen, at his freckled face with the wide, boyish smile. It looked genuine, as if he were smiling for real. I wouldn't have guessed a second ago that he'd been stone-faced.

I snapped the photo, tilting my head another direction for another.

Landon fumbled in his pocket for his own cell phone. "I should take one of you. Just you. You think?"

I nodded in agreement. "Could be good if anyone asks."

I fluffed my hair a little bit, shaking the bits of sand that'd stuck to the strands. It was weird to see him point his phone at me, weirder still to pose for him in my swimsuit. As he peered into his phone screen, I grinned a little at the thought of girls at Brentwood who would've killed to be me. Sitting on a beach with the untouchable quarterback? To them, I would've struck the lottery.

I struck another pose, this one to seemingly be more candid. I put a hand in front of my mouth with splayed fingers, like I was mid-laugh, stretching my other hand out toward Landon's phone, like I was saying *no pictures, no pictures*. Another snap of the photo. "I have another idea for one more. Is it...can I touch you?"

Landon blinked his ridiculously long lashes and nodded, and then, without any hesitation whatsoever, I laid down, resting my head on his crossed knee. My hair splayed across his bent calf, and he jerked as if it tickled him, his hand coming to brace himself on the blanket we'd laid out.

"Take the picture," I told him, looking up at his down-turned face. The sun was totally in my eyes, but his sparkled so intensely with the light, like they were the ocean water reflecting. "This position hurts my neck."

"You are really good at this," Landon said, but I couldn't tell if his voice was appreciatory or not. He lifted his arm above him, so the camera angled down on us. I raised two fingers in a peace sign, and when I thought he was about to take the photo, Landon shifted. He brought his arm down, laying it across my bare stomach, resting his hand on my hip. I sucked in a breath at the touch. "Smile," he reminded me.

The word echoed in my head, but I could barely get my lips to twitch up, and couldn't draw my gaze off the upturned line of his jaw. There were freckles there, too, trailing down his neck in a lighter fashion. He had his T-shirt back on, but it didn't obscure the shape of his shoulders, and certainly did nothing to hide his bicep. The bicep that was attached to the arm that currently rested on my stomach. My bare stomach.

Everything about me prickled hot, like I needed to jump back into the ocean.

When Landon lowered his phone, seemingly having captured the picture, I practically launched off him. I busied myself by quickly sending one of the selfies off to Hudson—***look how cute we are!!! Throwing up yet? ;)***—before I settled back down on the blanket, pressing my palms to my hot cheeks. "So, tell me," I said, clearing my throat, trying to sound as nonchalant as possible. "What is it about Madison that you like?"

"What do you mean?"

"Like, do you like her jokes? Do you think she's pretty? Did you have a fate moment that tied you to her forever?" *Why are we going to such lengths for one of the meanest people alive?*

"Fate moment," he repeated with a light scoff, shaking his head. "I guess, kind of. I mean... I don't know."

I rolled on my stomach and propped my head on my hands. "Let me be the judge, then. What happened?"

Landon pressed his lips together in thought, obviously debating whether or not to say anything. It wasn't like I'd use it against him. Ultimately, he continued to draw lines in the sand, letting it take his focus. "I think it was the fourth grade. We went to the same elementary together." He spoke hesitantly, repeatedly glancing at me. "It was Valentine's Day."

I poked him in the knee. "Aww."

"I made a box for my candy—because we used to pass out little cards in class—but...the kids in class took it and threw it in the cafeteria trash can before school."

I jerked my head up. "*What?* Why would they do that?"

"I was kind of a loser as a kid," he admitted. "My freckles were darker, my hair was redder, and I was the outcast. Even though I was a Settler, and my parents had a lot of friends, I didn't have any friends. Not until middle school when I got better at sports."

Squinting up at him, I tried to picture a version of Landon Settler where people *didn't* like him. *Didn't* gush about him online. A version that wasn't in the Top Tier. "I bet you were a cute kid," I said after a moment, feeling my heart pinch for the little red-haired fourth grader.

Landon reached up and combed his hand through his hair, shaking it out of his eyes. "Well, she—Madison—she gave me her box. With all the candy inside. The box and all the cards had her name on them, of course, but she said she had enough love to share with me. I guess, ever since then... it's always been her. "

There was a version of Madison that had a heart? Go

figure. I tilted my chin on my hands as I thought about it more, trying to picture the moment in my head. "Okay, fine, I deem that fate-worthy enough. It's definitely cute." Maybe that was why Landon still liked her, then—his past totally blinded him.

Landon let out a breath, blue eyes locking onto mine. He looked so relieved, like me accepting his little meet-cute was all he'd been hoping for. His gaze was steady—everything about him was unwavering, comforting, like my own shadow. "How about you?" he asked after a minute. "Have you ever had any fate moments like that?"

"Me?" A fate-worthy meeting? A meet-cute? I didn't think so. I tried to recall a moment where my heart fluttered—like, *really* fluttered. Nothing surfaced. All my years of school, I'd never really had a crush. I thought guys were cute, sure, but with the thought always in the back of my mind about moving away, I never really let myself develop feelings. If I'd had a crush, would I want to stay around to see what would happen, to avoid the "what ifs"? Would it be enough to get me to stick around?

"I don't think so," I said finally, answering both his asked question and my unasked one. "But I'm glad you had yours."

"Really?" Landon squinted at me, wincing against the brightness of the sun. "Nothing?"

"I don't think I had any elementary crushes, from what I do remember." Because what I remembered were the days Mom would drop me off at one of her friends' houses or leave me alone entirely. Days when I'd burn myself on the stove trying to heat up SpaghettiOs. Those days blended together. "No middle school ones, either. I was ugly in middle school."

"I doubt it."

I tried to fall back into the teasing, but thinking about Mom and the past had already opened the box of feelings, and I struggled to close it back up. Dread clung to me like dirt smeared across my skin, thinking about little Lacey. Days when I'd sit on the couch and watch one of Mom's favorite cop dramas because I couldn't figure out how to turn the TV channel. Nights when I'd hide in the closet waiting for Mom to come home, terrified that someone was going to break in. Time after time of crying by myself, patting my own back as if it provided any comfort.

I blinked back into focus to find Landon watching me silently, as if my past and pain were a movie he'd been able to watch the trailer of. Swallowing hard, I reached for my shorts. "You were right. We should get going if we want to beat traffic."

Landon dragged his fingers through his picture before I could see it, but from the second I did see, it didn't look anything like the wavy snakes from earlier. It almost looked like a face.

I worked the swing shift on Sunday, from two to seven, and my feet were crying by the end of the day. I sat in the grubby break room while I waited for my last table to leave, counting the rumpled tips I'd shoved into my apron pocket over the course of the day. Sundays were always the busiest with the church crowds and weekend brunches—the best days to make money. The satisfaction of a long shift came at the end when I could count out the bills.

"Bag it in tonight?"

I looked up to find Nate, one of the grill cooks, leaning into the cubby of a room, opening one of the square lockers that belonged to him. His dark curls seemed frizzy from the heat of the kitchen. "Of course," I said, repeating the number in my head to make sure I didn't forget where I left off. "You know weekends are always good."

"I've *heard* weekends are good," he returned, grabbing an energy drink from his locker. "Not that I've ever experienced serving firsthand. I'm perfectly fine with being behind the grill line."

I scrunched my nose. "You could try serving. You know, I've heard male servers get tipped more. Especially when they're handsome like you."

"Careful, your boyfriend will get jealous." With a teasing wink, he ducked out of the break room, leaving me to finish counting my money. I checked my watch, hoping that my last table would've left by now so I could clean it and go home.

Aaaaaand, nope. Still there.

"Why won't forty-two leave already?" I groaned, leaning on the server line with a frown. The two older ladies sat chatting in their booth, nursing their glasses of wine slowly. It'd been over an hour since I'd cleared most of the plates. They'd already paid their bill. Did a fish restaurant really offer them the ambiance they were looking for?

Raquelle, a server who only worked weekends, looked over at me as she loaded up her tray of food. "Hey, if you run my drinks to table twelve, I'll bus the table for you. Then you can get out of here."

I perked up like a dog. "Really?"

"Yeah, girl, you've been here long enough. I'm the closer, so I don't mind."

I patter her on the shoulders as I brushed past her toward the drink machine. "My feet thank you."

Raquelle laughed. "Tell your feet I said 'you're welcome.' That's two waters to table twelve."

I saluted her as she walked out onto the floor with her food, turning back to load up the waters. It was only a little past seven, which meant I had a few hours left to chill out before going to bed. I'd finished up all my homework, so the possibilities were endless when it came to figuring out what I wanted to do. Watch a movie with Paisley? Turn on the porch light and work on the van with Hudson? Call Landon?

The water I had under the spout began overflowing, running down the cup and onto my hand. Cursing under my breath, I sopped up the sides with a napkin, inwardly rolling my eyes. Call Landon, *pfft*. And talk about what? His offer of being able to call him on my drives home from work was probably flippant and off the cuff, anyway. I hadn't spoken to him since I dropped him off yesterday afternoon, and even then, we'd barely spoken on the ride home from the beach. He'd been too busy nodding off half the time.

Which, admittedly, was kind of funny to watch his head knock against the window.

Grabbing the two glasses, I curbed around the server line and walked out onto the dining room floor, mentally counting the tables as I passed them. Before I got to table twelve, though, I froze.

The woman at the table was slender and beautiful in a way that was almost movie-star worthy, with her jet-black hair furling over one of her shoulders. She had a tattoo along her neck that stretched out its butterfly wings, the intricate detail speaking volumes of the artist's skill. It was also instantly, achingly familiar, as was everything else about the woman, even down to the color of her fingernails.

It was my mother.

My chest caved inward, all of the air evaporating from my lungs.

I jerked back a step, and that was when my fingers spasmed. The glasses slipped from my grip, crashing to the ground with no forgiveness. The shatter seemed to echo throughout the entire building, everyone in the restaurant turning toward me.

Mom included.

I couldn't breathe when her eyes landed on me. My mouth opened and closed, but it did nothing to pull in air, chest spasming with desperation. Water soaked the toes of my shoes and clung to my pantlegs, glass shimmering around me. I took another step back, and my heel crunched on the shards. If any sliced through the rubber sole, I didn't feel it—I couldn't feel anything beyond the increasing pressure that threatened to crush my chest.

My world swayed as a fuzzy silhouette of Mom rose to her feet. Her painted lips were moving, but my ears rang too loudly for me to make sense of them. She started to take a step toward me, then stopped.

Wake up, I thought blearily, even though I knew I was wide awake—I knew this moment was real. The words were a frantic plea anyway. *Wake up, wake up.*

On their own accord, my feet began moving, whirling me around. I slammed into Maestro, who'd come up behind me with a broom and dustpan. I knocked the dustpan out of his grip, sending it clattering onto the floor with the glass. When he spoke, his voice was almost in slow-motion. "Lacey? Are you—"

I shoved past him, grabbing at the collar of my shirt and tearing open the buttons to get the material off my throat. I vaguely remembered rushing into the back of the restaurant to get my purse from my locker, vaguely remembered Nate calling something at me, but I didn't stop to listen. Autopilot had me moving at a pace that left no time to think. By the time I realized I was no longer in the restaurant, I was already in the front seat of Petunia.

My hands shook as I shoved the key into the ignition, and with a growl that mimicked one I felt building in my throat, the van roared to life.

And then I made my escape.

CHAPTER 13

I didn't know how long I drove for. Long enough for my fingers to ache from how tightly I clutched the wheel, long enough for my butt to hurt from sitting still, and long enough for my tears to dry. Then again, I wasn't totally convinced I'd cried. I didn't remember it, if I had. I felt suspended in the driver's seat, stuck in a realm between the real world and a breakdown. I knew I *should* cry—my whole body trembled like I could've —but those emotions seemed so far out of reach.

Even though I'd seen her a week ago at the shopping center across from Le Petit Bateau, the last place I expected to see her was at work. Five minutes from the end of my shift. Looking at me like we'd only been parted a few days rather than a few months.

I'd fantasized what it would've been like to face her again. I wasn't supposed to be the one running away crying.

The headlights of oncoming traffic had become easy to ignore at this point, like spotlights that I could block out. I hadn't remembered merging onto the highway, but I'd been on it for some time now, passing road sign after road sign that I didn't bother paying attention to.

What would it be like to just leave?

It'd been a question that lingered in my mind for as long as I could remember. When Mom stayed out late for work, that thought surfaced. When she came home and passed out on the couch, that thought surfaced. When the electricity was shut off. When I moved into the Bishop house—I thought about it each time. What would it be like to leave Brentwood and never come back?

Granted, I hadn't anticipated peacing out in my Le Petit Bateau uniform with no duffle bag or anything. All I had for a bed in the van was a wooden pallet with no mattress topper. I didn't even have my savings with me. The interior still smelled like wet paint. All I had was the one fifty in my pocket from tonight's tips and a collection of clothes that smelled like deep-fried cod. It wasn't the grand reset I'd been hoping for.

And then the hard reality settled in. Uncle Dean and Hudson would never let me go like this. I wasn't even eighteen yet. For all I knew, they could've even called the police by now.

I let up on the gas pedal, blinking at the dark road as I let the speedometer fall back within legal range. That was when I passed a road sign that had me jerking in my seat. *Welcome to New Jersey.*

Now, I slammed on my brakes, tires squealing on the highway's pavement. Thank God no one was behind me, but alarm bolted through me anyway. Realistically, I knew it only took a little over an hour to pass through the corner of New York and into New Jersey, but the thought that I drove over two state lines without realizing it was enough to thoroughly freak me out.

I took the first exit into New Jersey and followed the ramp to a dead road. There wasn't a headlight in sight. The loneliness of it all sunk heavily on my chest, extending to my bones. No one knew where I was. If I ditched the van, no one would be able to find me. That sort of anonymity was tempting but terrifying. That was something I'd never considered about leaving Brentwood—once I was gone, I'd be another face on the map. A no one with no one.

On the exit ramp to a pitch-black road, I rested my forehead on the steering wheel. My palms were sweaty, for no reason at all.

And I didn't know how long I sat like that, listening to the idle rumble of the engine. It felt like ages had passed before I slipped my hand into my apron pocket and took out my phone. At the perfect time, too, because it was lit up with a call. I turned my phone on silent when working, so the vibration was off. I went to answer when my gaze froze on the ID.

Slowly, I brought it to my ear, blinking in the darkness. "Landon?"

"Are you okay?" he asked, and the quality of his voice came clearer through the phone this time. The concern caused the inflection of his words to stab deeper, but his voice was still quiet, almost on the brink of whispering. "I— I've been trying to get ahold of you, Hudson's been trying to get ahold of you—"

"Hudson? You talked to my cousin?" *Those* words did not compute.

"He called me," Landon replied. "When you didn't come home. He thought you were with me."

I could understand Hudson and Uncle Dean getting concerned, but enough for Hudson to call *Landon*?

I pulled my phone away from my ear to look at my notifications. Everything was silenced from the setting I left it on during work, and my heart dropped at all the red alerts.

Hudson-7 missed calls

Uncle Dean-2 text messages

Hudson-5 text messages

Uncle Dean-5 missed calls

Landon-1 missed call

Landon-1 voicemail

Voicemail. He'd left a voicemail. I wondered what it said. "It's only eleven," I said as I pressed my phone back to my ear. My own voice clung to the defensiveness, but my chest felt warm, like the interior of the van turned way too hot way too fast. "It's not like it's three in the morning."

"You left work early," Landon said, and before I had a chance to ask him how he knew, he said, "Your boss called your cousin. He said your...your mom showed up."

Maestro and his big mouth. How he knew it was my mom, I had no idea. I felt sick at the idea of her saying something to him. My stomach rolled even more at the thought of Maestro telling my uncle that, the thought of them knowing that the worst had finally come to pass— Mom finally showed back up. I knocked my head against my seat, staring at the grainy path my headlights lit up. "Landon."

Something must've sounded strange in my voice, because he hesitated before answering. "Yeah?"

"You ever been to New Jersey?"

Another pause. "Yes."

"What state is past New Jersey?" I was too tired to picture it.

"Pennsylvania."

Pennsylvania. What was in Pennsylvania? Philadelphia. I'd never been there before, either. The thought of going now didn't exactly entice me, but the idea of going home, facing down Hudson and Uncle Dean...

"Where are you right now?" Landon asked.

I wondered what he would've said if I told him the truth. "On an exit ramp off the highway. Where are you?"

"In my room, sitting on my bed," he replied, clearing his throat a little. "Uh, Gemma's room is on the other side of the wall, so I need to be quiet. I didn't wash my hands after my drawing session, so I probably have graphite all over my sheets. I had the window open earlier, so it smells like nighttime. I...I wasn't going to go to sleep until I heard from you."

For a brief moment, as I idled on the exit ramp of the highway, I let everything he said wash over me. He was doing like he did before—letting his calming words distract me. I closed my eyes and pictured everything, down to the smudged sheets and the way Landon's body would imprint into the mattress. He would've been warm to lie next to. He would've felt safe. With how big his arms were, his hugs would've probably been next level. I let myself imagine it, letting it chase away the darkness that bloomed even before I'd closed my eyes.

"You should call your cousin," Landon said softly, as if trying not to spook an animal. "Let him know you're okay and that you're on your way home."

"I'm not sure I'm either of those things." The words snaked out before I had a chance to censor them. I rocked forward, knocking my forehead against the steering wheel. "I mean, yeah. You're right."

"You have to come home," Landon said, and I could hear the ruffle of his sheets on the other side, like he was turning over on his bed. "We haven't reached the end of our deal yet."

"You mean we haven't successfully made Madison jealous yet?" I smiled, despite everything. "I can't ditch you now, can I?"

"You would be a very bad fake girlfriend if you did."

This time, the world's tiniest chuckle escaped me—quiet, but genuine. I found myself wishing I'd called Landon before I left Le Petit Bateau—heck, even before I left Connecticut—because he had a weird way of bringing me back to the surface. I'd been bobbing up and down in the sea of blackness, but his voice was like a lifejacket, lifting me up.

"I'll call Hudson," I said, resting my hand on the gearshift. "And he'll probably chew me out—and then my uncle will want a turn—but then...would it be okay if I called you back? I've got a long drive ahead of me." Once again, I was too afraid to face the past, and once again, I wanted to use him as my shield. Or, maybe, I wanted to use him as my rope to reality, tethering me back. "I know you have curfew—"

He didn't miss a beat. "Yeah, call me when you're done getting your well-deserved scolding. I'll be up."

The soft breath Landon drew in seemed to echo through the phone, almost like it was directly in my ear. Despite how warm I felt, I shivered. I pulled the van back into drive, circling back toward the entrance ramp. "You know, you've got this boyfriend thing down. At least I don't have to worry about you fumbling the ball when it comes to Madison."

If Landon laughed, I didn't hear it. I didn't really give him time to reply, either. Instead, I drew my phone from my ear and ended the call, watching the numbers blink for a few moments before going dark.

Before I turned back onto the highway, I picked my phone back up, squinting against the bright screen. The notifications were still there, and even though I knew Hudson and Uncle Dean must've been worried sick, I found myself loading Landon's voicemail first, drawing in a breath that seemed to buzz in my lungs.

"Hey, it's, uh—well, it's me. Which you probably know. Your cousin called me—which, by the way, how did he get my number? But, uh, anyway. He said something happened at work today, asked if you were with me, and I thought I'd call you... I hope you don't think that's me being nosy. I mean, I guess I am being nosy, but I more just wanted to check in. With you. And make sure you're okay. Even if it's

after nine, you can call me. Even if we don't talk, I'll stay on the line. So...call me, Lacey. Okay?"

His uncertainty caused my heart to squeeze, along with everything that he said. I tried to picture what he might've been doing when he left the voicemail. Was he drawing? Pacing slowly around his room? Sitting on his bed?

Once again, Landon felt like a buoy I could latch onto to keep my head above water, and it was a brief gasp of relief.

Don't get too attached.

With that thought in mind, sobering the traces of my smile, I dialed Hudson, ready to face the music.

CHAPTER 14

I knew exactly what I'd been expecting when I got home last night. Yelling. Probably more from Hudson than Uncle Dean, but I was sure he'd have a few choice words too. When I called Hudson to tell him that I was coming home, he sounded frustrated, but didn't scold me then. He didn't stay on the line long, but told me to drive safe. I thought that as soon as I walked through the door, Uncle Dean would have his palm out, waiting for the keys to Petunia. Heck, I even expected Hudson to take his room back if only to make me suffer on the couch as punishment.

What actually happened was that I walked through the front door to a dark, silent house. It was almost one in the morning. Hudson was on the couch, covered up, his back to me. Uncle Dean's bedroom door was cracked, but I could see that it was dark in the room. I had swallowed hard, glad that they'd at least been able to go to bed early for work and school in the morning. As quietly as I could, I'd tiptoed to Hudson's room, shutting myself inside.

And then a minute later, I'd heard voices. They'd been hushed, but I eased the door open a crack to hear better.

"She get in okay?" It had been Uncle Dean, sounding perfectly wide awake.

"Yeah, she did." Hudson, whose voice also held no tinge of sleepiness.

I'd slumped against my door then, a new wave of guilt choking me.

I slept like the dead, though, and woke up to sunlight streaming in through Hudson's blinds, the rays of them slatting directly across my closed eyelids. Groaning, I tried rolling away from the brightness, my thoughts seesawing in and out of focus. For one of the first times since I moved in, I woke up with a firm grasp on my surroundings. I was in Hudson's bed, in Hudson's room, in Uncle Dean's house. I didn't want to emerge, didn't want to face them, didn't want to talk about last night. And I definitely didn't want to go to school.

School.

School!

The sun was *way* too bright for seven o'clock.

I threw the duvet cover off and tried to stand, my head rushing with a wave of dizziness at the movement. I tripped over my discarded serving uniform, the door catching my weight as I slammed into it. Cursing under my breath, I threw it open, hurrying out into the living room to find some signs of life.

And "some signs of life" ended up being Hudson, wearing his glasses, a pair of sweatpants, and a black tank top, sitting on the couch and watching a cartoon. He looked up at me. "Jeez, I was wondering if you were still asleep or had died at some point in the night."

My heart was racing from the sharp awakening, still unable to comprehend the image in front of me. "What time is it?"

"Like, noon, dude. How late were you up talking to lover boy?"

I shook my head as if to clear it, pressing my palms into my eyes. I couldn't tell if they still smelled a little like fish or if it was me imagining things. "Why didn't you wake me?"

"Dad gave us a free mental health day. I didn't question it, and didn't want *you* questioning it either, so we let you sleep." Hudson slouched lower into the couch and crossed his arms, staring at the TV. "Paisley went to school, though. We told her you were working late, that's why you weren't home for bedtime."

I waited for Hudson to say more—to ask at least one question—but his attention had been recaptured by the TV. Or he was *pretending* it was recaptured, anyway. I had questions of my own, too. What did Maestro tell him and Uncle Dean when he called? What were their first reactions? Did Uncle Dean get in contact with Mom? Did Mom...did she show up on purpose?

And there was one other pressing question. "How did you get Landon's phone number?"

Hudson turned down the volume. "Someone posted it on Babble once upon a time."

"*What?*" I raised an eyebrow, still standing in the middle of the living room. "You went on Babble?"

"Desperate times," he said, deadpan. "I typed

'Landon Settler' and 'phone number,' and someone had commented it on a post once upon a time. The internet is seriously a scary place. He should change his number. I'm surprised he doesn't get more late-night phone calls than the Grim Reaper's, honestly." He let out a long breath, and when he turned to me again, I saw the full depth of his expression. Hudson was an expert at masking what he was feeling, but it showed through in little cracks. "Listen, I'm not going to ask, because I'm not going to force you to talk about something you don't want to. But if you want to talk, I'll always listen. Dad will, too."

I wrapped my arms around my middle. Sometimes it was scary how well he could read me. Because I *hadn't* wanted him to ask. I didn't want to rehash that with him. Not yet. But I thought he *would've* asked. Once again, my expectations were wrong. "You should be a therapist," I said lamely, trying to lighten the mood.

Something about his expression turned stony. "Not like I'm that great with the relationships of my own."

My lips twitched. "How's your mentoring going?"

"Remind me never to talk to underclassmen again."

"That well, huh?"

Hudson's eyes rolled. I took a step toward him, intending to sit down on his other side on the couch, but Hudson lifted his socked foot out to stop me. "Why don't you go shower first? Or at the very least, brush your teeth."

Instinctively, I put a hand over my mouth. "No way you can smell my breath from here."

"No, but I can smell the fish grease that you never

showered off last night. Friendly reminder, you owe me new sheets when you move out."

I stuck my tongue out at him, kicking at his foot with my own. "Petty," I threw over my shoulder as I headed toward Hudson's room to grab a change of clothes. So, it *wasn't* just me. I really did still smell like fish.

The bathroom was cold as I shut myself in it, twisting the knob on the shower to get the water warm. When I turned toward the mirror, I nearly jumped out of my skin. How Hudson hadn't reacted upon seeing me was truly a mystery, because I looked *scary*. I didn't wash my makeup off last night, but most of it had come off as the tears flowed. I'd wiped my mascara, but smudges of black rimmed on my skin like I was going to a heavy metal concert. Foundation splotches were on my forehead and cheeks, and my lips were chapped. Totally not a good look.

My thoughts transported me to last night, to Mom sitting in front of me, staring up at me. Staring at my reflection, I realized that we had the same eyes.

Even though I didn't go to school that day, I loaded up into the van at three o'clock and headed for the building anyway, grumbling to myself the entire way. When I'd agreed to going to this, I'd definitely been half-asleep. Were agreements contractually binding if you were half-asleep? I'd argue *no*.

I threw a quick glance over my shoulder at the depths of the van, feeling a rush of endorphins flood through me at the sight. Since Uncle Dean gifted us a "mental health day," I wasn't going to spurn it by watching cartoons and brooding all day, unlike some people. No, as soon as I got all squeaky clean from my shower, I went outside and started to work on the renovation. I managed to finish painting the final few cupboards, and laid them underneath the car port to dry.

Now, everything was mainly décor. Once I got the mattress pad, it would technically be livable.

Which... I still couldn't wrap my head around it.

It was half after three, so Brentwood had calmed down pretty significantly from when school would've let out. The busses were gone, the parents lining the curb were gone, and there weren't any random students milling about. I drove to the school, past the student parking lot, and down a dirt road that led back to the football field.

Brentwood High's football stadium was about a five-minute walk from the school, which ended up being a minute drive. Several other cars were parked out here, like football players who didn't feel like walking all the way back to the main lot, or, like me, spectators watching the guys play.

Yeah. People did that willingly.

I thought back to my conversation with Landon last night, insides oddly fuzzy. He'd answered on the first ring when I called him back, and had stuck to his agreement of staying on the line until I pulled into the driveway. We hadn't talked about anything meaningful, but listening to his voice get progressively sleepier left me feeling...weird.

One thing he *had* talked me into—and I still didn't think it was ethical, making me promise something after midnight—was coming to his practice.

"It might make sense if you showed up once," Landon had said last night as I drove the last fifteen minutes home, his voice getting lower and lower with sleep. *"Just to...show us off."*

"Would it make sense for me to come if I made a whole stink about football on Friday?" I had asked.

"It would show how much you like me, then, wouldn't it?"

So, yes, that was why I was putting the van into park by the football field, here against my will.

After climbing from Petunia, I walked from the lot to the bleachers, grumbling. I could hear the cheerleaders calling out their little cheers as they practiced. The collision of shoulder pads on shoulder pads was also loud enough to hear without seeing it. All sounds that had me wanting to hightail it back to the van.

I lingered by the ramp that led up to the back of the stands, picturing myself turning back around. It was going to be me sitting by myself again like I'd done Friday night, only this time it would be *much* more awkward. I at least had a valid excuse for being there last Friday—this time, my excuse was *"I'm here because I want to see my boyfriend."*

I would totally look like a clingy girlfriend.

To my surprise, a *lot* of people were already sitting in the stands, and all of them were filling up the front few rows in the center. The majority of them were also girls, which didn't surprise me. There were a few guys ogling the cheerleaders, but a few of them were gazing off longingly at the field, too.

Landon owes me, I thought as I glared down at the field, gritting my teeth as I walked up the bleachers, not letting myself make eye contact. *He so, so owes me.*

"Oh my gosh, wait," a girl suddenly exclaimed, and when I turned toward her, I found her already staring up at me. "You're Landon's girlfriend, right?"

In fact, *everyone* on the bleachers turned to stare at me, and I had the briefest fear that suddenly they'd all rush at me. These were super fans—the sort of fans celebrities got bodyguards for, right? Was I going to die by fangirls and fanboys? "Um...maybe."

The same girl latched onto my wrist and tugged me down onto the bleacher, my butt jarring on impact. "It's *so* nice to meet you! We were talking about how insane it is that Landon has a girlfriend—Piper is super bummed, because she's been crushing on Landon for, like, *ever*—"

A brunette to her right threw a hand over her mouth. "Ashley!"

"—but we're all super happy for you. It's super cool, though, isn't it? Dating someone from the Top Tier?"

Everyone leaned in around me like whatever I was about to say next was going to be epic. The practice on the field had been long forgotten by this small group—everyone's attention was on me. When I looked over, I saw one girl with a notepad out. *A notepad.* Like, not even on her phone—a physical notepad.

"Uh...it's...super," I said, trying to keep my expression from appearing thoroughly freaked out. I'd never truly experienced the Top Tier obsession before. Sure, people stared at Landon and me in the halls, but it was my first time being bombarded alone. "Except I don't really look at him that way. As someone who's in the Top Tier."

Something about that must've been funny, because they all laughed almost in unison. "But he *is*," the first girl insisted, patting my hand. "Oh my gosh, though, Landon is like the most secretive of the Top Tier. Is it...is it okay if we ask a few questions?"

I looked at the silent girl with the notepad. Her glasses magnified her eyes to an almost bug-level appearance, giving me a clear view of the green irises focused on me. I shifted uncomfortably. "A few...is okay."

I regretted it almost as soon as the words came out of my mouth.

"What color are his eyes up close?"

"What's the wallpaper on his phone?"

"What cologne does he wear?"

"Does he wear mismatched socks?"

I stared down at the football field, trying to find the number ten jersey. *You so owe me.* But I would've thought the questions would've been normal, curious. But people really cared about Landon's *socks*? Yikes.

One of the girls—Piper—went on a tangent of how she thought Landon's eyes were more green than blue while I focused on the field. It was my second time seeing all the guys running around, and I really needed a cheat sheet or something, because I still couldn't tell who was who. They seemed to be running practice plays now, with Landon organizing the team into a line and positioning himself behind the guy who had the ball. Or something like that. I really had no idea how any of it worked.

The cheerleaders practiced their routines in front of the bleachers, like they did at Friday's game. Like they were performing for this meager crowd more than they were really intending to practice. Jade led the pack, of course, with Madison at her side, and both wore megawatt smiles that looked fake as could be.

Landon and Connor were off to the side of the field practicing his throwing while the rest of the team ran drills in the middle of the field. I didn't watch any of it too closely, unlike the others who sat around me. They leaned forward, invested.

I let my gaze settle on the quarterback, who only wore a black athletic tee instead of shoulder pads like the others on the field. He drew his arm back swiftly as he positioned the football to throw, twisting his body with the movement. From here, I could see where the sun glittered down on his arms, where it caught in the red strands of his hair. As Connor caught the pass, a grin stretched across Landon's lips, and mine mirrored it automatically.

The practice passed quickly, a lot quicker than I thought it would. The football players retreated to the locker rooms while the cheerleaders packed up their pompoms, and everyone on the bleachers began to rise.

"Now it's time to head home?" I asked Ashley with a tinge of hopefulness slipping into my voice. My butt had gone numb twenty minutes ago.

"Now we go wait for them to finish in the locker room," she replied, like *duh*, pushing to her feet. "We'll be able to talk to them afterward. Connor hasn't been sticking around lately, but the others have been."

Hang outside their locker room like they were celebrities? Like we were waiting for their autograph? I never wanted to do anything *less*. I'd have to wait for Landon, but I definitely wasn't waiting outside the locker room like an eager puppy. I could imagine the Babble posts now. *Lacey obsessed with her quarterback boyfriend!*

When everyone left, though, I realized I wasn't alone. The girl with the notepad still sat behind me, her nose ducked close to it as she wrote in tight scribbles. Even though I was close enough to see the ink, her penmanship was so messy that I had no chance of deciphering it.

She looked up and did a double take when she saw me staring, bug eyes blinking in surprise.

"The train left the station," I said, throwing my thumb toward where the fans meandered off to.

But she didn't quite have the look of an obsessed fan. Her eyes didn't twinkle with fascination, expression not eager at the chance of talking to one of the football players or cheerleaders. "You're still here," she replied, almost as if she couldn't figure out why.

"I'd rather not share my quality time with my boyfriend." That, and I didn't feel like putting on my romance face quite yet.

The girl gave me a not-so-subtle up and down look before she flipped the pad closed on her notebook, tucking it into her backpack. "I'm surprised they welcomed you so easily. Piper's obsession with Landon was so deep, I figured she'd fight you for him."

"How do you know that?"

"I just do."

Well, that sounded...weird. Borderline stalkery, but I'd let it slide. "What else do you know?"

The girl shifted on the bleacher, looking like she was about to rise to her feet, but paused at the last second. "I know you're not really the type to be hanging around the Top Tier."

"Is it that obvious?"

"Only if you're looking." She blinked, her long lashes batting behind her magnified lenses.

Before I had a chance to say anything else, a figure stepped into the main aisle with a fiery gaze. Madison's ponytail looked painfully tight up close. *Bobcat Babe* was scrawled across the chest of her cheer uniform, and her skirt caught with the wind as she stomped her way up the steps.

"Can we talk?" Madison asked me, expression holding no trace of the happy expression she'd been wearing minutes ago.

I gave an inward groan at the idea, but knew I couldn't say no. "Go ahead."

Madison's gaze cut to glasses girl. "In private."

She didn't flinch at the idea of being sent away, though, and the girl didn't say another word as she grabbed her bag and began descending down the bleachers, stepping on the seats rather than bypassing Madison to get to the aisle, her footsteps clomping.

I tilted my head back up to Madison, squinting against the sun. "That was rude, you know."

"You know, I wasn't going to say anything because I figured it would fix itself within a few days." She propped her hands on her hips, resembling her no-nonsense mother. "Stop messing around with Landon."

"I'm not."

"You coming here makes it obvious. You don't care about football."

I wiped my palms down my cheeks. "We're doing this again? Seriously? Is football *really* the only subject you talk about?"

Madison shocked me by reaching out and snatching my upper arm, hauling me to my feet. I was taller than her, but her gaze was far fiercer. "You shouldn't be here if you don't care."

"I might not care about football, but I care about—"

"You don't." She let go of my arm, but remained close. Her voice was deadly serious. "You don't care about Landon."

I blinked at the accusation, trying to figure out if I slipped up somehow and Madison learned the truth of our arrangement. If that was the case, wouldn't she have Jade as a backup dancer in this intimidation choreography? Except it was Madison by herself, a solo bullying act that didn't hold as much weight. I let her go on, though, keeping my expression neutral.

"You're messing with him because of what Jade and I said. Because of what you were voted." Madison drew in a deep breath. "You're messing with him because of what happened with Hudson in freshman year. The day after you're voted to never get a boyfriend, you start dating Landon? I see right through you, Lacey."

"Who knew you and Jade were such good matchmakers?" I said with a tilt of my head. "Why are you so protective over Landon, anyway? Do you like him or something?"

Madison backed out of her forward lunging stance, straightening her spine. She clenched her jaw as she regarded me. "He's one of the good ones left. He doesn't deserve to be used for your satisfaction."

"I don't know what *you* would do, but I'd never use someone for my own gain. I'd never throw someone under the bus just to get back at someone. Except that's like the Top Tier's MO, isn't it?" I leaned forward and gave her a wide smile, much like the one she'd sported on the field. "And maybe that's why Landon likes me so much in the first place."

Madison frowned, almost like she was about to send a retort right back, but she was cut off. "Lacey!"

Landon appeared at the stairs of the bleachers, finding us. A few of his football buddies came up with him— Connor wasn't among them, but Ashton and Kyle were, all with wet hair and different clothes on. Landon's hair looked much darker wet.

A new emotion surfaced upon seeing him, though —*shyness*. I thought of our conversation last night, filled with sleepy chuckles and breathy whispers. Like Hudson, Landon hadn't pressed for details on the situation. Though he hadn't quite *seen* me at a low point, he'd been a part of that moment in time, and facing him now almost had me wanting to run in the opposite direction. Swallowing the sudden tightness in my throat, I barely got out a "hi."

Landon greeted me with a warm expression. "Hi," he said, and when he was close enough, he wrapped his arms around me.

My body froze at the sudden full-on contact, momentarily blanking on what to do. His arms were solid around me, his palms flat against my back, pressing me firmer into him. I sucked in a breath as I tried to quickly reciprocate before my fumble became obvious, but a neon sign blazed in my head, blinking words that I couldn't think around.

This is the first time we've really hugged...and I like it.

His damp hair tickled my cheek, and he smelled like sharp bodywash, the kind that I had no idea what it smelled like other than *boy*. The kind that got my hormones going all wonky. And with him pressing me close like this, for a moment, it almost felt like he was my actual boyfriend.

And I like it.

The moment shattered apart when I lifted my gaze over Landon's shoulder and made eye contact with Ashton, who sneered.

Landon leaned back to push my hair from my face. "I missed you today."

Well, jeez, I guess us going to the beach on Saturday *really* helped in getting him more comfortable around me. We should've done that sooner.

"We were thinking of all going to see a movie tonight," he told me, reaching down to swipe my hand up in his. He tucked my pinky between his fingers, cupping my palm. "*Mirror Man* 2 is playing. Do you like scary movies?"

"Love them." It was rare that I got to see them anymore, since Hudson was an absolute baby with anything scary. I wasn't sure who *we all* were, but I had a feeling everyone going would be probably the group who stood around us. Stuck-up cheerleader included. "I have to work tonight, though." I puffed out my bottom lip, doing my best to walk the line between cute and cringy.

Landon's expression softened a little, mastering the bummed head tilt himself. "Next time, then," he said.

I slid my palm up his chest, feeling the warmth of his skin radiate through the thin workout tee. For a second, I thought I could feel his quick pulse. "I'm closing tonight, so I'll call you when I'm on my way home."

"I'll make sure to keep my phone close." Landon's hand slid down between us and swiped up mine, tucking our palms close. "Come on, I'll walk you to your van."

Thank goodness we weren't staying around to chat. "It was nice chatting," I said to Madison. Her sour face didn't change. "Catch you at the next practice?"

I wasn't sure who I was fooling, because I definitely didn't want to do this again.

Thankfully, no Top Tier members followed us, and none of Landon's fangirls did either. I held his hand tightly as we walked, debating on whether or not to bring up the showdown back there. It seemed like a good thing— Madison had gone from warning off Landon to staking her claim in front of me, which felt like a step forward in the "making her jealous" department. But then again, I didn't want to give Landon false hope.

"I was worried about you this morning," he confessed as

we walked, keeping his gaze straight ahead. "I couldn't get ahold of you."

"I forgot to charge my phone last night." And then I slapped a palm to my forehead as it occurred to me. "Did you wait outside for me this morning?"

"Only for a little bit, because then your dad came out and told me you were staying home for the day."

It took me a second to realize what he was talking about. "Oh, that's my uncle Dean. Wait—" This time, I stopped in my tracks. "You talked to him?"

Landon stopped, too, turning to me with his eyebrows raised. "Yeah. He asked me what I was doing in his drive-way, I told him I was your boyfriend, and he said that you were staying home from school." Slowly, Landon's expression morphed into something more like a scolded puppy. "Did I say something I wasn't supposed to?"

"No, no," I said. My voice was distracted, trying to picture the scene in my head. "How did he seem...when you told him that? That you were my boyfriend?"

"Normal, I guess. Like he already knew you had one."

I never had any plans to introduce Landon to Uncle Dean. There wasn't really a reason to. Convincing Hudson was the only intention—not Uncle Dean. The idea that Uncle Dean talked to Landon, even for a second, left me uneasy. The idea of talking about my love life with him felt beyond mortifying, and a little guiltily, I didn't want him to get his hopes up, thinking a boy would keep me in Brentwood.

I let out a little breath and resumed walking, and with my tight grip still on his, Landon followed. "I'm sorry you had to come all the way to my house. I slept in late, so I didn't get a chance to message you."

"It's okay." He glanced down at me. "I missed you at lunch today, though."

"You did not," I objected. "Because we both know we probably would've had a repeat of what happened on Friday."

Landon's eyes crinkled as he shook his head. "True. You couldn't even be alone with Madison for five minutes."

"*She* was the one that started it today." I scowled thinking about her stupid high ponytail and her snotty attitude. "Walked right up to me and told me to dump you. I feel like we're probably getting close. Has she talked to you again since Friday?"

"Not really. Not about you."

"But about something else?"

He didn't respond right away, and he didn't look over. "She texts me sometimes. About the Top Tier and stuff."

I felt my nose scrunch up at the idea of them texting each other. Did he ever spend nights with her like we spent last night? Whispering on the other end of the line, hearing each other get sleepier and sleepier? Were their conversations long?

My thoughts skidded to a stop, because I'd been driving way, way too close to jealousy-sounding territory. "Next time she tells you that you deserve better," I said, forcing my voice light, "you should say 'like who? Like you?' And see what her response is. That's a good opener—if she hasn't thought of it yet, she'll think of it now."

To that, Landon only nodded.

We crossed the distance between the football field and Petunia quite quickly, and Landon opened up the driver's side door for me, letting go of my hand. "Do you really have work tonight?" he asked, squinting against the bright sun. "Or did you make that up?"

"I really have work. And I can't call off, since I walked out yesterday." I grimaced at the thought, but before I climbed into the driver's seat, I turned to him. "I wouldn't lie to you, Landon."

He pushed some of his damp hair back, and from how close I was, I could see water droplets trickle down the side of his neck, soaked up by his shirt. Something about trailing the length of his throat with my eyes made my insides feel weird, like they were all jumbled up. "I don't really know much about you," he said after a beat. "And it's okay if you don't want to tell me more about last night. But I...I'd like to know you more, Lacey. I want to know as much of you as you want to show me."

Now my insides twisted and tightened, bordering on ticklish and painful. The feeling made me warm in a sore way, and I couldn't figure out *why* it was happening. "There's not much to know about me."

"I didn't know you lived with your uncle." Landon scratched the side of his neck, right above his collar. "Don't you think...I should've? In case someone said something?"

Of course I should've mentioned it. I should've mentioned it when we were establishing the important info about us on the first day. Even the day at the beach, I should've mentioned it. It wasn't even that fact that scared me, but it *was* the gateway tidbit about me. If I'd told him about living with the Bishops, only one question would follow: *Why?*

I lifted my chin and squashed the feeling down, trying to look at it from an analytical angle. "I'm not on speaking terms with my mom for a whole slew of reasons, but she showed up to my work last night. I went for a drive to clear my head." *And ended up in New Jersey.*

"How long have you lived with your uncle?"

"About three months. And, as you can guess from how small the mobile home is, it's pretty cramped."

Landon didn't ask me what spurred me to move in with him, surprisingly enough. "Is that why you want to fix up the van? To...sleep out in it?"

It was technically true. "Yeah."

"Hudson seemed like you 'going for a drive' was a bigger thing than you make it sound."

"It wasn't like I was in danger," I said with a scoff.

"Were you going to run away?"

My lips fell instantly. I leaned against the side of the driver's seat, intrigued by the laces on my shoes. The directness of the statement caught me off-guard, but what threw me even further was the sudden and insistent refusal to lie to him. I didn't know where it came from; all I knew was that in the split second the idea of lying surfaced, my brain shot it down. "It's not running away, for one thing. Besides, why would I?" I attempted to sound lighthearted, but my voice wasn't as strong as it'd been before. "I didn't have any of my things. If I was going to run away, I wouldn't do it in my work uniform."

"Would you have left if you had your stuff and different clothes?"

I opened my mouth, but the lie stopped on my tongue. I wanted to give him the right answer, the answer I knew my family wanted me to say, if only to clear the air before we faced all his friends. I couldn't, though. I couldn't lie. "I don't know."

If I hadn't been coming straight from work, would I have continued past New Jersey? If I had my savings and bag, would I have left and never looked back? If the van had been finished, furnished, ready to go—would I have gone?

Yes, I realized. I probably would've. At that moment last night, I would've been willing to call Hudson's bluff on him reporting the van stolen. Last night, I'd been ready to leave and never look back.

Suddenly, Landon moved. He braced his hand on the top of the van and leaned into my personal space, all of him instantly becoming all I could see. I sucked in a gasp, attempting to lean back, but there was nowhere to go. I was caught in the triangle he created between the van and his body. "There are people coming," he murmured in a low voice, blue-green eyes coasting over the planes of my face in a way that felt as delicate as a touch. "Is this...okay?"

My heartbeat fluttered in my throat manically, in a way that almost made it hard to breathe. He was waiting for my answer, though, and no matter how breathless, I had to give it. "Mmm...hmm."

A corner of his lips twitched up into a smile, a boyish

one that looked a little embarrassed. "We're crushing this fake dating thing, huh?"

Good God, we *definitely* should've gone to the beach earlier. Who knew the ocean had such magical, chemistry-inducing qualities? "You're doing much better, grasshopper. Your sensei approves."

The other corner of his lips lifted then.

My eyes lingered there, on the upward tilt. He had a nice-looking mouth. His bottom lip was fuller than the top, rosy in color, and...close.

Landon told the truth though, because not even a second later, cars began coming from the football field, and some even slowed to roll their windows down and catcall us. Landon ducked his head closer toward me, bringing us nearly nose to nose. "Call me first next time," he told me in a low voice, and it caused my skin to shiver. "Before you run, call me first."

Despite being mildly foggy in the head, a part of me instantly rebelled. "So you can talk me out of it?"

"So you won't be alone."

Our gazes locked. He was close enough that I could see every single long eyelash of his, could see when they swept down and then back up as he blinked. Close enough that I could count his freckles, even the faded ones. Nothing on Landon's face hinted any idea that he'd said something so serious. They were words that practically seeped into my body, settling over my chest like a weight. "Why?" I whispered. "Why do you care?"

In that moment, with the sun shining down on him, it almost felt as if I was dreaming. My body buzzed, foreign, tingling with the anticipation of his lips parting. Landon tilted his head to the side a little, almost as if the question seemed silly to him. "Because," he said slowly, voice dropping to a near-whisper as his words tickled my throat, "I'm your boyfriend."

And with that, he drew away. He dropped his arm from Petunia and took a full step back.

I stared up at him, reeling in the aftermath of the moment. The moment he seemed totally unaffected by. Goosebumps from his breath on my neck still lingered, and even though I *knew* that just happened, I almost convinced myself it wasn't real. That there was no way *shy Landon* could've stirred my pulse so easily, so effortlessly. So...seriously. The hug earlier had been a sneak peek at how affected I could be by him—and it freaked me out.

Landon tipped his head at the open car door. "You should get going," he said nonchalantly, as if he hadn't just pressed me up against the car a second ago and told me he never wanted me to be alone. "I'd hate to make you late for work."

Words were impossible to form, so I nodded like an idiot, knocking my knee on the door as I climbed into the driver's seat. And then proceeded to stare at the wheel dumbly, forgetting how to turn the car on. It wasn't even how close he'd gotten that really tripped me up, but what he'd said. The words burrowed in deep and made a home inside me, instantly and without permission. *So you won't be alone.*

They were words I'd wanted to hear my entire life, and

here Top Tier quarterback Landon Settler was, saying them with absolute certainty.

Once he made sure I was inside, Landon shut the car door and waved at me, smiling as he did so. I started the engine and put the car into gear, one thought in my mind:

Oh. My. God.

CHAPTER 15

I drove to work that night ready for the excuse to turn my brain off. I needed it *desperately*. To be able to flip a switch and go into full server mode, smiling at customers without a care in the world.

What I hadn't anticipated, though, was how nervous I'd be pulling into Le Petit Bateau carpark. Tension wound tightly behind my ribs, making it hard to breathe. The last time I'd been here, Mom had come too, and I never got to the bottom of *why*. Had she come to see me? Did she come for a meal? I couldn't picture that—Le Petit Bateau wasn't really her style.

But the biggest question that lingered of all—what if she came back?

I parked Petunia in my normal space and chafed the wheel with my hands. My heavenly escape, the one that built up my savings account for Van Life, now suddenly seemed much darker, like some of its light had been blown out. Like Mom's presence had left a stain on the brick and the boat-themed exterior. One of the reasons I'd started working as soon as I got my worker's permit was to get out of my house more, to forget about the fact that she couldn't care enough to spend time with me. The busier I was, the easier it was to shield the hurt with something else. Something bitter.

And now, I stared up at the building, the hurt surfacing like a buoy bobbing back and forth.

No. No, I wouldn't let her take it from me. I hated everything else in Brentwood, but I refused to let her make me resent LPB, too. She didn't deserve that victory.

With that thought in mind, I popped open Petunia's door, ready to face the night.

"Girl, what are you doing here?" Kelsi asked when I walked through the door, blinking at me in surprise. "You're not on the schedule."

I frowned. "Yeah, I am. Five to close."

"Was that the old schedule or the new one?"

"There's a new schedule?"

Before we had time to linger in the confusion, Maestro emerged from the back, doing his routine look over the dining room before his gaze skittered to mine. His casual expression pinched into something that looked serious. "You're off this week, Lacey."

At first, I thought he was kidding—that this was some rendition of a terrible joke. But Maestro didn't chuckle. "I'm not off," I objected automatically. "I work Monday, Wednesday, and Thursday this week."

Maestro marched closer, holding up a hand to stop me from slipping behind the server line. "I changed the schedule. You're off til next Sunday."

I sputtered a little at the bluntness of the way he spoke, how it left absolutely zero room for negotiation. I'd never known Maestro to be so firm, to not make any sort of conversation about something. "Why?"

He sighed, leaning his weight against the counter. "You're a kid, Lacey. With a lot on your plate. You need time off."

"I don't need—"

"Do you want me to say this is punishment for walking out yesterday?" he demanded, moving another chess piece in our back and forth. His felt eerily close to a checkmate. "Because I can say that. You know the consequences for walking out in the middle of your shift."

I did know the consequences. Walking out without clocking out meant immediate dismissal. Ice slipped down my spine. "You're saying you would fire me?" I demanded incredulously, causing Kelsi to turn and look over.

Maestro's eyes grew sympathetic. "You came off a summer of pulling nearly forty-hour weeks. Now you're back to school, still pulling fifteen-hour weeks—it's a lot, kid. Most kids would be kissing my hands for giving them a week off."

"I need the money."

"For what? You got bills? Because when I talked to your uncle, it didn't sound like you did."

Of course he'd talked to Uncle Dean. No wonder he was so firm—he had my guardian's support backing him up. If Maestro hadn't brought Uncle Dean into this equation, if he'd kept his mouth shut yesterday, I was sure I'd be on the floor already clocked in by now. But, no.

I fought the urge to snap at him, to tell him to just be my boss and stop putting his nose into my business. The words rang in my ears, ready to jump out. I clenched my hands into fists, staring my manager down. "Can I at least have a soda for the road?"

That was how I ended up on the curb five minutes later, slurping my to-go Sprite through a straw that I was ninety-percent sure had a hole in it. The cement parking block was cold against my butt, but I didn't move; I let it soak in as I glared at the restaurant that kicked me out. What really ticked me off was that now I had no idea what to do. I could've gone back home—and complain to Uncle Dean, who let me leave for work without explaining that he'd already made a deal with my boss.

I could've called Hudson, maybe see if he was down for a movie night or something.

I could've called Landon to see if he wanted to do anything, but—

No. No, I couldn't call Landon. Why would I?

I sucked my straw harder, angrily combating against the lack of pressure.

"What are you doing?" a voice asked, and I turned to find Nate walking up from the employee parking lot, twirling his car keys around on a finger. He took in my squatting figure and my angry drinking. "Kicked out, huh?"

"I'm debating on letting the air out of Maestro's tires."

Nate reached up and shook his hand through his hair, which wasn't as curly now as it'd be later on in the shift, when the humidity of the grill got to it. "I think you're the only one who is sad she doesn't have the day off. Call your boyfriend. Spend some time with him." He gave me a kissy face.

I gave him the finger. "I can't spend *every* waking hour with my boyfriend."

"Don't you want to?"

I sucked my straw again, listening to the whistle sound it made. "Is it normal to?"

"I dunno." Nate came closer and kicked the parking block. "I guess it's different for everyone. You've got this confidence about you, though. Something like 'ah, I'm too cool for relationship clinginess, I'll see you when I want to' sort of vibe."

"That doesn't sound that positive."

"Landon seems to like it."

The memory of this morning outside the locker room came back to me sharply. Landon's fingers grazing my skin. The curve of his lips as he did. The scent of him. "Can I ask you a relationship question?"

Nate looked at his wrist like it held a watch, but the only thing there was smooth skin. "Sure, I can make some time. My shift starts at five."

"Isn't it, like, five minutes after five now?"

Nate raised his eyebrows up and down once. "There's bad traffic today."

I scoffed at him a little, but quickly sobered up. This conversation was a weird one to bring up with him, but even though Nate was in the Top Tier, it didn't *feel* like he was. He was a junior, which already put him on a different rung than all the Top Tier seniors. And plus, we were work friends—I feel like that had to trump Top Tier buddies. "Is it normal to feel things for someone all of a sudden? Like, for the longest time, you didn't feel things, and then—*bam*. You feel...*things*. Suddenly. Is that normal?"

His expression went from curious to horrified in a slow descension. "Please tell me that you're not asking about what I *think* you're asking about. Please tell me you're not asking me about something you should've learned in health class."

"Not *that*. I'm talking just purely romantic feelings. Like, you look at someone for so long without all the heart eyes attached, and then suddenly..." *All you can see are heart eyes.*

Nate crossed his arms over his chest, palms pressed against his pectorals. "Not *me*, right?"

I kicked my foot at him, but he jumped back in time to dodge.

Nate dropped his arms and came up beside me on the parking block, stretching his long legs out in front of him. He hadn't cleaned his non-slip shoes from his last shift, and I could see bits of crushed, mushy food sticking on the side of his sole. "They say that the best relationships come from being friends first, but it's hard to know if feelings are *because* of that friendship or because that friendship evolved into more. I'm not the best expert in the field, as it turns out."

"Who would be?"

A smile tugged at Nate's mouth, exposing a dimple that sat in his cheek. His gaze was wistful. "Not sure." Then he turned to me. "Are you talking about Landon?"

"I like him, but I—I don't know if I like him or if I just

like that he's handsome and in the Top Tier." Or if it was a product of the fake relationship.

"Well, picture him ugly," Nate said simply. "Ugly and a loser. Picture him getting shoved into a locker. Do you still like him then? If the answer is no, then you totally only like him because he's handsome and popular."

I narrowed my eyes at him. "You're not helpful."

"I think if you're suddenly feeling things you haven't felt before, you have your answer. It's natural to like to hang out with someone. But if your heart flutters around them, and you find yourself thinking about them more than usual—in different *ways* than usual—I think the answer is obvious."

I shook my Styrofoam cup and listened to the melting ice rattle. I could still picture Landon leaning into my space earlier, how he effortlessly pushed my hair back. How my gaze dipped to his lips. If Landon had pushed my hair back on the first day we started fake dating, would it have made my heart flutter then? What had changed?

Call me first next time. Before you run, call me first. So you won't be alone.

My stomach hollowed as Landon's words resurfaced in my mind, matched with a trip in my pulse.

"I should get in there," he said as he pushed to his feet, stretching his arms overhead. "Before I get fired."

"Note to self: don't go to Nathan Tulane for love advice."

I'd meant it teasingly, but something serious passed over his expression, something that I couldn't quite pinpoint. "I'm not the best with relationships, but don't realize how important someone is to you too late."

"You know from experience?"

This time, Nate didn't smile.

The soles of my shoes slammed against the ground unforgivingly, my legs screaming out in protest as I pushed myself faster, faster.

Which, admittedly, wasn't that fast. Still wasn't a runner.

But Tuesday morning, I needed the ache in my chest to come from the run. And did it ever. My throat grew raw from the oxygen scraping past, meagerly attempting to fill my lungs before puffing back out again. It was so, so cold this morning—a stark contrast to the beautiful weather we'd had Saturday afternoon—and even though goosebumps dotted my skin, the sweat on my skin was frigid. My backpack slammed against my shoulder blades painfully. It was a lot different running on the first few days of school than it was now, with Calculus and History textbooks weighing me down.

I stopped at a redlight and practically coughed up a lung, fighting the urge to bend over and collapse on the concrete.

This was worth it, though. Space. I needed space.

Though Landon and I hadn't parted on bad terms

yesterday, I needed the morning to myself. My hormones or whatever had been totally confused yesterday. They were getting way, way too invested in this whole fake dating thing. I shook my head now, as if to clear it. No. No. This was strictly business.

So knock it off, stupid hormones.

The light went from a red hand to a green walking dude, and I resumed my self-inflicted torture.

I jogged toward the lit-up school, and as I approached the side door, I found that a broken brick had been placed in the jamb, propping it open a smidge. It was always funny how dead silent the school could get, and even now, the only sounds were my sneakers thumping against the ground as I made my way toward the gymnasium.

When I got to the door to the girls' room, I stopped. There was no sign on the door this time, but I still hesitated before entering. I glanced at the boys' locker room door, dancing down memory lane. If I thought really hard, I could still picture the way Landon's body took up the door frame. Could still remember his fingers splayed on the door, looking down at me with the even expression he always wore. He'd moved into immediate action to hide me from his friends, as if it never even occurred to him to do anything else.

I dropped my backpack down by the girls' room door and ventured down the hallway, bypassing the boys' locker room to where the weightlifting room was. As I approached the door, I could hear the soft clank of metal, hinting that someone was inside. I shouldn't have gone any closer. Really, there was no reason for me to. If Landon was even in there, I definitely didn't want to talk to him. Not while I was still trying to convince myself that last night's thoughts were complete baloney. So why was I approaching the door like I was hypnotized?

No clue, but when I poked my head into the window of the wooden door, I wished I hadn't.

Landon was in full view on the pullup bar, gripping it with both hands, his knees bent at an angle as he drew himself up and eased back down. I couldn't see his face from here, but his reddish-brown hair made it instantly clear who was doing pullups with ease. From here, though, I *could* see his biceps flex with each pullup, and I couldn't look away.

At least, not until a different face stepped up to the glass, one that was truly a jump scare. Ashton.

"I'll be right back," he called to whoever was in the room, and I jerked out of frame as he opened the door, coming out into the hall to join me. While Landon had a cutoff on, Ashton was completely shirtless, and I put a wide amount of distance between his bare skin and me. Sweat glinted on his chest, but unlike with Landon, the sight of it made my stomach turn. "You look different without makeup on. Almost didn't recognize you."

Don't hit him.

"So you finally let our boy join us today, huh?" Ashton asked, smirking at me in a way that made me uncomfortable in the dim hallway. "He's too busy picking you up for school now, he doesn't join us."

"Maybe he doesn't enjoy the company," I fired back,

holding my ground. If I gave him any sort of reaction, Ashton wouldn't let it go.

"That could be it," Ashton said, pursing his lips. "I'd much rather be with you, too."

I felt my features twist in disgust, glancing past him to the weightlifting door. I didn't feel too threatened, but he still made me uneasy. It was hard to imagine ever thinking this boy in front of me was cute—his slimy personality absolutely ruined any ounce of handsomeness in his face.

"You know, I'm surprised by you," he went on, leaning against the wall. "Last spring, you told me you'd rather die than date someone in the Top Tier. And yet Landon swayed you so easily."

"How could you not be swayed by those freckles?" I gave him an up and down look. "And I wouldn't compare you to Landon."

"Yes, he's better than me in every way." Ashton rolled his eyes before settling back on his smug stare. "So, have you truly fallen for those freckles yet? Do you smile when you see him? Does your heart flutter when he touches you?"

It creeped me out how close he was to the truth, but I knew Nate wouldn't have blabbed. "Obsessed much?"

"Believe it or not, I'm rooting for you two." He tipped his chin down. "I think after everything, you're getting what you deserve."

His words were icy on my skin, not ringing true. "You Top Tier people," I muttered as I took a step back, putting distance between us. "You're so freakishly intense."

"Part of our charm," Ashton said, and it was at that moment Landon stepped out into the hall.

Landon, in his Brentwood Bobcats cutoff and basketball shorts, looked between us with a surprised expression. Little wisps of his hair stuck to his temples, cheeks flushed from the workout. "What's going on?" he demanded, the question obviously directed at Ashton.

Ashton's smirk deepened. "Just talking."

"About what?"

"Oh, you're turning into one of *those* boyfriends?" Ashton shook his head. "The one who doesn't let his girlfriend talk to other guys."

The two boys stared each other down, though Ashton looked far more amused than Landon. I couldn't quite understand the intensity in Landon's eyes, until I remembered how he'd once said that we'd avoid Ashton because he made me uncomfortable. That had to be why he was shrugging on his protective boyfriend jacket right now.

Heart, don't you dare beat faster, I scolded as I took a step forward to lay a hand on Landon's arm. "Ashton was saying that we look cute together."

My words didn't seem to lessen the stony expression on Landon's face as he regarded his teammate. The hallway suddenly became way too tight with the four of us in it—Landon, Ashton, me, and the whole wall of tension between us.

I curled my hand around Landon's arm and pressed up against his side. His body was warm, and though he'd come from a workout, I could smell more of his deodorant than sweat. Normally teenage boys smelled terrible, but there was something about Landon's natural scent that made my head fuzzy. "Walk with me to the girls' room?"

It wasn't hard to get his legs moving. With one good tug, he followed, picking up my hand from his arm and wrapping his palm around it. "Have a nice makeout sesh, love birds," Ashton called after us. "Don't do anything I wouldn't do!"

"Idiot," I muttered underneath my breath, and led Landon around the hallway corner toward the locker rooms. Once we were a safe distance away, I rubbed my collarbone. Beneath my fingertips, my heart pulsed. "You did a good job playing the jealous boyfriend. Even I almost bought it."

"Don't hang out with him alone," Landon said, his hand tightening around mine.

I rolled my eyes. "Because he and I are besties as it is."

"I'm serious." Landon drew us to a halt just outside the girls' locker room and faced me, his brow knitted together. "He's...not nice. I don't want him to say anything that'll hurt your feelings."

"I'm not fragile. My feelings are made of steel." I said the last bit with a bit of a macho-sounding voice, but it didn't make Landon's lips lift like I wanted. I swung our hands between us, leaning closer. "Seriously, though. Don't worry about me. I can hold my ground with him."

"I know you can," he replied. "You can hold your own with the entire Top Tier. I just...know you don't like being around him."

I tipped my chin at him. "Yes, I'm going through many

hardships for you. I'm beginning to wonder what's in all this for *me*."

With his free hand, Landon suddenly reached out and slipped his fingers underneath a few loose hairs framing my face, grazing my cheekbone as he did so. I stilled at his touch, at the intimate trace that no one was around to see. He tried to tuck the hairs behind my ear, but they weren't long enough, and fell back against my face. That made his lips twitch into a smile. "I'll figure out something to make it worth your while."

I was Sweaty Lacey from running to school, with moisture on my eyelids and other various parts of my body, but Landon didn't look at me like I thoroughly disgusted him. I was bare-faced, in desperate need of a shower, but his smile never wavered.

I'll figure out something to make it worth your while.

I swallowed hard, and I would swear he heard the gulp.

Landon dropped his hand. "See you at lunch?"

"Right, sure," I told him, taking a sharp step back and sweeping up my bag from where I left it on the ground. "Um...lunch. After third period. See you then. At the Top Tier...table."

Without a backward glance, I escaped into the girls' room and leaned against the door to shut it, letting out a harsh breath. My heartbeat seemed to echo in the quiet space, or maybe it was just echoing in my ears. "Knock it off," I ordered myself sternly, scrubbing at my cheek to erase the memory of his touch. "Heart, hormones—whatever is going on, knock it off."

But why had Landon done it so *effortlessly*? Why even

in the first place? Was that him practicing to look good in front of others later? Did he think Ashton had followed us? Maybe he was thinking "hmm, her hair is in her face." Maybe it meant nothing. It probably meant nothing.

I'll figure out something to make it worth your while.

I scrubbed at my cheek again, shaking it all off as I headed toward the showers.

CHAPTER 16

 stood behind Hudson in the lunch line again Tuesday, this time on pizza day. I had a headphone in my ear and my phone in my hand in front of me, watching the YouTube video of a girl doing a van tour. Her van was the same model as mine, but it looked like something straight out of a Pinterest board.

"*I actually splurged and got a propane-powered RV-style oven,*" she explained, tapping the miniature stove and oven range. "*I'm definitely someone who cooks more than she eats out, so it seemed like a necessity.*"

I gasped, shoving into Hudson's shoulder blade as I reached an arm around him. "Look at this," I told him, holding the phone in his face. "It's like a legit range! I need it."

Hudson barely glanced at the video. "We've already built the cabinets, Lacey. You already painted them."

"It can't be that hard to cut out the one closest to the front." I tapped my screen. "Look, that's how she has it. I should've researched more—why did I let you talk me into getting a single portable cooktop?"

Hudson rubbed his fingers together before stepping farther up in line. "You wanted it on the cheap, remember?"

I shook my head in awe as the girl moved on to the beautiful black faucet she'd picked out, making me regret going with stainless steel.

It was hard for the lunch ladies to stiff Hudson on pizza slices, so we didn't trade once we checked out, but we did go our separate ways—him to his blessed lair, me to suffer through another lunch with the Top Tier. Admittedly, yesterday hadn't been as bad as the first day. Jade and Madison swapped seats to sit on the other side of Connor, farther down the line from me. Now Reed and another boy who remained silent throughout lunch sat in front of me, which worked a whole lot better.

I held my tray in one hand and my phone in the other, watching as I walked. Whereas I'd painted my cabinets a forest green, this girl had gone with a bright yellow—one that looked *really* pretty and happy. Hudson was right, though—even from a glance, it looked like she'd dropped serious cash into this remodel. Petunia wasn't Pinterest-board-level aesthetic, but she was affordable.

Landon stood behind our chairs, and when I approached, he turned to me. "Hey," he said with a voice that was a little louder than necessary, hinting to the fact that he was putting on a show. I became immediately aware of everyone around us, and how everyone tried their hardest to appear like they *weren't* listening. "Want to eat lunch somewhere else?"

I paused my video, leaving my headphone in my ear. Eat away from the Top Tier? He didn't have to ask me twice. "Sure," I answered cheerfully. "Where?"

"Somewhere more...private." He took my lunch tray with one hand, using it to gesture me forward. "After you."

Private. It sounded nice to finally eat lunch away from the prying eyes, like how it'd been with Hudson in Ms. Murphy's room, but something about the way Landon said it made my suspicions rise. I waited until we were out of the cafeteria to take my lunch tray back from him, raising an eyebrow at him. "So, where *are* we going?"

"Have you heard of the hookup closet?"

This time, both of my eyebrows shot up. "The what now?"

Landon's cheeks turned pink as he dodged my gaze. "The hookup closet. It's a sports equipment closet underneath the west staircase. It's where couples go to makeout on school grounds."

Oh, right, because kids couldn't wait a whole school day to make kissy faces with their significant others. They seriously had to dedicate an entire closet to making out.

And Landon and I were going there now. As a couple.

"For appearances, of course." Landon actually fumbled over his words at how quickly he tried to speak, still not quite looking at me. "I—I had the idea last night and I thought maybe it could work. To make Madison jealous. I'm sure that's where everyone thinks we're going, you know. *Private.*"

His nervous rambling was cute—and then I inwardly kicked myself for thinking it. Forcing out a chuckle, I said, "I mean, of course just for appearances."

"Of course."

"It's not like we're actually a couple."

"Right."

God, we were so awkward.

But then again, what *wasn't* awkward about eating our lunches in a closet designated by the school body for hookups? We'd be eating our lunch literally in the same spot someone had a tongue shoved down their throat. Which...so much for my appetite.

"What, uh—whatcha watching?" he asked as he glanced at my phone, which I still had palmed. The video hadn't darkened yet.

I picked up my dangling earbud and offered it to him. "Here, listen. Don't worry—I have clean ears."

He didn't seem worried in the least as he tucked the earbud into his ear, leaning closer to watch the video as we walked. His shoulder brushed mine. "Whoa, that's cool. So that's the van life you were talking about?"

"Mm-hmm. Hers is so much nicer than Petunia—that's my van's name—but she probably had a lot of time to work on it. And probably a lot of money." I rewound the video a bit and paused. "Look, it's an *actual* travel range. Isn't it sweet?"

Landon watched with an interest that I hadn't been expecting from him, so much so that I was the one who had to keep glancing up to make sure we weren't about to run into anything or anyone. "This is how your bed's going to be, isn't it?" he asked, reaching out and tracing his fingertip where the girl had built her bed at the rear of the van.

"Yep. I need to buy the mattress now and get some sheets."

Landon nodded slowly as he watched, but then his footsteps halted as we came to the west side staircase. "Oh. It's this door."

The closet was about the size I expected—small. If I thought about it—which I didn't—there was probably enough room for someone to lie down on the floor, but not much else. There were stacked boxes and a few scooters on a shelf on the far wall while a few rested on the ground, with one exposed lightbulb illuminating the narrow space. Landon shut the door behind us but didn't lock it, sitting a little in front of it. "That way if anyone comes in, they'll hit me first."

I sat across from him and set my tray on a nearby box, using it as a table. I nudged one of the scooters on the ground out of the way. "You think this is the most boring thing someone's done in here?" I asked him, glancing around at the stacked equipment. "Eat their lunch?"

"Could be worse," he said, unpacking his Tupperware. I watched as he used the nearest box to him as a table too. "You could have a tutoring session in here."

I snorted at the visual.

"Van life," Landon mused. He laid out his container of pasta salad and a turkey wrap, looking homemade and delicious. "That's really cool. I actually looked up a few videos after you mentioned it. It's really interesting, and seeing all the different possible setups is cool, too."

I blinked in surprise. "You looked up videos?"

"Yeah, well. I wanted to know more about it, in case it ever came up, which...I guess it wouldn't, would it?" Landon reached up and pressed the backs of his fingers to his cheeks, averting his gaze. "I can see how that sort of lifestyle is interesting to you, though. I could imagine you filming videos like that."

It made me happy to know that he'd done his own research on van life, to see the redness of his cheeks peeking through at the confession. As if it was embarrassing to admit he'd looked it up because I talked about it. "Could you ever see yourself traveling around in a van?"

"Not by myself." His eyes flicked momentarily to mine. "Maybe with someone."

As soon as he said it, I tried to stop myself from reading too much into it. He wasn't saying with *me*, just with *someone*. I picked up my slice of pizza, telling myself to get a grip.

"Are we friends?" Landon asked suddenly, startling me so badly that my pizza slipped from my fingers and landed back on my tray. A few specks of grease splattered.

"Friends," I repeated, grabbing my napkin and dotting at the grease on my legs. This morning flashed through my head, his fingers against my cheek. And then yesterday, him leaning against Petunia, smiling down at me. "I mean, y-yeah. I'd say we're friends."

He stabbed his pasta salad, but didn't bring a bite to his lips. He kept his chin down, as if talking to his food. "I feel like you're one of the only people around me who doesn't have an ulterior motive."

"So fake dating doesn't count as an ulterior motive?"

"But you're still honest in it all. You're still you."

Honest. Was I? Was I still honest if I never told Landon *why* I had to fake date him in the first place? Was it honesty even if I'd never told him about my messed-up family life? He'd said it himself—a secret is a lie, in a way. I watched him with a twinge in my chest. "You don't know everything about me."

"I want to." Landon lifted his eyes to mine and held them, earnestness leaking through the blue-green colors. "I told you I did."

See, it was when he said stuff like *that* that had my insides twisting in confusion. There was no one around now to listen in, no one to show off for. "Have you ever brought someone in here before?"

"In the closet? No."

"Honestly?"

"Honest." Landon took a bite of his turkey wrap and wiped his lips with his thumb, drawing my attention there. "You know I've had a crush on the same girl since the fourth grade. I never wanted to bring anyone else in here."

"Except me."

He paused, as if he'd only realized it. I couldn't read his expression. "It just worked out that way."

This was another first of his I'd taken. I didn't want to take any more, but he'd been the one to offer up this first this time. The only sound in the space for a few minutes after that was Landon's fork scraping the side of his Tupperware container or me chewing my piece of pizza. Sometimes with Landon, it was easy to forget he'd agreed to this in hopes of winning over Madison. He almost never talked about her—I had to pry all the information about her out of him. "Why hadn't you made a move before? On Madison?"

Landon's face screwed up for a split second before relaxing. "I'm not confident like that. It's a lot safer to watch from a distance than risk rejection, I guess."

"Tell me again, *how* are you in the Top Tier? I thought everyone was self-absorbed and had egos the size of Texas."

"Just lucky, I guess," he said a little ironically, lips curling up.

And then—whispers. On the other side of the door. They were impossible to make out, but they were there, like faint mice skittering about. Landon heard it too, and he turned toward the door, startled by the sound. His gaze found mine again. "*What should we do?*" he mouthed, and, using his hand to mime along with his words, he added, "*It's unlocked.*"

I waved my hand to beckon him closer, trying to think fast. If people were coming to find us, they were expecting to find us in a certain position, right? They expected to find us kissing, not eating our lunch. And while I couldn't kiss him—*wouldn't* kiss him—we could put on a good show.

Landon scooted as quietly as he could across the space toward me, and I reached out to grab his shirt near the collar to tug him closer. I stretched my palm out to brace myself, but it ended up landing directly on the scooter. The pressure sent the thing skittering backward, which sent me *falling* backward, and with nothing else to latch onto to steady myself, I ended up drawing Landon down with me.

No, not with me.

On top of me.

My back hit the floor hard, and Landon, with my grip still firm on his shirt, had no choice but to follow. His own hand shot out to brace himself, to keep his full weight off me, but it didn't stop his body from stretching out against mine, my knee grazing his thigh.

I stared up into his blue-green gaze, choking on the air that felt permanently frozen in my lungs. His eyes were equally wide as mine, and I could see my reflection in them. My heart thumped hard in my chest, so hard that Landon must've felt it too. But then again, was that really my heart racing? Or his?

"Hi," Landon whispered, cutting through the race of my thoughts.

Why was he saying that? What was he asking permission for? We were already touching—in several different places. Everything kicked into high gear with the one whispered word, like the world around me became hyper-focused. My eyes dropped to his lips, parted in surprise, inches from mine. They looked so soft. If I lifted my head a little, I'd be able to find out if they truly were.

My hand dipped on its own accord from gripping the front of his shirt to his hip, my fingers brushing the sliver of warm skin his shirt exposed. He had no outward reaction save for the fraction his eyes widened.

Kiss him.

My fingers tightened on his hip. "Hi."

We both held still, as if someone took a remote and

pressed *pause* on this moment. Until Landon ducked his head.

Landon pressed his face into the crook between my neck and my shoulder, his warm cheeks grazing my skin. His *lips* grazing my skin. His hand slipped between the floor and my back to press us closer together, painting the perfect visual of a couple caught in an embrace. He had to feel my pulse pounding at my throat—it had to be against his lips. It wasn't a kiss, but it was close enough. *Close enough.*

But not close enough at all.

With that thought ringing in my ear, the door to the hookup closet whipped open.

"Ah, my eyes!" someone screeched, followed by a flurry of gasps and giggles as everyone caught a view of the show. Landon launched off of me, but even without him hovering above and the peanut gallery gathering, my thoughts stayed hazy. Like they had a five-second delay. *You should've kissed him.*

But it was fake. Kissing him would've totally crossed a line.

Except that wanting definitely *wasn't* fake.

"Show's over," Landon said in a low tone, getting to his feet to shoo everyone out of the doorway.

Am I having a heart attack? I thought distantly as I stared up at the ceiling, drawing in a sharp breath. *Is that what this is?*

"Guess Landon is a good kisser," someone called—someone male. "Kissed her senseless, did you, dude?"

I could hear a girl's shrill laugh. "Never would've guessed!"

No kidding.

Everyone laughed and teased as if they'd caught us in an unintentionally compromised spot. They didn't know that it *was* intentional. That Landon played them.

Then again, I felt totally played, too. At least my body did.

I laid there on the skeevy hookup closet floor as Landon fought his friends back, pressing my hand to the side of my throat. Directly against the crook he'd had his face buried in.

When I finally gave one last look at the departing crowd, I didn't recognize a lot of the people who stood at the center of the open door. Not Connor, not Reed, not Nate.

But beyond the unfamiliar faces, before Landon shut the door, I did spot Madison at the very back of the group. Landon sealed me inside the closet before I had a chance to catch her expression, leaving me alone with our half-eaten lunch and a frantic, tumbling heartbeat.

CHAPTER 17

*I*f I thought I needed to run to school on Tuesday in order to avoid Landon, I really, *really* wished I could've avoided him Wednesday morning. It was almost laughable now. I thought him with his arm propped above me and leaning in was enough to stir weird feelings? Ha, try lying underneath him in a hookup closet, Lacey.

Like, *right* underneath him.

With his lips on your neck.

Ha.

It also, conveniently enough, was the only thing I could think about last night as I tried to fall asleep. I had absolutely no idea how I was going to face him without my face blazing firetruck red.

"You sure you don't want a ride?" I asked Hudson as I stood by the window, waiting for Landon's car to pull up. I tucked my fingers into my sweatshirt sleeves, already chilly from just looking at the rain. "You'll get soaked as you're waiting for the bus."

Hudson, standing slightly behind me, pulled his sweat-shirt hood up over his head, drawing the strings tight. "No thanks."

"I'm sure a short car ride wouldn't be so—"

"I said, no thanks."

I turned around and gave him and his stony expression a leveled look. "For someone who was pushing me to date, you could be a bit more supportive."

"I'm supportive. I just don't want to carpool."

"Or maybe there's someone on the bus you want to see?"

Hudson's countenance looked like that of a grim reaper —flat, unamused, slightly psychopathic. "Yes. Mrs. Savion."

"No," Paisley said suddenly, causing the two of us to turn. She stood at the mouth of the hallway with her yellow raincoat on, though her features were flat as she stared up at us. "His mentor."

My eyebrows rose, intrigued. "Your mentor rides the same bus, huh?"

Paisley nodded. "She even came over Monday."

I whirled on my eldest cousin, eyes widening. "Excuse me?"

"No one," Hudson said in an oddly tense tone, glaring at Paisley, "came over."

Paisley put a hand on her hip. "Yes, huh. She was waiting at my bus stop and walked with me back to the house because *someone* forgot to pick me up. She dressed like a grandma."

"Paisley." Hudson's voice was sharp, gaze intense. "Let's drop it."

I slapped Hudson hard on the arm, but he didn't even flinch. "Oh my gosh, you really had a *girl* over? I can't believe it. Is hell freezing over? Who are you and what have you done with my Grim Reaper?"

Hudson's scowl deepened.

"You should've told me earlier," I told Paisley, frowning. "Tell me everything. What did she look like? Was she pretty?"

Paisley's lips twisted like she wanted to smile, but stopped herself short. "Hudson doesn't want to talk about it."

Of course she'd take his side. I shouldn't have been surprised.

"Fine, yes, it was my mentor, okay?" Hudson said, detecting the tension. "My...buddy, or whatever. She stopped by. I walked her home. Nothing crazy."

Uh, it absolutely was crazy. Since I moved into the Bishop house in June, Hudson *never* had friends over. Not even his closest friends, Derrick or Tee. And yet he invited his mentor over? I wanted to pry—God, did I ever—but Hudson was like a stubborn toddler. Push at him too hard, and he'd stop what he was doing altogether out of spite. If I pried about the girl, he'd never tell me. Best to wait it out— or I could follow him after school one time and see the underclassman for myself.

"Your boyfriend's here," Hudson grumbled, turning toward his little sister. "We'll head out after they leave."

I patted Hudson on the shoulder. "Well, next time she comes over, let me meet her, okay?"

"It won't happen again," he called, but I was already

hurrying out the door and shutting it behind me, ducking my head against the rain.

When I got to Landon's car door, he reached over and shoved it open from the inside, saving me the trouble of grabbing the wet handle. "Morning," he greeted as I all but collapsed into the seat, giving an exaggerated shiver. He twisted the dial on the heat up.

"Good morning," I replied, squeezing my knees together, hating myself for the uncomfortable tension that filled the interior as soon as I shut the door. "Rainy one."

"It is."

Great, we were talking about the weather. This was going swimmingly.

I didn't look at him as I flipped my hood off, buckling myself in. "Will you have practice today?"

"Depends on if it keeps up like this." Landon hooked his hand on the back of my headrest as he twisted around to back up, his wrist at eye level. I could see all the veins underneath his skin, and if I traveled the arm up farther, I could see where the muscles of his forearms shadowed before his shirtsleeve hid the rest of it.

I shut my eyes, mentally grabbing my thoughts by the reins. *Stop it, Lacey.* "Should we...should we do something after school? If your practice is canceled, I mean. You know, in case someone asks?"

"We can say we did something together if anyone asks. I have to pick my sister back up from the school around four, so I don't really have time to do anything."

I spread my hands over my knees, digging my fingers into the damp denim. I had no idea why him saying that stung so much. It wasn't personal, and I knew that. It wasn't personal that he didn't want to spend even an hour together. With the rejection, something in my stomach hardened, like trying to protect itself. *See?* my thoughts whispered. *If you weren't dating, he wouldn't be hanging out with you.*

Landon had to flick his windshield wipers up a setting higher as we turned out onto the main road of Vista Villas, swiping water away rapidly. "But, uh, keep your Friday open, if you could. Bobcats have a home game, but then there's a Jocks Only party afterward."

I scrunched my nose. "What's that?"

"It's a party someone from the team throws for the football players and the cheerleaders. So basically the whole Top Tier will be there." He took a glance at me. "It'll be a good time to mingle, hang out, all that. It makes sense I'd bring my girlfriend there."

Of course it made sense to bring me, and of course the entirety of the Top Tier would be there. But unlike all the other times that it came to Landon's friends, I found myself curious, trying to picture us at a party together. "Who's throwing it?"

"Ashton."

And just like that, all curiosity evaporated.

"He's usually the one who throws them these days," he went on, unaware of how my mood soured. "Connor used to, but he hasn't thrown one since last schoolyear."

I wished Connor had been throwing it instead. I didn't know where Ashton lived, but I really didn't care to find out, either. For how grand his personality was, I wished he lived in a trash can. "If you think it's a good idea."

"Do we need to do anything to convince your cousin?"

"He's thoroughly convinced." A whole lot easier than I thought he'd be to convince, quite honestly. Then again, he had a lot on his plate with the mentor thing. "Now it's riding it out until it's time to break up."

Depending on how many more times Landon and I met up outside of school, it might've been a piece of cake. He nodded thoughtfully, slowing for a stop sign. "Do we want coffee this morning?"

"No, I'm okay."

The cab grew quiet again. We'd have a bit more time before school since we were skipping the coffee, so Landon drove slowly through the morning traffic. "You look...tired."

I was wound far too tight to get offended, especially because I knew he wasn't wrong. The truth was that I'd woken up *again* in a state of panic, but this time, it was at five in the morning. Hours before my alarm. The adrenaline that shot through my veins had made it impossible to go back to sleep even once it wore off. I didn't know why it was getting worse lately, but after having a hard time falling asleep and waking up early, I knew I had a rough day ahead of me. "I set my alarm for the wrong time."

Landon made a soft *mmm* noise as he nodded, reaching up and turning his air vent toward me. After a long moment, he cleared his throat. "You know, yesterday..."

The word *yesterday*—it had my insides jerking to attention, almost like all of my organs gasped. I wasn't delusional enough to hope that he meant something else, but whatever he wanted to talk about regarding the hookup closet, I *really* didn't want to. No doubt he'd tell me, "*Hey, listen, don't ever get grabby handy with me again,*" or, "*I hope you know that it meant nothing to me.*"

Which of course, I'd have to agree with. I'd tell him that moment in the hookup closet meant nothing to me either.

And me thinking about it all night *totally* meant nothing, too.

Was I...was I *really* developing feelings for Landon Settler? My body seemed to think so, flaunting its hormones whenever he was around. I mean, sure, the guy was nice, funny at times, and his shyness could be absolutely adorable other times... But liking him. *Really* liking him. Was that even possible?

"How did you get to school?"

I blinked, because that was *so* not the question I'd anticipated. "What?"

"Yesterday. You texted that you didn't need a ride." He fiddled with the heat dial again. "I was...curious."

"Uh, I used to run to school. Before I got a chauffeur. I'd run to school and then shower in the locker room. That's what I did yesterday."

"So that's why you showered in the guys' locker room that day?" he asked. "Because you ran to school?"

"No, that was because the girls' locker room was locked. Trust me, I'll never make that error in judgement again." Some of my guard lowered, and I looked toward him with a slightly amused expression. "Did you think the heavens blessed you when you walked in on a girl in a towel?"

"I thought *I'd* walked into the wrong locker room. I was waiting for you to start screaming at me."

A smile crossed my lips at the image in my head, and it slowly faded as something else came back to me. *How about you?* Landon had asked me once upon a time. *Have you ever had any fate moments like that?*

No, that wasn't a fate moment. Surely not.

"But we probably should talk about the other thing," he went on, clenching the steering wheel.

"It was an emergency thing," I cut him off, keeping my stare straight ahead. The sky was still dark, still a trace of the stars before they were covered by the rising sun. "If your friends saw us eating lunch in the closet, that would've been too suspicious. It was...necessary."

But was it necessary that I was still thinking about it?

This time, Landon's nod was vigorous. The relief that swamped his frame was clear as day, even by the way his shoulders relaxed, and it made me feel a little sick. "Agreed, agreed. I didn't mean to—I wasn't sure what to do—I just—"

"It was...quick thinking." I pressed the backs of my fingers to my cheek, trying to calm the flame there. No doubt I'd find mirroring fever spots on his cheeks if I glanced over. "Kissing my neck like that. I'm sure everyone bought it."

"I just wanted to make sure you didn't feel uncomfortable."

"We both said *hi*, didn't we?"

"Yeah, but—it's—your heart was beating fast, and I didn't know if—"

"Landon." The name came out almost sounding

desperate, and I forced myself to relax, to put on a show of nonchalance even if I felt miles from it. "Let's just...drop it."

"Dropping it," he murmured, and cleared his throat again.

The awkwardness was impossible to get past, as was the weight that felt like had settled in my stomach. *Of course he didn't think anything of yesterday*, my thoughts murmured, scoffing. *He doesn't like you like that. No one does. And no one ever has.*

It was similar to what the Top Tier would say if they found out the truth about our relationship. Madison and Jade, arms linked, staring me down with twin snotty expressions. *You, Lacey Churchill, are unlovable.*

We turned into the school parking lot in silence. It wasn't that full since we were so early, but it'd fill up soon. I was ready to get out of the car, to get breathing room.

"What are you doing tonight?" Landon said as he put the car into park.

I kept my gaze hyper focused on the school building, almost like I was talking to the chipped brick instead of the boy beside me. "I have to work."

A lie. It slipped off my tongue with minimal effort, surprising me. Before, the idea of lying to him seemed impossible—and even now, guilt followed on the heels of the excuse. The rock that sat on my chest still weighed too heavily for me to take it back, though. I needed it to be this way. I was getting too close.

Landon flipped the wipers off once we parked, which allowed the raindrops to pool on the glass. They blurred the school, and when I no longer had the structure to focus on, I looked over at him. His cheeks were still pinkish from our previous conversation, and his eyes were bright, focused on me. My heart gave an involuntary, heavy *thud*. "I'm going to eat lunch with Hudson today," I said tightly. "He's been feeling a little lonely, eating by himself."

"Oh—okay." Something shifted in his expression, but I couldn't look at him long enough to decipher it.

And with that, I popped my door open and stood, but it didn't stop the buzzing in my chest. I hurried toward the school as the rain poured down, not looking back to see if Landon followed.

Uncle Dean, Paisley, and I all sat in the living room that night watching a hospital drama that was way too mature for a girl her age, but Uncle Dean gave up fighting to get her to go to her room. She was the one who turned it on in the first place, and her little hand clutched the remote in a death grip. I sat on the couch beside her with my feet propped on the coffee table, whereas Uncle Dean sat in his recliner. He had his e-reader in his lap—he seriously never spent a moment without that thing—and multi-tasked between reading his book and watching the show.

Hudson emerged from his bedroom with his jacket slung over his shoulders, keeping his head down. "Derrick's here. I'm heading out."

Uncle Dean sighed. "Do you have to go out so late on a school night, Hudson? Really?"

"It's just to Tee's. They're having a bonfire—nothing crazy." Hudson looked at me, taking in my pajama bottoms and the baggy T-shirt. "You don't want to come...right?"

"You might as well have said, 'Please don't think about coming,' given your tone," I replied with a snort. "No, I'm good. Have fun listening to Simon's lame poetry."

Hudson rolled his eyes. "I will."

He headed out after slipping on his shoes, leaving us to resume our binge-watching. Paisley, though, wasn't too keen on paying attention anymore. Instead, she sat forward and stared—or, really, *glared*—at her father. "How come he gets to go out when it's my bedtime?"

"Because he's seventeen and you're seven," Uncle Dean replied, and then stared at her a little harder. "Speaking of which, it *is* bedtime. Past, actually."

Paisley flicked her eyes to me. "Lacey gets to stay up."

I pointed at myself with my thumb. "Seventeen." I pointed my index finger at her. "Seven."

"Please," she all but sneered, looking much more like a mean girl in high school than a harmless elementary schooler. "I'm more mature than you. At least no one has to worry about me running away."

While my jaw was too busy dropping, Uncle Dean stepped in. "Paisley Ann, apologize right—"

"You do, right, Dad? You worry about her running away. That's why you get up in the middle of the night and check to see if the van is still in the driveway."

"How did you know I—"

"You're the most—the most—the most *selfish* person I've met," Paisley fired at me, scowling further. "It's not good to be selfish."

After weeks of her hot and cold attitudes, I couldn't swallow it anymore. Not after the day I had. I gave the kid some leeway since she was so young, but I so wasn't doing it anymore. "What are you mad at me for? There's got to be a reason, since you're acting like a brat."

Uncle Dean's voice grew with apprehension. "Lacey..."

"You moved in with us and everything changed," Paisley said, standing up from the couch to glare at me. Her pink nightgown swayed with the movement. "My dad works more because of you. He doesn't pick me up from school anymore, and I barely get to see him! You kicked my brother out of his bedroom, got him in trouble over the summer. You *should* run away. Get in the van and never come back!"

And with that, she turned on her heel with dramatic flair to storm from the living room, leaving her father and me in her wake. My chest wound tight with half-fulfilled confrontation, but a different emotion seemed to suffocate most of my anger. *Selfish.*

I knew when Uncle Dean insisted I move in with them that it would put strain on everyone. Hudson had to give up his room. Uncle Dean bought more groceries because of me, even if I never ate them. He took on extra shifts to make up for what Mom never gave him. Paisley did see her dad less—he was gone to work most days before she woke up, and didn't come home until later at night. All because of me.

And then Sunday, leaving without notice but then coming back and acting like nothing happened. How long could I put them through the ringer because of me?

"I don't—I don't know why she's being like this sometimes," Uncle Dean said tiredly, turning off his e-reader and rubbing his eyes.

"*Sometimes*?" I echoed, a bite to my voice.

"A lot of times," he amended, kicking the leg rest of his chair down back into place. "I've been talking to her teacher, and she said she'll keep an eye on her in class. She recommended that Paisley meet with the counselor."

She needed it, given how much attitude was bottled up in that tiny body. "I've been trying really hard to be accommodating," I muttered.

"We're family, Lacey. No one needs to be *accommodating*." With a groan, Uncle Dean got to his feet, and for several seconds, he stayed standing still. The line of his shoulders was tense as he hunched forward, almost like he was too tired to stand up straight. "Maybe we all need to turn in early. Sleep it off. We'll talk more about it tomorrow."

"Sleep it off," I found myself muttering, glancing toward the hallway our bedrooms were in. "She gets free passes; that's why she's acting like this."

"Let me parent her," Uncle Dean said, but his voice wasn't unkind. It was tired.

He hadn't said it like one, but it felt like a scolding all the same, one that had warring emotions of shame and anger swelling in me. Everything in me was screaming to fight, to demand more confrontation, almost greedy for it.

Uncle Dean moved toward the opposite side of the narrow house, past the kitchen, where his bedroom was. "Did Mom ever send you the money?" I asked before he had a chance to walk away.

Uncle Dean's steps faltered, just as I'd wanted, but he stayed with his back to me.

"She didn't," I guessed after his silence stretched too long, a buzzing feeling blooming once more in my chest. Like bees had awoken behind my rib cage, fiery and ready to sting. "Of course she didn't."

When he turned, his expression was pained. "Lacey—"

"Does Paisley know that?" I asked him from the couch, body beginning to tremble. "That I'm not here on a vacation? That I'm here because my mom didn't want to deal with me anymore?"

"She's young, Lacey. Too young for adult problems."

"You said the same thing to me." This time, I did stand, wrapping my arms around my middle. "But just because we're young doesn't mean we're not forced to live through it."

The words hung between us in the air, harsh as they settled. I forced myself to look away from Uncle Dean, because this was the part that my anger always forgot—the guilt of snapping without considering how the other person would feel. It really felt like a good line, sounded like one in my head—but watching his face fall had me wishing I could take it back.

"You're right," I said after our long beat of silence, squeezing my lungs so tight that I couldn't draw in air. "We should turn in early for the night. I'll...see you tomorrow."

But even after shutting myself in Hudson's room, the pressure didn't let up. I leaned against the closed bedroom door, peering around the inside. My suitcase was half out from underneath the bed, and Hudson would've had to step over it to get his clothes from his dresser. The room was small—for three bedrooms in a mobile home, it had to be small—but the space was his. Posters, pictures stacked on his dresser. His bed with his sheets. His bedroom, one that I took over.

His family, which I did nothing but burden.

Closing my eyes, I let out a slow, shaking breath. Fighting with Uncle Dean was everything that I didn't want to do. He didn't deserve it. Out of everyone, he deserved it the least. Here I was, adding another rift through the middle of their household. I was the reason Paisley was acting like this. I was the reason Uncle Dean got up in the middle of the night checking to make sure I hadn't gone anywhere.

I felt as if I could throw up.

So that was why, despite how much I *really* didn't want to, I reached for my phone on the nightstand, finding the contact and hitting *call*.

It only took one ring for the line to connect. "You told me to call you," I said before he could speak, staring into the dark bedroom. My voice was flat, quiet, in case Uncle Dean could hear. "If I ever wanted to leave...you told me to call you."

"Where are you?" Landon asked without hesitation. He sounded like he was on the brink of whispering, but then again, it was already after his phone's curfew.

I closed my eyes at the sound of it, the buzzing in my chest quieting ever so slightly. "Hudson's."

Landon's end of the call grew noisy, like he was shuffling around. Drawing again, I guessed. "Can I call you back in five minutes? Don't...don't go anywhere."

"Where would I go?" I asked, aiming for a bit of my teasing spunk, but that well was dry. "I'll be here."

"Five minutes," Landon repeated, and then he hung up.

I moved away from the door to sit on the edge of Hudson's made bed, trailing my fingertips over the duvet cover. It had me thinking about my bedroom at home, the pastel pink sheets I'd left behind. *Everything* I'd left behind —everything that didn't fit in my suitcase, anyway. Before I left on the grand escape, I'd need to go home one last time, make sure I had everything I needed. Once I left Brentwood, I didn't want to have to come back in search of something. Once I was gone, I wanted to be gone.

The idea sounded so blissful, and I rested my head down on my pillow, imagining the day I'd stop being a burden on Hudson and his family. I'd stop having to be afraid of running into Mom. I'd stop feeling ready to fight at the drop of the hat. I'd finally be out from underneath the destiny that'd been assigned to me, free.

I pictured me sitting in the driver's seat of the van, window down, hair blowing in the wind. Nothing but the open road ahead of me.

Sounds lonely, a stray thought whispered.

Not lonely. Not really. Not forever. Besides, when had being alone ever truly bothered me? I'd been alone most of my life. In fact, now that I'd been living with the Bishops, I *wanted* to be alone. I felt too suffocated with the eyes on me, the attention, the pressure. Once I found a town on the coast, settled down, it wouldn't be lonely—it would be...perfect.

I stared up at the ceiling, strangely hollow even amidst my dreams.

Until my phone buzzed in my grip. "That felt longer than five minutes," I accused when I picked up.

"Sorry," Landon said, and this time, he no longer spoke in hushed tones. "Are you still at Hudson's?"

"Yeah."

"What's everyone doing?"

"We're turning in early for the night." I kicked the footboard. "Well, everyone but Hudson. He has a friend thing."

"Turning in early?" he asked in disbelief. "When it's barely nine-thirty?"

"Look who's talking, Mr. Cell Phone Curfew Boy." Landon laughed on the other end of the line, and though it sent shivers down my spine, I couldn't bring myself to smile. "Besides, it's not like I'm going to bed. I'll probably be scrolling on social media for at least two more hours. Gotta stay consistent with my nighttime routine."

"Ah, that makes more sense. I was going to say, the only person I know who goes to bed this early is my sister."

I made a face in the darkness. "By choice?"

"Eh. I don't know about that."

I listened closer to the background noise coming through my phone. There were a lot of thuds, like something kept bumping against his phone. "Your parents sound strict. Phone curfews, bedtime curfews, scolding you on your game performance—"

Landon sighed. "You heard that on Friday, huh?"

"It's okay. Them being strict means they care, right?" My voice took on a bitter edge.

"They care about something," Landon agreed. "Whether that be their kids or their image, who knows?"

I rolled onto my side and pressed the phone between the mattress and my ear, trying to imagine how that'd feel. If Mom cared more about image, would she have made half the choices in life that she had? If she cared more about image, would she have made sure I never moved out?

If only she'd cared more in general, I thought bitterly, and then shook my head. "Tell me more about your parents," I whispered, swallowing hard. "Are you afraid of letting them down?"

"Over some stuff," he answered. "Like football. Sports in general, I guess. I know they have high expectations of me. I know they like to be the parents of the quarterback— like to feel...superior, I guess, over the other football parents. And I don't want to let them down."

"Sounds like a lot of pressure."

"I'm lucky, I guess. All my parents care about with me is sports. Whether I'm overstriding or hanging on to the ball too long." He sighed a little. "My sister gets it worse, I think. Their hyper-attention."

It was funny that attention for some kids was frustrating, when that was all I ever wanted growing up. I understood him, though, and closed my eyes. "I'm sorry."

"Don't be sorry," he said quickly. "It's life. It could be worse."

Landon's life was filled with complications, ones I never would've imagined. He did a good job at keeping them underneath the surface, hidden from view. It was no secret that Landon was reserved, but I really had no idea how much he kept locked away. I wanted to dive deeper, to unlock the little things about him, bring them to the surface. I wanted to be the one he could confide in, so he at least had *someone*. I wanted to be his someone.

"Are you still there?" I asked him, nearly whispering.

"As it turns out," he began in a strange voice, "I had this sudden urge to go for a drive to look at the stars. The clouds from the rain have all cleared up. Care to join me?"

I blinked at the offer, at the flippant way he'd presented it. I waited for him to laugh, to say "just kidding," but he didn't. "I thought you had a curfew."

"Everyone should be rebellious once in their life, right?"

Now I sat up, as if that would clear my head. "I don't want you to get in trouble."

"Well, that's a shame." Something thudded against the phone, sounding suspiciously like a gearshift. "Since I'm already at your house."

I rushed to the window and forced the slatted blinds apart, peering out into the darkness. Sure enough, Landon's red coupe sat at the very end of the driveway with its lights off. It was too dark for me to make out anything other than the dark figure sitting behind the steering wheel. "No way," I breathed, blinking as if it would make the car disappear.

"Way." Landon flashed his headlights once, blinding me. "Still don't want to go for a drive?"

So many reasons had me nearly saying no. I was in my pajamas already. I'd already washed off all my makeup from the day. And then, probably the biggest reason, I knew it was a bad idea going out with Landon like this. With no one to impress, with no one to remind me that this wasn't real. Because if I went out with him tonight, it would be nearly impossible to convince myself that this was all pretend.

But there was one big reason that had me turning away from the window, and it was the way I *felt*. As if a magnet were lodged underneath my ribs, pulling me toward Landon's car with a force I couldn't deny. Whatever it was about Landon Settler that had me feeling calm, I needed it now. Before, I'd never really needed anyone, but tonight, I needed him.

I cleared my throat, reaching for one of Hudson's hoodies. "Give me a minute."

CHAPTER 18

"You have a lot of cherry Twizzlers on hand for a guy who doesn't like them."

Landon looked over at me where we sat on the hood of his trunk, both on the far ends of the car with the middle between us. The wind tugged at his hair, but his hair wasn't really long enough to fall into his eyes. Even still, he reached up and smoothed it down. "Weird," he agreed.

"Is this your mom's secret stash or something?"

"Probably someone's secret stash."

This bag wasn't a family share size, but a small one, and I shook the bag to shake the red goodness around. "I'd feel guilty if it were anything other than Twizzlers."

That made Landon laugh, and he pressed a hand to the back of his car, reclining. "Don't feel guilty. Finish the whole bag."

As I popped a piece into my mouth, I lifted my head to look at our surroundings. Landon had been right about the clouds from earlier having blown off, and the stars that shined down on Brentwood were clearer than ever. He'd parked up by Lookout Ledge, the tallest point in Brentwood, and one of the most beautiful. Most secluded.

The weirdest part about coming here at night was that couples usually parked here for other reasons—reasons that didn't involve Twizzlers nibbling.

The sweatshirt I wore of Hudson's was a bright yellow one, and I had the hood up over my head, strings drawn tight around my face. Not my most glamorous of looks, of course—especially not with the way my hair was still coming out of my hood to tickle my cheeks—but tonight, it was clear I didn't care about glamor. My red polka dot pajama pants and makeup-less face were a testament to that. The only thing that made me feel semi-put together was the perfume I'd spritzed on. I half expected Landon to say something when he saw me, to comment on my vastly different appearance, but he hadn't.

I glanced his way. "You didn't bring any snacks for you?"

"I'm not much of a snacker."

"What a boring life you lead," I said teasingly, tossing another piece into my mouth.

When Landon picked me up from the house, we didn't say much before traveling to Lookout Ledge. I'd crept as quietly as I could've through the front door, but I left a note on the table for Uncle Dean in case he had heard me. Despite needing some space, I didn't want him to worry.

But I felt relaxed with Landon, almost like the argument that happened in the Bishop household happened weeks ago, not just a mere half hour.

Almost as if Landon could read my thoughts to see what path they'd traveled down, he said, "So, what had you calling me tonight?"

I shook my bag again, contemplating my answer. "You told me to."

"To call me before you ran." Landon didn't look at me, but up at the sky, gaze roaming over the stars. "You wanted to?"

The cherry pieces were getting hard to chew from the cold, and it stole some of their flavor, but I didn't slow down on my consumption. "A little." It was easier to be honest without looking at him, and without him looking at me. I could almost pretend that I was talking to myself, in a way. Like even though I was sitting on top of his car, I could pretend that I was alone as long as I didn't look over. "Hudson has a little sister—she's seven. She made it crystal clear tonight that their lives have been messed up since I moved in."

"All of a sudden?"

"I don't know if she's felt this way for a while, or if..." Her harsh words echoed in my ears, and it nearly made me wince. The wind tore through the high ledge, and I tucked my fingers into my sleeves, shivering a little. "Or if what happened Sunday kind of made it worse. Then again, she's been a little spitfire since I moved in, so maybe it's been this way all along."

Landon drew in a deep breath and let it out, kicking his foot lightly against the side of his car. His gaze was still upturned when I risked a sneak peek, giving me a full view at his sharp jawline. It was too dark to see his freckles clearly, but I searched for them anyway. "Things are harder for kids to understand."

"It's all hard for *me* to understand. I can't imagine how it is for her." I thought of the way Landon had looked at me Monday as he walked me to Petunia. *I want to know as much of you as you want to show me*, he'd said, and even now, it gave me butterflies in a way I didn't understand. But the magnetized feeling was back, and instead of it being attached under my ribcage, it was attached to words that seemed to pull from my mouth. "I live with them because my mom...she didn't want me living with her anymore."

From the corner of my eye, I saw Landon lower his head from the stars.

"Well, I guess she didn't really *not* want me living with her," I amended quietly, peering into the Twizzlers bag. "But she didn't stop me when I left. She never called me after, either. Never texted. Then she canceled my phone plan. I had to get a new number, but at least that gave her an excuse for never calling."

"You don't have to tell me," he whispered, this time looking over.

I turned, too, and met his gaze straight-on. It was dark in this area of Lookout Ledge, with no streetlight in sight, and all I had was the moon and starlight to illuminate his face. It lit up the high points of his cheekbones and forehead, almost looking like a dream. "You said you wanted to know as much as I wanted to show you," I reminded him, scanning his expression for a hint of discomfort. The only thing worse than recounting my sob story would be to tell it to someone who didn't care. "Do you still want to know?"

He didn't even hesitate. That was one of the most beautiful parts about him, I decided. Even when things got heavy, he didn't hesitate. "Yes."

I hesitated, though. Because this was my sob story, and this would be my first official time recounting it. "Part of the agreement when I moved in with my uncle was that she'd give him payments for groceries and that sort of stuff. Child support, but without the legal requirements. She didn't pay this month. I'm not even worth that much, in her eyes."

"What made you leave?" he asked.

"It was summer, and our water got shut off. She hadn't paid the bill. The electric, either." I went from staring at my candy to staring out over the ledge, at the darkness that awaited below. If there hadn't been a moon, it would've looked like an abyss of darkness. "She never was good with money, and it only got worse when she got a boyfriend. Why pay bills on a house when she could crash at his place? Once Uncle Dean found out, he wouldn't let me live alone anymore."

I cut myself off, because picturing what happened the day after choked me like a physical vise. I didn't want to tell him about Allen's Alley, about the fight with Max, about sitting in the back of a police car. That felt like too much. He already had a pretty clear view of how train-wrecked my life seemed, but I didn't want him to see that part.

"At least, not until I'm eighteen," I said a little brighter, straightening my spine. "And then he said I'm free to do what I want. Stay, go back home...leave Brentwood altogether."

Something seemed to dawn on Landon. "So that's why you're fixing up the van. Not to sleep out in it in the driveway, but to leave town with it."

I tipped my head back and looked at the dark sky. The stars were scattered and jumbled, but though constellations meant nothing to me, they were still pretty. "Ever since I was little, I pictured what it'd be like to start fresh. To discover what life was like elsewhere. Somewhere where I'm not a burden or a bother. Just start my own life. You know?"

"You want to run away."

He hadn't sounded accusatory, but the urge to defend myself rose up. "It's not running away. You can think of it that way, sure. But haven't you ever imagined it? Picking up everything and leaving? To go to a place where no one knows your name, no one knows your history. A place where you can start over with no expectations, no preconceived notions."

Landon tilted his head to the side, gaze softening. "No."

I shouldn't have really expected another answer from one of Brentwood's prized boys. "I guess that's where we're different."

Landon angled toward me, resting his forearm on his leg as he leaned in closer, as if we were about to share a secret. "That's why you want to leave, though?"

The wind danced between us again, unrelenting in this moment. I peered down into my Twizzlers bag, but my appetite had disappeared. In fact, I almost felt a little sick. "My mom and I...we've never been close. Not in the way a lot of moms and daughters are. We've never painted our nails together or gone shopping together. But...not because *I* didn't want to, you know?" I glanced over to make sure he was listening, shaking my head. "She never wanted it. And I look around Brentwood, terrified of seeing her again. Running into her at the store. Sunday...she came into Le Petit Bateau."

"Did she go there on purpose? To see you?"

"I doubt it." If that were the case, she would've come earlier. If it'd been the case, she would've at least tried to call Uncle Dean afterward, tried to get in touch, but she never did. I zipped up the pouch of Twizzlers and set them on the trunk between us, sighing. "It's not just her, though. It's Brentwood in general. The Top Tier. Ashton and Madison and Jade. The gossipers and the mean girls. They drive me crazy."

I waited for Landon to tell me that there were crazy people everywhere. That was the argument Hudson always gave, that I needed to learn how to deal with the crazy here first and *then* leave. But Landon didn't say that. I didn't know how he always seemed to know what to say and what not to say, but he had the uncanny ability to read me like no one else could, like he was someone who truly knew me. One of the few. "Where would you go?" he asked finally. "When you leave here, where are you headed?"

"I don't know yet. I guess...I guess I'll know when I get there."

"Well, when you find out, let me know." He looked over at me, the moonlight brightening half of his face. "Maybe one person from Brentwood could come visit you."

Heat bloomed in my chest, instantly warming me against the chill. "Jade?"

Landon's face split into a smile, equally splintering the heavy mood that'd blanketed over us, if only for a second. Because that smile of his was like a second moon—bright enough to chase away any lingering darkness. "I'm sorry," he said when his lips drooped, startling me. "For making you hang out with the people you're trying to steer clear from of. Jade, Ashton, Madison...everyone in the Top Tier."

"Hey, I signed myself up for it. I agreed to help you win over the girl you were crushing on. Of course that meant I'd have to be around your friends."

"You said that you asked me to be your fake boyfriend because you trusted me." He flexed his fingers before curling them into a fist. "How do you know I'm not like everyone else?"

"What do you mean?"

The remote expression on Landon's face from earlier had dissipated into something that was a bit clearer, though it was filled with uncertainty. "How do you know I'm different than Ashton or Madison or Jade? How do you know there's more to me than football, or basketball, or whatever the next sport of the season is?"

I hummed a little as I thought about it. "You draw. That alone makes it clear how much more there is to you."

I realized immediately that it wasn't an off-the-cuff question for him. My answer didn't soothe him, and he shifted uneasily. "How do you know I'm different than the Top Tier?" His words came out faster, almost as if he were breathless with them. "I was in a fight with Hudson—I'm the reason he's outcasted like he is. How am I any different? How do you *know*?"

Landon's chest rose and fell quickly, and his shoulders were stiff, almost like he was braced for pain. I sat speechless for a long, long moment, staring. His eyes were bright with the urgency that'd accompanied his words, and I stared into them now, truly at a loss for words. The way he spoke, with the haunted look on his face, was as if these words had been bottled up for months, desperate to spill out.

And I was his someone he spilled it to.

The question seemed so obvious, but it was hard to come up with a straightforward answer. I angled my body toward him and reached out with both hands to place them on his cheeks. They were hot underneath my cold fingertips, and if his body had been tight with tension a second ago, he froze solid now. I wasn't sure he even breathed. "Landon," I said firmly, not letting him look away. "That very first day we met, anyone else would've taken out their phone and snapped a picture of me in the towel. They would've sent it to Babble. Jade would've probably stolen my clothes, and Ashton would've texted everyone the photo himself. But you? You grabbed all my things and hid me from your friends. You barely even looked at me."

With my hands on his cheeks, I could feel his skin grow warmer. "Sometimes even Jade is nice."

"And I'm sure sometimes you're a pain in the neck," I responded easily. "There's something so fundamentally different, Landon, and I can't believe you don't see it. You are not like them." I brought his face closer to deepen my stare. "I wouldn't fake date you if you were."

All at once, the atmosphere of the moment shifted into something different, though equally as serious. When I reached up to touch his face, I hadn't thought about it. I was so used to doing it to grab Hudson's attention when he wasn't listening to me, so used to Hudson knocking my hands away. I wasn't used to lingering in this moment, and I definitely wasn't used to it being Landon Settler looking back at me.

"I don't want to be like them." Landon shook his head a little, but still didn't try to break free. "More than anything...I don't want to be like them."

"Good, because I like you like *this*, not like them."

Landon blinked slowly, the movement of his brown lashes sweeping down and then back up. I replayed the words in my mind, realizing too belatedly what I'd said. *I like you like this.*

I dropped my hands into my lap, curling my fingers against the lingering heat. "We should—we should probably head back. It's—it's probably late."

I had no idea what time it was. All I knew was that it was dark. Sitting on the trunk of his car together, time seemed to stop, like we'd captured a moment in time and frozen it just for us. We'd both shared vulnerable snippets of ourselves tonight, in a way I hadn't been expecting. Knowing his fears, his insecurity, and sharing my own—it changed something for me. It made this feel dangerous.

"We should," Landon agreed, but was slow to slide off the trunk. He picked up the bag of Twizzlers and took a step closer. Since I still sat down, our eyes were now level, and for some reason, it made my heart skip a beat. "Thank you...for telling me about your mom."

"Thank you for telling me about how you're feeling," I returned, too aware that my leg was probably, like, two inches from grazing his hip. *Dangerous*, my thoughts warned, especially when my gaze dropped to the slight upturn to his lips. His soft-looking lips. *This is dangerous.*

Landon held up his hand, palm facing the sky, offering it out to me. "Thank you for calling."

I slipped my hand into his and let him help me off the trunk. I didn't need the help, I didn't need his hand, but I wanted it. *Dangerous.* "Thank you," I said, my fingers still curled around his. "For coming."

How could anyone not want to be around Landon Settler when he looked at you like that? Like you were the only person in the world. Like you were a star that belonged in the night sky? And maybe I was fooling myself —maybe he honestly was waiting for me to drop his hand— but I liked to think that in that split second that night, after we let each other see the saddest parts of ourselves, that him looking at me like this was real. That maybe, just for this moment, I was his star.

Landon smiled, and then after one final squeeze, he dropped my hand.

CHAPTER 19

I leaned against the lockers by Hudson's after school, watching as he loaded up his backpack. He wasn't looking at me, almost like if he didn't look over, I wasn't actually there. "You have your mentor thing today?"

He replied with a grunt.

"You didn't get home until pretty late last night."

"I told you." Hudson punctuated his words with the slam of his locker door, and he looked down at me as he hooked his backpack strap over his shoulder. "I lost track of time."

He had told me that, earlier today when we ate in Ms. Murphy's room, but I still wasn't convinced. Why? Hudson had his mean face down, but when he lied, he had the *worst* habit of blinking too frequently. It never failed. Each time I brought up last night, he'd blink three times before answering. A clear tell.

He started walking down the hallway, and I quickened my pace to catch up. "Maybe I can sit in with your little buddy lessons today? Please?"

"Don't you have a boyfriend to bother?"

I groaned, tipping my head back. "He wants me to come and watch him practice again. I'd rather take a pencil to the eye." And really, it wasn't like he explicitly asked today. It was lunch when the whole topic came up.

"You only came one time to watch Landon practice," Madison had pointed out, tipping her head in a superior way. *"What, he's not worth how boring you think it is?"*

"What does he see in her, anyway?" I muttered, glaring straight ahead as we walked.

Hudson glanced down. "What does who see in who?"

I looked in the opposite direction from the corner of my eye. "Uh, Connor. What does Connor see in Jade?"

Hudson shook his head, like he couldn't believe I'd stooped low enough to gossip about the Top Tier. I even had to cringe as the words came out of my mouth.

"Come on," I said as Hudson stopped in the middle of the hallway, and I leaned up to him. "Just let me sit in on your session. I'll be a fly on the wall. I'm dying to see who your mentor is since you said she came over."

Hudson stared straight ahead down the hallway of dispersing students, almost like his attention was caught on something.

"You said she's an underclassman," I went on, tapping my chin. "I don't know a lot of them, honestly. Is she on the Most Likely Tos? Ah, probably not, right? They normally aren't on the list."

Still no response.

"What are you looking at?" I asked, turning to look down the hallway. Most of the students had cleared by then, but there were a few stragglers, and it was clear why they stuck around. Wes Torres stood close to a few underclassmen girls with Trisha Clemms, his accomplice he sometimes made out with, and Trisha's friend stood behind him, closing in on the girl he paid attention to. I made a face. "For how old he is, he's way too attentive to younger girls. Seriously. He's been held back, like, twice, right?"

Hudson didn't answer. He was wholly focused on the group, still as stone.

"Do you know them?" I squinted closer at the underclassmen. The short-haired girl I didn't recognize, but the girl Wes zeroed in one, had nearly shoved up against the lockers, I knew her. Her long, dark braid hung down her back, and that alone gave her identity away. "That's Landon's little sister."

My thoughts began to scramble. *Should I go over there? I should, right?* I hadn't officially met Gemma because Landon said he wanted to keep us separate, but surely Landon would've wanted me to intervene in a situation like this. Right? Right?

Wes grabbed Gemma by the shoulder, and I sucked in a breath, taking a step forward before my second-guessing held me back. In response to Wes's touch, Gemma brought her knee up and slammed it between his legs—a beautiful connection, if I do say so myself—and Wes hit the ground. I went from anxious to impressed in a nanosecond, wanting to give her a pat on the back.

Wes got to his feet quickly, though, and that was when Hudson shot forward.

I opened my mouth to call after him, but he was already gone.

Out of all our years at Brentwood, I was certain that Hudson hadn't made one friend. How could he when no one was even willing to look him in the eye? I would've bet money that there wouldn't have been a single student he stood up for, intervened for. Until now.

Hudson shoved Wes into the locker beside Gemma, twisting his arm behind his back. I hurried over to them, because even though Gemma was now in the clear, the girl she'd been with wasn't. She was still on the ground, still in a fetal position. I walked up to the group that stood at a standstill, throwing my arm around Trisha's shoulders in a way that was more jostling than friendly. "Why don't you guys pick on someone your own size?"

Wes took that opportunity to sneer. "You offering, Churchill?"

This whole situation was bizarre. Wes picking on underclassmen wasn't new—he needed to be put on a watch list for when he was an adult, honestly—but Hudson positioning himself between Wes and Gemma was weird. I looked them both up and down.

All of that was running through my mind as Hudson took a step closer to Wes, his expression dark. "You touch her, and you deal with me."

My eyebrows shot up on my forehead before slamming down, and I looked at the scene with new eyes. Gemma didn't seem surprised the Grim Reaper was being her white knight. She didn't seem *afraid*, either. Even the girl on the floor didn't seem that shocked.

When Paisley had brought up the girl Hudson had over, he'd been quick to shut it down. Why did it matter who his mentor was...unless it was someone that I already knew. Someone that I would've been wary of.

No way. His mentor was *Gemma Settler*? Landon's *sister*?

Thankfully, the situation lost its tension rather quickly. I dusted the underclassman off while Wes and Hudson continued their bro-showdown, and I only half listened to it, still looking between Hudson and Gemma. Did Landon know they were meeting after school? Then again, it wasn't like he had a grudge against Hudson or anything. It was Hudson who'd gotten beaten up, not the other way around.

But why was Hudson keeping it a secret from *me*?

In the end, Wes and the girls ended up stalking off, leaving the four of us behind. Gemma kept sneaking glances at me, but in a suspicious way. Did she know who I was? Should I introduce myself? Hudson wasn't going to introduce me, so should I? Would Landon want me to? Probably not. It wasn't like Landon and I were *really* dating, and given the way things were between us now, I wondered if that would even last much longer.

Hudson convinced Gemma that they needed to go to Principal Oliphant, which I felt fifty-fifty on. Going to Principal Oliphant meant Hudson possibly getting in trouble, but then again, it might've been the least of his worries.

"Keep up the good leg work!" I called after Gemma, and awkwardly lifted my knee in case she didn't know what I was talking about. And then I wanted to smack myself for how cringe that was. And then I latched onto Hudson's arm, dragging him in the opposite direction of the girls, glaring up at him. "Gemma? Gemma *Settler*? She's your mentor?"

Hudson glanced back once before furrowing his brow. "It's not—"

"—like that?" I finished for him, unconvinced. "Seriously? Hudson, I mean, she seems super nice and all, but... there are so many reasons wrong with this, you know."

He scoffed. "You dating Landon is okay, but I can't have Gemma as my mentor?"

"*I* don't have a history with that family! Their mother doesn't know me. There aren't rumors about me. Landon is not a *sophomore*!"

"She's sixteen, I'm seventeen."

"Hudson, people will take anything you do and twist it into whatever they want. You *know* that." Which was why this choice definitely confused me. When Principal Oliphant paired them together in the first place, why hadn't he said no? Refused? Why hadn't *Gemma* refused? That had to be quite the story. "Wait, and she came over to the house on Monday?"

He closed his eyes, refusing to acknowledge the question.

"Is that why you didn't tell me? Because I wouldn't approve?"

"I didn't tell you because I knew you'd react like this. And you know, maybe I just wanted *someone* at this school. Tee goes to Jefferson, Derrick graduated—I only have you here, Lacey. And if you leave, I'll have *no one*." He hitched his backpack higher up on his shoulder, picking up his pace to stalk faster. "So sue me for trying to make at least one friend for when you eventually leave me in the dust."

I hadn't been anticipating the blow, and drew in a defensive breath too late. *It's a guilt trip*, my mind warned. *Don't fall for it.* Even still, it stung underneath my lungs. "I'm not mad about you making a friend," I insisted, hustling to keep up with him. "It's just, Gemma..."

"I could've said the same thing about Landon." When we got to the doors that led outside, Hudson stopped and turned to me, lips in a hard line. In that moment, he wore the Grim Reaper mask, and I'd always thought myself immune to it—until now. "I could've asked you why you'd pick one of the guys that had a hand in making my life hell. I could've asked you why, out of everyone at Brentwood, it had to be him."

I shrank back, filling with dread. It was funny how my body seemed to crave confrontation with everyone except Hudson, because at this moment, the urge to cry stung my eyes. "But you said you forgave him—"

"And I did." Hudson shook his head and looked away from me, like he couldn't hold eye contact any longer. "I'm just saying you're not in a position to be pointing fingers."

"I'm worried about you."

"How does it feel? How does it feel to worry about someone you care about, but they couldn't seem to care less? It sucks, doesn't it?"

If he'd slapped me, I didn't think it would've hurt as much. I stiffened almost as if he *had* hit me, looking up at my cousin as helplessness surged. He didn't stick around to listen to me try to piece together a response.

Without a word, he slammed the double doors leading outside open, and instead of turning left on the sidewalk toward the buses, he turned right.

My vision swam with tears unshed, but I refused to let them fall. The dig knifed through me. I *did* care that he worried—I didn't want him to. I didn't want him swept up in all of the insanity. It had happened once over the summer, and it wouldn't happen again. Didn't anyone get that? Couldn't anyone see that I was just trying to get out of their hair?

My backpack strap drooped off my shoulder as I stood motionless by the doors. In a matter of twenty-four hours, I managed to tick off every single Bishop family member. Of course, the one week where I would've taken work as a distraction was when Maestro decided to banish me. Because where was I supposed to go now? I couldn't go home. I couldn't face any of them.

It was times like this that I wished to be unknowable. I didn't want to leave because I wanted to hurt anyone—I wanted to leave so I *couldn't* hurt anyone. And no one seemed to understand that.

CHAPTER 20

shton's house was on the more expensive side of Brentwood. Not on Bleeker Avenue, but on an adjacent street with houses just as large and shrubbery that looked like animals. There weren't too many cars in his driveway—not nearly as many as I'd been expecting for a party—but then again, Landon *had* said this was a jocks only party. They probably all carpooled together from the game.

I slammed the shifter into park and stared up at the three-story structure, trying to imagine what someone would need with all the space. "How many rooms does his house have?"

"I don't know. Quite a few. And there's a basement."

I narrowed my eyes, hating the fact that Ashton had enough space to house five families while the Bishop house could barely hold one.

Landon looked over at me, his eyes searching mine. The ends of his hair had dried from his post-game shower—save for the tired look on his face, I never would've guessed he'd just had a football game. "We don't have to go in. We could go to Lookout Ledge again and look at the stars. We could go to the gas station and get some slushies. Could—"

"You do realize there's no point of a fake relationship if we don't *show off*, right?" I propped my elbow on my steering wheel. "At that point, we might as well be in a real relationship."

I'd said it to fluster him, but the boy seemed totally unaffected. "We show off every day at lunch. You come to my football practices and you came to the game tonight. We don't have to put on a show tonight."

There was something totally different about going to a party than going to lunch. No matter how much I wanted to take the out he offered, he had to see that. "Is Madison here?"

Landon paused to look around the driveway, and then he nodded. "That's her blue car over there."

"Then we're going," I decided, reaching for my seatbelt. "At least for an hour. And then I might take you up on the slushies."

"It's a deal," he agreed with a chuckle, climbing out.

It wasn't the sort of party that had music blaring the second you stepped out of your car, which was interesting. Not what I'd expected. Then again, the only party I'd been to was someone's eleventh birthday party. Maybe this was how high schoolers *actually* partied. Quietly with all the lights on.

Landon rounded the front of the van and swiped up my hand and fitted it perfectly in his, our palms pressed warmly together. I could feel his wrist bump mine, and when I looked down, I blinked in surprise at what I saw. His hand *did* look fine, but his forearms were filled with scratches and scrapes, and though some of them looked old, most of them looked new. "You're all scuffed up."

"Yeah, well. Comes with the territory."

"I don't like the territory," I muttered, smoothing his jacket sleeve back down to cover the injuries. It was funny how little scratches could leave me feeling so unsettled, but I couldn't get the image of Landon's head hitting the ground out of my mind. "You should stick to drawing."

"You haven't seen my work yet," Landon said, picking my hand back up and leading me toward the porch steps. "I could suck."

"Better to suck than have your bones broken. Or a brain injury."

Landon smoothed his free hand up my arm, a touch that was supposed to be comforting, but my skin trembled with it. "I'm careful, I promise."

When we walked into Ashton's large house, I heard the faint music, almost as if someone had it more for background music. The house had a very warm tone to it, like all the bulbs were more yellow than white. Landon led the way into the space, leaving me dragging my feet behind.

"God, *finally*," someone drawled from the grand living room, and practically everyone from the lunch table was sitting around the room. "There are the lovebirds. What, were you making out in your car?"

All of the seats on the couches were filled, and the overflow either stood around everyone or sat on the floor. Connor sat beside Jade on the couch closest to the door, and they craned their necks to look back at us. Madison sat on the arm of the chair beside Jade, but *didn't* look. Interesting.

"Wouldn't you like to know," Landon quipped, drawing me farther into the fishbowl of people. It felt like one giant sleepover, minus the pajamas.

"Landon, you can sit here," a guy who'd been seated on a plush chair said, hopping to his feet. "The winning quarterback ought to have a comfy seat for him and his girl."

I eyed the chair in question. It was big, but not big enough for us to sit side by side.

Landon didn't seem to question it, though. He sat down and made himself comfortable, his gaze slow to look up and meet mine.

As awkwardly as humanly possible, he patted his knee.

I stared at it for what felt like forever, but it had to have been only a second. I couldn't really sit on his *knee*, could I? Other than it being beyond uncomfortable, balancing on it would *look* weird, too. It wouldn't look couply. It would look forced. Fake.

All in or fold, my thoughts whispered, but I only had a second to consider before someone caught my hesitation. All in.

Instead of perching on the edge of his knee, I sat on Landon's lap, letting the arm of the chair support my back, trying *not* to let myself stiffen. If I thought about it, I'd be so beyond embarrassed, and everyone would wonder why my face was flaming. Heck, I was surprised Landon's cheeks hadn't turned red yet. Instead, he drew in a slow breath, resting his arm on the chair behind my back, his hand near my hip.

Sitting close to him like this had me thinking about the day in the hookup closet, and I absolutely *refused* to look at him. My heart picked up its pace in my chest. All of that probably took two seconds, but it felt like a lifetime.

"We were talking about homecoming next week," Connor said from his spot on the couch, smiling at the pair of us. He was the only friendly one in a room full of hostiles, and I latched onto him. "Did you hear we're on homecoming court?"

"You and Jade?" Landon asked.

"Duh," Jade said with a snort. "But you, too. You and Madison."

We both looked at the girl in question, who was too busy twirling her ponytail. Her expression was oddly tense, though, as if she was thinking about something else. "That's cool," Landon said appreciatively, but I could hear the effort he put into his voice. "So, I guess that means Madison and I are walking together?"

"I mean, yeah," Madison replied, blinking in surprise. "I'm sure our parents are planning it all out now, honestly. I wouldn't be surprised if they rigged it."

I stared at the cheer co-captain, thinking. I wouldn't have been surprised either—not if their parents rigged it, but if *they* did. The Top Tier. Jade, Madison. They had the weirdest ability to make everything go their way, and I wasn't sure I'd ever understand it. My fingers curled around Landon's shoulder, but I forced my voice to be light. "You know, I've been curious—who was it?"

Jade cleared her throat, a smirk still on her face. "Who was what?"

"Who did everyone vote for the MLTs?"

Landon's fingers came up to graze my hip, in a way I wasn't sure if it was in solidarity or scolding for bringing up the list.

"Please. Who remembers? It was weeks ago." Jade readjusted how she leaned on the couch beside Connor, and it was only then that I noticed they weren't touching each other. "We pick who we think would fit best."

"Wow, so Madison fits Peak in High School the best, then?" I bit down on my lip before tipping my head against Landon's. I got a big whiff of his shampoo he'd used in his post-game shower—a sweet lemony scent—and smiled. "I guess you got us wrong, though."

His fingers became a firmer pressure at my hip, thumb smoothing its motion gently. He ducked his head to kiss my shoulder, and when his lips brushed my jacket, he murmured, "Lacey."

Ah, so it *was* in scolding. Probably warning me to not let the situation devolve any further. The urge to dig my heels in, though, was almost intoxicatingly strong, but I backed off. For now. I moved my hand so I could thread my fingers into the wisps of hair at the nape of Landon's neck. "So, Connor," I said, changing the pitch of my voice. "Great touchdown today. You're so talented."

Connor rubbed his hand over his mouth. "Thanks, but I have to give it to my quarterback. Always with the great throws."

"My overstride was bad today again," Landon replied,

continuing to trace his fingers along my hip. His thumb was pushing the hem of my jacket around, almost sliding underneath. "You had to adjust to catch a few of the throws."

Connor raised an eyebrow. "Your parents tell you that?"

Landon just smiled.

Since there were so many people, there were also so many conversations happening around the room, all hushed, though. Madison was turned down to look at Jade, and her lips were moving fast, but I couldn't tell what she was saying. Jade looked over and met my gaze, eyes flashing.

Connor suddenly frowned. "Guys," he called to the room, drawing everyone's attention his way. "What the hell was up with the offensive line today? Why'd our quarterback take so many tackles?"

"He keeps the ball too long," Kyle, who was sitting on the ground by Madison's legs, piped up. His gaze was lazy as he looked at Connor. "We can't hold them back forever."

"You gotta be quicker with your decisions," Ashton added on. He was standing at the far end of the room, arms folded over his chest. "Maybe a tackle will teach you."

Landon lifted his chin, and when he drew in a breath, I could feel it expand against my side. "So you let the other team's players through on purpose."

Ashton gave a devilish smirk. "A time or two."

"So much for teamwork, huh?"

Ashton tilted his head condescendingly. "Hey, I didn't vote you my quarterback."

Landon clenched his jaw and broke eye contact, but

didn't respond like I wished he would've. In terms of hierarchy, Landon was totally above Ashton—so each time Landon let a snide comment slide, I wanted to jump in, even though I was sure Landon wouldn't have appreciated it. I slipped my fingers farther up Landon's hair, grazing his scalp. "You know what?" I said as Landon's eyelashes fluttered, probably worrying what I was going to say next. "Everyone has drinks—where are those?"

"I'll show you," Connor said, pushing to his feet. "Because if I stay in here a second longer, I'm going to punch Ashton's pretty face. Come on, Lacey."

"At least you admit I'm pretty," Ashton called cheerfully.

I withdrew my fingers from Landon's hair and got to my feet. "I'll get you something," I told him with a cutesy tone, hurrying off to follow Connor.

"I swear our parties aren't normally so...tense," Connor said as we walked down the hallway. The lights were on, of course, showcasing a horrifying display of yellow-patterned wallpaper cluttered up by expensive-looking art frames. Connor glanced back over his shoulder. "Then again, you bring a little trouble yourself, don't you?"

I didn't even try to stifle my laugh. "I take that as a compliment."

"You would." His voice was amused. "It's the fun kind of trouble, though. Ashton...he's the stupid kind."

"No argument there."

The kitchen was filled with dark wood and an orangey/yellowed color countertop, and despite how dated it looked, it was obvious it was expensive. Everything glimmered to catch the eye, showing off. There was an array of two-liter soda bottles lining the counters, a few stacks of red cups, as well as some other glass ones I didn't pay any attention to.

I picked up two red cups and flipped them over, inspecting the sodas. "You voted someone, didn't you?" I asked Connor, not looking at him. "For the list?"

"I did. But not Landon, if that's what you're thinking. And not you, either." He came up to the counter and leaned his back against it, looking at the wall. "Ashton put you down."

"Figures," I said with a snort. "I thought it was either him or your girlfriend."

Connor's lip twitched, but it didn't form into a full grin.

I picked Sprite, ultimately, since that was the only bottle left that was unopened. I broke the seal and poised to pour. "I'm disappointed, though. I thought you were one of the good ones."

"I like to think that I am." He frowned when he spoke, like he had a bad taste in his mouth.

"Do you regret it? Do you regret putting whoever you did on the list?"

Connor stared at me intently. I was so used to the happy expression he always wore, but this one was different. Less composed, more natural. I wouldn't have thought there'd been a difference if I hadn't seen him now. Ever so slightly, he nodded.

"Then I guess you're okay. As long as you regret it."

His eyes looked somber as he turned away, thoughts wandering.

"Hey, I've got a question."

He lifted his chin. "Shoot."

"Has there ever been anything...between Madison and Landon?"

I'd made sure to try and sound nonchalant, mildly curious, and I looked away from him as I asked. From the corner of my eye, I saw him shake his head. "Definitely not. Are you worried because they're on homecoming court together? Because—"

"I'm not worried," I rushed to say. "Really, I'm not. I just...I heard rumors that Landon used to like her. Since, like, elementary school or something."

"Where did you hear that?" Connor's eyebrows came together. "They didn't even go to elementary school together."

"Oh, I heard it somewhere—" I'd been so ready for the first half of his question that what he said following flew in one ear and out the other. And then it registered. "What did you say?"

"Madison and Landon didn't go to the same grade school. Madison went with me to Brentwood Elementary, and Landon didn't end up transferring to the Brentwood district until the seventh grade. I don't think he really even knew Madison until freshman year."

The revelation swirled around right along with confusion. I thought back to the day on the beach, Landon and I lying out in the sun. I'd asked him if he ever had a fate moment with Madison. *I think it was the fourth grade. We went to the same elementary together. It was Valentine's Day.*

I frowned, looking at Connor closer. He wouldn't lie. What reason would he have to lie? By why would *Landon* lie?

"So, yeah, you've got nothing to worry about with Landon." Connor reached over and nudged my shoulder, not noticing that I'd gotten lost in my thoughts, and I nearly spilled my soda. "That guy's head over heels for you."

My expression was reactionary—my server smile, the one I gave to customers when I knew they wanted me to chuckle at a lame joke they made, but didn't really feel like it.

Connor headed back into the living room before I did, and I slowly filled the second cup to the brim. No matter how many times I thought it over, it didn't make sense. So... Madison *wasn't* Landon's crush since elementary school, but he still liked her. Why lie about it? That would be the first thing I asked him as soon as we went back out to Petunia.

I shook my head as I grabbed the cups, heading back to the main room. I edged to the end of the hallway, the voices filtered to me, and I stopped around the corner of the living room. "I'm just saying," Jade said, sounding snooty as ever. "You guys don't seem *that* close."

"She was sitting in his lap," someone said defensively— I couldn't pinpoint the voice. "Which you aren't even doing with your boyfriend."

"Similar," Madison piped up. "You don't seem that *similar*."

"They say opposites attract," Landon replied, but even without seeing him, I could hear the waver in his voice. The nervousness of it. It had me inching forward. "But honestly, I'm the one dating her, so I don't see why you all have such an issue with it."

"No one has an issue," Connor tried to say, but Jade cut him off.

"You're only dating her because of the list. We all know it, Landon. If you're going to make us come out and say it, fine. But don't you think it's a *little* pathetic to stoop as low as *Lacey Churchill?*"

My fingers tightened on the plastic cup, and it bent, but didn't spill over. I pictured marching in there and dumping my Sprite on her pretty little ponytail, imagining the horrified expression on her face that would follow. It would ruin the couch, but it was Ashton's couch after all. Two birds. I was about to take a step forward, to charge into the room, when Landon spoke.

"Don't ever," he said, voice dangerously serious, "*ever* talk about her like that. Say whatever you want about me, but keep her name out of your mouth."

The entire room fell silent. I froze in my step forward, biting down on my lower lip. I'd never heard Landon's voice get so serious before. I didn't quite know he had it in him. The flush of warmth that soared through my veins was completely unexpected, because even though it was a good line, it was also in the way he'd said it. *Keep her name out of your mouth.*

I didn't need Landon defending me, but wow, oh wow. Hearing a guy who wouldn't stand up for himself stand up for *me* was so stupidly attractive.

It had effectively stunned the room, too. I took their

prolonged silence as my cue, and with a firm hold on the cups, I sauntered into the living room.

"So," I said sunnily, ignoring the tense atmosphere. "What were we talking about?"

Everyone stared at me as I approached Landon, *except* for Landon. He still stared Jade down as if waiting for her to say something else. I noticed a few girls leaning into each other to whisper something on the far side of the other wall, and Ashton had moved to lean against the back of the couch Connor sat at, his hands curled into the cushion. "You," he replied with the same amount of nonchalance. "You and Landon."

"Have you two even kissed yet?" Jade asked as I once more sat down on Landon's lap. Weirdly enough, it wasn't awkward this time, even though everyone was staring. Maybe it was because Landon's voice was still lingering in my ears.

I held onto the two cups, because Landon made no move to grab his yet. "Of course we have," I replied to her with a scoff.

"Prove it. Kiss him right now for us."

I arched my eyebrow at her. "You're into that sort of thing?"

Ashton rested his hands on Jade's shoulders, jostling her in her seat. "Jade, here, is curious how much your relationship's progressed, that's all. Isn't that right, Jade?"

Her response was a sour-faced expression.

"Go ahead and give her a peck, Landon," Ashton prodded. He lifted his chin toward me, "I'll give you five bucks."

"I'll give you ten," Connor added with a smile, though

his was friendly. It almost looked teasing. "Not that you need the incentive, but I'll help fund date night."

I gripped the plastic cups tighter, my heart starting to pick up on the situation we were finding ourselves backed into. I tried to get out of it. "You know how shy Landon is—"

"You don't want to kiss him?" Jade asked, looking like a cat about to swallow a mouse.

I shifted, causing Landon's leg to stiffen underneath me. I waited, but the guy never opened his mouth. Why wasn't he objecting? Why wasn't he pushing back? Was he going to let it happen? We didn't talk about how far was too far when establishing our fake dating rules, but I fully assumed kissing would be off the table for him. Because...I mean, *yeah*, it was just a kiss, but I didn't expect him to even consider it.

I turned to Landon, but he didn't look as embarrassed as I thought he would've. He met my gaze evenly, making it impossible to tell what he was thinking.

All in or fold. This time, my decision-making process was a whole lot slower. I'd had my first kiss back in the sixth grade, but if he'd been obsessed with Madison for who knew how long, would this be *his* first kiss? Was he okay with that? Was *I* okay with that?

But if I wasn't, if I backed away, then it was over. Everyone in this room would know we were faking it. Everyone's suspicions about Landon having a fake girlfriend would be confirmed. And while I didn't care about what his friends thought, I knew he would. It would be all over Babble, the talk of the school. Hudson would find out, would figure out I'd been lying, would never give me Petunia.

And even though I might've been able to leave and escape the fallout of the entire school knowing, Landon would be stuck in the middle of it. And maybe that was why he wasn't protesting—because in the end, the choice was either kiss or let everything fall apart.

I swallowed hard. "Hi?" I whispered, but it definitely came out as a question, one that also sounded more like a breath than an actual word.

I didn't think he'd do it. As Landon searched my face, I didn't think he'd actually do it. I thought he would finally make an excuse and turn away. Claim he had a cough. Say his lips were chapped. Fake a bathroom break. Never in a million years did I think Landon Settler would actually kiss me.

Until he did.

Landon's hand came up to rest on my cheek as he leaned in, pressing his lips to mine.

Once upon a time in a locker room, I thought this boy was bold for grabbing my hand without permission. And now, with the way that he kissed me, I realized him grabbing my hand was total child's play.

It wasn't a quick peck. Despite the eyes on us in the room, Landon kissed me deeply, firmly, like he'd done it a hundred times before. My heartrate, which had been beating fast before, absolutely hammered against my chest now like I was about to pass out. His lips were firm but soft, his fingers trembling a little against my skin. I clutched the cups of soda tighter, holding perfectly still so they wouldn't spill.

In the back of my head, I knew there were people around us, but for the brief moment in time, it was like we were the only two in the world.

Landon broke away with a sharp breath in, leaning back enough to look into my eyes. The flecks of green seemed deeper in the blue now, darker almost, like shadows bloomed in his irises. He blinked once, his reddish-brown lashes fluttering, before he turned to regard the room. My head swam, almost like I was dreaming—or drunk.

I shoved one of the red cups into Landon's hand, which he barely had his fingers wrapped around before I let go, and turned to the room. Unlike how it was the other day in the hookup locker, no one had their phones out now. Unlike then, no one was tittering and grinning, poking fun at the spectacle we made. No, in fact, almost every single person looked shocked as well, like what just happened wasn't something they expected in a million years.

Everyone except Connor, who grinned like an absolute fool. He was truly a Lacedon fangirl.

Clearing my throat, I looked between Ashton and Connor, reaching a shaking hand out, palm facing the ceiling. As evenly as I could, I told them, "Pay up."

CHAPTER 21

Safe to say, Landon and I didn't stick around long after that. Really, that seemed to dissolve the party. Who knew a kiss in front of twenty people would be so...awkward?

Literally everyone with a brain knew. But the Top Tier brought it upon themselves.

Landon's hand was stiff in mine as we made our way to the van, exiting the party with a few cheerleaders right behind us. They giggled about something, and the only way to keep my face from flaming was to convince myself they were laughing at something *other* than Landon and me. Even though it was unlikely.

I took my hand out of Landon's and rounded toward the driver's side, pressing my palms against my cheeks before opening the door. "That was fun," I said in a voice that was deceptively cheery, stabbing the ignition a few times before I could get my key in. "Super...fun."

Landon settled into the seat, not replying. He instead

looked down at the fifteen dollars he latched onto it as if it were a lifeline.

I started the engine, my headlights automatically sweeping over Ashton's stupid front porch. "What was that all about, pressuring us to kiss?" I asked as I pulled out of Ashton's stupid driveway, leaving him and the rest of the stupid crowd behind. Stupid, stupid, stupid. "Like, I would never want to see Connor and Jade kiss. I would have nightmares. Scarred for life. Why would they want to see *us*?"

"They didn't believe we were really dating," Landon said quietly, still staring at his money.

"Your friends are all pervs, *that's* why. Did you see Ashton egging you on? Total skeeve-city."

Landon didn't look up as I turned out onto the main road, leaving the rich neighborhood behind. "He's like that."

"And why didn't *you* say anything to stop it? They might've thought we were faking, but they would've backed off if you pushed it. No one expected you to actually—to actually—" *Kiss me.* Except I couldn't get the words out.

Landon shifted, almost as if he couldn't stand the idea himself.

I knew I needed to stop talking, but since Landon *wasn't* talking, my brain thought it needed to pick up the slack. "You prostituted our first kiss, you realize that? You and your fifteen dollars over there."

"I, uh—yeah. I guess...I did." He lifted his fistful of cash. "We can go halves."

"We *better* go halves! And while you're at it, you can explain to me why you lied about liking Madison since the fourth grade. Connor said you didn't even go to the same school with her."

Landon's head practically whipped toward me, the neck-breaking speed swift from the corner of my eye. "What?"

"Were you embarrassed you didn't have a fate story? You didn't need to have one. But you also didn't have to lie to me. You *shouldn't* have lied to me. With such an elaborate story, too."

Landon's hand tightened around the money; I could see his knuckles pale in the lights from the dashboard. "I didn't mean to lie, I just—you're right. I wanted a fate story. Make it look less...pathetic. That Valentine's Day story was the first thing I thought of."

I still made a face at the roadway in front of me, flipping on my blinker toward Brentwood's center. I felt jittery, jumpy, like I'd drunk a cup of coffee. Maybe it was because no matter how hard I tried, I couldn't stop thinking about what happened back there.

Keep her name out of your mouth.

And then his mouth.

On mine.

I slammed on the brakes to turn left, away from Brentwood, causing Landon to propel forward in his seat. The belt kept him from hitting the dash, but he slapped a palm to it anyway. "Where are we going?" he asked, sounding appropriately nervous.

Now it was my turn not to answer. And it didn't take Landon long to figure it out either, because once I turned onto Lookout Drive, the destination became pretty obvious. I accelerated up the winding hill, practicing my speech in my head as I did so. The more I thought about the words I had to say, the more the emotion built inside me, feeling almost like a dam about to burst. My body was ready for the battle, prepared for it, and it was ready to lay everything out.

The van slid as I braked across the gravel, stopping on the shoulder of Lookout Ledge. I left the engine running as I swung my door open, relishing in the peak of drama as I stepped out, but there was a legitimate reason I wasn't doing it in the van.

No way was I going to christen my independence-mobile with a breakup. Total bad juju.

Landon followed me out into the windy night, shutting his door behind him. "Where are you going?"

"Listen," I began, swatting my hair away from my eyes as I whirled around to face him. He stood half in the way of the headlights, his shadow reflecting against the stone of the bridge. "I think we should stop here."

Though it was mostly cast in darkness, confusion swept across his face. "Stop?"

"This." I gestured between us. "Us. Our fake relationship."

Landon took two large steps forward, his expression becoming clearer with each inch. "If it's because I kissed you—"

"Of course it's because you kissed me!" Now I threw my hands into the air, the dam breaking. "It's because you kissed me, and you made my heart flutter, and because you say kind and caring things to me, and it's making me all—all —*jumbled*. You're supposed to be the reserved one. You weren't supposed to kiss me."

Landon's lips parted. "You said hi."

"Yeah, but—but—" But he wasn't supposed to actually *do it*. "I *know* you were trying to be nice, saying I could call you on my way home from work and talking to me about my life problems. I know that everything you were doing was to be nice, but I can't deal with niceness right now. I thought I could help you win over Madison and walk away, but—" I shook my head, trying to clear the fog, but it was endless. There was no escaping, and no slowing down my ramble. "I don't think we can do it, Landon. If we haven't changed Madison's mind already, I don't think we can convince her like this, and I can't...I can't kiss you and walk away."

The wind swept past us again, tearing through my hair, at my clothes. I knew it was cold—it was late September at eleven o'clock, of course it was cold—but I didn't feel it at all. My skin was burning, probably hot to the touch. I curled my hands into fists as I stared up at Landon, my confidence slipping with each second that passed and he didn't respond.

"Then don't," he said, blinking rapidly. When Hudson blinked fast, it was a telltale sign he was lying. When Landon blinked fast, it was like he was trying to *think* fast, but too stunned to do so. "Don't walk away."

I narrowed my eyes at him, tilting my head. "You can't just fake date me forever."

"What if—" Landon stopped, drawing in a sudden, swift breath, cutting himself off. "What if it wasn't fake?"

I didn't think my frown—or my confusion—could get any deeper, but it did. "What about Madison?"

"You said yourself that we couldn't convince her."

"Oh, what, so I'm a good *backup*?"

"No!" Landon closed his eyes as he frowned, shaking his head. "*No.* These past few weeks have been really fun with you. I've liked it. Getting to know you, being close with you. And seeing how Madison's reacted to you changed things. She's not who I thought she was."

It was nice to hear, of course—it made me question his judgement less, if he didn't like the she-devil's sidekick— but I was hesitant to believe him. I stared at him skeptically. "You changed your mind awfully fast."

"Honestly?" Landon shifted on his feet, leaning like he was about to take a step forward. "I didn't really like her that much in the first place." I opened my mouth to protest when he rushed on, stretching his hands out. "I just wanted to get everyone off my back. I'll admit it now. I said yes because of the Most Likely To list. I said yes because I'd be proving my friends wrong."

"I distinctly remember you making it sound like people who proved the Most Likely To list wrong were shallow."

"That's why I made it sound like I liked Madison." His gaze was earnest as he looked at me, and in the depths, I could see the urgency behind his words as well as a tinge of guilt. "Your bet with your cousin was separate from the list, so it's not the same. I didn't want you thinking I was shallow. But...of course being on the Most Likely Tos bothered me. Voted by my friends that I'd never get a girlfriend. That's...hurtful."

I reeled with all the information, stuffed so full that I was sure brain cells leaked out my ears. My heart still had its arms folded, afraid to let go of the defensive shield, afraid to give in. "That's why you made up the Valentine's Day story," I said, looking at him warily. "Because you wanted to make it seem like you liked her?"

"I didn't make it up exactly. It was about a random girl in my class who'd done that. I—I shouldn't have lied. I should've been honest about why I agreed to the fake relationship, should've told you the further we got into it, I just —" Landon smiled a little, the boyish expression causing my heart to loosen its defensive stance. "I started having fun, too. And everything I said...it wasn't just to be nice."

Landon finally took the last step forward, the one he'd been hesitating on, and reached up to smooth my hair back from my face. His palms rested on my cheeks lightly, the size of them swallowing my skin in a way that made me feel delicate. "I shouldn't have kissed you," he said, blue eyes darting between mine. "Because it wasn't pretend for me anymore."

"You're not just saying that," I whispered, swallowing hard. My pulse stirred in my chest, hyperaware of how close he was. How his fingertips felt against my skin. "You mean it."

They were statements, ones full of doubt with the fear

of hope. I could've walked away. In that moment, I still could've done it. It would've been hard, and I might've had the lingering "what if" question for a while afterward, but I could've done it. If Landon backed off now, told me he only saw me platonically, I could've left Brentwood and never looked back. I had that thought a split second before he answered, but by then, it was too late.

"You can't walk away," Landon murmured gently, sweetly, his fingertips brushing against my temple. "I haven't drawn a picture for you yet."

And just like that, the moment between us felt sealed in time. Without hesitation, I grabbed a fistful of his shirt and tugged him hard toward me, crushing his mouth to mine. Before, when he'd kissed me, I held perfectly still, too stupefied to react. Now, I took full control of the way his lips pressed against mine with an urgency that had been building, peaking. He kissed me back with equal eagerness, allowing me to hold him in place while his hands still held my cheeks. His gentleness startled me, but it shouldn't have. It was so *Landon.*

Kissing him now, without any prying eyes...it was different in a weird way. My body still arched toward him on its own accord, and he still tasted the same, but it felt so much *realer* now. Two teenagers, making out on the side of Lookout Ledge, throwing all of the pretending out the window.

And it felt right.

This time, I was the one to draw back first, taking in his dazed expression before he had a chance to hide it. I fought to pull in a level breath, lungs aching. "That'll be fifteen dollars," I told him.

Landon let out a breathy chuckle, tucking my hair once more behind my ear, staring into my eyes. "Worth it," he replied, lips tipping up. "Definitely worth it."

CHAPTER 22

The next morning, I pulled into the driveway of a red two-story house, trying not to block in the minivan parked in front of the garage door. The front door was open, giving me a peek into the seemingly cluttered house. I reached for my seatbelt, but Paisley, still dressed in her unicorn pajamas, appeared on the other side of the glass and peeked out. She squinted, but recognized her father's car, and she hurried to gather her stuff she must've left close by. She rushed out of the house with her head down, hoisting her duffle higher up on her shoulder.

When she got to the backseat and hauled the door open, she stopped, gaping at me. "What are you doing here?"

I glanced over the seat. "Picking you up from your sleepover."

"You're in my dad's car."

"The van doesn't have a backseat with a seatbelt, and you're too young to ride in the front."

Paisley still hadn't climbed in. "Why didn't he pick me up? Or Hudson?"

"Your dad needed to shower after his shift and Hudson didn't come home until, like, after the sun came up." And he hadn't been quiet about it. He bumped into the doorway, and then the kitchen table, and then the coffee table, before collapsing onto the couch. Eventually, I nagged him enough to get him to go into his bedroom. He looked like a zombie, but he passed out before I had a chance to ask. I even had to take his boots off. "Climb in, Paisley."

No one could hold a grudge like a seven-year-old. She threw her duffle in with a vengeance, and when she was sitting down, she slammed her door shut, pressing as close to it as she could. As far from me as she could.

Think about this rationally, I thought as I backed out of the narrow driveway, forcing my shoulders back. *You were an angry kid at her age, too. How did you want to be talked to?*

"Listen, I'm not putting up with the cold shoulder," I said firmly, not looking in the rearview mirror. "We're not going home until you talk to me about what's going on."

"So you're kidnapping me then?"

"If that's what I have to do to get you to listen to me."

Paisley's jaw made an audible sound as it dropped open, and when I finally caved and looked in the rearview mirror, she was glaring at me. "If you're going to kidnap me, you should put me in the trunk, because I'm not listening."

My fingers tightened on the steering wheel. *You can't hit children.* "You're mad at me because I worried your brother and your dad by leaving last week, right?"

"No, I'm mad because you're messing up everything and you're not who I thought you were."

Now it was my turn to frown. "What do you mean?"

"I thought you were cool and fun, but you're not. You're selfish and mean."

"*I'm* mean?" I demanded, stunned. "The other day, you told me to leave and never come back. That's a whole lot meaner, don't you think?"

"You're mean to your mom!" she fired back. "You left her all alone and now you're making my family suffer for it."

Impulsively, I turned the steering wheel to the side and veered along the curb, slowing the car to a stop. I made sure to keep the doors locked, though—I didn't put it past the little gremlin to open the door. "I didn't leave my mom alone."

"You have a mom," she said, voice still livid. "You have a mom, and you don't even care. All you care about is leaving Brentwood, and you don't even care about the people you're leaving behind."

"I care—"

"You don't! If you cared, you'd still live at your house. That's why I hate you—if I had a mom, I'd never leave her alone."

It stung something fierce, listening to a kid tell you that they hate you. In Paisley's case, it stung, but it also made me unbearably sad. Out of all the reasons why she could've been mad at me, it never even occurred to me that it was because she didn't have a mom. In her eyes, it *would* look like I abandoned Mom. She was only seven—she couldn't possibly understand.

I turned around to face her, the seatbelt scratching my throat. "I didn't leave my mom, Paisley. She wanted me to leave."

It was clear she didn't believe me at first. Paisley's little features twisted into a livid frown. "Why?"

I bit down on my lip. Uncle Dean had said Paisley was too young to know the details, and I couldn't defy him on that, not totally. But there would be no bridging this gap with Paisley unless I could be a little bit honest. "You know, sometimes... Sometimes people are moms and dads when they don't want to be. And my mom—well, she was ready for me to grow up so she didn't have to be a mom anymore."

"You never stop being a mom or dad," Paisley pointed out, her voice softening, even if it was only marginally. "Even when Hudson and I get big, Daddy will still be our daddy."

"You're right, you're right." I half turned toward the front of the car, peering out the windshield. "My mom was just ready for me to get big too early."

I'd been in the third grade when I could remember the first time Mom talked about me growing up. It had been one of the rare times she took me out for ice cream, and I remember her being *happy*. Or at least looking it. Her eyes had been soft as she looked at me, like I was a cute puppy she wanted to take home. "*You're so independent*," she had said to me. "*I won't have to worry about you staying home past eighteen, thank goodness*."

I hadn't understood what that meant then, but the line

stuck with me. It stuck with me until I was old enough to understand what she meant.

I turned back around to find Paisley's expression faraway, like she was thinking about something hard. "I couldn't live with my mom anymore, and your dad didn't want me going off on my own, so that's why I'm living with you for now. It's not forever, but just for now. And I never, ever wanted to mess everything up. I never wanted to be selfish. I never wanted things to be so upsetting for you, Paisley, and I'm sorry."

Something like worry flashed across her big eyes. "Does my daddy want to be a dad?"

I unclicked my seatbelt and turned to face her, lowering my voice. "Your daddy *loves* being a dad. That's why he took me in with no hesitation. He loves your game nights, and hanging your drawings on the fridge, and listening to you about your day. He loves tucking you in at night. Uncle Dean is a great dad—he's the dad I never had."

"Then why did you leave the other night? Why did you make him worry?"

"That *was* me being selfish." A sudden pressure built behind my eyes, throat stinging with the taste of tears before they'd even had a chance to form. "I wasn't thinking about anyone but myself. But I was...I was just very sad."

Paisley stared at me, the anger that'd scrunched her brow for the past weeks finally letting up. With it, some of the weight on my chest disappeared, though not completely. Talking about my mom always left me feeling disconcerted, like I was sand that had yet to settle at the bottom of a stream.

"I know all mommies aren't good ones," Paisley said eventually, picking at her fingernails. "Oakley says her mom spends more time with Braxton's dad than their family."

I looked to the side. "Uh—"

"But I didn't know your mom wasn't a good one. No one told me."

"When you're older, people will tell you more. They're just afraid of scaring you." I reached out to her and squeezed her knee, right over a unicorn on her pjs. "But don't ever worry about your dad, okay? He's as good as they come."

Paisley put her hand over mine and gave it a measly squeeze. "My mom was a good mommy, right? When she was alive?"

"She was an amazing mommy." The stinging came back behind my eyes. "She used to come by for sleepovers or bring me over when my mom was busy. She'd buy the good ice cream bars. She taught Hudson how to braid your hair. The *best* mommy."

I expected Paisley to look sad, but she didn't, not really. She didn't know anything other than life without a mom— she didn't know what to miss. That was how I'd been at her age, before I realized my life didn't look like other kids' lives. When I realized that my normal wasn't really normal at all. One day she'd realize it, though. She'd feel the pinching pain of moments she wished she had her mother. I knew she would, because I did.

I turned back toward the front and gripped the steering wheel, swiping at the tear that had fallen onto my cheek.

There were signs of life in the Bishop household when we pulled into the car park. The door was open and letting in fresh air through the screen, and when I opened my door, I could hear something clanking within. "You go ahead," I told Paisley, slipping my cell from my pocket. "I'll be inside in a second."

She hoisted her duffle bag over her shoulder and nodded. "You think my dad will make us pancakes?"

It was only nine-thirty, so not out of the realm of breakfast time. "Doesn't hurt to ask."

As she ventured into the house, I made my way over to the van, popping open the back. The mattress pad was still bare without blankets, but I hopped up onto it anyway, letting my legs dangle over the side. I glanced around the space, something uncomfortable tugging behind my ribcage. Confusion. It caused my lungs to ache as they expanded.

Ever since agreeing to the bet with Hudson, I'd had a clear end goal with an even clearer D-Day: Convince him I had a real boyfriend so I could ride off into the sunset on my eighteenth birthday. My checklist, my rest stop research, my mapped-out routes—I had all of it ready for a week from today.

But Landon's face popped up behind my eyes. If I left Brentwood in a week, I'd be leaving him behind. It shouldn't have mattered. As much as I liked Landon, and as fun as these past few weeks were, he couldn't sway my decision. Suddenly having a boyfriend didn't invalidate every other reason I wanted to leave. Having a boyfriend shouldn't have affected my plans in the least.

And yet...

I unlocked my phone and opened up the photos that Landon and I had taken together. My lips twisted a little at our very first—very awkward—photo, where I'd sidled up alongside him after his football game. His smile was small, and looking back, mine was my serving smile—no true emotion behind the eyes. When did it happen for him, I wondered. That day at the beach? When did it stop being fake and start being real?

I loaded back up the photos from the beach and studied his freckled face and squinted eyes, almost as if I were committing it to memory. Next week, on my birthday. Could I walk away and leave it like this? Say *see ya* to the first guy who'd made me feel something? On paper, the answer was easy. Of course I could. It wasn't like we were soulmates. We were in high school. We'd been fake dating for two weeks, and only *seriously* dating for less than twenty-four hours. I didn't understand why my heart braced itself at the idea of leaving, digging its heels in.

Annoyingly enough, I remembered this was exactly why Hudson made the bet that I needed a boyfriend in the first place. This was exactly what he wanted to happen. For me to doubt.

Impulsively, I loaded Landon's contact info and pressed the call button. My stomach flipped at the prospect of hearing his voice, but as it rang, I flopped down on the bare mattress, readjusting my phone against my ear. Was he still asleep? Was he the type to sleep in on weekends?

And then—"Hey, sorry," Landon said right before the

voicemail kicked in, sounding breathless. "I didn't hear my phone."

At the sound of his voice, lightness replaced the weight on my chest. "That's okay." I kicked my feet against the back of the van. "Whatcha doing?"

"Weightlifting."

"Jeez, you don't even take weekends off?"

"I haven't been doing it much since I pick you up in the mornings," he said, but his voice was kind. "Gotta keep the throwing arm in shape."

I reached up and traced the metal of the ceiling with a fingertip. "*Just* your throwing arm?"

It made Landon laugh suddenly in my ear, the sound tickling down my spine.

"I work tomorrow from eleven to four. You could stop by." I drew the words out like they were an incentive, tipping my head back and forth. "If you wanted. I can get you twenty-five percent off on any entrée of your choice."

"Twenty-five?" he asked in a shocked voice. "What a steal."

I pressed my palm over my smirk as if it could shrink it. "In exchange for you drawing me, of course. It could even be on the back of a napkin."

"I think I can do better than the back of a napkin," he replied, but then sounded muffled. "I—think—would you knock it off? It's a five-minute break, give it a rest."

Someone replied, but I couldn't make out who it was. "Football buddies?"

"Yeah." He sighed, like that fact annoyed him. "What

time did you say you were working tomorrow? I'll swing by. Can't pass up the twenty-five percent off shrimp poppers."

"Eleven to four." It was my first shift post-banishment, and thank goodness it was a shorter one. I was sure my legs had forgotten what it was like to stand all shift. "We could always do something after instead. It might be boring to come in while I work."

"How about I come at the end of your shift and wait until you're done."

I smiled at the ceiling. "Deal."

"Deal," he echoed, and even though I couldn't see him, the grin in his own voice was plain as day. "I should go before Ashton decides to drop a weight on my foot."

Before I had a chance to respond, there was a scuffling sound over the phone, and a second later, it wasn't Landon's voice in my ear. "You can talk dirty to loverboy later," Ashton said with devilish amusement. "I'm keeping him busy right now. Unless you want to put it on speaker."

I sat up, slouching over so as not to hit my head on the ceiling. Without replying, I ended the call. It would've been a perfect world if Landon didn't spend any time with Ashton, but I'd only just become his actual girlfriend—I didn't want to bring up talk about him cutting people out. If I did, I didn't think I'd be able to stop with Ashton.

Someone knocked on the side of the van with their knuckles, and a second later, Uncle Dean appeared around the open back. "Hey, kid."

I brightened. "Hey. Did Paisley convince you on pancakes?"

"She did. I've got the pan heating up now."

The way Uncle Dean lingered made it clear that there was something he wanted to say, but I figured I'd start first. "I told Paisley about Mom. Not the full story, but enough so she won't be so angry with me anymore."

"It's what we should've done from the start." He pressed his lips together, causing his smile lines to stand out. "I didn't realize keeping it from her would cause so many problems."

"You wanted to protect her. She's seven. You can't really fault that."

"I wanted to protect you, too," he said, holding my gaze. His watery blue eyes were serious, but filled with a gentleness that reminded me of Hudson without his Grim Reaper mask. "But you were right. Just because you're young doesn't mean you don't have to deal with adult problems sometimes."

"I *am* almost an adult, you know. One week from today."

"True." Uncle Dean leaned against the edge of the van, his gaze peering around on the inside. I wasn't sure the last time he'd seen the progress, but he took it all in now, eyes flicking about the interior. "Have you, ah—have you decided what you're doing for your birthday, then?"

I wasn't sure if he meant how I would celebrate, or where I'd be. Whether or not I'd be in Brentwood. Whether or not I'd be on the road. "Still thinking about it," I answered, kicking my feet once more. "But I'll be sure to let you know."

"Dad!" Paisley's voice came in piercing through the moment. "The pancake is burning!"

"I didn't put one on," he called back, straightening.

Paisley's voice rose again, this time sounding more nervous. "I, well—I sort of did, but I can't flip it, and now it's burning—"

Before she could get another word out, Uncle Dean raced away from the van and toward the house, leaving me chuckling in his wake. It felt good to be on the same page with Paisley after months of tiptoeing around the issue, and it felt good to clear things up with Uncle Dean.

I had a week to make a decision about what I would do on my birthday, but no matter what the outcome would be, I'd make the most of this week. No matter what.

CHAPTER 23

$\mathcal{A}$h, Le Petit Bateau. The smell of fish and fryer grease. The ungodly amount of garlic bread. The servers fighting with the grill cooks. Maestro hiding out in his office until he was needed. Was it weird that it felt like home?

"Behind," I called Sunday afternoon as I swooped my loaded tray behind Cha's back. Instinctively, she pressed against the counter, not pausing her typing in the computer. The smooth linoleum from behind the server line switched into the short carpet of the dining room, and the noises of silverware clattering filled the air as I approached my table. I readjusted the way I held my tray as I unloaded it, making sure to keep it balanced throughout the whole process. "This smells heavenly today," I said as I laid the plate of seasoned salmon in front of the woman. I watched her eyes light up. "You'll have to let me know how it tastes."

"Oh, she will," the man said with a laugh. "She'll let everyone know."

"This place has the best salmon," she said happily, picking up her fork. "You're the best, dear. Thank you."

I gave her a grin.

"I'm impressed," Cha said as I made it back to the server line, tapping her pen against my chin. "You've kept your smile on your face all day. You haven't slacked once. Not even when that old lady said your nose ring was unprofessional."

"People need to be more original." I collapsed against the obscured counter beside her, taking my break from the public eye. My feet ached something fierce, and I rocked onto my heels to try and alleviate the pain. "You'd think my nose ring had fallen into their meals with how upset people get over it."

"I wouldn't mind it falling into my food," Cha said as she leaned in closer, inspecting it. "It's pretty. And shiny."

I tipped my head back, not even wincing when it struck the side of the computer. I had about an hour left of my shift, which meant Landon would be arriving any second. I'd be taken off the rotation soon so I could clean my station—today, I was assigned to keeping the drink station clean—and roll my silverware. I might not be able to serve him, but he could sit across from me as I rolled silverware. I couldn't imagine Maestro complaining about that.

When I lowered my chin back down, I had a straight view into the grill line through the warming window, where Nate had his head bent. He had a beautiful hairnet on, and I had the strongest urge to take out my phone and snap a picture.

He looked up and caught me staring. "Did I miss a food ticket?"

I waved my hands. "Nope. The rush is over, Nate. Take a breath."

He made a dramatic show of raising his shoulders and letting them slump. "Your shift almost over?"

"Thankfully." I patted my apron pocket, where all of my bills were stashed. "And I was tipped good today."

"How good?"

I actually didn't know. For the first time probably ever, I didn't pull my tips out mid-shift and count them as they piled up. Normally it was such a habit, taking all the bills out and straightening them into one clean fold, imagining adding it to my savings the second I got home. Today, I didn't even keep track.

The door to the back of house slammed open as Maestro walked through, surveying the scene the way a captain would survey the waters. He then looked over at me. "How many tables you got?"

"One. I just served their food."

Maestro checked his watch, pursing his lips. "Seat the door, and they can be your last table. How are your outs?"

"I still have to fold my silverware. I'm waiting to restock the drink station til the last minute."

Maestro lifted his fingers and saluted me. "Cool, cool. Cha? Think you can hang on until Kelsie gets in?"

I peeked over the partition to see how many people were waiting by the door, and beamed when I recognized the boy. Swiping up one roll of silverware, I rounded the server line and made my way to him. "Perfect timing," I greeted, tucking a piece of hair that'd come free from my braid behind my ear. Thankfully, I hadn't been running around like a maniac since an hour ago, so if I was sweaty, it dried. "You're my last table."

"I'll go easy on you, I promise," he replied, coming close like he was about to reach for me.

"Now it's my turn to warn you not to get too close—I'm betting fish grease is a worse smell than sweaty football player."

"Don't bet on it," Landon teased back, returning my smile with one of his own. "You look so cute."

"It's the pigtails," I said, tousling one as I picked up a menu with my other hand. "Booth or table?"

He pretended to think about it. "Booth."

I led him through the aisles to one of the booths available, but the one farthest from most of the other tables. When Landon sat down, I slid into the booth seat on the other side of him, leaning my forearms onto the table. "I have a few minutes if you want to get started. My left side is my good side."

I expected Landon to laugh it off, but he surprised me by taking his roll of silverware and unwinding the napkin, flattening it on the table. "Like you have a bad side," he said with a shake of his head, pulling an ink pen out of his pocket.

"Are you really going to do it?" I leaned farther across the table, blinking at him. "You're going to draw me?"

"You said you wanted me to. You can't laugh if it looks bad."

"Let's see if you have a career other than football."

Landon lifted his gaze to mine and searched my face. "What if I only like drawing you? Can I make it a career, drawing different renditions of Lacey Churchill?"

I laughed. "I'll singlehandedly fund your career."

Landon's freckles were illuminated by the Le Petit Bateau lights, and they made his hair look redder, too. As he tipped his head to look up at me, I sat still for a moment. Once upon a time, he'd told me about how when he was little, he had more freckles and redder hair, and that he was picked on for it. A flash of what he might've looked like as a little boy danced through my head, almost like I knew firsthand.

"When did it happen?" I asked.

"When did what happen?"

"When did you realize you liked me?" I pinched my lips together a bit, trying not to feel awkward as I asked. "That it wasn't fake anymore."

Landon blinked three times as he processed the question, but even though he parted his lips, he didn't answer right away. His gaze dipped to the left, and I had the weirdest thought. *Is he thinking about it or is he about to lie?*

"I'm not sure," he said eventually, slowly, his pen lifting from the napkin.

"Is that bad if you don't know?"

"When did *you* realize?"

"There were a lot of moments where I wasn't sure," I told him, leaning my cheek against my fist. "Like you leaning into me against the van. Or when you buried your face in my neck in the hookup closet. But I think I knew for sure that I liked you the night we sat out and looked at the stars."

"I think it was the same for me." Landon reached across the table and took my face delicately in his hands. I could feel the cold press of his class ring against my cheek. "When you grabbed my face like this. Honestly, I thought you were about to kiss me when you did that."

My heart fluttered. "Oh, you thought so?"

"I wanted you to." He dropped his palms to the table, but the heat remained in my cheeks. "I really, really wanted you to."

The confession was a soft collection of words that caused my skin to heat. I bit down on my lips to keep them from curving, and the corners of his lips turned up as our eye contact continued, causing other thoughts to surface. I needed to get up, to make sure that my table didn't need me, but I allowed myself another moment to consider the boy across from me, freckles and all. I knew I needed to say something about my birthday, but admitting that I was on the fence with my decision felt...wrong. How could I tell him I was thinking about leaving still? What if he took it the wrong way?

Then again, was there even a *right* way to take that?

"What are you thinking about so hard?" Landon asked gently, tilting his head to the side, lips taking on a teasing tilt. "You're thinking about kissing me, aren't you?"

My own mouth split into a smile. "The employee parking lot of Le Petit Bateau will be empty after my shift. We could kiss a little then."

Landon cleared his throat, and I watched his cheeks

grow pink. "That's—that's an option. A good option. A great one, really."

I laughed as the atmosphere lightened, closing my eyes as I leaned deeper into the booth. "I have to go home," I told him.

"Home? Why?" He started blinking fast. "Did—did I seem too eager about what you said?"

I snorted again. "No. If you seemed any less eager about kissing me, I would've been offended." I opened my eyes and placed my palms on the table. "I meant I have to go back to my mom's house. Not after work, just...sometime."

Landon reached over and slipped his hand underneath mine, palm to palm. Silent support, and it made my heart squeeze. "Why?"

"There are only so many times I can wear the same outfits, and I need to get some things for the van." I actually had a list of the things I wanted to get. Clothes. My birth certificate. My bedding. And really anything else that looked important. I hadn't been in my bedroom for months, so there obviously wasn't anything *too* major in there, but I couldn't remember if there was anything I wouldn't want to leave behind. "But I don't want to go. I don't want to see her, or see the house. And I don't want to go alone, but I know Uncle Dean won't *want* me to go, and I can't ask Hudson." The last time I asked Hudson to come with me to see my mom, it'd landed the both of us in the back of a cop car.

"I could go with you," Landon suggested as he brushed

his thumb along the back of my hand. "That way you aren't going by yourself. I could wait in the car."

"Why would you want to?"

"Just to be with you."

I looked at our hands, and the way we held them together. It felt like yesterday when I held his hand for the first time, figuring out which way it felt most comfortable. I never thought I'd be doing it now, with no eyes around to see it. "You always say the right thing." I narrowed my eyes at him, fighting to keep my lips from curling. "It makes me suspicious."

It was almost astounding how different he was from the other Top Tier members. I thought everyone lived in their little self-absorbed bubbles, but it was like Landon was from a different friend group entirely. Like he'd been spared from the drama-loving mindset that came with the popular clique. He was just...normal. I wondered if it was because he said he was picked on when he was little—if that stuck with him enough to keep him more down to earth. I couldn't imagine any of the others being bullied.

"You meant it," I said after the beat of silence, one in which the tacky music playing over the speakers took over. "You would come with me when I'm ready to go?"

The question held far more weight than he could've ever known, mostly because the act of going home was... huge. It seemed impossible to face, especially alone. But he offered to come. The boy that seemed to balance out the feelings and fears and anxieties. He was the one person I felt like I could show everything to, the one who would listen to it all.

When Landon spoke, my chest caved with the words and the soft way he said them, like they were a promise. "I'd go with you anywhere. When you're ready, let me know."

I slipped out of the booth then, because I'd been sitting down too long, pressing my luck—Maestro was bound to do his rounds any minute. But before walking away, I took a quick glance around the restaurant, and once I made sure no one was looking—and made sure Maestro had retreated back to his office—I slipped out of my booth and bent down to give Landon a kiss. Our lips only touched for the briefest moment, but electricity seemed to zing between us, and I grinned against his mouth. "This can be your payment," I said when I leaned back, tapping the bare napkin in front of him. "For the drawing."

"I think your card was declined," he said, reaching up and looping his hand around my wrist. He tugged me closer. "You should try again."

This time, there was no fighting the grin. "I'll get you a water," I told him, hurrying off toward the server line before he had another chance to sway me.

Cha was inputting another order into the POS system when I approached, shaking her head at me. "I saw your PDA out there. I'm torn between high-fiving you and slapping you in jealous rage."

"Definitely slap me," I said, moving to the drink station. "Turn our workday into an episode from a soap opera."

Cha smirked at her screen as the front door chimed again, and people moved into view. "A four-top?" She glanced over toward the door, her jaw dropping. "Oh, whoa. No way."

I turned to look closer too, freezing as I filled Landon's water. Ashton, Kyle, Jade, Madison—the four people I wanted to see the least. They were less noticeable without Brentwood spirit gear on, but equally as insufferable.

The water from the glass overflowed onto my hand, and I yanked the glass back with a swear. "Tell them we're closed," I said as the host made their way over to the group. I watched Jade point at where Landon was sitting. "You've got to be kidding."

Of course now that we've decided to stop faking was when Landon's friends decided to butt in. And of course they wanted to be added to my table, my *last* table, which meant my one-top suddenly turned into a five-top.

Cha, at least, looked sympathetic as I gathered four more rolls of silverware. "More tips," she tried to say cheerfully, but we both knew the truth.

"I'd be shocked if any of them *did* tip," I muttered, and with the silverware and Landon's drink in my hand, I made my way back to the table.

Madison slid into the booth beside Landon, with Jade and Ashton on the other side. Kyle had pulled up a chair on the end of the table, blocking the aisleway. It was technically a fire hazard, but I wasn't going to say anything. "Look what the fisherman reeled in," Jade said when I got close enough, fluttering her fingers at me. "And you even smell like fish. This place is *super* authentic."

"Aw, look how cute you look with those pigtails," Ashton said. He looked like all the typical rich boys who came into Le Petit Bateau, with their collared button-downs and fancy-looking boat shoes. "I might've come to see you at work sooner if I knew."

I fantasized about how lovely it'd be to flash him my middle finger, and I totally would've, if I could've been certain a customer wouldn't have seen. Instead, I looked at Landon, who had stashed his napkin and gave me a help-less look. "Welcome to Le Petit Bateau," I said in a dull voice, plastering on a watered-down version of my server smile.

"Ashton overheard Landon mentioning he was coming to visit you at work today, and Jade thought we should tag along," Madison said as she looked up at me. I didn't know why she felt the need to explain, but I could've kicked her for it. Just because. "You're not mad, right?"

"They're not staying," Landon said, glaring at his friends. "Or eating. So you don't have to worry about them."

Kyle muttered something about wanting fish sticks, but I didn't listen. "Wave me down if you need anything," I said instead, and without another word, I went to check on my tables.

It doesn't matter, I tried to tell myself. They could keep Landon company while I worked, but it wasn't like they'd stick around to hang out afterward.

I checked back on Salmon Lady—who was totally blissed out as she devoured her fish—and dropped the check off on my other table. As I passed by it, I could hear the voices of the Top Tier carry, and I slid into an empty booth to listen in.

"Seriously, though, why?" I heard Landon hiss, voice exasperated. "Why are you seriously butting into *everything*?"

"That's what friends are for." That was Jade. "Besides, you're here to watch her work? How boring."

"I bet *she* finds it flattering, though, huh?" Ashton said, sounding quieter. "What'd her face look like? Was she excited to see you?"

"*Stop.*" Landon's voice was low and threatening, just as it'd been for the briefest instant Friday night. "In fact, just leave. Because you're not helping."

"I can't imagine we'd *hurt* anything," Ashton replied. "From what I saw Friday, she's totally into you already."

I made a face at the empty booth across from me, straining to hear Landon's next words, but they were too quiet. Whatever he said, though, caused Kyle and Jade to laugh, their volume much louder than it needed to be.

I slid out of the booth and made my way back to the serving line with my hands balled into fists. Nate ducked down to peer at me through the warming window. "Did I see Ashton and Kyle?"

"Unfortunately." I walked up to the warmer and leaned in, letting the heat melt my face. "How do you do it?"

"What?"

"Stay sane around those people."

Nate smiled, but it almost looked like more of a grimace. "I have one more year left with the worst of them. It helps to think happy thoughts."

Nate got back to work as I turned to peer over the parti-tion, finding the heads of the Top Tier as they bent together, talking. Landon was facing the server line, so I could see his serious expression, but I couldn't read his lips from here as he talked hurriedly. Could I really stand the rest of the schoolyear around all of them? It wasn't like they were fabulous friends to begin with. They put him on the Most Likely Tos, for crying out loud. They obviously didn't have his best interest at heart.

I looked at the way Madison was sitting beside him, leaning in, looking at him as he spoke. It was stupid that jealousy sprang up. Beyond stupid. Landon had already assured me Friday that there was no reason to worry about him having feelings for Madison, but seeing them together caused something uneasy to stir within me, like I was looking at a trap being set.

Cha came out from the back to load her food up to serve, catching a look at my expression. "Your smile's gone," she pointed out.

I forced my lips to lift, but even I could feel how plastic and fake it was.

CHAPTER 24

*H*omecoming week started off as a major bummer, mostly because Landon and I barely saw each other. Since I worked the closing shifts at work, clocking out when Landon's curfew went into effect, we could only deal with stolen phone conversations, whispered so no one could hear. I could only really see him at school and during our lunch period, and even then, that time was taken up by the Top Tier members and their snarkiness. Weirdly enough, though, Jade wasn't on an insult kick like usual, but that probably had to do with the fact that Madison had stopped sitting at the lunch table.

"What's with that?" I asked Wednesday afternoon as Landon and I walked hand-in-hand to lunch. Something about the grip felt different, but I couldn't put my finger on it. "Why isn't Madison sitting with the Top Tier?"

Landon shook his head. "Not sure. Connor said Jade and her have been touchy lately. I doubt the competition for them to be homecoming queen is helping."

"Ugh, they *would* fight over that."

"It's silly," he agreed. "At least Connor is obviously the shoo-in for king. I think I'd have a panic attack over the attention."

"You never know what'll happen," I pointed out, shifting my grip on his fingers, and then I realized why our grip felt different. I looked down, lifting our hands. "Where's your class ring?"

I'd only seen Landon without his ring at his practices or at games; otherwise it always adorned his finger. I couldn't believe it took me this long to notice it was missing.

With the question, Landon stopped in the hallway. I half expected him to be shocked, worried, as if he hadn't noticed its absence either. Instead, he glanced around the hall, at the kids who sidestepped around us, not-so-subtly eavesdropping. "It's cheesy," Landon said finally.

I blinked. "What's cheesy?"

"And I know I already asked once before, but that was before we were official. It's okay if you still don't want to, but I figured—"

"Landon." I cut him off with a tilt to my lips, tipping my head at him. "You're rambling."

Taking his hand out from mine, Landon reached into the pocket of his jeans, and with what seemed like a steeling breath, he pulled something out. When he opened his palm, he revealed his class ring in it, with a thin silver chain threaded through it. It pooled against his skin. "It wouldn't fit on your finger," he said softly as we both peered at the ring, "but a necklace would work. If you wanted to wear it."

Something inside me went soft and gooey, like a piece

of chocolate left out too long in the sun. Maybe it was the way he spoke, in a tentative murmur, or the way his gaze would hold mine for a second, flit away, and then come back. Maybe it was the class ring in general, something that had seemed cheesy until this moment. *I feel like that's something you should give your girlfriend*, I'd said back when it wasn't real, but it was real now. This was real.

With a strange pressure in my throat, I lifted my chin as an answer.

Landon picked up the chain and used his fingers to ease it over my head. The chain was long enough that the ring fell in the middle of my chest, like a pendant. I reached down and brushed my finger across the stone immediately, tracing the *SETTLER* engraving. Things could change so quickly in such a short amount of time—it was still hard to believe.

When we got to the lunchroom, Landon went off toward the Top Tier table while I went to join the lunch line, still staring down at the ring. It was a small thing, me wearing his class ring, but it made my skin warm.

Today was hamburger day, though the smell was less than enticing—burnt, greasy meat didn't smell all that appetizing—I was ready to eat anything in sight. I stood in line alone, tapping my fingers against my plastic tray, bouncing on the balls of my feet.

"Lacey, right?"

I jumped at the voice in my ear, turning to find a girl standing on her tiptoes behind me. It was the girl from Landon's practice that one day, with the big glasses and notepad. She didn't have a notepad now, but her glasses were low on the bridge of her nose as she blinked up at me. "Oh. Hey," I greeted, pressing a hand to my chest. "You scared the crap out of me."

"I know Brentwood is big, but I didn't realize how hard it'd be to cross paths with you."

I eyed her up and down, but something about her put me on edge, like I had to be extra careful what I was going to say. She sought me out individually. Creepy. "What's up?"

She leaned in closer, causing me to fight the urge to lean back. "It's about your boyfriend."

My heart instinctively jumped at the mention of Landon and the ominous way she'd said it. I looked out across the lunchroom, spotting the Top Tier table—and our empty seats. "What about him?"

She leaned in farther, letting me catch a whiff of her sweet floral perfume. It was so much prettier than my Target perfume, leaving me wondering where she'd gotten it. But all thoughts of perfume vanished with her next words. "He's not really your boyfriend."

I jerked back from her this time, shocked. "What?"

"He's faking it," she whispered, expression growing earnest. "He's only pretending."

At first, her words caused my stomach to feel as if it dropped, but only for a second. Because as I realized what she said, a smile spread over my face, one filled with relief. "Oh. Yeah. I know."

Now it was her turn to frown, and her eyebrows disappeared beneath the rim of her glasses. "You know?"

I gestured for her to come closer, to which she complied. "Because I was pretending, too."

The poor girl was clearly and obviously confused, eyes darting back and forth like she was watching a tennis match. She reached up and tugged her fingers through her hair, tapping the back of her head. "I don't get it."

"It's okay. But I appreciate you telling me if you thought it was true." I patted her shoulder, but then frowned. "Wait—how did you know that, anyway?"

The girl lifted her chin. "I have my sources."

"Stalking?"

"I'm not a stalker. It's not like I'm *sitting* on this information. Everything has a purpose."

"And your purpose is...making the most epic yearbook for the Top Tier once senior year is over?"

She rolled her eyes a little, shuffling forward with me in the lunch line. "Classified, I'm afraid. But...well. I didn't realize you knew."

I set my tray down on the table when I got to it, and watched as the lunch lady set a hamburger on it. I plucked a cookie up off the shelf near the register and paid quickly, offering the treat to the girl. "I appreciate you wanting to tell me, though. Really."

The girl took the cookie slowly, almost like she expected it to bite her. When she looked up at me, her big eyes softened. "Thanks."

I'd have to tell Landon about that interaction in case it ever came back up, but it'd have to wait until we were alone. With a wave to the girl, I turned toward my table.

Ugh, *my table*. I couldn't believe I considered it that.

The two spots were still empty as I approached, but Landon's lunch bag had been set down in front of his seat. I frowned, looking at where Jade sat across, imagining the conversation I'd have to keep up waiting for Landon's return.

Connor grinned at me as I sat down. "Hey, hey."

"Hi," I said warily. "What's up? Why do you sound so...excited?"

He looked across the Top Tier table—where everyone, to my horror, was already looking at me. "Oh, nothing," he replied, still smiling. "Just...waiting."

Something heavy sank in my stomach, especially when other people at the table giggled. Dread sank its teeth into me, and for a long second, all I could think about was that I was somehow, someway, about to become the butt of a joke they'd tell. For a wild moment, I thought the girl had been talking about something else entirely. *He's not really your boyfriend. He's only pretending.*

And then I looked up and found Landon walking into the cafeteria through the doors like he had a few minutes ago, but this time, he had his hands full.

I ducked my head toward the table, unable to fight the cringe.

In one hand, Landon had what looked like a mini football-shaped cake on a platter, chocolate frosting covering it. It almost looked homemade. In the other hand, he held a poster that curled a little as he walked closer, but it was still easy to read with the blocky letters.

Let's Have A BALL At Homecoming

There were little footballs drawn all over the board,

varying in sizes. It would've been cute if it weren't in front of the entire cafeteria.

"I know," Landon said when he came close enough, stopping off to the side of my chair. I looked up to find a pained smile in place, like he was posing for a picture. "They put me up to this. I was going to ask you this morning, when I picked you up, but—"

"We wouldn't miss this adorable spectacle for the world," Ashton interjected, but I didn't turn to look at him. "Make sure you get his good side, Connor."

"I'm making sure," Connor said, angling his phone at Landon.

Jade watched it all, silent, which was all kinds of bizarre. Not even one snarky comment.

"Lacey Churchill," Landon said with a grandiose flare that I honestly did not expect from him, but his reddening cheeks hinted at how embarrassed he felt about it. "Will you go to homecoming with me?"

I bit down harder on my lip, but I couldn't stop the laugh that came out. I put my hand over my mouth, looking at him like he was crazy.

"Please?" he asked. "Please say yes so I can sit down and stop everyone from staring."

I laughed in earnest now, nodding at the spectacle. "Yes, I will go to homecoming with you."

I should've braced myself for the literal applause the cafeteria broke into. I jumped a mile at the sound, looking all around at everyone—which, since it was Country vs City Day for spirit week, I made eye contact with a lot of farmers. Before Landon could sit down, though, Connor gestured at me. "Wait, wait, Lacey, stand up. We need a picture of the two of you with the sign."

"Don't you know how it's done?" Jade asked with a little bit of a sneer, tapping into her old mean-girl routine.

"I didn't realize it was a big deal," I said as I painfully got to my feet. I could see why Landon begged to sit down—standing above everyone else while they stared was borderline traumatizing. "I haven't seen your homecoming proposal yet, so I didn't know."

Judging by how Jade's expression soured—and Connor's froze—I had a feeling I accidentally stepped on a hot topic between them.

Landon passed me the cake so he could hold the poster, and I smirked down at the little football. Someone had piped white frosting for the little stitches, and there were green M&Ms used as the grass around the ball. "This is adorable," I said as he wrapped his arm loosely around my waist. "Who made it?"

"Contrary to popular belief, I did. So I can't promise how it's going to taste."

Gosh, this boy constantly found ways to make my heart expand in my chest. It was almost ridiculous. It'd only been a few weeks—and most of those days, we'd still been knee deep in faking our relationship—but I'd never felt so completely and totally overwhelmed with a feeling like this before. Like I'd gone my whole life missing the other half of myself. Like I'd finally found *my person.*

"Say 'quarterback,'" Connor said as he pointed his phone at us.

I leaned into Landon's side, careful not to nudge the

cake, and wrapped my own arm around him. Despite the people staring, and how awkward this was, I had the world's largest smile on my face. I hadn't been this happy in a long, long time, and I wasn't sure anything could take it away from me.

"Quarterback," Landon and I said cheesily at the same time, and with a grin of his own, Connor snapped the picture.

CHAPTER 25

The day I left my mom's house in June, I'd packed everything in my room in a blind daze. Uncle Dean had agreed to wait for me outside, and even from my bedroom, I had been able to hear the rumble of his engine as the car idled. I'd grabbed random clothes, toiletries, my makeup bag—but I'd never stopped to do a final once-over.

It was after my shift at Le Petit Bateau that I knew Wednesday was the day. Maestro cut me from the floor early, since we had next to no customers, and I ended up clocking out a little after six. Homecoming festivities would pick up starting tomorrow, and I still had to go shopping for a dress, so today was the only day to bite the bullet before my birthday.

And so, with a determination I didn't feel, I decided to go home.

Landon drove Petunia up the steep climb of Grimes Avenue now, both of us sitting in silence. It was odd to see him behind the wheel, but my hands shook far too strongly for me to be the one to drive. Landon hadn't forced me to say it, though—when I asked him if he'd take me, his response had been immediate. *"How about I drive?"*

He had one hand on the steering wheel and the other wound around mine, and it felt like just enough to hold me together.

"If she's home..." I began, but trailed off, the words taking my breath away. "If she's home, then I don't want to stop. We'll go back."

Landon nodded. "Got it."

I didn't expect her to be home, though. Aside from the fact that she bartended most nights, she'd probably be at Max's or out with friends. Her visits home had been few and far between toward the end, and I doubted she'd come home at all now that I wasn't there.

And I'd bet accurately. "It's the blue house," I said, pointing off to the right. "The one with no cars in the driveway."

I didn't want to look at Landon's expression. I didn't want to see him look around at the crumpled house, at the overgrown lawn, the broken front porch. I wanted to tell him that once upon a time, it looked better than this—that Mom used to keep it maintained—but the words died on my lips. After all, what use was there in defending it?

Landon eased the van into the muddy driveway, killing the engine but not reaching for his seatbelt. He looked at me with an open expression. "I'll wait here?"

"You can come in." My response came too fast, too breathless. "If you want."

By way of an answer, he popped his seatbelt undone and reached for the doorhandle.

The air was quiet outside, almost like the wind was afraid to blow too loudly. *She's not here*, I told myself, rubbing my arms as we rounded the house. *She's not home. Max isn't home. There's no reason to be uneasy.*

Landon followed close behind me as we walked up the back porch, dodging the broken step without me having to instruct him on it. I pulled the house key out of my pocket, sticking it in even though I was pretty sure the door would be unlocked.

"Don't judge, okay?" I whispered, fumbling to twist the lock.

A sudden, slight pressure touched the crown of my head; Landon had kissed it. "Don't worry about me, Lace."

The breath I let out shook, and I finally managed to get the door open.

The house smelled like cigarettes, even though Mom never smoked inside. Maybe that was something that changed after I left. Maybe Max did. I stiffened as I ventured farther into the dark house, looking around the space. I half thought the space would be in disarray—dishes piled up in the sink, cans and bottles littered throughout. Even a pizza box or two. That had been the way I left it.

What I found, though, was a house that was filled with half-filled moving boxes. There were a few crumbs on the counter when I looked close, but otherwise, it was like a cleaning crew had come through and removed all traces of lonely memories, sealing them up in the cardboard containers.

The memories clung to the walls, though. I couldn't see them, but I could feel them.

My room was on the very back side of the house, so I led Landon through the kitchen, through the living room, fighting the urge to look back at him. I wondered if he was looking around, noting the boxes as I was.

Even though the other rooms were semi-packed up, my bedroom had remained untouched. My dresser drawers were open, my bed was unmade, and there were random books and magazines on the floor. It looked like someone left the room in a hurry, uncaring of the mess they left behind. Exactly how I left it.

Suddenly, light came on in the room, causing me to flinch. The ceiling fan started to spin too, and I whirled around to find Landon with his finger paused on the light switch. He froze at my sudden movement. "Should I—is it supposed to stay off?"

"No." I blinked. "It's just...the electricity's on."

Something passed over Landon's expression. The last time I'd been here, it hadn't been. It was one of the reasons that drove me out. And now...it was on.

"My room's messy," I said, stating the obvious because I was too embarrassed not to.

"Not judging, remember?" Landon walked up to the corkboard where I'd pinned up photographs. Most of them were of Hudson, me, and his friends, but there were a few random magazine clippings that I'd pinned up. He reached out and traced a photo of me that'd been taken during middle school.

"I was my ugliest in the seventh grade," I said, shaking

my head. "My mom let one of her friends cut my hair, and they basically gave me a mullet. With pink highlights. *Cringe.*"

"You were cute," he insisted, smiling a little. He unpinned the image and brought it closer. "You liked changing your hair up, huh?"

I reached up and patted my grown-out roots. "It was fun to pretend I was different. Like, with each new hairstyle, I could be a different person. Except I totally would've skipped the mullet phase."

First thing was to collect more clothes. I went over to my dresser and picked out the things that looked the most versatile—like blank tees, jeans, leggings. And then I moved to my tiny closet to find any sweaters I might've wanted, since the cold season was approaching. I stacked everything on the top of my dresser, turning to survey the room.

"The bedding needs to come," I said, moving to fold the fluffy comforter into a puffy square. "And the pillows."

Landon volunteered to run them to the car, loading them into his arms with ease. I found a garbage bag in the kitchen that I was able to pack my clothes into, and Landon came back to study my room while I figured out what else I wanted to keep. There were a few yearbooks on my shelf that caught my eye, but I didn't care about them enough to pack them. I'd leave Brentwood behind but carry a yearbook with all the memories with me? No, thanks.

"What elementary school did you go to?" I asked him suddenly.

"Elementary?" He sounded confused. "Why?"

"Connor said you didn't go to Brentwood Elementary with them, so I was curious."

Landon hesitated before answering, but I couldn't figure out what about the question was so sensitive. "Evergreen."

My jaw dropped. "Me too! We went to the same school?" I whirled back to the shelf with renewed interest. "I'm pretty sure I have a yearbook. I can't remember if it's from the third grade or—"

The second my fingertips brushed the Evergreen Elementary yearbook's spine, Landon latched onto it and yanked it away from me. "I told you," Landon said, holding the book high in the air. "I was an ugly kid."

"Please, you saw my *mullet phase.*"

"I was worse, trust me."

"I bet you were *adorable.*" I reached for the yearbook, stretching onto my tiptoes. I still wasn't anywhere near the book. My fingers barely grazed his wrist. "Jeez, are your parents super tall or something? Or were you given radioactive vitamins—when you were younger—"

I hopped up to try and snatch the book, but when I came back down, my foot slipped on the slick magazine on the floor. I grabbed Landon's shoulder to balance myself, but his free hand shot out and wrapped around my waist, pressing against the small of my back, holding me to him. The moment went from playful to charged in an instant, transitioning as the distance between us disappeared. Chest to chest, breath to breath. He tried to back away, but I wrapped my arms around his neck.

"Smooth," I murmured, tilting my head, momentarily forgetting about the book. "Real smooth."

"You were the one that slipped." His voice was adorably breathless, and the hand that had pressed me to him had yet to move from my back. I could feel all five of his fingertips against the thin material of my dress. "I caught you."

"Is that why you're blushing?"

Landon closed his eyes and shook his head a little, like he was cursing his cheeks and the cuteness of them. I brought one hand out from around his neck to touch his face, stomach flipping at the fire there.

He opened his eyes to look at mine, but his gaze snapped to something behind me. His arms went from around me to pulling me aside in an instant, tucking me half behind him, and then I saw what drew his attention. My mother's boyfriend, Max, took up nearly the entire space of the doorway, his stare cold and emotionless. He clutched a metal baseball bat in his right hand, propped on his shoulder like he had been thinking about swinging.

My hands curled into fists at the sight of him, but I had to fight the urge to press deeper into my bedroom. This was how close he'd been last time I saw him, last time everything fell apart. "Hey," I offered with obvious disdain.

"I saw the van out front," he got out, glaring between the two of us. "I thought someone broke in. Who's the boy? You got a little boyfriend?"

"I'm just here to get my stuff—"

"You stealing now?" Max gripped the bat tighter as he took

a step forward, but at the same time, Landon wrapped his hand around my arm and drew me to the side, out of the warpath of my mother's boyfriend. Landon didn't step between us, didn't shove me behind him, but he did tuck me close against his side. Max's eyebrows shot up. "Oh, *and* he's a gentleman?"

"What makes me a gentleman?" Landon asked, his voice level. Almost like the man in front of us didn't wield a weapon and a murderous gaze to match. "Because I'm not threatening a girl with a baseball bat?"

"I wouldn't be stepping in for her, if I was you," he replied, using the bat to gesture to me. "She attacked me in June, and she let her freak cousin take the blame for it. I'm sure she'll let you take the blame for this too." Max ducked his head to peer at me in the eye. "After getting arrested, I guess you'll let boys do your dirty work for you, huh?"

My whole body shuddered, not because what he said was true, but because Landon heard it. If there was one thing I wanted to take to the grave with Landon, it was mentioning the whole arrest situation. I never wanted him to know—to see the side of my life and the people in it that were truly ugly.

But I wouldn't let Max look at me like he was a big dog bearing down on a kitten. "No, this time, I'll be sure to actually land a decent punch."

Max's lips curled into a sneer.

"What's going on?"

The growing tension in my room froze, like ice had spread over all three of us. Max turned toward the doorway, and even though I didn't want to, I followed suit, my world dropping out from underneath me.

In some ways, I liked to think I looked like my mother. She was beautiful—always had been. Her warm brown hair was long and healthy, curling around her chest. I was taller than her, but she had an air of authority to her that made her seem larger. The T-shirt she wore exposed both of her tattoo sleeves, different colors and images that I never had enough time to memorize.

Mom's mouth dropped open when she saw me standing in my bedroom. "Lacey?"

The name was like a dagger sliding through my ribcage, and when it pierced, I couldn't breathe. Suddenly, I was in the fourth grade, sitting on the couch with my hands over my ears, waiting for my mom to walk in the door. I was in the sixth grade, cooking soup on the stove, searing my fingertips on the burner. I was seventeen, packing up my suitcase to leave home.

Back then, I'd been so angry that I couldn't think straight. Now, I felt like I was going to throw up.

"You didn't come back," Mom stated. It took me several seconds to realize she wasn't talking to me, but to Max. "I was waiting for you to come back outside. You told me not to call the cops, but I got worried—"

"We were having a little reunion," Max replied, voice *worlds* different than what it'd been before. Gone was the low, threatening tone, now replaced with something softer, more awestruck. A complete flip of a switch now that my mother was in the room. "I was just coming to get you."

Nothing about Mom looked surprised to see me, nor all that *interested*, either. She took a step forward into the room, not even looking at me. "Who's this?"

I sucked in a breath. As soon as Mom walked in, I'd completely forgotten about the boy beside me. I turned to look at him, heart pounding. He regarded the scene before him with a blank look, staring at Mom with a vaguely polite expression. "Landon Settler," he replied, not stretching his hand out to shake hers.

"Does your uncle know where you are?" Mom asked, turning back to me. Curiosity stirred in her gaze, but no tears. I waited for them to pool up, to glisten the light brown of her eyes, but they never appeared, and I hated her for it. "You're not supposed to be here without his permission."

"Please," I tried to sound tough, but it came out more as a quiver. "If you cared about Uncle Dean, you would've paid him the money you owe him for taking me in."

She tilted her head. "We agreed to not talk about that with you."

I inhaled to fire off the retort dying on my lips. *Why would you bother to agree? It's not like you talk to me anyway.* But at the last second, the words fell apart.

I'd played this day over and over in my mind for so long. On nights when I couldn't fall asleep, when Hudson's bed was too hard and the house was too quiet, I pictured this moment. The day I finally came face to face with Mom again. I'd rehearsed every mean, angry, spiteful thing I wanted to say, throwing it all in her face as I watched her crumple. The part that she abandoned wanting nothing more than to see it all now—to finally see the tears fill her eyes. That side that loved confrontation begged for it, as if bloodthirsty.

I'm not afraid of her, I'd told Hudson once upon a time, and maybe this wasn't fear, but it was something different. The side I'd been shoving down, resisting, pretending didn't exist reared its head now. The side that wasn't angry over Mom's abandonment—the side that was unbearably and irreparably heartbroken.

"I was just getting the last of my things," I said through the tightness at my throat, and collected the garbage bag I'd packed the remainder of my things into. It was miserably light. "You can throw away the rest. I won't be back."

With my free fist clenched, I walked past Max and Mom, holding my breath as I did so. I didn't expect either of them to reach out, but if Max tried touching me, I would follow through on my promise.

But it wasn't Max that grabbed my wrist—it was Mom. Her fingers were cold around my skin as she brought me to a halt. "I'm going to sell the house," she said. Her eyes bounced around my face uncertainly, almost like she wasn't sure where to look. "Are you sure that's everything you want?"

I took an involuntary look back at the room, looking stripped, ransacked. Nothing in it screamed to me—then again, with the ringing in my ears, I wouldn't have been able to hear it anyway. My throat tightened. "I'm sure," I eventually got out. "You can throw everything else away."

She still hadn't let go. "You look thinner."

"I'm surprised," I replied, voice sharp. "You'd have to remember what I looked like before to notice."

Mom had no reaction, almost like she didn't realize what I'd said. Like she wasn't listening. "I'm glad you're happier over there with Dean and the kids," she went on, patting my wrist. "It...it worked out better this way, didn't it?"

I felt weighed down to the floor, like someone was pressing down on my shoulders. The longer I stared at her, the heavier I felt. *It worked out better this way, didn't it?* When she looked at me, she thought I looked happy. With me, she never stuck around long enough to see what my unhappiness looked like.

But my mother...she looked beautiful. Well-rested. Happy. I'd been gone three months, and my mother looked *happy.*

Something cracked inside me, something that seemed to shatter in my ears. No one else reacted to the sound, and I couldn't understand why at first. Only I could hear my heart breaking.

"Mail Uncle Dean my birth certificate," I finally managed to get out, and what a miracle that was. But my words were full of glass slivers, broken and bleeding. "If you did that...I'd be happy."

With that, I jerked my hand out of her grip and practically fled the hallway.

In all the scenarios that I'd played in my head of meeting Mom again, I had thought she'd ask me to come back home. I always imagined her saying that she missed me, or that the house was too quiet without me, or that she at least wanted to meet up a few times a week to get dinner together. Something. Something that showed that my absence in her life affected her. The selfish part of me wanted it to be a gaping hole left in her heart, but I would've settled for even the slightest bit of sadness. Even just a glimmer.

But she well and truly was okay with me being gone.

It worked out better this way.

I didn't even remember making it outside, but I snapped back to the moment as I slid the van's backseat door open with all the force I could muster, half surprised the door didn't fling off. I threw my trash bag of belongings inside, hearing something crunch, but too far away from the moment to care.

And then Landon was there, his hand trying to catch at mine. "Lacey, let me drive—"

I brushed him off, swallowing the suffocating feeling, and slammed the door shut. "I'm fine."

"You're not fine."

The words were soft, little pinpricks poking at my heart, but I shoved it down and rounded the front of the van. "If you don't want to ride with me, whatever. You can walk back."

By the time I got into the driver's seat, Landon was already sitting beside me, buckled in.

I gave one last look at my mother's house, wondering if what I'd said had been true—wondering whether or not I'd really never be back. The longer I stared at it, the harder it became to breathe. She didn't even come to the door to wave goodbye.

Gravel kicked up as I slammed my foot down on the gas pedal, reversing out of the driveway so fast that I nearly clipped one of the neighbor's already dented trashcans. "It's funny, isn't it?" I asked Landon as I switched into drive, peeling away from the house. "She—she didn't even say she *missed* me. She didn't even say she *loved me.*"

Landon turned in his seat to face me. "Lacey."

"You'd think she's a stranger." I blinked at the roadway, at the lines that seemed to weave in and out. "Not my mother. Not the woman who gave birth to me. Not the person who's supposed to raise me and support me. And all she could say was that I've *lost weight?*" I gave a crazed, incredulous laugh. "Does—does she not care? Not even a little bit? Of course she doesn't. If she cared a little, she would've checked in at least once, don't you think?"

Landon said something, something that I only recognized as a hum in the background, heart thrashing too loudly in my ears to hear him.

"It won't matter," I said, the determination washing over me like ice. "In a week, it won't matter, she won't matter, Brentwood won't matter."

"Why not?" This time, Landon's words pierced through the fog.

"Because I'm leaving." *And I'm never looking back.*

"You can't run from what's going on—"

"Why not?" I demanded, hitting the brake hard so I could make the turn. It slammed Landon's shoulder against the window. "Why can't I, huh? Why is it so wrong to?"

"Just because you can put miles between the location of the problem and yourself doesn't mean it can't follow you," he insisted. "Just because you ignore it, doesn't mean it will go away. If you run from it, it'll eat away at you until—"

Now I slammed on the brakes hard, using both feet, causing the van to cry out its protest. The tires screeched against the dry pavement, heaving at the sudden stop, and if I'd been going any faster, we definitely would've spun out. I gripped the steering wheel so tightly that I was surprised the thing didn't bend under my will, feeling my nails grind into the leather. When we came to a halt, I whirled on Landon. "It'll eat at me?" I said, voice trembling with the severity I'd packed behind the words. "If I don't leave, it'll *suffocate me*. I'll be afraid of running into her at the grocery store, or the mall, or the movie theater, and I'll have to think about what she's doing at every single moment in time. Is she having dinner with her boyfriend? Is she laughing with him? Did she forget about me? Did she forget she had a daughter who loved her despite everything?"

I tried to draw in a breath, but it was like all the air lacked all oxygen, doing nothing more than searing my throat. I was like a balloon filled with too much air, seconds from bursting. The pressure in my chest caved in deeper, attempting to swallow me whole.

I stared at Landon, suspended in the urgency in his eyes, the desperation that mimicked what I felt swelling. In the silence that stretched out, my mind played back the moments in the house with merciless precision. Max had spoken to me more than my own mother. She'd only said a handful of sentences. None of them had been *I miss you* or *I wish you'd come home*. None of them had sounded like something a mother would say to her daughter after months of no contact. She hadn't asked about how I was doing—she didn't care enough to think about it.

And then that balloon popped.

"She was happy," I whispered miserably, voice finally breaking and echoing the crack that consumed me in the house. It triggered hot warmth to sting down my cheeks, eyes finally spilling over at the realization I finally said aloud. "She was happy without me. I didn't...I didn't think she'd be *happy*."

Landon's face twisted as if he were in pain, but that was all I saw before I closed my eyes and began to cry. They were the huge, painful sobs that I'd kept dammed up since moving into the Bishops', ones that I choked on and could barely breathe around. Landon's hand disappeared from my cheek, and distantly, I knew he got out of the van, but my awareness was too quickly overwhelmed by how much everything hurt.

It was one thing to suspect something all along and another to be faced with it. One thing to assume something was the truth and another to have it confirmed. One thing to think my mother never cared about me, another to have it thrown in my face.

My driver's side door pulled open, revealing Landon standing on the shoulder. He took me into his arms without hesitating, crushing me close. I wrapped my arms around his neck, my legs around his waist, and clung to him. I felt Landon kiss the side of my cheek, my temple, the top of my head—light, tender kisses that only made me cry harder.

On the side of the road, I mourned the relationship that had been severed, one that left me damaged and broken. I cried the tears I'd kept bottled since I was a little girl and came face to face with the truth I'd never wanted to confront. It was easier to be angry and never know. But now I knew, and there was no going back.

On the side of Lookout Ledge, Landon held me while I cried, uncaring of the tears that soaked into his collared shirt, smoothing his hand down the back of my head, rocking me back and forth.

And we both stayed like that for a long, long time.

CHAPTER 26

*L*andon lay beside me on the mattress in the van, both of us staring up at the metal ceiling as the wind tugged in from the open back door. My head rested on his chest, and I allowed myself to be lulled by the rhythmic rise and fall of his breaths, letting the movement calm me. Sometime during my crying session, when I'd spiraled so deep that the world around me darkened, Landon brought me back here. I clung to him even then, tucked against his side, unable to stop the wave. It felt like I'd cried for hours. But eventually, the well of tears had run dry, leaving my insides twisted like a wet towel.

Landon never stopped running his fingers through my hair, though, and still lightly touched my head now, the world's softest massage. He must've laid down the comforter when he brought it out to the van initially, because we lay on the yellow plaid printed blanket now, cuddled up on top. My arm was around his waist, fingers hooked on one of the loops of his belt. "What are you thinking?" I finally asked him, breaking the silence that had become too thick.

"What am I thinking?" he echoed quietly, continuing to trace patterns against my scalp. "I'm thinking I can see why you wanted to fix the van up," he said. "I know I said I never thought about it before, but I can see the appeal of packing up and just...starting new."

He could understand it now since he'd met Mom. A part of me felt relieved at the prospect that at least *someone* could understand me, but the other part felt wholly mortified that he'd had to see me at my worst. My head weighed heavier against his chest.

"What are *you* thinking?" he asked.

My thoughts were sluggish now. "I'm embarrassed."

"Why?"

"Is that really a question?" I gave a hollow laugh. "I'm a trainwreck, Landon. My whole life is one, and you just got to see it in all its glory. You're probably already thinking of how you can jump ship."

Landon squeezed my arm firmly enough to be serious, and it drew my gaze to his. There was no trace of discomfort in his expression, nor judgment. It was open and wide and filled with earnestness. "Don't joke."

"You think I'm joking?"

"You want to know what I'm really thinking?" He didn't wait for me to answer. "I'm thinking that I wish I could've told your mom off for not treating you better, for leaving you alone, for making you feel like you're not good enough. I'm thinking about how lucky I am to get to be here for you right now. That I get to be the one who holds you when you need it. That it was me that you chose to be your fake boyfriend and not some other guy at Brentwood."

A fraction of a smile crossed my lips, thinking about the day outside of Le Petit Bateau that sparked him to be my choice. My hand wrapping around his button-up, pulling him closer to shield me from view. Mom had been there that day, across the street. It was funny that things seemed to go back to her once again. My well was truly dry, though. I had no more tears left in me.

"You're not a trainwreck," Landon said in a softer tone. "And even if you were, I want to be in the wreck with you."

The words snaked around me, as warm as his arms were. I could hear his heartbeat thump steadily underneath my ear, and when he drew in a deep breath, my head bobbed with it. I peered up at him again, sniffing. I knew I had to look like a hot mess—my lips and eyes puffed up like crazy when I cried, and my makeup had to be *totally* smeared. But he didn't even blink. "You have this way of making me feel...*quiet*. Like everything bouncing around in my head sort of slows down when I'm with you, and you bring me back from spiraling. Like you're the tether and I'm the balloon."

Landon looked so sad as he gazed at me, and he reached out and smoothed the pad of his thumb underneath my eye, absorbing whatever tears had yet to dry.

Out of anyone that had to have been with me in that moment back at the house, I was so glad it was him. Glad it was him, my tether, who had been there when I broke loose. Landon said he was lucky that I chose him, but it was almost laughable how lucky *I* was. The one guy at Brentwood who dove into everything, no question. The one guy in the Top Tier who would've held me while I cried.

Yeah, it wasn't Landon who'd gotten lucky. It was me.

"I had told you I never thought of running away before," he said as he threaded his fingers through my hair, voice soft. "When I was a kid, I wanted to. When everyone picked on me and made fun of me, I wanted to run away. I felt so alone...and I guess I really do see now how alone you must've been feeling all this time."

My eyes prickled again for no reason. I sniffed. "I want to go back in time and give younger you a hug."

"I'm sure he would've appreciated it." Landon brushed his lips along my temple. I could feel his lips tip up. "But he wouldn't have appreciated it as much as I do right now."

I snorted and pushed at him, the mood lightening ever so slightly. After a moment, I sat up and swung my legs over the side of the mattress, staring out the back of the van and at the tops of the trees I could see. "Do you want to do something tomorrow?"

"I know we planned on going to the homecoming party after the game Friday, but let's go to the party tomorrow instead," he said as he coasted his hand back and forth across my shoulder blades. "And then, after the game, we'll do something just us for your birthday. Watch a movie, go to the beach, go for a drive—something just you and me."

"It'll be late after the game," I said, kicking my heels against the platform. "I'm sure you'll want to celebrate with your friends after homecoming."

Landon came up behind me and rested his chin on my shoulder, wrapping his arms around my waist. Hugs were something I wasn't used to, and they surprised me every time, but despite everything in that moment, his closeness made me relax. Landon was such a touchy person, and it never failed at making me feel comforted. He pressed his face against the back of my neck. "I want to spend it with *you*."

The words trickled their way inside me and made themselves a home there, warming me up. "Homecoming," I echoed, scrunching my nose up a little. "I never thought I'd go to a homecoming game."

"Bet you never thought you'd be dating the quarterback either."

I didn't respond, because of course he was right. I knew we needed to go—my uncle would be expecting me home soon, and Landon's curfew was creeping closer—but I wanted to stay in this moment forever. In the van that was my escape, cuddling with the one person that actually made me want to stay. My life seemed to be going in a completely different direction than I'd always thought it'd go, but I didn't hate it. In fact, with Landon's arms around me, with his lips kissing the top of my spine, I didn't mind it one bit.

Yes, I was the lucky one, indeed.

CHAPTER 27

The cab was absolutely silent.

Hudson had his hands curved over Petunia's wheel lazily, but his stiff spine hinted that he was more tense than he wanted to let on. Then again, why wouldn't he be? Though Paisley and I had had a good talk on Saturday, finally clearing up some of the air, Hudson and I had gone almost a full week of the edgy back and forth. I couldn't remember a time where things had felt so *awkward* around him before, but as he drove down the road, I fought the urge to roll the window down to let the tension out.

"You'll turn on Willow," I told him, my impulse finally winning out.

"I know," he replied.

So much for a conversation starter. "The week's been so long," I went on, rubbing my palms along my knees. "I'm so glad I'm done with work for the week."

Hudson's gaze never deviated from the road.

"You've had a rough week, too. The superintendent finding your pocketknife and all."

The week had started out with quite the bang when Uncle Dean was called into the principal's office. Like my uncle had always warned, Hudson got caught with his pocketknife on school grounds, and had nearly gotten kicked out of Brentwood for it.

Again, though, the topic didn't kick off a conversation like I'd been hoping. Hudson's fingers simply tightened around the wheel.

"Can you stop being mad at me?" I asked him, turning in my seat to face him as he slowed for a stop sign. I curled my fingers around each other, pinching hard. "I shouldn't have told you to stop seeing Gemma. I shouldn't have tried to control what you do."

He sighed as his foot closed over the brake, and we came to a standstill. The intersection was empty, with only one couple walking down the sidewalk eyeing the van with suspicion as they passed. "I'm not mad," Hudson said, surprising me as he slumped into the seat. "I'm...I'm trying to figure out how to bring something up."

"What?"

"You went home."

On instinct, I froze, only blinking. With everything going on, I hadn't told him or anyone about last night. When I'd gotten home from dropping Landon off, my tears had long since dried, and the puffiness around my eyes had died down enough to conceal the evidence. "What makes you say that?"

Hudson tipped his head toward the back of the van.

"Your blankets. You left those at home."

I turned around as if I had no idea what he was talking about, and found my yellow comforter draped over the mattress where Landon had made it. If you looked closely, it was clear to see the ripple in the sheet, almost like two people had been down there.

"How...how did it go?"

"The cops weren't called, so I'd say it was a success." It was a joke—a truly terrible one—and it rang awkwardly in the air. Hudson still had his foot on the brake at the stop sign, not leaving without more elaboration. "I feel like...I feel like I got it out. Everything that I've been bottling up. Like that was a big hurdle, and now that I've cleared it, I feel...lighter."

I could feel his probing gaze on me, but I focused on the scratches on the dashboard. As weird as it sounded, I *did* feel lighter now. Almost as if crying it all out with Landon had been what I needed. To face everything with Mom one last time, to cry, to mourn, to move forward. She no longer felt like a shadow monster in a closet. I'd turned on the lights.

"I always thought I was angry, and I guess I was," I went on, curling my fingers into my jean-clad knees. "But seeing her yesterday...it was like I let myself really, finally feel sad."

"Did you go alone?"

I paused, but only for a second. "Landon...came with me."

The importance of it wasn't lost on Hudson. I wasn't sure if he ever doubted me, but this had to convince

Hudson. Beyond a shadow of a doubt. Because if I could trust someone with my past, things must've been real. "You like him," he said finally.

"I do. I really do." I turned to give him a defeated sigh. "You won the bet."

"I was hoping I would." Hudson reached over and shoved my shoulder hard, cutting through the sentimentality as naturally as ever. "With your rock of a heart, though, I wasn't sure I would."

Honestly, I hadn't expected him to win. When we agreed to the timeline weeks ago, I had thought I'd have all my things packed up and in Petunia right now, waiting for the clock to tick down to midnight. But as Hudson pulled up along the curb of the Settler residence, I could've laughed at how differently things had played out.

"I'll tell Gemma you're out here if she wants to say hi," I said as I unclicked my seatbelt, sliding out onto the sidewalk. "Since, you know, I'm fully in support of you two now."

Hudson rolled his eyes. "Better late than never."

Letting out a slow breath, I started up the walkway to the door. Cue another thing I thought I'd never do—meet Landon's parents.

When Landon's mom had seen him baking the cake, he said she'd practically begged him to bring me home so she could meet me. Begged. I really hoped he wasn't being dramatic, because I honestly doubted that I was the type of girl his mom would want him bringing home. Not that I was that bad or anything, but if she was expecting a girl like Madison, I was so far from that.

And it terrified me.

I stood on the welcome mat with my heart running a mile a minute. If I had one of those fitness watches, I'm sure it'd say my pulse was well over one hundred beats per minute. Surely.

I turned around to find Hudson still parked in the van at the curb of the road. He flicked his palm at me from behind the driver's seat, like saying *knock on the dang door*.

I shot him back a look that said *please save me*.

Hudson pointed at the steering wheel, and with exaggerated lip movements, he mouthed *"I'll honk."*

Wide-eyed, I whirled around and knocked on the door.

And literally, not even a second later—almost like she'd been waiting on the other side for me—the door burst open, and Mrs. Settler stood over the threshold. She looked exactly as she had that day at the restaurant, with her fiery red hair loose and spilling over her shoulders. "You must be Lacey," she greeted warmly, causing some of my panic to melt.

"Y-Yeah," I said, and then barely held back a gasp as she wrapped her arms around me in a quick hug. I hurried to awkwardly pat her on the back, smiling when she eased back. "It's nice to meet you, Mrs. Settler. You too, Mr. Settler," I added once I spotted him standing near the kitchen doorway.

"*So* nice to meet you," she replied, shutting the door behind me. And thankfully, my awkwardness didn't have to be endured for long, because suddenly Landon was there with his sister in tow behind him.

This moment in time was beyond surreal. Thinking

back to when we'd begun our fake relationship, I could remember him clear as day telling me he didn't want his family to know about it. About us. Back then, there really hadn't *been* an us for them to know about, but now...now there was. And he wanted to share me now.

For some reason, this moment made me think of my mother. What it would've been like if things had been so vastly different. She hadn't even introduced herself on Sunday when she met Landon. She hadn't hugged him. If life were different...

I stopped myself there. There was no use for the "what if" statements.

Landon crossed the room to me, and my thoughts instantly brightened. "Hi," I said.

He picked up my hand with his left and cupped it like normal, giving it a squeeze. With a secret smile, and stars in his eyes, he murmured, "Hi." And then he straightened his shoulders, looking around to find his family staring with strangely knowing expressions on their faces. "This is Gemma," he told me, stretching a hand out toward his sister. "I think—you've met her before, right?"

Gemma bobbed her head of dark hair. "Yeah, she helped me out during the whole situation in the hallway with Morgan."

"It's nice to properly meet you," I told Gemma, patting Landon's arm. After a moment, I said, "Hudson's actually waiting outside, if you wanted to go say hi."

Gemma asked her mother for permission, and on her way out, she touched my pink sweater's shoulder. "It was really nice to meet you," she said with a genuine expression, eyes wide and kind. "Hopefully we can chat again soon sometime."

"Definitely," I said, leaning in. "We can secret swap about the boys."

Landon drew in a breath to object, but Gemma beamed. "Deal."

After that Gemma hurried outside to go meet my cousin, and this time, I was sure I had a strangely knowing expression myself. After everything in life Hudson had gone through, he deserved to be happy. I also, selfishly, had already begun to think about all the double dates we could go on. And all Hudson's embarrassing stories I could tell.

"Well, come in, come in!" Mrs. Settler insisted, maneuvering around the coffee table to lead into the kitchen.

Mr. Settler, who'd been lingering on the edge of the room the entire time, turned to me. "Are you hungry? I made a few sandwiches."

"A sandwich sounds great," I said as we entered the kitchen. It was so much homier than I'd been expecting. For how high up in the Top Tier Landon was—and for the fact that Mrs. Settler was one of the most popular ladies in town—I was shocked by how warm their house felt. It wasn't ultra-fancy like Ashton's, and it wasn't empty and cold like Mom's kitchen was. There were mismatched hand towels and two-toned rugs on the floor, with some clutter on the counters, but not too much.

"Have a seat, I'll grab them for us," Mrs. Settler said, gesturing at the table that sat on the far side of the room. "Oh, I'm so happy to meet you. Truly. Landon's *never* brought a girl home. And I've been waiting."

"Mom. Please." Landon's face was pained as we sat down.

"We're happy for you, Landon, that's all," Mr. Settler said as he sat across from us, giving me his best fatherly expression. It was so strange to see them like this, all smiling and happy, when I could remember how they berated him about football. I tried to put it out of my mind. "Be grateful your mom hasn't broken out your baby scrapbook."

Landon looked sharply at his mom, as if he expected her to bolt for whatever closet the album was stashed in. I patted his knee. He seriously had nothing to worry about—when it came to rough experiences with family, I doubted his mom could top mine.

"Tell me a bit about yourself," Mrs. Settler said as she came over with the sandwiches on a plate. She set one down in front of me and one in front of Landon, but brought nothing for herself. "I'm assuming you go to Brentwood?"

"I do." I sat up straighter, almost like I was beginning a job interview. "I'm a senior, like Landon. I'm a server at Le Petit Bateau in Jefferson."

"Oh, we go there all the time!" She looked toward Landon as if wanting confirmation. "How fun. Oh," she said again, and this time, it was more hesitant. Her smile faltered a little. "The thing in your nose is...pretty."

I could tell she didn't really think so, but I could still appreciate the effort. Even though her smiles were fake, it was more than how my mom greeted Landon. "Thank you."

"What about college?" Mr. Settler leaned an arm against the tabletop. "What schools do you have your eye on?"

I pinched my fingertips, knowing the right answer to his question. It sat on the tip of my tongue. After all, what would it hurt to tell a white lie now? If it meant making a good first impression, it would be okay, wouldn't it? The only problem was that if I lied, Landon would hear it—and know it.

"She's taking a gap year," Landon answered for me, picking up his sandwich. "Travel the country. See what she wants to do, where she wants to go."

"Oh." Both Settler parents blinked a few times, probably because that hadn't been the answer they were expecting. Their initial expressions weren't too judgmental. Mrs. Settler leaned forward. "Well, that's quite interesting. How are you traveling around?"

"In a van," I replied. "I've renovated one so that it has a bed, a mini fridge, cabinets—"

"*Oh.*" Though it was the same word, it sounded completely different. Now her expression was more reproachful. "You're going to *live* in your *van?*"

Though it was far less judgmental than how Jade and Madison normally spoke, something about the emphasis triggered my old defense habits. I looked at the turkey sandwich in front of me, trying to think as quickly as possible how to respond.

"She is," Landon said, and this time, he reached over and put his hand on my knee. "You should see her van sometime, Mom. It's amazing what she's done with it."

Mrs. Settler tapped her lips. "Still, a young girl traveling alone..."

"There are so many ways to make sure you're safe when traveling," I rushed to say. "And I've mapped out where I'm going—"

"And she's not traveling alone," Landon said confidently, taking a bite of his sandwich as if we were talking about the weather. "I'm going with her."

I sucked in a gasp as I whirled on him, a sound that was drowned out by his parents' unison cry of, "*What?*"

Landon was so calm as he chewed, not looking at any of us as he did so. He acted as if he sat in the kitchen alone. "A few weeks in the summer, maybe. To see what it's like. Seeing more of the country would be a fun adventure."

The more he talked, the wider my eyes got—and the lower his parents' jaws dropped. I was in such a state of disbelief that I had no idea what to even do beside stare at him and listen to the craziness he was saying.

"Are you—are you joking?" Mrs. Settler asked, face pale.

"Of course he is," Mr. Settler responded for his son, and opposite of his wife's face, his grew red. "Our son isn't that irresponsible."

"It's not irresponsible." Landon put his sandwich back down on his plate. "I'm not saying I'll skip the school year, just explore the world a little. Find out more about myself."

This was quickly going from bad to worse, judging by the looks on his parents' faces. He didn't even seem to notice, lost in his world of insanity while the three of us looked at him as if he were a different person. Maybe he was. Maybe he'd been abducted overnight and replaced by an alien. I had no idea where this was coming from.

"You—you'll have summer football practices," his dad insisted. "CCSU starts their practices—"

"Are you saying this because of Gemma?" Mrs. Settler glanced at me rapidly, turning back toward her son. "Or because of...something else?"

I didn't know what she meant "because of Gemma," but I knew what she meant by "something else." *Someone* else, more like it. I wanted to object immediately, to say I had absolutely no part in this, but Landon spoke first. "I don't want to settle. I just want to find out more about myself. Like Lacey's finding herself. And I'll be eighteen," he added, expression firm, "so I *can.*"

Both of his parents turned to me at once, almost at the same time. My eyes bounced between them both nervously, afraid to spot the sudden bloom of animosity. Because it had to be there. Their darling son was suddenly rebelling, all due to a girl. I had to be public enemy number one in their eyes.

Mr. and Mrs. Settler looked from me to each other, and Landon's mom was the first to give. She shot him a look, an obvious promise of "later," but nodded. "Ahem. Well. Lacey dear—aren't you going to eat your sandwich?"

I ducked my head and picked it up, feeling nauseous at the idea of taking a bite, but doing so anyway. It was delicious, but my stomach still flipped unsteadily. Landon chewed away happily in his seat, as if completely unaware that he'd dropped a bomb on his parents, the blast hitting me.

It was safe to say that the rest of the time was awkward. Mr. and Mrs. Settler didn't have too much to say, so time was filled with silent chewing and small talk passed back and forth. I almost brought back up the baby album if only to possibly lift their spirits, but the atmosphere was far too awkward. Maybe I had been too confident when I thought that our meeting couldn't have been any worse than Landon meeting my mom.

When we got outside, safely out of the sight of his parents, I turned on him. "Landon, what in the world?" I demanded as we walked to his car. "Going on the road with me? Are you *trying* to get your parents to not like me?"

"Of course not," he replied, twirling his keys around on his finger far too nonchalantly. "I was only thinking about what it'd be like."

"Thinking about it and dropping it on your parents are two totally different things!" I rounded the car and stared at him over the roof. I wasn't sure my eyebrows could've gone higher if I tried. "You never said anything to me about coming with me."

Landon rested his forearms against the roof and leaned in. "I've been thinking about it. I know you said you wanted to leave soon, but what if you waited? What if you waited until the summer, and I went with you? What if we kicked off that adventure...together?"

I blinked at him. That was all I could do. There was no way I could speak, not with the sudden and instant inability to pull in air. Again, who was this and where was Landon Settler? I gaped at him like a fish out of water, opening and shutting my mouth.

And then I yanked open the passenger door and slid in, leaving him outside. Of course, he followed me a second later, now much closer, with only a console between us. "You hate it," he stated, though his brightness hadn't quite dulled.

"Summer is so long away. Why...why are you thinking about summer?"

"I don't want you to leave." Landon picked up my hand and pressed our palms together. "What you said yesterday... I don't want you to disappear after your birthday. I want to spend Christmas together, and Valentine's Day, go to prom—"

I squeezed my fingers around his hand. "Landon."

"You said I was your tether," he pointed out. "I don't want to let you fly away, not yet. Not when we're in the middle of a chapter."

"I'm not leaving," I told him firmly, shoulders slumping a little as what I said last night hit me. He'd been thinking about it since—that was why he'd done a kamikaze on his parents. I lowered my voice. "I said what I did about leaving last night because I was upset. I'm...I'm gonna stick around. Until graduation. To put my trip on hold until then."

Some of the urgency seeped out of his gaze as he listened, and when he spoke, his voice was soft. "Really?"

The decision felt right when I said it aloud—I could see the future stretched in front of me, and for the first time, it didn't seem so horribly overwhelming. Yes, there was Landon now, but I'd meant what I told Hudson. It was like facing Mom, allowing myself to really cry, altered something in me. Like one of the biggest things driving me out didn't seem so scary anymore.

I cleared my throat. "I mean, as long as I have my tether, I'm pretty sure I can survive one more school year at Brentwood High. I've been doing it for this long." I narrowed my eyes at him. "And I can't leave yet. You *still* haven't drawn me. I'm beginning to think you're faking this artistic ability you have—"

Landon cut me off by letting go of my hands, clasping my cheeks, and kissing me. I gasped a little in surprise at the sudden contact, but quickly melted into the feeling of his lips against mine. It was short and sweet, and when he pulled back to look at me, his face had been lit up with happiness and something that looked like relief. "I'll draw you ten times," he said, smoothing my hair back out of my face. "A hundred times. You'll get sick of it."

"Doubt it," I said with a laugh, reaching out and tracing his starburst of freckles. "Too bad I hadn't told you that earlier, and maybe you *wouldn't* have given your parents the shock of a lifetime."

Landon laughed before letting go, turning to put his key in the ignition. "No, I needed to say it."

"Why?"

"To be my own person," he replied, and turned toward me one last time. "And to remind myself of that."

I'd be lying if I said I completely understood what he meant, but asking him seemed wrong in that moment. Not with that boyish happiness on his face, with the stars in his eyes. So, instead of asking, I rested my hand on my knee, settling into my seat. "I like the sound of that."

CHAPTER 28

*L*andon had been right—the pre-homecoming party was *completely* different than the Jocks Only party from last Friday. In fact, the two probably weren't even comparable. What was a party of maybe thirty people max last Friday turned into a party of what felt like a hundred, spread out *everywhere*. The front yard, the back yard, the main floor, the second floor, the third. There were *so many people*. And I guess it made sense—Brentwood High was a school that had nearly a thousand students. Of course people were going to come.

And extra especially since the Top Tier would be present.

When Landon and I arrived, it took us a while to find anyone we recognized. The first person had been Reed, who was chatting with a few football players near the far wall. "You guys made it!" he greeted over the loud music.

"I didn't know parties were actually like this," I confessed, looking around uneasily. "Seriously. I thought that was only in movies."

"The parties Ashton throws are *like* the movies," Landon said with a shake of his head. "I don't even want to think about the cleanup."

No kidding. I locked eyes with the girl Reed stood beside. "Why don't his neighbors call the cops?"

Reed rubbed two fingers together, and then rolled his eyes. "Or so he says. It's the higher-end district. Everyone's got each other's backs, I guess."

Landon wrapped his arm around my waist and loosely held me close, like this was his relaxed position. I looked around the living room I'd been in a week ago, shocked by how different it looked. All of the furniture had been pushed up along the walls, creating a wide, empty space for people to mingle and dance. Some of the paintings had been taken down off the walls, too—the valuable ones, I assumed. Ashton might've sucked, but apparently he appreciated the arts.

Landon leaned in close, and his lips grazed my ear in a way that sent a shiver down my spine. "Want a drink?"

"I think it's against the law to be at a party without a cup in your hand," I replied with a smirk. "If he has Sprite, I'll take that."

"Aye-aye," he replied, kissing my temple. "I'll be back."

I watched him dissolve into the crowd, dodging the dancers and the elbows as he made his way toward the kitchen, like it was a football play and he needed to dodge a tackle.

"So, Lacey," Reed said as he took a step forward. "How's everything been?"

"Good," I answered automatically. "How's, ah...how are things with you?"

"Equally good," he replied, tapping the edge of the soda can he held. "Landon was so psyched you said yes to his hoco-proposal, you know. He called me while he was baking it, as if I was the one that came up with the recipe."

I smiled at the thought of Landon stirring together a bowl of cake batter, and then laughed at the idea of him attempting to frost it. "He was pretty proud of it."

"As he should be. I didn't think the boy had it in him, but it didn't taste too bad."

Everyone at the lunch table had been curious what Landon's chances of a baking career had been, so I allowed everyone one forkful. The only person who didn't try any was Jade. Shocker.

"I'm glad fate finally brought you two together," Reed went on with a bob of his head. "You two are perfect for each other."

"Finally?" I echoed.

Reed's lips stretched into a wide smirk, exposing a dimple in his cheek. "He didn't tell you?"

"Tell me what?"

Reed took another step closer, ducking his head. "Landon's been in love with you since, like...the fifth grade? The fourth grade?"

It was the second time that night that I'd been stunned absolutely speechless. I jerked my head up and stared at Reed hard, sure I'd heard him wrong.

"He's always been too chicken to ask you out," he went

on, chuckling. "*Totally* chicken. I'm glad he finally worked up the nerve. It only took him until senior year."

I had slowly begun shaking my head as he was speaking, finally able to find my voice. "I think you've got the wrong person." What I really wanted to say was *no way*.

Reed pointed at his head. "You had pink highlights once, right? In the...seventh grade? I remember him pointing you out to me, telling me he had a crush."

I let out a little gasp, one that got swallowed by the beat of the music that reverberated through the entire house. The seventh grade *was* when I'd had the pink highlights. How else would Reed have known if not for Landon? *I remember him pointing you out to me.*

I started running back through all our interactions together, looking for a sure answer for the theory Reed posed, but I couldn't find one. That first day Landon saw me in the towel—had he hid me in the stall because he was a nice person? Or because he'd always had a crush on me? What about the fake relationship? Did he agree to it because he wanted to stick it in his friends' faces like he claimed, or because he liked me?

There were several reasons why I adamantly didn't think him crushing on me was the case. He'd been hard to convince about the fake relationship. He'd been so awkward around me at first. He hadn't wanted to tell his family about me right away.

But...we *had* clicked. So easily. He seemed to get me like no one else, like he already knew me.

Or just liked me for a very, very long time.

"I totally spilled the beans," Reed said, eyes wide. "Whoops. Blame it on Connor, okay?"

The butterflies in my stomach took off in a frenzy, unable to stay still. The girl beside Reed picked up the conversation again, leaving me to wade through the revelation on my own. A smile popped to my lips at the idea of Landon pretending not to have feelings for me. At liking me all along. When I'd been stressing about my feelings growing for him, he'd already fallen long ago.

When my gaze focused, I saw Madison weaving her way through bodies in the room, looking oddly out of place as she did so. Maybe it was the fact that she didn't have Jade glued to her hip like normal. Maybe it was the slightly dazed expression on her face. Or maybe it was the fact that she walked right up to me, stopping within arm's reach.

"Hey," she began awkwardly, gaze shifting from me to Reed and then back. "Can... Can I talk to you for a second?"

At any other moment in my life, I would've laughed without even thinking about it, because talking with Madison in private? On my "yeah, right" list. But there was something about her expression that stifled any laughter that tried to bubble up. It was far more muted than I'd ever seen it, her eyes almost looking...haunted.

I glanced around the party, hesitating. "Now?"

Madison gave a silent nod.

The fact that Jade was nowhere in sight should've had me hesitating—surely this was them setting up a prank or whatever somewhere, right?—but I couldn't look away from Madison's face. I'd always thought Madison easy to read, but in that moment, there wasn't a trace of the girl I'd come to loathe.

Something caught at my wrist the second I took a step, tugging me back. Reed dropped his fingers immediately, but his voice was low. "I...wouldn't," he said in a low tone, gaze flicking cautiously to where the cheerleader stood.

My gut was warning me against it too, but ultimately, I shook my head. "It's all good," I assured, and he let go. "Tell Landon we'll be—"

"In the guest room," Madison finished for me, and then without another word, she turned on her heel and walked away.

I didn't expect such a fast getaway, and scrambled after her, keeping my gaze locked on her blonde ponytail as it bobbed through the people. The way she was speed walking made it clear she didn't want anyone to see me trailing after her, which almost had me giving up and returning to wait for Landon at Reed's side. Curiosity, though, was what linked me to her, even though it felt like a bad idea.

Madison ducked through a door in the hallway and waited for me to follow in after her before she sealed it shut behind us. I scanned the room, trying to ignore how ominous the *click* sounded. The room was clearly a guest bedroom, as Madison had said. There was a bed, a side table, and a closet, but no personal belongings. Which was a good thing. I wasn't sure I'd be able to stomach it if she forced us into Ashton's bedroom or something.

I nudged open the closet door, peering at the emptiness inside.

"No one's going to jump out," Madison said.

"Can you blame me for checking?" Turning back around, I crossed my arms over my chest. "We're not exactly besties that gossip together at parties."

Away from all the prying gazes, it struck me again how *weird* Madison looked. Now, though, I could see her better. Under the bright lights of the bedroom, it almost looked like her foundation had smudged underneath her eyes, black specks of her mascara sticking to the skin. Like she'd been crying. "Jade knows."

I glanced to the side. "Knows what?"

"About you and Landon. About your fake relationship."

Hearing those two words—*fake relationship*—had my body stiffening instinctually. My mind halted instantly, and then sped into high gear. "We're not—"

"Save it," she said, but her voice was more tired than harsh. "She and Ashton both know. I don't know how, but they were talking about it tonight. I heard them."

That mental image wasn't a pleasant one, but I still fought for my calmness. "I don't know what you heard, or what they heard, but it's not fake. We really like each other. I know you're probably hoping he'll dump me and go for you, but—"

"I'm not." She let out a sigh that shook a little, squaring her shoulders. "Jade's out for blood. I thought I should tell you."

I regarded her again, trying to find the crack in whatever façade she had on right now, because no way was the Madison Oliphant I knew this nice. "Why?" I demanded when it still made no sense. "Why not just giggle your head off with the Top Tier when it blows up in my face? Why warn me about it?"

"Because you don't deserve whatever they're planning."

"Careful." I raised an eyebrow. "It almost sounds like you're going rogue."

Something flashed across her expression—not anger, but shock. It was a fleeting spark, but one that softened the lines between her eyebrows and loosened the tightness by her eyes. She looked to the side, away, sealing it off. "I don't want another person to get caught in the crossfire," she said after a moment, and before I could ask her what she meant by that, the guest room door swung open.

Madison and I both turned toward where Jade now filled up the threshold. Whereas Madison seemed off tonight, Jade looked exactly like her calm, snotty self, half smirk resting on her lips and all. She glanced between the two of us twice, lifting her brows. "So, this is where the real party is at, huh?"

I shouldn't have expected Madison to say anything in return, because now that the ringleader had shown up, gone was her display of breaking from the mold. Her hands were in fists at her sides, but otherwise she looked more like a puppy facing down its vicious owner now.

"She was trying to tell me one last time to lay off Landon," I said, not really knowing why I was sticking up for Madison, but the words coming out anyway. "Another pathetic attempt. You need to work at training your cronies on blackmail."

A sudden, broader smile split across Jade's face. "Blackmail. Funny you mention that."

In hindsight, it was that moment that should've made me realize nothing good was going to happen from there on out. In hindsight, it was that moment that I should've left to find Landon. But I didn't have enough time to think.

Ashton came through the door Jade hadn't bothered to close, finding us around the room with a smile on his face. "Just the ladies I was looking for," he said in a grand voice, focusing on me as he sealed us in the room. "What are we gossiping about?"

Madison came up behind me, close enough to appear out of the corner of my eye. I found myself staring at the door. Was it dramatic to say that it felt like I'd been trapped in a room with three snakes? Probably, but it felt like at any moment, one of them would strike.

"We were just about to talk about how Lacey is Landon's *fake girlfriend*," Jade called after me, voice taking on a smug tone.

Without Madison's head's up, that statement would've knocked the air from my lungs. Even now, with my hand on the doorknob, it was jarring enough to make me hesitate.

"You're not even the least bit curious how we found out?" Jade continued on. "Landon told us."

"Technically, Landon told *me*, and I told you," Ashton replied to Jade. "And I only did that because you kept whining about not knowing our secret. Don't add yourself into the equation."

Jade scoffed. "Wow, a math sentence—I'm shocked. Did you get a tutor, too?"

As they bickered, I stared down at the silver knob in my grip, knowing I shouldn't turn around, knowing that Jade was dangling bait and waiting for me to bite. Logically, I knew Landon never would've told them about the fake relationship. Never. But how else would they have known about it?

It was bait I shouldn't have bitten.

"It's a long story," Ashton said, and I turned around to find him sitting down on the edge of the bed, patting the top beside him. "Come sit, and I'll explain."

I felt my face twist with disgust. "I'd rather drop dead."

"So mean." Ashton chuckled as he said it, tipping his head. "I see right through it, though, don't worry. I can tell you're practically shaking on the inside waiting for me to spill."

It was the mocking way he said it that had me gripping the doorknob with renewed anger, twisting it, intending to leave the three musketeers in the dust.

"I was at your fishy little restaurant the day you asked Landon to fake date you," Ashton said before I could open the door more than a few inches, rendering me motionless once more. "Desperately, might I add. Once I heard you asked him out, I wondered why you, a Top Tier hater, would try to woo our quarterback. I thought I'd tag along, listen to how awkward our golden boy would be on a date. Lo and behold, I hit the jackpot of pathetic."

Jade popped her hip out. "You put on such a show about the Most Likely Tos not bothering you, and yet you got into a fake relationship because of it. Pathetic."

There was absolutely no point in attempting to argue the *why* behind my fake relationship motivation. None. They wouldn't listen anyway, and I honestly didn't care to change their minds. But Ashton was there that night. That was how he knew the truth. It made more sense than Landon telling our secret, but I still couldn't wrap my head around it. "You knew this entire time?"

Ashton batted his lashes at me. "The *whole* time."

"Which I'm still pissed about," Jade interjected, kicking his foot where he had it stretched in front of him. "Keeping secrets is *totally* against the spirit of the Top Tier."

"You would've blabbed your mouth the second you found out," he said, sounding irritated. "We had to hold out until homecoming."

"Why?" The exact feeling that had risen up yesterday at the lunch table, moments before Landon came in with his homecoming proposal, surfaced now, except a lot more potent. "Why homecoming?"

His gaze slid back to mine, sparking. "Because that's when the bet ended."

For a second, I thought he was talking about my bet with Hudson, getting a boyfriend by homecoming. It was Jade who voiced the question for me. "Bet? What bet?"

"I bet Landon that he couldn't get you to fall for him by homecoming. Fall for him for real." Ashton sneered. "I guess he won that, huh? He barely had to do anything, and you just latched on."

I didn't think I'd ever felt more confused in my life. Despite my palms itching to smack the smirk off his face, I forced myself still. "A bet to get me to fall in love? Why do you care about me getting into a relationship?"

"The pieces aren't clicking yet." That amused him, enough that he had to look away as he chuckled. "The end of the bet plan was never a happily ever after for you. Running off into the sunset with the quarterback on your arm? Does that really sound like something I'd do for you?"

On their own accord, my gaze flicked to Madison where she'd stood silent the entire time. At least she wasn't joining them in the attack. I hated the way my heart beat faster. "Then what?"

"Landon was going to win you over and then dump you," he said bluntly. "Like the trash you are."

I'd never doubted that Ashton was off his rocker, but I almost couldn't believe what he was saying. I nearly laughed aloud at the prospect, for so many separate reasons, but one made its way out first. "All because I said no to your prom-posal?"

"It is a lot of effort for her," Jade muttered, folding her arms tighter across her chest.

"You're asking why?" Ashton asked. "Why *not*? I don't need a reason to put you in your place and have a little fun while I do it. Apparently, lover boy didn't need a reason either, since he agreed."

"You're the pathetic one," I told him, turning to Jade. I clenched my jaw so tightly that my teeth ached, but I held still. "All of you. You think I'm going to believe you and not Landon? Believe you all, who wouldn't know kindness if it bit you in the—"

Ashton carried on as if I hadn't spoken. "We could've had fun with it, too. Him and me. Could've made it symbolic or something. 'I can see now why you've never had a boyfriend—I don't want you, either.' How fitting would that have been?" Ashton sat forward on the bed and laid his forearms across his knees, linking his fingers together. "Come on. You think I don't know about the late-night phone calls, the pretending in the hookup closet, or your little 'hi, hi' thing you do? You think Landon didn't tell me about your mommy issues?"

It was like time stopped. Jade gave an amused huff, going so far as to put a hand to her mouth as the words struck me like an arrow to the chest.

Ashton saw whatever reaction I had and latched onto it, unyielding like a dog with a bone. "You have to live with your cousin now because of it? She called the cops on you and everything? Your family's a hot mess, you're a hot mess... You really, *really* believe that a guy like Landon Settler—anyone—wants a girl like *that*?"

The poisonous words pierced my heart mercilessly, and if I hadn't been holding my breath already, I would've gasped at the impact of the pain. Weirdly enough, in that moment, I had the strongest feeling of déjà vu. Back when things had still been fake between Landon and me, I'd had the briefest picture of this moment. I didn't realize it would be so painful. *You, Lacey Churchill, are unlovable.*

And it wasn't even just what Ashton said that hit so hard—it was the fact that he knew. He knew about my relationship with my mother. He knew about the incident over the summer. He knew about Landon's and my code. Secret after secret. This time, I wasn't stupid enough to wonder how Ashton knew something only my family and Landon did.

My lungs suddenly felt three sizes too tiny.

"What the hell is *wrong* with you?" Madison

demanded, taking a half step forward toward Ashton before skidding to a stop. She looked between Ashton and Jade almost desperately, chest rising and falling fast. "Why—why are you being like this? What are you doing?"

Ashton didn't even flinch at Madison's tone—then again, why would he, when all he had left to do now was bask in his win? Because that was what this was. A victory lap around the girl they managed to string along for weeks.

It was like I was back in Hudson's bedroom, waking up in a panic as I didn't recognize my surroundings. Each time, I wondered where my old bedroom went—my yellow sheets, my photographs on the wall, the yearbooks in the corner. Every time, I was stuck in a limbo of dread as reality took its sweet time to sink in.

And now, even though it took its sweet time, realization set in like a cold chill.

"I'm surprised," I said in a voice that sounded dead. "You're not recording all this? Don't want to send this to Babble?"

"Of course not," Jade replied, folding her arms across her chest. "The Top Tier has its fun where no one can see it."

Ashton came closer to me, entering my personal space and causing my blood to heat. "But go and tattle, if you want. 'The Top Tier made a bet to get me to fall in love with Landon Settler.' See who'll ever believe you about our quarterback."

"But you know what they *will* believe?" Jade took her phone out and waved it in the air a little. "That you used

Landon for his popularity. Used him to get rid of your Most Likely To title. *That'll* be front-page Babble news."

My lips twisted into a smirk as I stared at her. There wasn't anything funny about the situation, but a laugh bubbled up anyway. "It's like I said. It's pathetic how much you make Brentwood and Babble and the Top Tier your entire personality."

"Says the girl who was fake dating the quarterback."

"No," Ashton whispered, ducking his head to me. "Says the girl who thought the quarterback fell for her. How does it feel to find out he was the one stringing *you* along in the end?"

My brain instantly rallied against the thought, trying to defend Landon, but Ashton's voice still lingered in my mind like a sickening song. *'I can see now why your mom didn't want you—I don't want you, either.' How fitting would that have been?*

The guest bedroom door flung open again, the momentum so hard that it slammed into the door stop on the wall with a loud crack.

Landon surveyed the scene only briefly, regarding his Top Tier mates with little interest, and stopped looking when he found me. And just like that, the moment our eyes met, my red-hot anger melted as if I'd jumped into an ice bath. I'd held tight to the fury like a lifeline, letting it drag me through, but as soon as I looked at Landon, the rope slipped through my fingers.

"Well, there's the guest of honor," Ashton drawled as he straightened back from me. "How'd you know which room we'd be in?"

It was funny how different he looked, standing in the doorway. How hollow I felt looking at him. I wanted Landon to say something—to dismiss all of my doubts and deny all of Ashton's claims. To say it was ridiculous, a bet to get me to like him. The silence that filled the room was loud, as was the blood roaring in my ears, and I knew I wouldn't have been able to listen to him if I tried.

"You all can go to hell," I said, and shoved past Landon, not caring about my shoulder slamming into his in the process. I didn't look back and didn't slow down.

Everyone in the crowd of partygoers blurred as I moved past them, uncaring if anyone was jostled or hurt in the process. I drew in a sharp breath, needing out of this house, away from these people, into the fresh air, before I well and truly lost my mind. The front door was open, and I sailed through it, drinking in the night air, letting it sink its teeth into the burn of panic. It didn't take it away—not nearly— but it did enough to keep the world from spinning on its axis. *Get out*, my thoughts still chanted, still rattled and broken. *Get out, get out, get out.*

I made it down the front porch steps when Landon caught my wrist, holding me in place. "Lacey, wait, wait," he pleaded, stepping around in front of me and holding his hands out in front of him. Landon was normally such a broad guy, whose height was impossible to miss, but in that moment, he looked so *small*. Like he, himself, was broken, too. His chest rose and fell rapidly. "What—what did they say?"

"What do you *think* they said?" I demanded, my voice coming out like a slap.

Landon reached out and brushed his fingers against mine, curling them around. "I—I don't know, but—"

I jerked my hand out of his so hard that I nearly stumbled back a step. "When I asked you to be in a fake relationship, was Ashton there? At the restaurant?"

It was a simple question, but it seemed to hit Landon hard. He stilled on the grass, cheeks leeching of color. "I can fully explain," he said after a beat

"Explain?" I echoed, the word not making sense. "*Explain?* What's there to explain? Was he there or wasn't he?"

"He—he was, but—"

"Why? Did you know that ahead of time?"

"If I knew, I would've suggested we meet somewhere else," he insisted, blinking fast. "I wouldn't have stayed if I knew he was there. I wouldn't have agreed to the fake relationship if he was there."

I lifted my chin. "Why not? Since you went ahead and told him everything about us anyway." I knew there were people standing around, listening in, but I was so far from caring. I wasn't sure I'd ever care again. "You told him I call you on my way home from work? You told him about how we say 'hi' before touching? Did you show him our text messages, too?"

"I—"

"You made a bet with him to date me for real, Landon?" My heart started racing faster, forcing my thoughts to keep up. I jerked back a step, the confrontation stirring dangerously within me. "A bet to get me to *fall for you?*"

All the questions hit him so fast, and it was clear he struggled to keep up with the most pressing one. Landon reached up and pressed his hand to his chest, as if there was pain there. "Ashton was going to tell everyone that you were looking for a fake relationship, Lacey. He was going to run you through the dirt. I was trying to stop him, so—so I said 'wouldn't it be fun if I won her over for real?'"

"*You* proposed the idea?"

"It—it wasn't a bad thing!" he rushed out, voice loud enough for anyone around us to hear. "I didn't mean it as a bad thing. But Ashton was going to turn the whole school against you for trying to use me, and you *know* them, Lacey. It would've worked."

"So, you said 'hey, I've got an idea on how to make her seem *less* pathetic—convince her I fell in love with her, and then dump her at the end.'"

His eyes widened further. "I *never* agreed to dump you!"

"What did you expect, Landon? That Ashton would turn nice and support us? That he'd buy us couple T-shirts and say how cute we looked together?"

"I didn't think it through—"

"You think?" With that, and with fire building underneath my skin, I stomped past him, leaving the house and the staring students behind. "Guess you thought you were quite the charmer, huh? Making a bet to get me to fall for you. That's just...wow."

I knew Landon followed me close behind. "Please, Lacey, it's not—it's not how it sounds."

I wasn't sure there was anything he could say to argue

it. The fact didn't change that he'd made the bet. That he'd told Ashton about my home life. That he wasn't who I thought he was. "How am I supposed to believe *anything* that comes out of your mouth?"

"I've never lied," he insisted as we walked. His long legs kept pace with me easily. "Everything I've said—I've meant it."

"Oh, yeah?" When we reached the first row of cars, I stopped again. Electricity built up in my body, heating my veins, making me want to scream. "So you *did* like Madison?"

Landon recoiled as if I'd smacked him. "That—that was the one thing. The only thing."

There was zero energy left within me to argue, not anymore. It felt zapped out of me. Ever since Ashton stepped into that guest room, anger had been on top of all the other icky emotions. Now, though, in the coolness of the night with Landon looking at me like a wounded puppy, the anger began to recede, leaving something icy in its wake. Something more defeated. Images of the Top Tier laughing at every moment painted across my mind. Reed making up the story of Landon liking me all along. Ashton bet Landon five bucks to kiss me, knowing the truth about the fake relationship. The bet.

And Landon kissed me anyway.

"How could I have faked that, Lacey?" Landon whispered. His eyes fluttered shut for a second, as if realizing the straws he grasped were now few. "How—how could I have faked any of it with you?"

"I'm sure it was second nature to you, right? To *all* of

you. I was wrong before when I said you were different from the Top Tier. You're not different. In fact, you are all *exactly* alike." My voice cracked, the perfectly curated mask breaking apart as my eyes began to sting. "Except it's almost worse. You know better, but you went along with it anyway. You don't start things, but you don't stop them either. Just like freshman year."

Landon rocked back as if I'd shoved him, chest caving as he let out a breath. The night at Lookout Ledge, with my bag of candy and the stars above us, I could remember his voice with perfect clarity. *How do you know I'm different than the Top Tier?* His urgent expression, eyes filled with something like fear. Vulnerability. Desperation. I'd put my hands on his cheeks and brushed off his fears so confidently. *You are not like them.*

I couldn't believe how wrong I'd been.

I reached up and lifted the necklace over my head, his class ring rocking on the chain. A part of me wanted to chuck it into the night, forcing him to scour through the bushes for it. In a perfect world, it'd take him until dawn. Instead, I was merciful, gathering the necklace in my palm before tossing it to him. "Go back inside," I told him. "Go back to where you belong." *Because it isn't with me.*

I wasn't sure Landon could've looked more heartbroken if he tried, and in that instant, he looked like a boy with reddish brown hair, freckles, and the saddest face in the entire world. He opened his mouth, but I cut him off. "Don't," I said, but the word cracked. I held my hand up, warding him off. "Just...don't."

And he didn't. He sagged back, the tension between his

shoulders evaporating with defeat. Even now, staring at him, my heart cried out to surge forward, but my body held firm. The fact of the matter was he truly *wasn't* the person I thought he was. The night had shattered so many things, and it all lay between us now, too broken to cross.

He was the saddest boy that I turned away from, and I didn't look back.

CHAPTER 29

The Bishop house was silent when I walked in.

The lights were off, and there hadn't been anyone in the driveway. Not Uncle Dean's car, not my van. Hudson wasn't back from Tee's yet. I wasn't sure where Uncle Dean would've gone with Paisley, but their absence felt too perfect, in a broken way. An open door for me to walk through. The perfect chance.

Uncle Dean had turned off the air conditioning days ago, but the air felt icy and stagnant, and I waded through it almost in a daze. The entire walk back to the house, I'd been numb. Almost like the late September air had frozen me solid, keeping my thoughts scattered and my emotions at bay. Now inside, out of the cold, it all began to thaw, dripping little drops of sadness and anger.

Not now, I willed almost desperately, entering Hudson's room and dropping to the ground. I yanked my suitcase out from underneath his bed and grabbed some of my discarded clothes from the floor, shoving them inside, not caring that they were dirty. Not caring about anything.

I unzipped a flap in the suitcase and found my savings stashed inside, the little sandwich bags filled with bills and coins. I hadn't found a better way to store it all, but it was all there. There, and ready to go.

I'd just gotten to my feet when I heard a vehicle in the driveway, and I took my suitcase up with me, gripping the handle tightly. I'd know the sound of that engine anywhere.

I met Hudson on the threshold, and he lifted his head when he realized I blocked him. "Hey," he began, and then cut off, gaze going to my suitcase. "What are you doing?"

"I'm going for a drive."

"With your suitcase?"

The accusation in his voice was obvious; he hadn't tried to hide it.

"Lacey." Hudson pushed into the house with alarm growing in his eyes, which forced me back a few steps. "What—what happened? Where's Landon?"

Back at the party, probably laughing with his buddies about how easy it was to get Lacey Churchill to fall in love. "It doesn't matter," I said, holding my hand out. "Can I have the keys?"

I did a good job of holding it all together, but the tape and glue quivered the longer Hudson stared at me. I hated myself in that moment, because time and time again, he told me not to leave, and I was finally doing it. Practically telling him his feelings didn't matter. They *did* matter, but I couldn't do it anymore. It felt like I'd entered survival mode, fighting to hold my head above water.

I watched the helplessness cross Hudson's expression, like he was about to make a decision he'd regret. He stepped past me and into the kitchen, reaching up into one of the cabinets they hardly used. "Your...your mom dropped this off while we were at school today."

Hudson brought over a tan-colored envelope, passing it over to me with a grim frown. I took it hesitantly, pulling back the unsealed flap and peering inside. In the official scrawl, I found the words. *Certificate of Birth.*

The urge to laugh a little bubbled up at the document. The one thing I asked of Mom that she actually did. The last thing I asked of her. She didn't fight me to stay, refuse to give it up—her palm was spread wide, waiting for me to fly away first. The pieces were finally falling into place, but my legs suddenly felt too heavy to lift.

"Even after everything," Hudson began softly, "you still want to leave?"

I nodded. *I don't want to*, I thought distantly. *I need to.*

Hudson took a step closer to me, his eyes softening. "Tell me what happened. Something had to have happened, since you were fine a few hours ago. Did Landon do something?"

I scrunched my face up, trying to grab onto a mask of frustration so the burning in my eyes wouldn't transform into tears. "I dumped him."

Suddenly, Hudson wrapped his arms around me and squeezed. I stiffened from the contact, trying to remember the last time we hugged. When his mom died, maybe. The Bishops and the Churchills weren't huggers. Especially not me. My arms hung like deadweight at my sides, my eyes wide as they stared over his shoulder, vision beginning to grow blurry.

Hudson patted my back slowly, like a mother trying to soothe a baby. "I know your mind is set, but I want you to stay," he said. "Paisley would want you to stay, and so would my dad. If you're waiting for someone to say they want you, we do."

It was like an arrow directly to my heart, piercing and nearly causing me to double over. I pushed at Hudson until he let go, breaking out of his grip and taking a large step back. "I have to go," I insisted, taking the van keys from Hudson. "The money for Petunia's in the top drawer of your dresser. I'll come back to officially transfer the title."

Hudson looked off toward the living room. "You don't have to buy the van off me. It was going to be a graduation gift."

"Keep it. You can think of it as payment for everything." The blurriness in my vision faded a bit, and I blinked quickly. "I'll call you. Your dad—"

"I'll deal with him." Hudson looked off toward the living room, fixated on something, with a hard line to his jaw. "I bet that if you got a boyfriend by homecoming, I wouldn't stop you from leaving. You won. I'm not going to threaten you to stay. You turn eighteen tomorrow. It's not like it's even going to matter then."

The bet. The stupid, stupid bet. The reason I began fake dating Landon in the first place, the reason I opened my heart to have the Top Tier quarterback and his friends crush it to pieces. But ultimately, it was the bet that let me get away with nothing holding me back. In a way, I was grateful.

"It was a good effort," I said, gripping the handle of my suitcase tightly.

"I want you to be happy." Hudson's voice was resigned, a weary sigh following. "Whatever that means."

An ache crept up my throat, squeezing like it was about to cut off my airway. *Not yet*, I willed, lifting my chin. "I'll call you," I repeated, and with that, I headed outside.

The van was warm since Hudson had been driving it, and when I looked down, I saw the gas gauge was on full. Hudson must've filled it before coming home. It was almost laughable—I'd been fighting for so long to leave Brentwood, and now finally tonight, things were falling into place. Everything was. There wasn't a single thing holding me back.

I settled into the driver's seat once I picked up speed, focusing on the road, the signs, watching them pass by in a blur. I never passed a *Now Leaving Brentwood* sign—did the city even have those?—but I felt the liberation like it was a physical thing anyway, leaving behind the lights and the houses and merging to get onto the highway.

I picked up speed, something building in my chest like it was a live thing. The numbness had thawed, opening the holes in my heart the ice had filled. Leaving Brentwood meant leaving so many other things. Jade and Madison and their stupid insults. Ashton and his creepiness. My mother and her motherless nature. Landon.

How could he? After everything—everything he said, everything he did. When had it become such a joke in his eyes that he thought it would be funny to rip my heart out? Or had I just been a joke all along?

Each time I smiled at Landon, held his hand, sat with him at the lunch table—they had to have been laughing on the inside.

And when Landon kissed me in front of everyone... I closed my eyes for a brief second, shutting out the visual, flinching against the painful twinge in my chest.

I drove and drove and drove, until I passed through New York, entered New Jersey, and came close to Pennsylvania. My eyes burned with tears unshed, but I didn't slow, putting as much distance between Brentwood and myself as I could as the memories rang through my head like gunshots.

Landon sitting with me on the trunk of his car, staring at the stars.

Landon looming over me in the hookup closet, eyes wide with surprise.

Landon kissing my temple while I cried, pressing me close as if he could seal me inside himself to protect me.

You said I was your tether, Landon had said. *I don't want to let you fly away, not yet. Not when we're in the middle of a chapter.*

And all of that was *fake?*

The length of the day poured over me, and mixed with the sting of tears, it had been hard keeping my eyes open. When the dash blinked a little after one in the morning, I pulled off at a service plaza off the interstate, feeling my heart kick up in anticipation. My first ever stay in the van— officially. From what I'd researched, rest stops were a maximum of a two-hour stay, but the bigger service plazas had a twenty-four hour stay limit. At least in this state.

I made sure to park underneath a lamppost and went to work doing exactly as I'd always prepared to do. I attached my Velcro window blockers on the front windows and windshield, keeping out prying eyes. I made sure I had my pepper spray and pocketknife close, locking the van up tight, and settling in.

But I hadn't expected to feel so *empty* going through the tasks. What was supposed to be the big adventure of my life felt so...hollow now.

What if we kicked off that adventure...together? Landon's words caused my insides to brace. His voice had been so happy then, hopeful. Like he'd truly wanted to come with me, truly wanted me to stay. How had we gone from that to the truth in a matter of an hour?

I stared at the dark ceiling of the van with only a little battery-powered nightlight on the countertop to light the space up. The service plaza wasn't too loud, with the rumbling of trucks as they idled and then the mild white noise of those still driving on the interstate. Despite the lack of noise, I couldn't close my eyes, couldn't get my mind to shut off.

My phone was pressed against my hip, the glass screen cold against my skin from where my T-shirt had pushed up. I shouldn't look at it. Shouldn't. I had an idea of what it might've held, but then I also was so desperately afraid of what it might *not* have held. Afraid of the texts waiting for me, but even more afraid of the texts that might not have been waiting for me. But I knew for a fact I'd never be able to sleep unless I checked.

So, with slow movements, I wrapped my fingers around

the rectangle, slowly bringing it up. There were several texts, but Uncle Dean's—which came in an hour ago—was the most recent.

UNCLE DEAN

I'm not mad, kiddo. Text me when you're somewhere safe for the night, and we can talk tomorrow.

Tears pricked at my eyes, and I shared my location with my uncle through our Friend Finder app. I flipped the setting to make sure it stayed on.

LACEY

Just shared my location with you. I'm safe. Thank you for everything, Uncle Dean. Tell Paisley I love her and that I'll call her tomorrow.

The thought of my littlest cousin realizing that I was gone caused another rift to open in my chest, one that ached like an actual wound. We'd just gotten to a good place after everything, and I abandoned her all over again. For good, this time.

You're like your mother in that regard, a thought hissed, and the words came like a slap to the face. It was so shocking that I found myself sitting up, hair flying into my eyes.

The thought made me sick, and the sickness only compiled when I saw the next notification.

Landon – 1 missed call

Landon – 1 voicemail

No texts, just one missed call and one voicemail. A part

of me felt offended at the fact that he only tried to contact me once—I wasn't worth the double text?—but the other part, the larger part, was too consumed with what the voice-mail might've contained to really care. There would be no cutting him off this time. If I pressed play, I would have to listen to all of it until the end.

My thumb hovered over the *Delete* button. Whatever he said, I couldn't possibly trust it. But could I really delete what could possibly be the last thing I ever heard Landon Settler say? Could I delete something from the boy I'd given my heart to? He'd broken it, but the pieces still lay around me, radiating the pain.

"Tomorrow," I whispered to myself, leaving the voice-mail untouched and locking my phone. "Decide tomorrow."

With the wind swaying Petunia ever so slightly, and the droning hum of idling semi-trucks keeping me company, sleep didn't find me for a long, long time.

CHAPTER 30

I sat with my legs dangling out the open back of Petunia, letting the cold morning breeze stir my damp hair. I'd gone into the rest plaza to shower and grab a few snacks, and they lay on the comforter beside me, untouched as I watched the sunrise. It wasn't pretty. Thick clouds covered whatever colors there would've been, and the morning looked...gray. There wasn't really another way to describe it. Gray clouds in a gray sky, creating a gray morning. When I pictured this moment, the first morning on the road, the sky was filled with so many beautiful colors —oranges, yellows, pinks, all blending into a breathtaking view.

I didn't get any of that, though. Just gray.

Tugging a corner of my comforter over my legs, I turned to my snacks. A bag of trail mix, salt and vinegar flavored chips, and a bag of strawberry Twizzlers. They didn't have cherry.

This time three weeks ago, none of this would've bothered me. The idea of scouring rest centers for good road trip snacks had been exciting. Being able to wake up in the van, to feel the wind pass through the vehicle once I opened the doors, was enough to keep me eagerly working on it. Weeks ago, the sky could've been a baby puke green for all I would've cared—the fact that I got to experience it would've been worth it.

And now I sat with my pitiful breakfast watching a sunrise that really didn't exist, hating myself for feeling disappointed.

In three weeks' time, my beautiful dream was ruined.

Before, I never considered it running away. I'd simply been eager to start over. Now, though...now I *was* running away.

I turned my phone over in my hand, tapping it against my fingertips. A minute and eleven seconds. It sat on my phone like a timebomb, waiting for me to detonate. I might've been in Pennsylvania, but there'd truly be no escaping him unless I answered it. Unless I laid everything to rest.

All in or fold. With Landon, it had only ever been one choice.

I pressed play, bringing my trembling hand up, lifting my phone to my ear.

"I know you might not listen to this," Landon's voice said. I stiffened even though I'd been expecting it, instantly transported to last night. "You might've even blocked my number already. I wouldn't blame you. God, I've made such a mess of things, and it's—*I'm* pathetic. I swear. The bet with Ashton—and it was stupid—but I never meant for you to find out about it."

I kicked my feet hard against the back of the van. "No kidding," I whispered as if he could actually hear me.

"I know how it looks. What it sounded like. I needed to tell you that none of it was fake to me."

I lay back down as his voice grew in earnestness. If I closed my eyes, it would've almost been like I'd gone back to Wednesday, with my head on his chest, his voice soft in my ear. Only now it was filled with far more sadness.

"Even back to the beginning, when you first asked me to Le Petit Bateau. I never told you, but I was so *stupidly happy* that you asked me. That day in the hallway, I thought I was dreaming. I thought my friends put you up to it because they knew how I felt about you. How I *have* felt about you. I've—" Landon drew in a gasping breath, one that sounded sucked between his teeth. "I've loved you since the fourth grade, and I know you don't believe me—I wouldn't believe me either. Underneath the passenger seat is some sort of proof, though. And if you ever decide you want more proof, or to talk..." He let out a little breath, one that trembled even through the phone. "You can call me. Curfew or not."

All of the times Landon said that raced through my mind, echoing like he spoke them now himself.

You know, if you ever want to talk on your way home from work, you can call me. Curfew or not.

Even if we don't talk, I'll stay on the line. So...call me, Lacey.

Before you run, call me first. So you won't be alone.

I sucked in a breath, gripping my phone tighter, but

Landon didn't speak again. The minute and eleven seconds were up.

Still staring up at the ceiling, I didn't lower my phone. Everything he said bordered between making sense and insanity, leaving me reeling. *I've loved you since the fourth grade.* The L word—he'd spoken it so easily, so freely, like it'd been a truth he'd kept bottled up and it finally spilled out. *Underneath the passenger seat is some sort of proof.*

I bit down hard on my lip, turning my head toward the front of the van, even though I couldn't see anything. When would Landon have had time to put anything under the seat? Then again, would he have told such an easily provable lie?

Slowly, I sat up on the mattress, hating myself for being so easily enticed. *All in.*

I fell to my knees at the back side of the passenger seat, and I slipped my palm underneath, tapping around. At first, all I felt were crumbs that I'd done a terrible job of vacuuming up, apparently. There was a screw, too, left over from the construction process. And then—something slippery. Thin. A book.

I pulled out the Evergreen Elementary book, staring at the green and gold color scheme on the front cover with shock radiating through me. Landon must've picked it up from my bedroom floor before following after me outside.

Picked it up and stashed it underneath the front seat.

I flipped open the cover, confused and breathless as I skimmed for my grade. I'd been wrong before when I thought this was my fifth-grade yearbook—it was my fourth grade, and I found myself easily. In the fourth grade, my hair had been a near strawberry blonde, a color I assumed I took after my father. For picture day, I'd worn it in the world's highest ponytail with two thick pieces hanging out to frame my face.

I scanned through the meager list of students until I found him, and my heart gave a painful squeeze.

The boy looked skinny, lanky, nothing reminiscent of the broad football player he was now. His face was full of brown freckles, concentrated across his cheeks, accented by his vibrantly red hair. It was pushed out of his eyes with hair gel, spiked up to reveal his smile. It was the kind of face that most little kids had—awkward, showing all their teeth without really lifting their lips. He wore a blue collared shirt that was buttoned all the way to his throat, with even a little vest over that.

Despite everything, Landon Settler was the most adorable fourth grader I'd ever seen.

As I traced his portrait, something flashed in my memory. The same little boy hunched over his desk.

I flipped a page in the yearbook to our spread of classroom photos. I searched for the red-haired little boy in them, but they were all filled with kids I didn't recognize. I was in one of them, holding a paintbrush in an art class with a green plastic apron covering my clothes.

The next photo had me pausing. It was Valentine's Day —it was obvious from the decorations that hung in the background of the photo. All of the children had lined up to take the photo, all holding their Valentine's Day boxes. Everyone except one.

On this day, my hair was down. I beamed widely at the

camera, exposing my gapped teeth and sparkling eyes. My arms were wrapped around the boy beside me like I had been giving him a hug, but had stopped and turned for the photo. The boy didn't look at the camera, but at me, and even through the photo, the fourth grader's awestruck expression was clear. The box he held was all pink and purple, with a girl's name scripted across the front.

It was Landon, holding a Valentine's Day box with my name.

The box and all the cards had her name on them, of course, but she said she had enough love to share with me, Landon had said that day on the beach, barely looking at me. *I guess, ever since then...it's always been her.*

He hadn't been talking about Madison, and he hadn't made up the story. He'd been telling the truth.

It had been about me.

I've loved you since the fourth grade, he'd said in the voicemail, and there hadn't been a trace of hesitance in the words. All at once, my mind flipped back through the weeks, trying to find something that would contradict him... but coming up empty.

He's always been too chicken to ask you out, Reed had said at the party, smiling fondly. *Totally chicken. I'm glad he finally worked up the nerve. It only took him until senior year.*

That hadn't been a lie. It'd been the truth.

I held the realization between my hands and didn't know what to do with it. I lingered in my doubt, in my skepticism, because that felt like the only way I could protect myself. Just because I gave him my Valentine's Day box didn't necessarily mean that he had loved me the entire time. It only meant that that hadn't been a lie.

I went to shut the book, but the laminated pages flipped together, exposing the back spine where my classmates had signed their names. I looked at the chaotic handwriting that had partially faded or smudged, trying to remember it. It was a vague memory, passing around yearbooks at the last day of school—a memory that could've belonged to any grade, not just the fourth. But the image of that red-haired boy bent over his desk cleared in my mind, and he hadn't been bent crying—he'd been bent signing a yearbook.

I found his signature, tracing the messy, boyish writing with my finger.

Thank you for being my first friend. I know it looks goofy. I'll draw you prettier in the future. – Landon Settler

And underneath the words was a stick figure of a girl with a wide sideways C mouth, two circles for eyes, and two lines for hair.

But he never had a chance since I moved at the beginning of the fifth grade, and even though we started going to the same school again in the seventh, our paths hadn't crossed again until senior year.

I let out a breath that shook, matching the way my hands trembled as I gripped the yearbook. I didn't remember it—try as hard as I wanted to, I couldn't remember Valentine's Day of the fourth grade. What had been a memory that hadn't stuck in my mind had stayed in Landon's. *Ever since then...it's always been her.*

I checked, but Babble didn't post anything about the fight Landon and I had in front of Ashton's house last night. I waited all morning for a post. Even though the Top Tier said they wouldn't air their dirty laundry, I still wasn't sure that someone wouldn't leak it. I was going to use that as my final decision maker. To go back or not to go back. I had been sure someone would've had to submit something about it—there were enough listening ears, after all.

Because if there was one thing Babble completely wigged out over, it was homecoming.

I walked the fragile line of indecision. It was safer to run, to never look back. Safer to leave Brentwood and everyone in it in the dust. To never have to deal with a Jade or an Ashton or a mom again.

But I'd also be giving up the Hudsons, the Paisleys, and the Landons.

Starting over meant starting fresh, leaving the pain in the past.

I never wanted to start my trip of freedom off with running away. I always tried to frame it in my mind that I wasn't running away, but starting fresh, starting anew. But this—leaving without knowing the full truth—was running away, and I knew I couldn't do it.

As the gray clouds parted in the sky, revealing a sliver of glimmering, yellow sunlight, I knew for certain: I was going back.

It took me a little over five hours to get back to Brentwood, since traffic picked up once I got into a construction zone. The landscape was so vastly different in the light than it'd been in the dark last night, and as I drove east, it was like the clouds began parting further, exposing more of the beautiful blue.

I ended up pulling into the Bishop driveway a little after two o'clock, easing underneath the car park and behind Uncle Dean's car. Paisley's bike was leaning against the side of the trailer, and the main door was open, letting wind funnel through the screen door. A part of me felt ashamed for showing up, for putting them through everything and then waltzing back up like nothing happened. I couldn't help but smile at the familiarity of it all, though, and at the warmth that bloomed behind my fluttering heart.

Drawing in a steeling breath, I popped my door open and hopped out.

I had stepped on the top porch stair when the house door opened, revealing Paisley and her braided pigtails. Her eyes widened as she saw me, eyebrows shooting up on her forehead. "It's Lacey!"

I sucked in a breath as another figure appeared behind her—taller, blonder, one with a face that mimicked his little sister's. Hudson. "You're back?"

"I'm back," I said somewhat awkwardly, opening the screen door and stepping into the house. "What are you doing home?"

"Half day for homecoming," Hudson returned, and he was awkward too. Then again, the note we left on last night wasn't exactly chipper.

Weirdly enough, it seemed different, like something changed in the last twenty-four hours. Nothing *looked* different, but the air felt different. Less stiff and stifling, less like a stranger's house. It almost felt like coming home. "Where's your dad?"

"Here." I turned to find Uncle Dean emerging from his

bedroom, holding his e-reader. He seemed just as shocked to see me, though he fought to hide it more than the other two did. "Happy to see you, kiddo."

"Happy birthday!" Paisley said, rocking back onto her heels. "Hudson said you got to skip school since it was your birthday, but Dad says I can't do that for mine."

I looked up at the boy in question, who sort of shook his head.

"Only big kids get to skip on their birthday," I told her, reaching out and nudging her shoulder. Uncle Dean and Hudson still hovered on the edge, staring but not saying anything. I ducked my head like I stood before a judge. "I'm sorry for last night. For...everything."

Uncle Dean reached out and lightly laid his hand on my shoulder. "Don't apologize. Please. You have nothing to be sorry for."

"Besides, it's your birthday," Hudson added, resting his hand on the top of Paisley's head, despite her frown. "You get a pass."

"I shouldn't get a pass." I glanced around the room, throat tightening as I took in their expressions. The surprise was still there, but on each of their faces was something warm that made me want to fall into their arms and cry. "I made you worry. I didn't take what you all thought into account. I was so desperate to get away from everything that I forgot who I was actually leaving behind."

"We're family." Uncle Dean shook my shoulder affectionately. "We make each other worry. It's what we do. Isn't that right, Hudson?"

Hudson rolled his eyes a little. "How many times do I

have to apologize about taking the pocketknife to school, Dad?"

"Until I forget that you nearly got expelled for it."

I bit back a laugh, blinking against the haziness in my eyes. "I do have one condition, I guess you could call it, if I come back," I said, sniffing back the tears. "Hudson gets his room back and I sleep on the couch."

The three Bishops looked around at each other, and then Paisley stepped forward. "What if you slept in my room?" she asked, batting her eyes. "We could get bunkbeds and you could have the top one. It would fit perfect."

"We had talked about it earlier in the week," Uncle Dean said, tipping his head. "Paisley came up with the idea."

"You came up with it?" I reached out and nudged her arm. "That's a pretty good idea."

"Agreed," Hudson piped in, sliding his hands into his front pockets. "I wasn't going to say anything, but I think I *am* developing a hunch."

Uncle Dean shot his son a look.

Paisley walked forward and wrapped her arms around me first, and then Hudson and Uncle Dean followed suit, picking up on what I needed without me even saying anything. All the sniffling and clearing my throat hadn't helped, because a tear rolled down my cheek now, but I didn't try to wipe it away and hide it. "We're always here for you, kiddo," Uncle Dean murmured in the group hug. "Don't ever feel alone. We're always here."

I closed my eyes, settling into the warmth of the hug.

My idea of family had evolved these past few weeks. Family wasn't someone who didn't want to be there. It was someone who stuck around through thick and thin, someone who still loved you no matter what.

And I was so glad I realized it before I'd strayed too far.

When we parted, Uncle Dean asked for a moment alone to talk to me, and we walked out to Petunia and popped open the back door. He didn't climb up to sit on the mattress, but rather peered around at the insides. He never seemed too interested in the progress over the past few months, but never hesitated to ask if I needed anything. Power tools. Screws. Paintbrushes. He'd been a silent supporter in it all, and lingered around it now, expression serious.

"You know," he began softly, nodding as he avoided my eyes. "You're a lot like your mother."

I knew it wasn't an insult, but I felt myself stiffen anyway. "How so?"

"She never wanted to stay in Brentwood either." Uncle Dean patted the propped-open door, smoothing his hand up it. "Traveling around in a van wasn't really popular when we were growing up, but she definitely wanted to leave town. Brentwood's big, but she always said it wasn't big enough for her."

"I didn't know that. That she wanted to leave." I rubbed my palms over my knees, not sure that I wanted to know the answer to the question I was about to ask. "Why didn't she?"

"She got pregnant with you." Uncle Dean's lips quirked up a little, but it wasn't exactly a smile. "She was excited, you know. Especially to be pregnant the same time as Renee."

It was strange to hear him talk about my mom so softly, especially after the months of *not* talking about her. Even before everything fell apart, stories of my mom when she was younger were few and far between. When Aunt Renee was still alive, she'd tell me some things, but never Uncle Dean. He always said thinking back that far was a blur.

"I don't think she was really prepared for how much it took to be a mom," he went on. "Not really. Does anyone really know until they experience it? It's hard. There were two of us raising Hudson, and it was hard. And your mom did it on her own."

That much, I knew, of course. Mom getting pregnant out of wedlock, her one-night stand wanting nothing to do with a baby. It was her story and mine, even though she hadn't really shared it with me. Not really. Mom's past before my memory was shadowy—if I did know it, those memories collected too much dust to remember.

"She's never been the motherly type, either. She struggled a lot after you were born. I think once you were old enough, and we started watching you more—once Lizzie got a taste of her freedom again—it was hard for her to go back."

He didn't say it, but my mind filled in the blank—she let herself imagine what it'd be like to not be a mother. She missed the life she lived before me, mourned the life she could've had without me. I'd always known it. All the times I made dinner for myself. Waited for her to come home.

Listened to her talk with her friends. Motherhood wasn't for everyone...and it hadn't been for her.

Uncle Dean cleared his throat and kicked his work boot in the grit of the driveway. "She didn't do things right by you. There were a lot of things she could've done differently. She doesn't deserve one of those *Best Mom Ever* mugs."

A ghostly grin touched my mouth now.

"I'm not saying to give her a free pass. I'm not saying to forgive her. I want you to know that it was never you. It wasn't anything you did or didn't do. You're a good kid, Lacey. It was always her."

It was never you. It was always her. The words triggered something contradictory inside me, like relief and discomfort at the same time. Hot and cold. Happy and sad.

Uncle Dean reached into the cab then and awkwardly wrapped his arm around my shoulders to give me a squeezing hug. I froze, motionless with the most affection he'd shown me. "I'm proud of you, Lacey," he murmured, giving me a squeeze.

I ducked my head closer to him, letting myself bask in the moment. It'd been a long, long while since I'd had a parental hug like this. I couldn't even remember it. *Uncle Dean is a great dad—he's the dad I never had,* I'd told Paisley, and I believed it wholeheartedly. I never knew my father, but Uncle Dean fit that role perfectly. Absolutely perfectly.

CHAPTER 31

$\mathcal{I}$t was no secret that I wasn't Brentwood High's biggest fan. I never belonged on the cheer squad, stood out in the student section, and probably didn't have an ounce of spirt in my body. Even in years past, I could count the number of times I went to sport games on one hand. Though it wasn't the first homecoming I'd been to, I never had someone to watch on the field before. Never had a reason to care.

I could hear the roaring crowd at the Brentwood High football game even before I opened the door to my van. And that was me having parked all the way in the senior lot five minutes from the field. It would've been near impossible to find parking up close, and I didn't even want to risk it.

"*Aaaaaand* touchdown by number 22, Connor Bray!" the announcer called, and his voice reverberated through the speakers, carrying over. "And that's halftime, folks! Which means it's time for the halftime show by our very own Brentwood High marching band and cheer squad! Let's give them a hand!"

I swung my legs out to hang over my seat, staring at the football field with the stadium lights. Halftime. Which meant that once the marching band was finished with their songs, the homecoming court would come out onto the field. Landon would be there with Madison on his arm.

I almost didn't show, which was why I'd missed half the game. The scoreboard was hidden by the bleachers from the angle I'd parked in, so I couldn't even tell if the Bobcats were winning or not.

You didn't come all the way here to sit in Petunia, I scolded myself, drawing in a breath as I hopped out.

I walked up to the field while listening to the awkward blare of the band, bundling my jacket tighter around my shoulders, tucking my chin beneath the collar. I paid at the ticket booth and walked toward the fenced edge of the field where a few others leaned against it. I hooked my fingers through the chain link and scanned the field, trembling.

"Okay, Bobcats," the announcer cut through the tail end of the band's song, excitement in full blast. "Before we get back to the game, let's take a second to recognize the Brentwood High homecoming court!"

The underclassmen representatives for homecoming court came out first, freshmen and sophomores I didn't recognize. When the junior reps came out, I spotted one person I did recognize—Nathan Tulane. Nate wore his football gear with his helmet off, revealing a sweaty head of hair. He had his arm awkwardly crooked for Riley Huntington, who was dressed in a baby pink gown with sequins I could see glitter even from here. I wondered if that meant they'd gotten back together—I hoped not.

Since I was positioned close to where they walked down, Nate spotted me by the fence, giving me a little wave. I saluted him back, shaking my head in amusement. He wouldn't be able to win since he wasn't a senior, but he would've been on my list for the crown if he could've had it.

"Oh my gosh," a woman at my arm exclaimed as the announcer voiced the next reps. "Look at how adorable they look together!"

The couple I'd been waiting for came next. Landon and Madison walked down the middle of the football field, causing people to cheer louder as the announcer gave their names. They really did look like a cute couple together—the perfect high school cliché. Madison's floor-length gown glittered like gemstones underneath the football lights, and it clung to her body in a way that made her look more mature.

She looked like a million bucks hanging off of Landon's arm, in a way I never could.

"They're the perfect pair," a man replied to the woman, clapping. "Ah, Clayton must be so proud of his son."

I was slow to shift my gaze toward her partner, my insides bracing. Like Nate, Landon still wore his football uniform. Especially paired with Madison's blue, the gold accents on his jersey really popped. He had a small smile on his face, one that, if you knew him, made it clear how uncomfortable he was with all the attention. He leaned to say something to Madison, causing her to laugh.

Perfect pair, I echoed in my thoughts at the exact same time Landon's gaze slid to mine.

Landon's lips fell, the discomfort transitioning as his shock upon seeing me settled in. I sucked in a breath, backing away from the fence, letting the adults around me swarm in my open spot. I hadn't expected him to see me—I hadn't even decided whether or not I wanted him to.

I made my way toward the concession stand, getting in the line. Everyone else was out there watching the homecoming court get announced. "One hot chocolate, please," I told the cashier, passing over a handful of bills at the exact same time the crowd began rising in volume. Like something dramatic was going on. I watched as the little old man grabbed the hot chocolate thermos, wondering if there was a homecoming brawl over a plastic crown going down on the field.

From the corner of my eye, I saw someone cut around the concession stand with their cleats sliding on the gravel. I didn't notice the blue and the gold that swamped them until I turned, finding Landon standing there, chest rising and falling rapidly.

"What are you doing?" I demanded, glancing around as if expecting a coach to be chasing after him. "You're —you're—"

"You're here," he said in what almost sounded like awe. "I thought—I thought I imagined you on the sidelines. I thought I was going crazy."

I bit down on my lower lip at the confession, unsure how to feel. "You're supposed to be out there for the homecoming court—"

"Connor is busy doing a homecoming proposal, and no one was looking, so I—"

"He chose *now* to ask Jade?" It was a cool grand gesture, I guessed, but I was a little miffed that it was the she-devil who got it.

Landon shook his head and came closer, not looking anywhere but me. "You're really here. I didn't...I didn't expect you to be."

The little old man passed me my Styrofoam cup of hot chocolate while his gaze darted between us, obviously intrigued. I picked it up, the temperature warming my fingers, feeling a little more grounded now that I had something to hold. "I found your proof."

Landon opened his mouth when the little old man set another cup of steaming liquid on the counter. "For you, Mr. Quarterback," he said with a cheery face. "Hopefully this cup will help you to win the game."

Landon hastily picked up the cup. "Thank you, sir," he said, and then stepped away from the counter and turned to me. "Can we—can we talk? Over here?"

I hesitantly followed behind him as we left the old man, going to a corner near the backside of the bleachers where no one stood. Everyone was too busy paying attention to the field to even come searching for Landon. I kept a bit of distance between us, too nervous to get too close. "How did you remember that Valentine's Day photo was in our yearbook?"

"It was the only trace of you I had. In the fifth grade, I looked at the picture all the time to remember you. I was probably creepy." He closed his eyes and winced. "And it's embarrassing to say aloud, but I'll tell you anything, Lacey. Everything."

"Now isn't the time," I said, because *duh*. He was literally standing in his football uniform while the halftime clock ticked down. "You're in the middle of the homecoming game. We'll talk—"

"I couldn't care less about the game." To punctuate this, Landon tugged his shoulder pads off, revealing his black athletic shirt underneath. He dropped the pads uncaringly, taking a step closer. "I wasn't even sure I was going to show up in the first place. How could any of that matter after you left?"

I couldn't look away from the shoulder pads for a long moment, staring at how they were resting in the mud. "Landon—"

"I'd trade all of that for you in a heartbeat," he went on, voice still firm and unwavering. "Quarterback, Top Tier, popularity—if it meant that I got to be yours, I'd never look back."

If I got to be yours. Not *if you got to be mine.* I lifted my cup to my lips to hide a bit of my expression, feeling the significance of the word choice tickle my insides. "Have you really liked me since the fourth grade?"

"Yes," he said without hesitating. "And I can prove it to you."

Could he? He'd been able to prove that he might've liked me *during* the fourth grade, but how could he possibly prove that he's liked me since? I was desperate for the answer, though—to be able to push past the one thing holding me back. "Where is it? Your proof."

"My house." Landon held his hand out to me tentatively, palm facing the sky. "Let's go."

I blinked in surprise. Uh, he was in the middle of something right now, did he forget that? I stared at his upturned palm, imagining sliding my hand into it, wrapping my fingers around his in the way we always did. My pinkie between his index and middle fingers. A perfect grip just for us. Instead, I reached out and curled his fingers inward, gently pushing his hand away. He might not have known it, but this moment, him offering to walk away from his senior year homecoming game was proof enough.

"Finish the game first," I said, lifting my eyes to his. "Then we'll talk."

He didn't turn away. His cleats remained rooted to the ground, as if he hadn't heard me. The people in the bleachers were cheering about something, and when I looked over, I saw the scoreboard ticking down how much time was left for the half. I was surprised no one came searching for their quarterback yet.

I nudged his shoulder pads with the tip of my boot. "Put those on, win homecoming, and then you can show me."

"You won't leave," he whispered, but it came out sounding more as a plea. "Right?"

The sad quality of his voice had me wanting to reach out to him, to wrap my arms around him like he did me when I was upset. "I won't," I promised as I took a sip of my watered-down hot chocolate to ease the sudden pressure in my throat. "I won't leave until we talk."

Landon gave a small nod, but still didn't seem

convinced. He bent down and picked up his shoulder pads, gripping them by the collar. "I'll meet you after, then."

"I'll be by the fence," I said, pointing to where he'd spotted me earlier.

Another nod.

"Break a leg," I told him, and then paused. "Is that something you say in football?"

The worried line of his lips broke as the corner of them tipped up a little. "No, because it could actually happen."

I laughed a little, too, though it sounded awkward. "Good luck, then."

Landon walked backward toward the field for several paces, nearly clipping a few kids playing in the grass, before ultimately turning to jog the rest of the way. I sipped more of my hot chocolate as I stood in place. Hopefully seeing me and anticipating our conversation later wasn't going to throw him off for the last half of the game. There was no way I'd have been able to focus if it was me. I could still picture his face as our gazes locked, the wide-eyed shock he hadn't tried to hide. Disbelief...relief.

How could I fake that? he'd asked me last night, and in that moment, it was clear that everything on his face had been real.

As I made my way back to the fence, I realized I'd made the right choice this morning, turning back. Just to see that expression on his face.

CHAPTER 33

Like I promised, I waited against the fence after the game, watching people file toward the parking lot in droves. Every Bobcat in sight was relishing in the win of their homecoming game, chattering about each seamless pass and epic touchdown, and the post-game party practically *everyone* was attending. I eavesdropped as I rocked against the chain-link, nerves stirring in my stomach.

A group of cheerleaders walked past me, too engrossed in their own whispering conversations to glance my way. Jade and Madison weren't among them. In fact, even though I'd been keeping close watch on the area, I hadn't seen either cheerleader.

The football players began emerging from the locker room slowly, quickly intercepted by their family or adoring fans. Nate spotted me first and hiked his shoulder pads up, heading over. "Good game," I told him once he was close enough to hear.

Nate ducked into a dramatic bow. "Thank you, thank you. Now it's my turn to congratulate you." He lifted only his eyes. "Happy birthday."

I peered at him over the lip of my jacket collar. "Did you come bearing gifts?"

"Unless sweaty shoulder pads count."

"Pass."

He glanced back to the locker room. "Landon's showering, so you'll have a sweet-smelling boyfriend to hug."

I studied him closely, trying to gauge whether or not he knew what happened at the party last night. I would've thought everyone in the Top Tier would've heard about it by now. Ashton didn't want to post to Babble to tarnish their reputation, but they had to have giggled about it amongst their friend group. Nothing in Nate's expression hinted at anything that serious, though. "Did you hear about what happened last night at the party?"

"I heard Madison and Jade had a fight, but I didn't catch what it was about. Why?" Nate shifted his shoulder pads to his other hand. "Did I miss something else?"

I tipped my head back to look at the night sky. With the field lights still on, it was too hard to see any stars. "No, nothing else."

Landon wore a pair of blue and gold sweatpants and a Bobcats T-shirt when he emerged from the locker room, and I watched his head swivel as he searched the crowd. He carried his shoulder pads in one hand and a duffle bag in the other. He finally turned toward the fence line, spotting me. Even from here, I could see his shoulders drop almost as if he'd let out a relieved breath, and without wasting a second, he started toward me.

Nate turned to look toward where my attention had been snagged. "Ooh, looks like my turn for your attention is over," he said teasingly, taking a step back. "I've got someone of my own to find. See you at the party?"

"We're not going," I told him, watching as Landon crossed the distance between us quickly. "We've got our own plans."

Nate waggled his eyebrows and took another step back. "I won't ask, so don't tell."

"Don't tell what?" Landon asked as he arrived before us, glancing back and forth. His hair dripped onto the tops of his shoulders, and his freckled cheeks were flushed in the light.

Nate mimed him zipping his lips shut. "See you two Monday," he said, and with a quick salute, he turned on his heel to head toward the parking lot.

I followed his movement for a moment before turning back to Landon, who had his eyes fastened on me, as if when he looked away, I'd disappear. With my hands firmly in my pockets, I tipped my head toward the parking lot. "Proof?"

"Proof," he agreed, and together we walked toward where I'd parked Petunia.

It was weird to be with Landon and not reach for him. He had his hands full with his stuff anyway, so it wasn't like we could hold hands, but the weeks of trying to sell our fake relationship had led me to expect the physical touch, to anticipate it. Even look forward to it. Now, too much space stretched between us for me to be able to reach out, both physically and metaphorically.

Landon stashed his things in the back of the van before climbing into the passenger seat, letting out a breath as he stretched the buckle across his chest. "So, you found the yearbook?"

I started the van up, and it growled out its protest before settling out into a hum. "I don't want to start there," I told him firmly, backing out of the parking space. "I want you to start with the bet."

"Right, right." He rubbed his palms along his knees, nodding at the same time. "So, uh—back to the beginning. Ashton overheard about our date, and showed up at the restaurant to listen in. I think he thought I'd make a fool out of myself. But then...then he caught you suggesting the fake relationship."

Prime creep behavior, but I never should've expected anything less.

"He came to my house that night with the grand plan to expose you for wanting the fake relationship—he wanted to spin it like you cared about the list, not that you had the bet with your cousin," he went on, fidgeting in the seat. "I thought if Ashton told the school that you wanted a fake relationship, you'd think I was the one that told him. He just wanted to embarrass you in front of the whole school. You're not the first they've messed with for laughs. They kept it between themselves. They keep everything between themselves. And to me, this was my one chance with you, and I thought I was going to lose it."

"So you told Ashton you'd get me to fall in love with you by homecoming?"

He gave a small nod. "I told him that maybe we could make it more interesting. To keep it...between us. The Top Tier. That way, he wouldn't embarrass you in front of the whole school."

Ashton had the opportunity to embarrass me in front of everyone, but chose to do it just in front of his friends. "Why?"

Landon's hands curled over his knees, fingers digging into his sweatpants. "He said embarrassing you wouldn't be as fun as 'this.' In hindsight, I should've known what he meant, but I swear—I didn't know he was going to spin it like that. I didn't know he thought I was going to break up with you in the end. But...I should've expected he'd do something like that. I should've questioned it, but I...I didn't want to. All I could think about was that this was my chance with you."

I drew in a slow breath as I focused on the road, processing it all. "That's why you were so shy in the beginning," I mused aloud. "Because you *were* nervous around me. Because you...liked me."

"So much. I wondered if Ashton would change his mind sometimes, though. Tell everyone at school that you proposed the fake relationship. That's why I had you around us more. Brought you around all *my* friends. Sat at *my* lunch table. Came to *my* practices. Kissed you in front of *my* friends. That way, if it ever got out, I could say that I was the one who asked for it first, since I was the one who benefitted the most."

That was true, at least in the sense that we were more public for his sake. So it wasn't because he was trying to make Madison jealous, but to create a backup plan in case everything fell apart. When I swallowed, my throat was tight. "And no one else knew it was fake?"

"Just Ashton. He didn't even tell Kyle. Ashton told him and Jade last night before the party, but before that, only Ashton and I knew. I said I didn't want it getting out."

I mulled it all over as I turned onto a side street that'd lead to his house, still unsure how to feel. It didn't surprise me that Ashton targeted me, though. After what happened between him and Hudson freshman year, it was clear he relished in hurting people. Beating up someone and then convincing the entire school that he, himself, was the victim. Psychological warfare was his strong suit, and after rejecting him, he'd turned it on me.

"So, what was your plan?" I asked as I turned on Landon's street. "I'm assuming you *weren't* going to dump me."

"Of course not," he said immediately. "I was going to tell you, I swear. When I said I wanted to hang out after the game tonight, that was when I was going to do it. To show you...what I was going to show you."

My pulse stirred at the unknown prospect as I pulled up in front of his house, staring at the dark structure. We'd beat his parents home. Landon turned to me, eyes bright. "I'll be right back." Again, it sounded almost like a question.

"I'll be right here," I promised, turning the engine off.

The time he took to grab his things from the back and jog into the house had my insides twisting in a knot, one that cinched tighter each second he didn't emerge. His excuse. His proof. Proof that he'd liked me all along, proof that would let me to believe him. I wasn't sure what it even could've been, but in that moment, I hoped it was enough.

It took him probably two minutes inside his house before he reemerged, carrying something in his hands. He tucked it underneath his arm to open the passenger side door, and as the light flicked on, I saw it was a shoebox. A child-size shoebox.

"Let's go to Lookout Ledge," he said as he climbed in, shutting the door. "That way my parents won't interrupt us when they get home."

Landon's knuckles were white as he clutched the box to him, staring down at the surface of it as we drove. I kept taking peeks, curiosity warring with my nerves. I couldn't tell if anything was jostling around inside the shoebox—Petunia's engine was too loud.

Thankfully, Lookout Ledge was only a few minutes' drive from Landon's house, and I pulled off to the side quickly, putting Petunia in park. I reached up and turned on the dual overhead lights, illuminating the space. And Landon's nervousness. "Don't...run away screaming," he said.

My eyebrows shot up. "What, do you have locks of my hair in there?"

"Not that bad." He clutched the box tighter. "But maybe...close."

I unbuckled my seatbelt so I could turn to face him fully, my heartbeat stirring in my chest. The anxiety was clear on his face, knitting his brow and tensing the area around his lips. Whatever it was, it was something he felt uncomfortable sharing. "I won't run away screaming. Promise."

With a slow, shaking movement, Landon set the shoebox on the console between us, turning so the lid would open toward me. Even though the shoebox was obviously old—dents in the corners, scrapes along the sides—it wasn't dusty, almost like it'd been brushed off or frequently used. Landon's hands snaked to either side of the box, and without a word, he flipped it open.

Several folded-up pieces of paper were inside, enough to cover the bottom of the box. I sifted through them with a finger first. "I'm terrified," I tried to tease, but neither of us laughed. Glancing at Landon, I picked up one of the papers, and as I lifted it, the fold fell open, revealing an image drawn on the surface.

My first thought was that it was a beautiful drawing. There were a few finger smudges along the edges, but the graphite and shading created a picture that practically dripped skill. It was a girl with her hair twisted in two braids, ones that barely hung past her shoulders. She was smiling widely, so wide that her eyes were squinted with happiness. There was a stud in her nose—one that was instantly familiar.

It was me.

"I drew that after the beach," Landon explained in a

halting voice, the tremble in his words obvious. "There's—well, there's a date in the corner."

I looked, and sure enough, it was dated after the beach. I lifted my chin to look at him and narrowed my eyes. "So you're telling me this entire time that I've been asking for a drawing of me, you've already done one?"

Landon's attention dropped back to the box, silent.

All these papers...

No way.

I set the smiling picture down and picked up the next paper, quick in unfolding it. It was another drawing of me, though this time, I was in my serving uniform with a tray full of drinks balanced on top. I had my hair in braids again, but this time, my smile was different. Instead of the wide, crinkled mouth from the first image, this one held a grin that was more refined, more focused. My serving smile captured perfectly.

I checked the date—the day the Most Likely To list went out.

Realization washed over me, and Landon confirmed it. "That was the day my family went to Le Petit Bateau. I'd never seen you working before. I thought...it could be interesting to try and draw."

"It's really good," I said earnestly, tracing the pencil strokes, lost for words. I set it down and picked up another image, this time checking the date first. It was from last year, and it was a drawing of me slumped in a school desk, hand propping my head up, eyes drifting shut. The angle was partially sideways, as if the perspective was from someone who sat in the same row as me. "You made it sound like you were terrible. You said you'd be embarrassed if anyone ever saw."

"I think you can guess why I'd be embarrassed."

I looked up and found Landon's freckled cheeks flushed, and something stirred in my chest.

"Ever since the fourth grade, I've been drawing," Landon said as I picked up another image. This time, from sophomore year, an image of me standing in front of a locker. "I drew some, but you were the one who told me to keep drawing, as long as I drew you."

The next picture was from freshman year, and it was of me standing behind a volleyball net, crouched with my hands positioned in front of me. There wasn't as much detail in this one as there was in the previous ones, clear by the shakier lines and the harsher shading.

"Whenever I drew, I always wanted to draw you," he went on, running his fingers across his knuckles. "But only whenever our paths crossed. When I was sitting beside you in class, or watching a volleyball game, or passing by you in the hallway. I couldn't bring myself to talk to you...but I could draw you."

The eighth-grade drawing was of me hanging upside down on monkey bars, hair stretching down to the ground, eyes staring directly at the viewer.

What if I only like drawing you? Landon's voice from the past crept through my mind now, a delicate whisper. *Can I make it a career, drawing different renditions of Lacey Churchill?*

There were a few other drawings, but when I got to the last one at the bottom of the box, my breathing slowed a bit.

The drawing was obviously done by a child, with the uneven eyes and basic mouth. There was absolutely no resemblance to me at all. I traced the boyish scrawl in the bottom corner, the signature of a child who'd yet to steady his hand, noting the date.

I was paired up with this girl and had to draw her, Landon had told me once upon a time. *That first picture sucked, but I liked it enough to keep drawing.*

Do you still have it? I'd asked. The drawing?

I could still remember the way he avoided my eye as Landon replied. *Probably in some box somewhere.*

"I've always liked you, Lacey." Landon attempted a glimpse of a smile when I finally looked at him, with all of the drawings of me before us on the bed. "I liked seeing how you'd dye your hair, or seeing you passing in the halls, wondering if that would be the day you'd finally look at me. I've always wanted to thank you for being so nice in the fourth grade. I've never forgotten it."

I looked back down at the drawing from the seventh grade I still clung to, mind whirling. I couldn't even settle on a single thought—they all flew around me in a flurry, leaving me dazed and confused and something else that felt lighter. "Why didn't you tell me?" I asked him, resting the image on my lap. "When we agreed to be together for real, why didn't you tell me?"

"I was scared to," he admitted, cheeks deepening in their color. "I was afraid you'd be freaked out that I still remembered something from elementary school. Afraid you'd be freaked if I ever told you about the drawings. I was too afraid to risk it."

"*Freaked*," I echoed with a little snort, looking at the drawings. "I mean, maybe if you'd brought it up while I was still standing in my towel, then I'd have gotten bad vibes. But not after we kissed."

He glanced around at the drawings too, at the opened pictures of me. "Bringing up Valentine's Day that day on the beach, I guess that was my way of...testing the waters, I guess. To see if you remembered it, remembered me. But it's okay that you didn't—the only thing that mattered was that I remembered it. I could remember that day enough for the both of us."

I stared into his earnest blue-green eyes, feeling the need to hold my breath. I wished that I could've remembered that day, if only to remember what boy-Landon's expression would've been like. Everything he was saying caused the walls I'd built up in my mind to fall, tumbling over with every explanation. "I was going to leave," I told him, carefully putting the drawings back in the shoebox. "I *had* left. I'd gotten all the way to Pennsylvania."

"What had you turning back?"

"In my mind, I never could see how me leaving town was running away. Hudson said it was, and you said it was, but I never could see it. I didn't want to start my fresh start by running away, so I guess I never looked at it that way." I let out a light breath. "But I *was* running away. Running away from you."

Landon was silent as he watched me.

"I asked myself if I could go my whole life without looking back. Without knowing the explanation you wanted to give me." I turned away from him and leaned my head against the headrest, staring out the windshield. "You were right. If I ran, my problems would've still followed me. *You* would've still followed me, at least the thought of you. I would've wondered about you all the time. Would've wondered what your proof would've been. And then I thought about how the next time I'd see you would probably be at a high school reunion, and you'd be married to Madison with five kids—"

Landon's eyebrows shot up. "*Five?*"

"—and it'd be too late to hear you out," I finished, swallowing hard. "And I knew I'd regret that forever."

My chest ached thinking about that alternate reality, at how drastically different that course would've been. I never would've gotten to see the snapshots of my life through Landon's eyes. Years that I'd been so lonely, there he'd been, a silent spectator in it all.

Once upon a time, I'd wondered if I'd ever had a fate moment, where it was undoubted and undeniable. Back then, I'd been certain I'd never had such a moment. Never had a meet cute.

But I'd actually had a fate moment, and he'd been there with me all along.

Landon's voice was soft. "What are you thinking right now?"

"I'm thinking that I'm sorry for not hearing you out last night. Would've saved me a lot of miles on the van."

A startled laugh burst from Landon, and I softened at the sound, at the hopeful look that lingered on his freckled face. "I'll make it up to you. I'll make everything up to you. Tell me how, and I'll make you forget all about this."

Now, with the drawings between us, the answer was obvious. "Kiss me," I said.

Landon wasted no time in answering. He leaned forward and pressed his lips to mine, sealing the forgiveness between us with the light pressure. I wanted to sink into it, into him, but he eased back way, way too soon.

I grabbed a fistful of his shirt and held him from pulling away further, raising an eyebrow. "That wasn't the kind of kiss I meant."

Landon's eyes darkened, glancing down to my hand on his collar. "Have I ever told you," he began in a low tone, "how much I love when you do this?"

I smirked and tightened my fist. "It's because you're mine."

"I'm yours," he said, and really, *really* kissed me.

One of his hands reached up and cupped my cheek, using firm enough pressure that it made the butterflies in my stomach flutter. I lifted the console up to open the seat between us, knocking the shoebox of drawings onto the backseat floor, scattering images of me everywhere. Neither of us noticed. Landon's arms swept around me easily, pressing me against his body like we were two puzzle pieces that couldn't be separated. The lingering way his lips trailed against mine made it impossible to break away, impossible to think about anything other than this moment in time.

I kissed him deeply, warming something that felt long too cold. The past twenty-four hours had left me feeling hopeless, but with each kiss, with each graze of his fingertips, I could feel the happiness resurging within me, along with the feeling of relief that I'd dodged something massive. I had been right—if I'd walked away for good last night, there was no telling what could've happened. No telling when I'd ever see Landon again.

And now, here we were, in each other's arms, right where we always belonged.

EPILOGUE

The air was cold as I leaned against the van, listening to the *glug-glug* of fuel shifting from the pump to my van, watching the numbers tick upward. This gas station had a little speaker installed for motorists to listen to while they got gas, and I listened to a pop song crackle through, bopping my head to the beat.

The long weekend had kicked off officially an hour ago when school let out, and I was ready to take it all in. Halloween was on Monday, and since Brentwood High wasn't a normal school, they gave students the day off claiming "fall break." Not that I was complaining that much. A long weekend meant the perfect time for a road trip adventure.

My phone chirped in my jacket pocket, and I pulled it out to peer at the screen. "What did I forget?" I asked, toeing my shoe in the pavement.

"Your phone charger," Hudson replied evenly. "It's still plugged into the wall."

"I'm staying in the van, Hudson. Which has a car phone charger."

He was silent for a long moment. "Oh."

"You're going to miss me, aren't you?" I smirked even though he couldn't see it. "Me and my awesome jokes."

"You mean you and the hairs you leave all over the bathroom floor."

Dang. I thought I'd gotten better at picking them up.

"It's more like I'm afraid you're going to leave and never come back," Hudson went on, still sounding like he was grumbling. "You're going to Maine, right? Not Vegas?"

I rolled my eyes. "Yes, *Dad*. Fun camping and hiking, and maybe catch the last of the leaves changing color. I showed you the pictures of up there—it's *beautiful*."

The gas pump gave one final *glug* as it kicked off, and I balanced my phone between my shoulder and my ear as I shook the last drops of fuel from the nozzle. "Besides," I went on, "it's three days. What would I do in Vegas? I'm not old enough to gamble."

"It was a joke, Churchill," Hudson returned, sighing. "If I have to tell you why it's funny, it's too sophisticated for you."

I scowled. "If you have to explain your jokes, it means they aren't good."

"Uh-huh. Tell it to your passenger—I'm sure he'd get it. Actually, wait, don't do that. Don't mention it to him. No one needs any ideas."

I hooked the nozzle back on the fuel pump, pressing *no receipt*. "I'll call you when we get to the campground. It'll probably be late."

Hudson paused, and from the other line, I could hear a faint murmur. "Dad says to make sure to stop and rest if you have to. Paisley says that she loves you and to remind you to bring her back a keychain."

"Keychain, check," I said as I hauled open the van door, hopping in. "Mug for Uncle Dean, check. And you said all you wanted was a postcard?"

"Very funny."

I laughed at his deadpan voice. "I'll pick you up some cutesy Maine-themed gift too, don't worry. Talk to you later."

"Drive safe," Hudson said seriously, and then hung up.

I started up the van and ran my hands over the steering wheel, taking a quick glance back at the van. The bed was made with the cheery yellow comforter, the counters were clean of anything that would've fallen off in transit, and on the floor there were two duffle bags. Ready for adventure.

The passenger door popped open, and I turned to find Landon climbing into the seat, holding two plastic bags. He held one of them awkwardly cradled in his arms. "The handles broke, but I've got the goods," he proclaimed, turning to me with a proud expression as he unloaded his finds. "I got four Sprites—two for now, two for later. Snacks galore, naturally, and of course—" He took out a red family size bag. "—Twizzlers."

"You always get me the massive bags," I said, though I was *so* not complaining.

Landon pulled out a bag of trail mix before setting the other bags on the floor by his feet, settling into his seat. "I have to make sure my girl's well-stocked."

My girl. Now there was no fighting my smile. "What did your parents end up saying about our road trip?"

"Now that football season's over, they're letting me do what I want." He raised an eyebrow at me. "I told you they're not making me sign up for basketball this year, right?"

"Good." I turned my head toward him. "That opens you up more for me."

Landon returned my smile with a warm one, and it lit up his eyes. He looked at me like I was the only girl in the world, and it never failed to make me want to crawl into his arms.

"Do you have your sketchbook?" I turned toward the road and tapped my right cheek. "This is my good side."

A second later, Landon stretched across the console and pressed a kiss against my cheek, and before I had a chance to react, he was already falling back into his seat. "It is a good side. Not that you have a bad one."

I reached out and grabbed a fistful of his shirt, stretching him back across the console, kissing him on the lips. It was funny how Landon always drew in a breath when I kissed him, like he was left so thoroughly shocked by the initial touch, but then a second later, he'd kiss me back with the same amount of enthusiasm I put in. A month into our relationship, and it was the case for every kiss we shared—and each kiss never failed to leave me breathless.

It felt like such a gift to have found him. But then again, I *hadn't* found him, not really. He'd found me first. He liked to say he was lucky, that fate was on our sides, but I was really the lucky one. Lucky to have stuck around in Brentwood long enough to see past all the hurt and pain in order to see *him*. Lucky to have seen him before it was too late.

The night before homecoming, when I left, that had almost been it. I almost hadn't looked back. Our story could've ended there.

And now, as I smiled against Landon's soft lips, I knew the truth.

Our story was truly just beginning.

LANDON'S POV

I measured my school days in interactions with Lacey Churchill.

They say that if a big enough event happens to you as a kid, you'll remember it with perfect clarity for the rest of your life. And for me, that was true.

Fourth grade. Valentine's Day. Lacey's big brown eyes as she gave me her box.

I have enough love to share.

I'd been sure she'd been joking. That she couldn't have possibly been talking to me, the class freak. Lacey Churchill, the prettiest girl in class, couldn't possibly be talking to little fourth grader Landon, who'd had his own Valentine's Day box ruined by his classmates. And yet she had been. With her gapped smile and bright expression, despite the whispers from everyone around her, she had been talking to me.

I have enough love to share.

I hadn't known what love was in the fourth grade, but I knew in that moment that I'd do anything for the girl with her outstretched arms, the first classmate to show me kindness.

"You know what I love the most about being a senior?"

Ashton asked from where he leaned against the dumbbell rack, admiring his slight bicep in the mirror instead of actually working out. He hadn't broken a sweat all morning. "Seeing how scared the freshmen are of us. Have you noticed?"

Kyle, he only other boy in the weightlifting room, nodded. At least he had a pair of dumbbells in his hands, though he stopped doing his curls a long time ago. "Their eyes get so wide."

I focused on the ceiling as I readjusted my grip on the barbell, trying to empty my mind to finish my final reps. Ashton was supposed to be spotting me, but I'd given up trying to call him back over. Not that I trusted him much to help me if I needed it, anyway.

"I swear, Madison's legs got longer over the summer," Kyle said, letting out a low whistle. "Shame that Jade forced her way in as co-captain of the squad. Madison would've looked good front and center, don't you think?"

Ashton laughed. "Hey, Madison is Landon's girl. Cool off."

"Not my fault if Landon doesn't make his move," Kyle called in an obvious way, but I refused to look over. "You just stare from afar, like a creep."

Drawing in a breath, I pressed the barbell away from me, muscles flexing with the weight. The frustration of his comment bolstered me, tightening in my chest. My arms trembled when I extended my arms, and I brought the barbell back down with a sharp exhale.

The comment hit too close to home. Not with Madison, but it was easier to let them go on thinking it was her I looked for in the hallways. If they knew the true source of my attention, they'd never let me hear the end of it. Worse, they'd never leave her alone.

They didn't wait for me to chip into the conversation, knowing I wouldn't. Instead, I breathed through another rep as I tried to reorganize my thoughts.

Like a creep.

The barbell slammed against the support when I brought it back down, relaxing against the bench. I knew it was creepy, drawing someone who didn't even know you existed. I tried to rationalize it, though, grasping at the straws like they would make my compulsion better. It was just drawing practice. It wasn't like I *stared* at the pictures afterward—I put them in a box, completely out of sight. I didn't even let myself pull them out again once they went in. They were never *weird* pictures, either. It was fine. It wasn't creepy.

My hopeless rationalization would only ever last a few seconds before I cringed again.

I'd only started drawing her after the seventh grade, when our paths crossed again. When I saw her, I remembered the promise I'd made her. But I hadn't been satisfied by the crude drawing—it looked nothing like her. So I'd told myself I'd draw her until I could get it right.

Each time I drew her, though, it brought me back to the moment in the fourth grade, with her Valentine's Day box in her grip. Her gapped smile. Each time I drew her, it was like I was transported back to that moment, when I'd felt so happy to be shown a shred of kindness that I could've cried. When, for a few months, I'd had my first friend.

Even as my skills improved, there was always some-thing wrong with each drawing. The shape of her eyes, the arch of her throat, the shading of her hair. Never quite right. So I drew her and drew her and drew her, feeling comforted at just the memory.

Like a creep.

I swung my head out from underneath the setup and straightened, shoving to my feet. "I'm going to shower," I announced, suddenly feeling too grimy with the sweat layering my skin.

"Wait—I have ten more reps, though," Ashton called after me, and in the mirror, I saw tug his T-shirt's sleeve back down. "You're not going to wait?"

"I'm not waiting all day." Bringing my shirt up to wipe my chin, I called back, "Spray down the bench for me, will you?" And then walked out.

Even though I'd had such a fond memory of her, I never spoke to Lacey again. Three years had passed when I saw her again in the seventh grade, but she'd never looked at me twice. She hadn't remembered me. And then after, throughout the years when our paths crossed, I couldn't bring myself to take the step. I let myself watch her in snip-pets, like when we passed each other in the hall or when we were in the same class, but never approached. My world revolved around her the way a planet revolves around the sun—close, but never touching. Never engaging.

Until now.

I walked into the locker room, barely hearing the sound of the shower over my thoughts. If I'd been paying atten-tion, I would've noticed it was weird that the shower was on since we were the only ones in the workout room. If I'd been paying attention, I might've noticed that a floral scent clung to the air—smelling like women's bodywash instead of men's. I'd been too caught up in my memory, though, and walked around the lockers toward the showers.

Where I stopped dead in my tracks.

For the briefest second, I thought I was hallucinating Lacey standing in front of the showers with a large towel wrapped around her, hair dripping onto her bare shoulders. The thought of her had been haunting me all morning— surely she wasn't here now. Water from the now shut off shower head still dripped, and steam wound through the locker room like smoke.

She didn't move as she stared at me, but a corner of her lips lifted. "Uh, hi."

She was real. She was real, and in the men's locker room. In a towel.

I jerked my head sharply to the side, the tension immediately gripping my shoulders. My pulse was a wild beat in my ears, and I forced myself to study every dent in the metal cabinets. "You—you need to leave," I told her in a voice that had to sound strangled.

"I was here first," she quipped back, as if this situation wasn't bizarre. "But trust me, I'm not sticking around to watch you shower. And I'm not giving you a free show of watching me get dressed either. So, if you could hand me my—"

"There are others." Definitely strangled now. It was a wonder she could understand me. "Coming into the locker room. They were right behind me."

Everything happened at a rapid pace. Ashton and Kyle's voices were suddenly loud as they walked into the locker room, still concealed by the wall. In my mind, I could see the scene play out before me—the boys rounding the corner, finding a girl in a towel, and all the dirty remarks that would follow. The gossiping with the Top Tier. The scandalous Babble posts. Lacey's name, dragged through the mud.

"Landon, I know you finished your set, but you could've waited for us to finish ours, too," Ashton called to me, closing in. "What, you not like us anymore?"

I snatched her backpack up off one of the benches between the locker and stuffed her clothes back inside without care, adrenaline making my movements jerky. I finally allowed myself to look at Lacey, but focused on her face as I crossed the steps toward her—and saw as her expression melted from nonchalance to *fear*. She tried to shut the shower curtain between us, but I stopped her hand. "This is where they're coming," I whispered, and after a moment of hesitation, I gently grabbed her arm.

With the bathroom stall door shut, I wanted to fall against it, to let out a gasp of relief, but Ashton and Kyle stepped into view, forcing me still. Ashton's expression was a scowl. "What's the point of working out together if you're not going to hang around until we all finish?"

"Not my fault if you both are slow," I replied, fisting my hands to keep them from shaking. Lacey was silent on the other side of the stall, almost as if she disappeared the second the door shut. "I'm not going to skip a shower because you two take forever to do your reps."

Just get in the shower, I willed them. With the noise of the water, Lacey could get dressed and I could get her out.

Ashton and Kyle both turned to their lockers when something on the ground caught Ashton's eye, his head swiveling down. When he spoke, his voice was laced with glee. "Wait, woah. What do we have here?"

At first, I was too focused on keeping calm to really listen—until I looked at what he had in his hands, and then I stiffened all over.

"Dude, who had fun in the locker room?" Kyle asked as he stared at the neon pink bra in Ashton's hands. He gripped it crudely, both hands cupping the front. "Left behind their *unmentionables*. You think it was Bray and Jade?"

Ashton shook his head, lifting it up as if weighing it. "It's not Jade's. She'd have to stuff that bra to get it to fit."

I suddenly could not look at it. I could not think about the bright floral-patterned thing in Ashton's hands. I could not think about it *fitting* anywhere. But Ashton's hands on it, though, left me feeling equally unsettled, and Lacey needed it. With a tight breath, I stalked over and looped a finger around the strap, yanking it from Ashton's groping grip. "You taking it as a trophy, Landon?" he demanded, looking annoyed as I backed up. "We all know it doesn't belong to your girl—you know, because you don't have one!"

"Neither do you," I fired back, too embarrassed at the entirety of the situation to feel true anger at the comment. Even though I held the bra by the strap, I couldn't help but feel a little mortified by the fact that this lightweight thing was once touching Lacey Churchill's body. And in a few seconds, it'd be touching it again. I shook my head to shake the thought from my mind. "I'm putting it in my locker until Connor or whoever can grab it. You know Tito—he'll probably take it home with him."

Kyle snorted. "And add it to his collection."

I walked up to my locker as if to spin the combination, but the boys moved to the showers then, pulling the curtains aside and starting the water. Neither of them questioned why the floor was already wet. I hurried over to the stall while they were distracted. With my eyes closed, I slung the bra over the top of the bathroom stall, feeling it bounce against something. A second later, Lacey snatched it away.

My cheeks would set on fire any second now. I was sure of it.

I stood in front of the stall door as if standing guard, forcing my eyes on the lockers again. This was not how I thought my first interaction with Lacey since the fourth grade would go. Then again, I'd never really let myself *truly* envision it. The first day of my senior year was three days ago, and I'd gone through the entire day holding my breath, waiting for her to walk through any one of the classroom doors. Surely I'd have at least one class with her. Surely our last year of high school together we'd have at least *one* class together.

She never walked in, though. For each period, the teachers never called her name for roll call.

Then, I'd thought fate was cruel. Maybe it still was.

I jumped when she poked my shoulder, whirling to find

her fully dressed with her hair dripping onto her T-shirt. She huddled her backpack to her chest, staring up at me with the same big brown eyes she had all those years ago. Her expression was none of the same, though—there was far too much distrust now. But staring at her, I couldn't help but marvel at the fact that she was looking back at me. That our eyes were meeting. The feeling I got when I drew resurfaced then—despite the situation, those brown eyes brought me comfort.

"Landon," Ashton called, and I heard the shower curtain clink as if sliding aside. "What are you doing over there?"

Without thinking, I shoved into the stall, pushing Lacey backward. She slipped on the tile though, evident by the sudden widening of her eyes, and I reached out without thinking and pressed her against me. Her backpack was between us, but as my hand settled on her lower back, my mind empty, the surreal moment rendering me speechless.

This is not happening, I thought as I blinked down at her, close enough that I could see how her lashes fanned outward, could see the way her eyes darted back and forth. *She's—I—this—this is not happening.*

Lacey only held still in the embrace for a moment before she got her footing and wedged me back, and I backed away as far as possible in the stall, trying to give her space. She probably thought I was a creep, a freak, and that realization was enough to leave me feeling grimy all over again. Her eyes flared, but I couldn't read the emotion. "How—"

I pressed a finger to my lips before she spoke more,

offering my other hand out tentatively. "I'll get you out," I promised her, trembling at the idea of her smacking me away.

Lacey's eyes dropped to my hand and stared at it, almost as if she didn't know what it meant. Her eyes were slow to trail back up to mine, the gaze feeling as if it raked over my skin. I swallowed hard as she finally looked at me again. As she slid her hand into mine, a small smile worked its way over her soft-looking mouth, sending a rush through me. She gave a trusting nod.

As we ducked out of the stall and hurried toward the locker room door, it struck me once more how insane this moment felt. That after so long of just watching her, revolving around her like the sun, *this* is how we finally collided. This absolutely wasn't how I thought our paths would cross, but I was glad it was me who found her. Glad for this moment, even if I felt like I'd burn up at any second.

And yet, despite finally meeting, I still could do nothing more than stare at her once we got out of the locker room. She put on her shoes, and I could do nothing but stare. She warned me about telling others, and I could do nothing but stare.

Lacey leaned forward, her floral scented bodywash filling my nose. A droplet of water slipped its way down her throat, but she didn't notice. "Thanks for an exciting start to the morning," she said in a cheerful voice, raising her eyebrows as she gave me a teasing grin.

This is it, I thought in a daze, staring down at her with

my pulse once more stampeding in my throat. *Say something. Say anything. This is your chance.*

I only could go as far as parting my lips, the words cowardly disappearing on my tongue.

Lacey patted my hand that was braced on the door before she turned around, taking the fire and adrenaline with her, only turning around once to grace me with her smile once more. Then she disappeared around the corner, leaving me gasping in the men's locker room doorway as if I hadn't breathed the entire time.

A mixture of disbelief and disappointment crept its way through me, a slow trickle through my veins. After all the years of simply seeing her from afar, I'd finally gotten to see her up close. *Talk* to her. Would I ever have the chance again? Was this the last time I'd ever speak to Lacey Churchill?

No. A situation would come up. In that moment, no matter what happened, I vowed to not let the opportunity pass me by again. If I ever got the chance again, I'd go to Lacey first. No matter what.